Scorn to be Guilty

Scorn to be Guilty

Finnegan Gilhooley
Book 3

R.F. Ryan

Scorn to be Guilty
Paperback Edition

Wolfpack Publishing
1707 E. Diana Street
Tampa, Florida 33610

www.wolfpackpublishing.com

Paperback ISBN 979-8-89567-261-7
eBook ISBN 979-8-89567-260-0

"Have no altercations with the Pinkerton men. Keep away from them when there is danger of a rupture. Remember that every man of you is being watched, your footsteps are being dogged, and even a joking remark may serve to fasten upon you a crime of which you would scorn to be guilty. By taking this course you will strengthen our hands, and public opinion, always fickle, will be borne to your aid by the shifting winds."

—Terence Powderly
Grand Master Workman, Knights of Labor, 1886

"They can be carried in quantities about the person; they can be thrown by hand or by sling. Nicety of aim is unnecessary. Whatever they strike they pulverize, and kill all within a certain radius. They can be manufactured cheaply, secretly, and readily. Any manufacturer of bad smells in the basement of a soap factory can turn out more means of destruction in a day than Krupp could in a century. Nay, the work can be done in any back-kitchen. If the devil delights in the horrors of war he must be in ecstasies over these new inventions."

—Captain James Chester
Dynamite and the Art of War, 1884

Scorn to be Guilty

Chapter 1

ST. LOUIS, ILLINOIS

April 29, 1886

The avowed anarchist had proved slightly more spry and considerably more aggressive than Finnegan would have credited him. As suspected, Alfred Fritz Brahms had entered the railyard in St. Louis dressed in the general guise of a switchman early in the morning. Of course, Mr. Brahms was not a switchman, but an out of work shoe cobbler and frequent contributor to German-language newspapers in Chicago. Finnegan had been following the chap around for two days, having come to suspect that Mr. Brahms was responsible for the shooting of a deputy during a strike riot a week earlier. Seeing Mr. Brahms enter the railyard, where he had no business being, had given Finnegan just cause to arrest the man, search him, and hopefully gain a confession to the murder of the deputy.

As always, Finnegan had aspired to put the man in custody without undue labor, but Mr. Brahms had opted for a different course of events. It might have been that Finnegan appeared out of place in the railyard. It might have been that Mr. Brahms had developed something of a sixth sense over the years he had spent engaged in labor agitation. Whatever the reason, as Finnegan had been approaching the man on the railway platform, Brahms had turned and fired three shots with a revolver. Finnegan had leapt behind a set of benches to gain cover. When he had his gun drawn, he emerged to see Brahms fleeing across the railyard.

Finnegan had looked down at the man assigned to assist him while in St. Louis, a rather portly gentleman by the name of Richard Gander. The Pinkerton preventive wore a wholly shocked expression. "I didn't think the man would have a pistol in his possession."

"Did you believe he killed that deputy with crude language? Get up, we must pursue him." Finnegan had not waited for Gander to right himself, but had instead jumped from the platform and gave chase. Halfway through the yard, Finnegan had tried a shot and had been lucky enough to nick Brahms in the elbow. The anarchist had turned, fired three more shots, then sought shelter inside a shed the railroad used to store tools and switch grease. Finnegan took up a position behind a large stack of ties only about thirty yards from the shed. All around, various railroad workers were gathering on the periphery of the yard as Gander came trudging up, covered in sweat.

"Got him penned up in there, Mr. Gilhooley." Gander threw himself against the ties and sank to the ground, apparently overtaxed from the run.

"Yes, he is in the shed there, Mr. Gander. Your assistance has been invaluable."

The preventive wiped sweat from his brow with one sleeve and failed to notice any sarcasm. "That's what they pay me for, sir. Happy to help."

"Saints preserve us." Finnegan brought his attention back

to the shed. "Brahms! Can you hear me in there, Mr. Brahms?"

"I can, but I have no interest in speaking with you, you wretched Pinkerton assassin."

"For the love of Pete." Finnegan slipped the two spent shells from his Remington revolver and reloaded the weapon. "This is foolish, Mr. Brahms. I can only assume you have come to this railyard to shoot a few scab laborers or to do some minor wrecking, but it begs credulity that you believe you can continue. Can I assume the reason you have not tried a shot at me just lately is because you have run out of ammunition?"

"Go to hell, Pinkerton."

Finnegan sighed. "Oh, come, now. Be a good little communist and do what is best for everyone. If you come out now, I promise I will see to it that you are given a lovely spot in the prison at Joliet. It is an imposing edifice, but I am told the inmates can be quite gregarious."

Gander glanced up at Finnegan. "Joliet ain't so bad. I did a stretch there some years back. Nice breeze all summer. Reasonable warm in the winter."

Finnegan shook his head and returned to negotiating. "Mr. Brahms, it is silly to persist in this. You have been shot and you have no more ammunition. Leave off of this."

"I am still armed." The man's voice lacked much conviction as it drifted over from the shed.

"Are you?" Finnegan fired a round at the edge of the shed. "Fire back, if you can, Brahms." The Pinkerton detective shook his head once again. "Yes, I rather thought not." Finnegan looked down at Gander. "He does not wish to retaliate."

"Perhaps he has found religion." Gander wiped more sweat.

Finnegan rubbed his eyes. "Oh, enough of this absurdity." He stepped out from behind the ties and took a few steps toward the shed. "Come out of there, Brahms. I am not going to sit out here all day while you take your time bleeding to death in there." He took another step forward and could just barely hear a soft hissing sound of some sort. "Brahms?" The shed exploded, flinging Finnegan to the ground and covering him in a mixture of splinters, dirt, and burning grease. "Bloody hell." He began rolling and had made it back to the ties before the flames licking around his clothes were extinguished. The detective stood, still swatting at his coat. Gander was staring at him with a dull look of disinterest. "My apologies if that woke you from your nap, Richard." He gave his pants one last round of slapping.

"That fella exploded, Mr. Gilhooley."

"He did, indeed."

"Do you reckon he done it on purpose?"

Finnegan looked around and located his missing slouch hat. "Yes, I imagine he did."

"Why would he go and do a thing like that?"

"I assume he acted with the intention of killing me, avoiding Jolliet, and ruining my wardrobe." Finnegan checked his pistols to make certain they were still with him. "I must say, that came as a damn shock." He dusted off his hat, thankful it had not been burned. "I have not seen something blow up like that since the war."

Gander rubbed his face. "The war between the states?"

Finnegan raised an eyebrow. "Yes, Mr. Gander."

"Hey, what side was the Irish on in that war, anyhow?"

Chapter 2

CHICAGO, ILLINOIS

May 2, 1886

Finnegan sat facing the office door that formerly had the name of Allan Pinkerton stenciled on the frosted glass. There had been a time when Finnegan rarely, if ever, had to wait for admittance to that particular office, but times change. The door now bore the name of William Pinkerton. Since the passing of the firm's founder, many things had changed. Aside from the signage, the whole office had a decidedly different atmosphere to it. The senior Mr. Pinkerton had always made the offices those employed within could proudly call their place of work. By '86, Finnegan had begun to sense a certain paranoia, if not some outright shame, from some of those who labored within the offices. Given the type of men currently employed by the firm, and the labors they were commissioned to perform, Finnegan could not help but understand why some paranoia or misgivings might be warranted.

Growing bored, Finnegan first adjusted his guns to be more comfortable in his chair. When that proved a short-lived amusement, he looked over William Pinkerton's secretary to assess the chances she might offer something in the manner of intelligent conversation. He rated the chances as minimal, so he withdrew a cigar from his pocket and began looking around for the spittoon that the elder Pinkerton had always kept in the anteroom so that those unfortunately forced to linger there could at least pass the time in a civilized manner. While he was scouting the room, he heard the secretary's rather nasal voice.

"Smoking is not allowed in these offices, sir."

Finnegan stared unbelievingly at the woman for a long moment. "You will excuse me, madam, what did you say?"

"Mr. Pinkerton does not allow smoking in these offices."

"Madam, I have been smoking in these offices since the original Mr. Pinkerton hung the sign on the building. As a matter of fact, I helped Mr. Pinkerton hang the sign and, as I recall, we celebrated with a good cigar. Now, I do not know what you have been told, but the very notion of disallowing the smoking of tobacco in an office is simply..."

"Finnegan..." Robert Pinkerton, the youngest son of Allan Pinkerton, stood in the inner-office doorway, smiling. "Finnegan, we are ready for you now. If you are not too busy discussing matters with Thelma."

Finnegan scowled at the secretary and stood. "Certainly not." He straightened his coat and walked into the office. Inside, he found the oldest son of Allan Pinkerton, William, sitting behind his father's large desk. The man wore a look that made Finnegan's visage seem gleeful. Finnegan closed the door behind him and turned to the two Pinkerton descendants. "Robert, I do not know if you heard, but that vile harpy out there just told me the most preposterous thing. She claimed that smoking was no longer practiced in the building. Can you credit that?" Finnegan chuckled and placed his cigar between his lips.

"Not only can I credit it, I damn well told her to inform the employees of it." William rubbed his eyes and stared at Finnegan from across his desk blotter. "If you wish to smoke that wretched thing, do it outside."

Finnegan raised one eyebrow at the rebuke. "You dislike smoking, William?"

"I believe, quite fervently, that it contributed to my father's early demise. As such, I have disallowed it in the building."

Finnegan slowly placed the cigar back in his pocket. "William, I have heard many tales in my life, but I have yet to have anyone tell me that cigar smoking can kill a man. What in the name of St. Peter gave you the notion that it killed your father?"

The heir sighed. "I would really prefer not to discuss it with you at this time." He rubbed one temple. "I assume you have come to deliver news of the incident involving the deputy in St. Louis?"

Finnegan shrugged. "Naturally."

William rolled his eyes and stroked his jowls, which were beginning to become prominent. "There has been a resolution to the matter?"

"Yes." Finnegan glanced to Robert Pinkerton. "You did not inform him as to the content of my telegram?"

"My apologies, Finnegan, it may have been lost in the shuffle around here." Robert smiled sheepishly.

"Well, since you stand right here, perhaps you could tell me of the telegram's contents." There was an edge to William's voice Finnegan did not appreciate.

"Very well." Finnegan adjusted his gun belt. "Albert Brahms is dead, and I feel confident he can be rightly held responsible for the death of the deputy, as much as the dead can be held responsible."

William stared coldly across the desk. "You killed him?"

"No, but not from lack of an attempt." Finnegan looked from one brother to the other and back. "I wounded the man, he sought refuge in a shed. I moved to capture him and...well, he must have possessed some sort of explosive..."

"An explosive?" William sat forward a bit further.

"Well, yes. As far as I could discern." Finnegan shrugged once more. "He entered the shed, palavered for a moment, then the shed exploded. I can only assume the man died by his own hand or as the result of an accident with whatever powder or dynamite he possessed."

"Dynamite?" William sounded incredulous.

"Or some manner of blasting powder made to act as a bomb, yes." Finnegan reached for a cigar before remembering the injunction. "It should not come as a great surprise, William. Such items can be purchased at most any store carrying the goods of an average working fellow. Railroad men, miners, even farmers have need of dynamite."

William sneered and looked to his brother before answering. "Well, if you say it was so..." He grunted. "Just keep it to yourself. It is one thing to let it be known you killed the man. That, of course, will help to keep that damn rabble in their place, but we don't need the newspapers causing a stir by claiming these anarchists have begun to use dynamite. No man will board a train if he has to worry about some communist dynamiting a trestle to spite the railroad." He drummed his fingers on the desk blotter. "On the other hand, such news might convince a few of those more tightfisted railroad men to pay for preventatives at the depots and trestles." He motioned to his brother. "We will have to choose our moment, Robert."

Finnegan sighed and hooked his thumbs into his gun belt.

"Yes, well. Speaking of preventatives, there is a matter regarding them we must discuss."

William grimaced. "What matter?"

"To be perfectly honest, William, if it is a choice between working alone and being assigned one of those useless slugs, I would rather run the hazard of working alone. This last dizzy bugger you saddled me with freely admitted to having been a guest at Joliet. I would imagine the late Mr. Brahms would have proved more trustworthy as a partner. You really must see about finding some better men if you intend to continue pursuing the more vicious or intelligent sort of criminal, sir. I dare say your father would have never allowed such a man to participate in a detective's assignments."

"Really?" William sat back in his chair. "You believe you have a better understanding of my father's business practices or wishes for this business than I?"

Finnegan grinned. "Well, I did work for the man longer than you did, William."

"Of all the impertinent, damned..."

"William..." Robert Pinkerton took a step closer to his brother. "I am certain all Finnegan was attempting to convey is that the work of preventatives differs greatly from that of detectives." Robert smiled at both men. "That is all you meant, is it not, Finnegan?"

Finnegan stared at the younger Pinkerton quizzically. "I meant exactly what I said, as I always do."

"I am certain you did, Finnegan." William sat forward in his chair and rubbed his temples. "I have never known you to do otherwise." He sighed. "Now that I think on it, I do not know if I ever heard you question any commission my father gave you. The man only need to point out a fellow and you would soon enough see to it that the fellow was no longer with us. In all the years you were at his beck and call, I never heard him complain of your performance."

Finnegan nodded. "Is there some conclusion you are suggesting there, William?"

"I am merely pointing out that it is a might hypocritical for a man who has worked as an assassin his entire life to go about commenting on the moral failings of others."

"Assassin?" Finnegan nodded very slowly. "William, let me inquire something of you. If you know to a certainty that a man is an assassin, and thus holds life quite cheap, do you believe it is wise to impugn that man's character to his face?"

William Pinkerton took a moment to think back on some of Finnegan's previous duties. "I meant no insult, Finnegan." He swallowed and grunted. "It was wrong of me to cast aspersions on your work. My father was always proud to have you in his employ...in whatever capacity." The elder Pinkerton let out a small cough, seeming to feel he had escaped any danger. "That being said, we all need to face a few harsh realities around here if this business, and it is a business, is going to continue in operation, grow, and thus provide for its employees."

Finnegan rubbed one side of his face and grimaced. He did not enjoy such talk. "Harsh realities, William?"

"To begin with, in case you have not noticed, we are very nearly out of the detective business, at least here in the environs of Chicago and the east. Before this last bit with the dead deputy, what did we have you doing?"

"I was investigating the theft of some bonds in Cicero."

"And before that?"

"I was in Texas and then Mexico looking for Dave Rudabaugh. The railroad and the one bank still wished to have the man brought in to face punishment for crimes committed in Arizona."

William rolled his eyes. "And did you capture this Rudabaugh?"

Finnegan shook his head. "No. I had managed to narrow my search down to a single town and was correct in my deduction. Unfortunately for myself and Mr. Rudabaugh, several of his old acquaintances discovered the man first. They shot him down in the tavern he had been running. The Mexican constabulary placed his head on a pike in the center of town to discourage others of his ilk from moving there."

"So, you did not capture him?" William seemed a bit accusatory.

"Well, no."

"Did you discover the thief who had made off with the bonds in Cicero?"

"No. You called me off that endeavor to investigate the dead deputy before I really had a chance to begin."

"Ah, yes, that brings us to the deputy." William looked to his brother and back again to Finnegan. "You settled on this fellow Brahms as a suspect and now he is dead, so we will never truly know whether he was the man we sought or not."

Finnegan chuckled. "William, in my experience, when a man would rather blow himself to smithereens than be arrested, it is a very safe assumption he was the guilty party."

"That is hardly the point, Finnegan." William was beginning to sound a might churlish. "The point, Finnegan, is that there is damned little profit to be had in this detective ridiculousness anymore. We cannot continue on as father did, chasing desperados and penning nickel books. The largest corporations in this country depend on this firm for their security and their continued operation in the face of an onslaught of threats. We simply cannot afford to have you chasing after petty thieves such as this Rudabaugh man or skulking after a single anarchist when an army of them currently threatens the city. These are times for broadswords, Finnegan, not pen knives."

Finnegan sighed and longed for a cigar. "William, for a man who wishes to get to the point, you are doing a fine job of dancing about."

"Very well, I will get to the crux of the matter." He swallowed and ran a hand over his face. "You have always served this firm in the capacity of a detective, of sorts, correct?"

"Correct."

"Currently, this firm has little need of detectives. We require more preventives and infiltrators every day. Do you have any interest in serving this firm in one of those capacities?" Finnegan slowly shook his head. William continued. "Well, then, I suppose we have come to the crux of the matter."

Finnegan leaned toward the heir to the Pinkerton firm. "William, are you trying to tell me, that after all these years, after all the blood I have shed and given for this firm, you are terminating my employment?"

William Pinkerton's lower lip quivered. "I have offered you work, and you have said it does not suit you. I...uh...you are not terminated. We will contact you when your services are again required. If you seek other employment in the meantime, that is your prerogative as a free man in a free country."

"William, ah, if only your father could see you now." Finnegan sneered.

"You cannot say what my father might say regarding this. He always kept the best interests of the company as his cornerstone."

Finnegan grinned malevolently. "It would not be difficult to arrange things so you could ask him yourself."

"Gentlemen, gentlemen." Robert Pinkerton came

forward and placed one hand on Finnegan's shoulder. "I believe our passions are running too high today. Perhaps it would be better to discuss these matters some other time, before one of us makes a statement he might later regret." He offered a placating smile to both men. "Finnegan, as my brother said, you are not terminated. We would never let a man of your experience go. We are merely in a slump of sorts when it comes to detective work and, as such, do not have an assignment for you, currently. Is that true, William?" The elder Pinkerton nodded. "There, now. I will walk you out, Finnegan. It has been too long since we have had a chance to talk."

William coughed again and extended his hand. "Yes, well put, Robert. Until we meet again, Finnegan."

Finnegan took the elder Pinkerton's hand. "I will assuredly see you again, William." He turned and walked out of the office with Robert Pinkerton following. The two men descended the two stories to the street. Once out the door and on the cobblestones, Finnegan took out a cigar.

Robert grinned. "Might you have another one of those?"

Finnegan shook his head and handed the man a smoke. He found a new one for himself and struck a match for both of them. "Your brother bandies about strange notions these days, Robert."

The younger Pinkerton waved smoke away from his eyes. "Yes, I suppose. Although, you may recall that I often chided father about the company finances when he was alive. Now that he is gone, William is simply trying to make the operation as profitable as possible." Robert frowned slightly. "Father was, not unlike Barnum, a great showman. William is a businessman who holds his ledgers in the highest regard. Some aspects of the firm are bound to change when it is passed into new hands."

Finnegan puffed his cigar. "Robert, I, of all men, can understand that your father's passing must change things. It does not vex me that your brother has assumed control. It does not vex me that he might wish to no longer employ me. It truly does not even vex, much, that the daft bugger has banned the smoking of cigars in the building. It is his building, after all. There is one item of arithmetic that I find worrisome, though, Robert."

The younger Pinkerton blew out smoke, still grinning. "I have never known you to indulge in much worry, Finnegan. What troubles you now?"

"Simple numbers, Robert. I have been perusing the papers ever since I have found myself mired here in Chicago and I have noticed a few items that are a bit disturbing."

"What numbers?"

"The number of preventive thugs your brother has been hiring during this most recent strike. William has shown a great deal of fervor collecting every armed drunk and derelict hoodlum between here and New York. As you well know, these men have been responsible for several ugly scenes already and more are sure to follow."

"Finnegan..."

The gunman raised a hand to stop his old friend. "Robert, I know that when two large bodies of impassioned fools collide, terrible things are bound to occur. That is not what worries me."

Robert arched one eyebrow. "Ah, yes, you are concerned with numbers."

"Yes, Robert." Finnegan tapped the ash from his cigar. "A quick tally will reveal that your brother currently has preventatives in his employ which number nearly twice those men enrolled in the state militia." Finnegan gave his friend a slap on the shoulder. "It is only an observation for you to consider."

Robert appeared a little grim. "I suppose I had not considered it from that perspective."

"I am not the first man to refer to your new minions as a private army, Robert. I should think it would have been noticed by you long ago." Finnegan shrugged. "Well, it is not my place to discuss such weighty matters."

"Finnegan..." Pinkerton continued to frown. "Does it truly not matter to you whether or not you remain in our employ?"

Finnegan gave the man a pat on the shoulder once again. "It was your father I owed a debt to, Robert. I am fond of you, and I would not have an objection to continuing in my current role for your company, but I will not sink to...whatever this new business of your brother's is. If you have use of a man such as myself, call on me. If not, it has been a pleasure to know you, Robert." He nodded and walked off down the street.

Chapter 3

CHICAGO, ILLINOIS

May 3, 1886

Above all else, Finnegan detested boredom. Perhaps more explicitly, he detested boredom as the result of not having a purposeful commission. His first thought after leaving Robert Pinkerton had been to cast about for a new venture. If the Pinkerton firm no longer had need of his services, surely others would. Finnegan had a level of experience and reputation in his field that few others could lay claim to. His first inclination had been to visit the offices of other detective agencies. Thumbing through the directory had made that appear to be a rather dull endeavor. His next inclination was to pen a letter to his too-long estranged friend, Molly Meagher. He could announce to her that his attachment to the Pinkerton firm had been severed and he was enroute by the fastest train to discover if Molly's inclination toward his previous proposals had changed. Finnegan got so far as removing the paper from his writing desk before changing his mind yet again.

In the end, after a small burst of frenzy, he settled on thorough consideration as the best course of action. Finnegan knew the dangers of rash behavior all too well, and did not intend to fall into the same trap he had witnessed so many men stumble into before. Startling events called for calm contemplation, not frenetic panic. As a gunman, Finnegan knew these things to a certainty. Instead of seeking new employment or penning missives that promised an uncertain future, he opted for a quieter path.

The next day, Finnegan was up early and made the rounds to the various banks he grudgingly placed trust in. There seemed to be no safe place for a man to hide his money, so spreading it around was the only real option. After reviewing his savings, he checked his various deposit boxes at each bank and drew up a list of the various items, bonds, and stocks he had invested in. He also wrote a few short missives inquiring as to the financial state of the cattle enterprises he owned a percentage of. By sundown, his entire financial empire was in proper order. Finnegan enjoyed having things neatly organized, but was somewhat depressed to realize it had only taken one workday to review all his worldly property. He slept fitfully that night, contemplating his future, but not precisely in the considered manner he had intended. Finnegan had never welcomed change.

Chapter 4

CHICAGO, ILLINOIS

May 4, 1886

Growing weary of the fair offered by his landlady at his boarding house, Finnegan had left his abode and sought breakfast at a café. After eating, he remained at his table, sipping coffee and flipping through the paper he had purchased on his way over. He was on his third cup of brew and about halfway through the Times when he noticed a familiar face peeking through the café's front window. He smiled at the young man and raised a hand to him. Finnegan continued to smile as he approached. "Good morning, Abijah. Take a seat and join me, if you have the time."

Abijah Smith pulled out a chair and sat at the table. "I surely have the time, Finnegan. I have been sent to fetch you, so there is little else that demands my attention."

Finnegan slowly shook his head and closed his paper. "You have come to fetch me. I would have thought it would take more than a day for the Pinkerton brothers to notice my absence. I have only been allowed to enjoy one full day of being without work, Abijah. Should a man not be given a bit more of a rest after being so unceremoniously let go?"

Abijah chuckled and motioned to a waiter. "William Pinkerton did not mention that he had removed you from employment."

Finnegan shrugged. "It is more as if he approached removing me, and then paused for fear he might cause a row between us. Instead, he chose the less decisive option of placing me in abeyance."

Abijah sat back as the waiter set a coffee cup in front of him and filled it. "Thank you, that will do." The waiter departed. "William is often less decisive than his father was. You always told me it was a poor habit in this business. Perhaps someday it will tell on him."

"William Pinkerton is not in the same business we are, Abijah. Well, not engaged in the work I taught you to do, at any rate." Finnegan sipped his coffee and pulled two cigars from his pocket. "He offered me a choice between working as a preventive or doing some of the infiltration that I have been told you excel at."

"I take it you turned him down."

"I did."

Abijah contemplated his coffee. "You still hold a low opinion of infiltration work?"

"I believe a man should do the work he is best fitted to, and I see no reason to discuss it further." He proffered the cigar. "You have grown into a very capable man in the time I have known you, Abijah. I am proud to say some of your better attributes may be the result of what little tutelage a man such as myself can offer. Do not think my opinions regarding the Pinkertons in any way reflects on my opinion of you."

Abijah took the cigar. "Of course, Finnegan." He nodded. "Thank you."

Finnegan struck a match. "No trouble, these are quite

affordable." He lit his and held out the match for the young man. "So, what has prompted the great William Pinkerton to send you in search of me? Does he require a detective? Has he misplaced the key to his liquor cabinet?"

Abijah stifled a laugh. "I would assume it has something to do with the dustup that occurred at the McCormick works last afternoon. It was quite the spectacle between the union men and the Johnny Laws."

Finnegan nodded grimly. "There was some shooting?"

"Yes, some."

"That is unfortunate. The day will come when men will miss the good times when the unions would only throw a brick or two and the police were only equipped with batons. Things escalate too quickly now that all on both sides have guns and who knows what else."

Abijah lowered his cigar. "Robert Pinkerton informed me that you had a man blow himself up while you were pursuing him the other day."

"Indeed. The man put up a fine scrap first, and made no attempt to curry mercy at the end. If he had not previously committed the cowardly act of shooting down a deputy, I would say I respected how the fellow conducted himself. Kept his nerve to the bitter end, that one."

"And you suspect him of being associated with the anarchists and the foreigners?"

Finnegan smiled and pointed one chiding finger at the young man. "Careful with your talk of foreigners, boy. A loyal son of Hibernia may take offense."

Abijah mimed remorse. "Certainly, I meant no offense. You are a citizen of the whole world, Finnegan, and could not be considered a foreigner anywhere." He puffed his cigar. "But, the fellow was likely in with the Germans and the communists?"

"Thick as thieves. Brahms, the fellow's name was Brahms, had penned several lengthy editorials to one of those Teutonic newspapers. I had no hope of reading them, of course, but his name was at the bottom, nonetheless."

"Most of the agitators operating locally here seem to be some breed of bohunk. They rile up the workingmen with their rantings, either from the bed of a wagon or in those damned newspapers. Then there is a riot, the police shoot some down, and they rant all over again to repeat the process. Strange how the men stirring the pot never seem to be present when the bullets begin to fly."

Finnegan knocked some ash to the café floor. "Yes, well, that is life, Abijah. I noticed an oddity much the same during the war. Now and then, as I huddled in a ditch or behind a spare corpse, I would be overtaken by boredom and find myself looking about for someone to make conversation with. In all that time, looking about to my left and to my right, I never once saw Abe Lincoln or Jefferson Davis huddled anywhere nearby."

Abijah grinned. "Very strange, Finnegan."

"Yes, quite."

Abijah sighed. "Well, I suppose we should make haste to the home office to see what it is William Pinkerton requires of you. I am sorry your retirement was so short-lived. You probably did not even have the opportunity to purchase a rocking chair."

Finnegan snapped his fingers. "I knew I had forgotten something." He pointed to the cigar in Abijah's hand. "You had best put that out before we reach the office. As I am sure you are aware, Mr. Pinkerton The Second has banned smoking inside the holy environs of his lair."

Abijah let out a laugh. "I have been made aware of that. Has he told you his reason for it?"

Finnegan blew out a plume of smoke. "Yes, he believes it killed is father."

Abijah continued to laugh, having a hard time ending the revelry. "Ah, where does that man get such ideas?"

"I do not know, but if he will buy into such foolishness, I shudder to think what will become of the agency."

FINNEGAN FOUND himself standing in front of the desk he had stood in front of not two days previously. William Pinkerton was once again looking dower while Robert Pinkerton appeared more nervous than ever. Standing with his thumbs hooked into his gun belt, waiting for William to finish scribbling a letter, Finnegan noticed that a change had occurred in the office furniture.

"Where have the chairs gone?" Finnegan looked to Robert Pinkerton.

"Chairs?" Robert glanced about.

"The two leather clad chairs your father kept here for... well, forever. They were quite comfortable. I spent many an hour in them taking my leisure. Your father and I swapped many yarns and a few outright lies seated in them."

William took his letter, placed it in a ledger book and slapped the cover shut, causing a loud clap. He glared at Finnegan. "I had them removed."

"Removed?" Finnegan squinted at the man. "Whatever for?"

"I had them removed so that men would not place themselves here to enjoy their leisure and waste my time. This is a place of business, even if my father preferred to treat it like the drawing room of a private club. I have no interest in swapping yarns or listening to lies. As such, I have no need for chairs. From now on, the men who enter this office will state their business and move on. There is no need for them to lounge about."

Finnegan rubbed his eyes. "I am sure that will lead to greatly improved efficiency, William. In that spirit, would you mind telling me why you sent poor Abijah to find me? I am certain the boy has better things to do than running errands."

Robert Pinkerton cleared his throat. "Ah, that was my notion, Finnegan. I thought you might be more amendable to...well, I thought you might enjoy a visit with young Abijah."

"I see." Finnegan turned back to William. "In the interest of efficiency, William, what is it you require?"

William Pinkerton snatched a sheet of paper from a corner of his desk and cast it toward Finnegan. "Those have been appearing in several languages around the city."

The gunman picked up the sheet and looked it over. "Yes, that German newspaper produces this tripe. They are fond of calling in all workingmen with these circulars. What of it?"

"What of it?" William stared, aghast at his employee's lack of comprehension. "You cannot grasp the danger such a...such an inflammatory circular represents. My God, Finnegan, what you hold in your hands there is no less than a call to arms, the spark that wishes to ignite an insurrection."

Finnegan chuckled. "Perhaps there is more of your father in you than you give yourself credit for, William. He would often become equally agitated when reading these ramblings. They produce ten of these a week, each more farfetched than the last. They are the work of deluded men wishing for unrealistic change."

William lowered his eyebrows into a glare. "What

occurred yesterday at the McCormick works was quite realistic, Finnegan."

"A bit close to home for you, William? Had you been hoping this strike would wane somewhere near the railyards?"

"Quite droll, Finnegan." William adjusted himself in his chair. "If it had not been for the quick actions of the police, the incident might have gone completely out of control. This city rides on a razor's edge this day."

"Yes, well, it has been my experience that the peelers do a fine job of keeping most of the citizenry of Chicago on edge, these days, William. What is it you want of me?"

The elder Pinkerton motioned to the circular. "Go to the damn Haymarket at the appointed time and observe."

"Observe what, pray tell?"

"You claim you wish to serve as a detective, go to whatever place that is they refer to as Haymarket Square and detect some damned anarchists. Identify the main agitators. Follow them to ascertain their associates and locations." He shook his head. "After that, well, do as you wish. If you believe you can shoot a few of them down without being seen, have at it."

"Shoot them down, William?"

Robert cleared his throat once more. "My brother jests, Finnegan. There was a time when you and my father jested in just such a manner."

Finnegan shook his head. "Your father was always quite serious involving such matters, Robert." He turned back to William. "Do you wish for a written report of my findings?"

"Do not bother me with it. Inform Robert and...well, inform Robert. I have far too many other items to deal with presently."

"Very well."

"Oh, yes," William frowned, looking stern. "The police will undoubtedly be in attendance at that meeting. Do not forget which side your bread is buttered on, Finnegan."

Finnegan arched one eyebrow. "My bread, William?"

"I seem to recall an incident, years ago, when you were dispatched to Pennsylvania to work with the Coal and Iron Police. You shot several of the officers, if I am not mistaken."

Finnegan took a moment to think back. "No, not several. If memory serves, I shot one Coal and Iron Captain and, I believe, a county sheriff. What does that have to do with the meeting at Haymarket?"

"If there is shooting, direct it toward the anarchists, not the police." Robert Pinkerton smiled.

"As always, gentlemen, I will direct my fire at those who are firing upon me." Finnegan gave a small nod to both men. "Good day, sirs."

EVENING WAS APPROACHING as Finnegan took up a position on the far side of the street from what many Chicago citizens referred to as Haymarket Square. Finnegan could not say for certain if the place had once resembled a square, in the sense that Trafalgar Square is designed as such. As Finnegan gazed across at the place, it more closely resembled an empty building lot which no one had found a use for as yet. He had no way of knowing that he was perfectly correct in the assumption. The fact that Haymarket Square was unused property made it a fine place to hold meetings, especially for labor movement agitators who could not afford to rent a hall every time they felt the urge to harangue a crowd.

The Pinkerton agent was more than a bit astounded to see so many people crowding into the small space. The rantings of unsuccessful revolutionaries were hardly the sort of thing Finnegan would have chosen to listen to on a fine May evening, if he was not being paid to do so. As the crowd grew larger, Finnegan pulled from his pocket the copy of the circular that he had been given at the office by the two Pinkerton brothers.

> Revenge!
> Workingmen, to Arms!!!
> You have for years endured the most abject
>   humiliations.
> You have worked yourselves to death.
> Your children have been sacrificed to the
>   factory lord.
> In short: you have been miserable and
>   obedient slaves all these years.
> Why?
> To satisfy the insatiable greed?
> To fill the coffers of your lazy masters?
> When you ask them to lessen your burden,
>   they send bloodhounds to shoot and
>   kill you.
> To arms we call you, to arms!

It went on to ask all the workingmen of Chicago to report to Haymarket Square the evening of the fourth so that a plan of action might be discussed, and a course of action adopted. Finnegan folded the circular and put it back in his pocket. He shook his head and mumbled under his breath. "A call to arms, William. You always were quite literal."

He stared across the street covered in large wooden blocks that served as paving stones. The place was filling with people, and he did his best not to react when he saw Abijah Smith arrive and take a seat with several other men on a pile of discarded lumber. The young man laughed and joked with the bohemians around him as if they had all grown up together somewhere in eastern Europe. The boy truly did have a talent for insinuating himself into the good graces of those around him and gaining trust. On the one hand, Finnegan found the practice distasteful. On the other, it was a skill he had never accrued, so he had to grudgingly congratulate Abijah for learning it.

A man had climbed into the bed of a wagon and was doing his best to whip the crowd into a frenzy of sorts, and Finnegan was already becoming bored. Finnegan could do without rhetoric. He had grown weary of it from far too much exposure. His father's friends and neighbors had spouted rhetoric in the shanty they had dwelled in back in Ireland. The officers had spouted similar rot in the Army. Wherever Finnegan traveled as a Pinkerton, there seemed to be a few men obsessed with climbing soap boxes and expounding. In all his born days, Finnegan had never seen the words amount to anything of note, but the spouters continued in their labors and showed no signs of giving up. Finding the current speaker tiresome, he dug out a cigar and had just withdrawn a match when a fellow in the dusty working clothes of a mason approached.

"Vood you mind giving me tinder?" The man's thick German accent made his lineage unmistakable.

"Aye." Finnegan struck the match and held it out as the man placed a half-smoked, cheap cigar between his lips.

"Tank you."

Finnegan lit his own cigar. "Once it is struck a man might as well get some use from it."

"That is vise."

The two men stood smoking and listening to the speaker for a long few minutes by Finnegan's reckoning. He did not find the fellow entertaining and disliked being in the section of Chicago most of the eastern Europeans had settled into. It was not so much that he disliked Germans or Slavs, although he did feel more comfortable around other Irishmen, but more that he kept catching whiffs of sauerkraut, which he detested.

"Vat do you think of this man?" The mason motioned to the speaker.

Finnegan sighed. "He seems quite similar to the previous man, and my prediction is that he will have a fair resemblance to the next man."

"You do not like vat he is saying?"

"I have not truly been paying enough attention to say that." Finnegan puffed his cigar.

"If you do not like him, and you are not listening, vie are you here?" The mason looked Finnegan up and down, perhaps thinking he had stumbled upon one of the dreaded infiltrators the German newspapers claimed infested the city. Of course, they were correct in the assumption, but Finnegan was not about to help give the rumor credence.

"I cover the news of Chicago for the Dublin Evening Mail."

The man stared suspiciously. "Shood you not write down vat the man is saying, if you write for the news?"

Finnegan shook his head. "Newspaper readers will only be interested if there is a riot, my friend. Carnage is all people care to read about."

"These people are not to be rioting." The mason laughed. "I do not tink you vill get your story."

Finnegan smiled. "Perhaps I will make up a riot. I doubt anyone in Dublin will know the difference."

The mason grinned. "Ah, you a smart one, eh?"

"I do try to be." Finnegan nodded to the man. "Never believe anything you read in the papers, my friend."

"Damn vell never do."

Finnegan stood around with the mason for the better part of the next two hours. His predictions regarding the speakers were largely correct and as storm clouds began to gather and the light began to ebb, Finnegan began to get the sense the mason was growing as bored as he was. The normally dogged detective was just about to resign his commission early, when he happened to peer down the street and see a face he recognized. It was not uncommon for Finnegan to see people he knew about town. He had lived, off and on, in Chicago for many years. What made this acquaintance of interest was that the man was not dressed as usual.

Finnegan turned to the mason and handed the gentleman a spare match. "For later, sir." He tipped his hat, and the mason tipped his cap. Finnegan only needed to stroll down the street a hundred yards or so before coming up next to the familiar fellow he had caught skulking about. He gave a quick look around to make certain no one was within earshot and gave the man a pat on one shoulder. The fellow just about jumped out of his coat. "Andrew Boyer, you are peeking about as though a husband is hunting for you."

The rather cherubic young policeman in street clothes appeared in a bit of a panic. "Mr. Gilhooley, what are you doing here?"

"Much the same as you, Boyer. I might suggest you get a little closer. From here you can barely tell what is occurring.

It could be a meeting for the temperance league, for all you know."

Boyer licked his lips. "I know perfectly well what is occurring and who is attending that meeting, Mr. Gilhooley. I am not here to observe them, only to make certain the street is largely clear before Captain Ward brings the rest of the men down."

Finnegan arched an eyebrow. "The rest of the men, dear Andy?"

"The captain has almost two hundred men; he means to disperse the crowd."

Finnegan chuckled. "Two hundred, Andy? That is ridiculous. There cannot be more than three hundred or so gathered down there. Have you peelers gotten so that you must have the odds even when you face an adversary?" Finnegan smiled, but the young policeman did not see the humor. "Andrew, where is this captain of yours?"

"A block over and one down, sir."

"Run and tell him to send the boys off to the tavern and save the city its money. These fools here are only a danger to my pleasant disposition. They are about to disperse of their own free will to flee the storm clouds gathering."

Boyer shook his head. "I am to report back, Mr. Gilhooley. If you wish to tell the captain something like that, you had better come with me. I have never known a captain to give my opinions much weight."

Finnegan rubbed the bridge of his nose. He did not wish to waste his time interceding with the police on behalf of a gaggle of unwashed anarchists any more than he wished to continue listening to the tripe of the speakers, but it seemed a pity to let conditions worsen without cause. "For the love of St. Peter, very well. Take me to your captain, boy, and I will speak with him."

The young policeman and the more aged Pinkerton detective made their way through a series of alleys and sides streets that did not warrant paving. By the time they made it to the place chosen as a staging area by the police, the storm clouds above showed the occasional flash of lightning. Most Chicago policemen made do with only a blue jacket, given to them upon hiring, but the man who stood at the forefront of the assembled police squad sported a full uniform, complete with pants and a jaunty cap that appeared to be of his own design. Young Officer Boyer went straight to the well-dressed man. "Captain Ward, Mr. Gilhooley of the Pinkerton Agency would like a word, sir."

The police captain slowly extended his hand to Finnegan. "You are a Pinkerton man?"

Finnegan nodded. "I am, sir, dispatched here to observe the meeting at the Square."

The captain nodded. "And I have been dispatched here to disperse it." The captain looked down at Boyer. "Is the street leading to the Square clear of obstructions?"

"It is, sir."

"Ah, good. I had feared these communist bastards might have built some sort of barricade." He shook his head, smiling. "They adore such things, though it never seems to do them much good." He motioned over his shoulder. "We had best get to our business. If you would like to accompany us, Mr. Gilhooley, an agent of Mr. Pinkerton is always welcome. I would imagine you have a bone to pick with these anarchists, given what they perpetrated at the McCormick works." He slipped on a pair of black leather gloves.

Finnegan removed his hat and rubbed his head. "Captain, do not misunderstand me, I enjoy giving those who vex me a good drubbing, same as the next man, but this all seems a bit gratuitous at this point."

"Gratuitous?"

"Yes." Finnegan let out a small chuckle. "You have all these men hid away here in an alley, making ready to charge a half-starved rabble of fools you very nearly outnumber. A storm is threatening, many are already leaving of their own accord. There is no need to cause a row."

The captain pulled a baton from his belt and hefted it in one gloved hand. "Mr. Gilhooley, are you suggesting I should simply allow those people to meet, plot more trouble, and then go about their evil deeds unchecked?"

"I am suggesting you let a small group of rather ineloquent blowhards and a large group of bored workingmen go their own way."

"I cannot believe what I am hearing from a Pinkerton man." Captain Ward raised both eyebrows. "Those men down there, the speakers and the crowd, are insurrectionists. They are holding a public meeting, flouting the laws of the decent citizens of this city. I will not stand for it."

"Captain, there are women and children in the crowd." Finnegan was doing his best to remain calm in the face of the man's stubbornness.

"Mr. Gilhooley, what would women and children be doing attending an anarchist rally?"

"I would assume they are the wives and children of the men attending. Captain, my former employer, Allan Pinkerton, always paid close attention to the reputation of his firm. I would assume your police chief has the same concerns regarding the reputation of his officers. How will it look if you are seen to be beating women and children, sir?"

"Oh, poppycock, Mr. Gilhooley. We are not in the practice of beating women or their brats. I intend to disperse that meeting up there and inform these bastards they cannot orchestrate their crimes where and when they please. Now, if you wish to accompany us, I would ask you remain in the rear, lest your peculiar notions cause difficulties for my men."

"Captain, you would truly risk these men when there is no purpose to it?"

"There is no risk, Mr. Gilhooley. You yourself just said they are a foolish rabble."

"The graveyards are full of men who failed to see risk, Captain." Finnegan shook his head. "Good day, sir. I wish you luck." He moved from the alleyway at a walk. When he was out of sight of the police squad he broke into a run, retracing his steps through the alleys and side streets back to the Square. Finnegan knew it would take much longer for the slow-moving police squad to close the distance. For some strange reason, Finnegan had a deep sense of foreboding regarding the approach of Captain Ward and his men.

When he made it back to the Haymarket, Finnegan paused and looked around to locate Abijah. The young man still occupied the same spot on the lumber pile he had occupied earlier. He sat, feigning rapt attention to the speaker on the wagon bed. With no preferable option, Finnegan decided that old tricks were the best tricks. He approached the lumber pile and pulled the small Cloverleaf Colt he carried from a vest pocket. When he was within arms-length of Abijah he jammed the revolver into the young man's ribs and moved between him and the speaker on the wagon.

"You gamble with your life when you play cards with a man like me and run off without paying, sir."

Abijah blinked a few times and finally found an answer. "You mistake me, sir. I do not play cards."

"The only mistake is that you continue to try and slip your debts." Finnegan looked to the men who sat around young Abijah. One or two of them seemed to have been taken in by him so well that they wished to act in his defense. "This is not a matter of concern to you men." Finnegan scowled. "Your attempts to intercede will only lead to this fellow having a hole in his gut. Get up off your backside, we are going to have a talk and locate your wallet, sir."

Abijah nodded and slowly stood from the lumber pile. "This gentleman has me confused with someone else, friends. I will go with him, and reason with him. He will come to understand. In the meantime, make no move toward him. I would hate to see you boys hurt over a misunderstanding." Abijah motioned to the street. "Lead on, sir."

"You first, young sir, and do not attempt to depart from my company. I assure you, your back is as fine a target as the front of you, and I make no distinction." Finnegan swung the young infiltrator around and jammed the Colt into his back. "Get moving."

Finnegan pushed Abijah along, out of the Square and into the street. One man from the lumber pile followed enough to watch them turn into a nearby alley. Once out of sight, Abijah turned and threw his hands in the air. "Finnegan, what in the hell can be so important as for you to risk this? Do you know how long I have been drinking godawful beer with those krauts and listening to their damned nonsense?"

Finnegan placed his diminutive Colt back in his vest. "You may resume your activities tomorrow. That is, if any of the men on the lumber pile still live, and are not too busy convalescing."

"What is afoot, Finnegan?"

"A rather irritating peeler captain by the name of Ward is currently on the march toward that shoddy square with no less than two hundred men. Their intention is to disperse the crowd and teach the agitators a lesson they will not forget." The sound of footfalls like low rolling thunder could be heard coming down the wooden paving blocks. "Ah, there, they approach."

"What?" Abijah peeked around the alley corner to see the police turning toward Haymarket Square. "What the hell are they doing that for?"

"They are bitter regarding the men injured at the McCormick works." Finnegan pulled Abijah back out of sight of the street. "It is a simple matter to indulge in the practice of taking an eye for an eye when you begin as a blind jackass." Finnegan shrugged and pulled a cigar from his pocket. "Would you care for one?"

"Finnegan, some of those men speaking there today have brought their wives and children."

The more experienced Pinkerton shrugged again. "Aye, but a man cannot save the whole world from itself, Abijah." He struck a match and lit his smoke.

"You intend to stand here smoking while the peelers attack women and children?"

Finnegan shook his head. "My young friend, I have already attempted to dissuade Captain Ward from entering the Square. Finding him to be intractable, I removed you from the Square so that the agency will not have a good man needlessly wasted." He tossed down the used match. "At all events, I doubt there will be much of a row. Even the likes of Ward and those drunken peeler swine will surely not have the nerve to beat women or children in public where some newspaper man might witness the act. Have no fear, Abijah; if someone falls under a baton today, it will only be some of your beer swilling compatriots from Bohemia, and not their offspring or spouses."

"This is madness, Finnegan. It is needless. Is Mr. Pinkerton aware of what these fools are doing?"

"If he is, he did not mention it when I was dispatched

here. Abijah, a highly esteemed idiot by the name of Ebersold is in charge of the peelers, presently. He takes his direction from the mayor who takes his direction from whatever robber baron is currently flush enough to afford the bribes. One of the men in that chain of command has become incensed with these damn union agitators and labor communists, and wishes to see them receive a good drubbing. It is such matters that make up the ebb and flow of life in the great city of Chicago. There is little two such men as ourselves can hope to change regarding it." He puffed his cigar. "I find it best to help who I might, and hide in alleys smoking once I have done all I can."

"Finnegan, we must, at least..." The muted sound of an explosion stopped the young man midsentence. Both Pinkertons leaned forward to look out into the street where they saw a large plume of dust and smoke drifting over the tops of the lampposts. "What in hell?" The soft pop of gunfire could be heard within the Square. "My God!" Abijah took off at a dead run.

"Ah, bloody hell." Finnegan let his cigar drop and gave chase after the young man. "Ward is not the only jackass about today." Following some fifteen feet behind Abijah, Finnegan saw the young fellow disappear into the smoke and followed up to where he had seen his associate vanish. Once in the smoke, Finnegan came almost to a stop, paused, and drew his Remington from the high-riding hip holster he kept it concealed in while working in the city. Stalking forward, he could hear the sharp snap of a revolver firing, could see the occasional flash in the smoke, and he could hear what sounded like Ward's voice hollering out rather disjointed commands. What he could not see was Abijah.

No direction seemed better than another, so Finnegan began walking forward through the smoke toward what he felt might be the rear of the square. He passed a badly mutilated policeman, passed two shot workingmen, and could just barely make out the remnants of the wagon formerly occupied by the various speakers. A woman lay near the wagon and was struggling to make it to her feet as a policeman ran up and grabbed her by the hair. The peeler jerked her head back and appeared ready to strike her with his baton when Abijah came out of the smoke and knocked the policeman down onto the paving blocks. Knowing the average member of the Chicago police would not suffer such treatment lightly, Finnegan ran forward. The peeler was struggling to pull a small revolver from his pocket while Abijah moved the woman away from the wagon. Standing over the policeman, Finnegan leveled his Remington on the man. "Cease digging for that pistol, sir."

"I'll be damned if I will." The peeler pulled on the butt of the gun.

Finnegan shot the policeman in the shoulder, reached down and tore the small Smith & Wesson revolver from the man's pocket, then grabbed Abijah by one arm. "Do something so foolish again and I will leave you to your fate." He pushed the younger Pinkerton into a doorway many members of the crowd had fled to. Wrenching the door open revealed a saloon devoid of patrons.

"Those blue bottle devils..." Abijah kicked over a chair. "That is a massacre without cause, Finnegan."

Finnegan groaned and pulled a chair over to him. Slowly taking a seat, he withdrew a fresh cigar. "Abijah, I do not know what occurred out there. I do not know what begat this damnable scene. What I will tell you is that it seems unlikely Captain Ward threw a bomb into the midst of his own men. It was clearly an explosion we heard before the firing began, was it not?"

Abijah calmed some and took a seat on a table. "Yes, the gunfire was proceeded by an explosion."

"Yes. It sounded to me much like a mortar shell, without the mortar, of course." Finnegan lit his cigar. "I cannot say what has just occurred, my friend, but I would venture to guess that it will sound repercussions for a long time to come."

"Yes, I suppose so." Abijah glanced to the door they had entered through. "That peeler, the one I hit, did you kill him?"

"He should live, assuming too many of his brethren do not take precedence over him at the surgeon's table." Finnegan took the Smith & Wesson from his coat pocket and tossed the gun to Abijah. The young man awkwardly caught the weapon. "That is a darling .38, the man must have given a fair number of dollars for it. From now on, keep it on your person at all times. I may not be near the next time you choose to do something so foolish as cuffing an armed man on the chin."

"Uh, yes." Abijah placed the gun behind his back. "Thank you, Finnegan."

"Yes, well, perhaps there are a few things a gunman such as myself could teach you infiltrators, at least if you should choose to stray into the realm of my profession." Finnegan stood and looked around the saloon. "My goodness, this is a shabby sort of hole in the ground, is it not? We should be off before someone comes barging in here and sees us together." He motioned to the rear of Abijah. "Go back behind the bar there and see if the keep has a box of cigars worth stealing, then let us be off."

Chapter 5

CHICAGO, ILLINOIS

May 5, 1886

By the time the sun crept over the city of Chicago, the telegraph wires had informed the world of the Haymarket Square Massacre. Neither Finnegan nor Abijah could fully appreciate the fact, at the time, that they had witnessed history, albeit purely by accident. As the underpaid paperboys of Chicago flung out headlines announcing the deaths of somewhere between five and a hundred police officers, the two Pinkerton operatives had little time for reflection. Abijah was expected back at the tavern he spent most of his days loitering in so that he might feel out the men he had ingratiated himself to in the passing weeks. Finnegan was about more direct business, as was his common practice. Contemplating the meaning of events would keep for later. As the few roosters left to Chicago crowed on the fifth of May, there was work to be done.

In the very wee hours of the morning, Finnegan had sat through a short briefing from a Lieutenant Shea. While the majority of the Chicago police were to make a showing in the streets and to be on the lookout to stomp down any further rioting before it began, a select few men were being charged with the duty of discovering those individuals responsible for the bombing at the square. Luckily for the investigators, there was little question as to who needed collecting. The speakers from the meeting at the square, and those who had been bandying about anarchist rants were well known. Those anarchists who readily promoted violence and suggested revolution had been under surveillance by Pinkerton agents for some time. In truth, Finnegan had frequently mocked both Allan Pinkerton and his son William for wasting the resources of the firm on men who, to Finnegan's way of thinking, seemed to pose little danger, aside from possibly boring a fellow to death. As always, the admission of being wrong came grudgingly to Finnegan.

"So here we have it." Shea puffed his pipe a few times, the very picture of a proper Irish copper. "Do any of you ne'er-do-wells know these men by sight?"

Finnegan smiled and nodded. "I know Spies, Fielden, and Parsons. I have followed them all about many a time." He struck a match on the brick wall of the police station basement the men were meeting in. The bedlam of prisoners in the jail could be heard down an adjoining hallway.

"You have been following these men?" The question came from a midsized, rather plucky-looking fellow with a clean suit and a mop of black hair on his head.

Finnegan nodded again. "They are all well-known communists and Mr. Pinkerton the senior had made something of a hobby of tasking us with their observation. Parsons, in particular, has been about his rabblerousing the better part of a decade now." Finnegan extended his hand. "We have not met, that I know of. I am Finnegan Gilhooley."

"Detective James Bonfield." He shook Finnegan's hand.

"Bonfield?" Finnegan grinned. "You are not the only

Bonfield employed by the city of Chicago. Is the other your father?"

The young detective shrugged. "John Bonfield is my brother." He scratched the back of his head. "He was commanding at the McCormick Works when the trouble broke out."

"Yes. Your older brother I have met once or twice. He has quite the reputation for strike breaking." Finnegan puffed his cigar. "If he continues on his present course, he will either be mayor or be lynched in short order."

"I have told him much the same thing many a time," Bonfield scowled.

"We can discuss the Bonfield family legend later." Shea arched one judgmental eyebrow. "If you know these blokes, you might as well have your pick of them."

Finnegan chuckled and looked to the other men present. Most were police detectives swept together because they lacked anything pressing to occupy them otherwise. He was the only Pinkerton agent. Any other Pinkerton men with knowledge of the anarchists were firmly embedded and needed to remain in position until the structure of the conspiracy became clear. "Well, gentlemen, as far as I recall, Fielden should not be difficult to locate. He has a good business in freighting and will not be apt to flee his property. We should try for him at his home this very morning." Finnegan rubbed his chin. "Spies -- the damnable cur -- we will surely find him at his printing house when it opens. He will wish to expound on the events from the Haymarket in his paper. We need only watch the building and wait for him to arrive."

Shea laughed. "You think this man will truly come into the office this morn' as if nothing of much interest occurred last evening?"

Finnegan tapped the ash from his cigar. "Spies will be

jolly as hell when he rolls out of his bunk today, fellows. Last evening was the first step toward his much-awaited revolution. He would not miss this morning for the world. Better to spend it at the paper than tromping through some field as a fugitive. Besides, he will be proud to be arrested. In his cell, he will eagerly await the toppling of the jail by his brethren in arms."

Shea tapped out his pipe. "The fellow sounds quite mad, Finnegan."

"You will see, soon enough." Finnegan looked over the men around him. "Send some of your peeler detectives here to watch the printing house. It is only a block or two down Fifth from this building. Only send one or two so that they will not be obtrusive. Have the rest begin watching Albert Parsons' house. He will be the most difficult one to obtain. I would bet my last dollar he has already fled."

Shea began refilling his pipe. The man looked as though he had not slept at all between the bombing and the early morning briefing. "What makes you think Parsons will prove a difficulty?"

"He is the most long-lived of the group. The elder Mr. Pinkerton called him the most dangerous man in Chicago some ten years ago. He has now outlived Mr. Pinkerton. He is also the only man you search for who is not an immigrant. Parsons has a large family living in various parts of the country. He can find a shady spot to hide when in need of it."

Shea let out a groan. "Very well, Finnegan. I will defer to you in these matters, I am sure you know best." Shea jammed the pipe in his mouth. "You wish for these fellows to watch the printer and Parsons' home; what will you be doing?"

Finnegan pointed to one side. "I will take this surprisingly chipper Detective Bonfield with me and collect Mr. Fielden." Finnegan smiled at the young investigator. "Have you ever a captured criminal before, dear James, or have you only heard stories of it from your brother?"

Bonfield cleared his throat. "Up to this point I have only followed along behind my older sibling and sometimes been given the honor of holding the comealongs, but I will try to assist you as best I can, Mr. Gilhooley."

"It is good to hear you are eager." Finnegan dropped his cigar to the floor and stepped on it.

Bonfield straightened up rather proudly as the rest of the men began shuffling out, headed for their varied assignments. As the last of the men were leaving, he cleared his throat once again. "I may be of more use than you imagine, Mr. Gilhooley. I speak German passably well, sir."

Finnegan smiled and nodded to the young fellow. "That may be of use as we bring in more and more men from the ranks of these anarchists and communists. For today, we will get by without it. Spies and Parsons both speak English quite well, and, to my knowledge, Fielden does not speak a word of German."

Bonfield glanced about to make certain they were alone. "Mr. Gilhooley, I must confess, I have heard many a rumor regarding you over the years. Is there any truth to what people claim?"

Finnegan laughed. "Young James, I do not know how I might confirm or deny any allegations without you first telling me what is claimed."

"Well, sir, I only bring the matter up as it may pertain to our work. I have been told that you rarely bring a man before the bar and we require these men to be held up as examples at trial, so that the public might view their wickedness and see their despicable deeds for what they truly are, sir."

Finnegan licked his lips and shook his head. "Ah, you are an eager fellow, James." He grinned. I give you my word as a gentlemen, here and now, that I will not remove my pistol from the holster unless I find myself in danger of losing life or limb. Not only that, I will continue to abstain from firing upon our suspects even if you are in danger of losing life and limb, since you are so very sincere in your wish to bring these men in alive and well." He continued grinning. "I must say, it is a fine thing to meet a young man with such dedicated principles."

Bonfield swallowed with an audible click in his throat. "Well, I do not know if I will wish to hold to my principles quite that far, Mr. Gilhooley."

FIELDEN'S HOUSE was located just behind the small stables that housed his horses and freight wagons. The house was a well-kept little structure. The place bespoke of a man who had made some money, but was not yet rich. Given some time, the ever-enthusiastic Samuel Fielden might have grown his freight business into one of the corporations he claimed to despise. Finnegan doubted that would occur now that Fielden had become formally embroiled in the dealings of his anarchist friends. The future looked rather dim for the lot of them.

A quick reconnoiter around the house revealed that only two people were inside, both illuminated by the light of an oil lamp in what appeared to be the main bedroom. Finnegan made use of his pocketknife to pop open the lock on the house's back door. The two men slipped inside and slowly came to the bedroom door with light spilling out from the crack at the floor. Listening for a moment, they heard what must have been husband and wife speaking back and forth in agitated but hushed tones. Finnegan slowly pulled his Remington from the holster and Bonfield took his much smaller Smith & Wesson from his pocket. In one quick movement, Finnegan spun the doorknob, flung the door open, and surveyed the room.

Two figures, a man and a woman, were inside the sparsely decorated bedchamber. The man reclined with an injured leg and a pile of bloody rags lumped on the end of the bed. The wife, a lady with grey hair, wore a frightened look. Fielden, the husband, showed only an angry scowl over his leathery freight master's face. Finnegan took a step closer to see that neither person was armed. He placed his Remington back in the holster and hooked his thumbs in his belt. "Mr. Fielden, Mrs. Fielden. My apologies for the crude entrance, but there are more than a few men in the city who would care to speak with Mr. Fielden."

"You tell them I am not inclined to give audiences today, Pinkerton." Fielden winced and clutched at his leg.

Finnegan inspected the injured limb. "Ah, you have gone and gotten an extra hole added to your carcass there, Samuel. Was it the bomb or the bullets at work on you?"

"It is a bullet, likely placed there by you, Pinkerton." He winced again as his wife placed another compress on the wound.

Finnegan moved a bit closer to investigate more. "Ah, well, you are still with the living. Some hot iron slapped to that will make the bleeding cease. You may well live to attend to the business that lies before you. Oh, by the way, I am not a member of the Pinkerton family, only an employee of the firm. Finnegan Gilhooley, by name." He smiled at both the husband and the wife. "In case you were confused as to my business here."

Fielden sneered. "I have heard the name Finnegan

Gilhooley. You were among the railroad bastards who hung the Mollies."

Finnegan shook his head and gently shooed the wife back so that he could inspect Fielden's wound firsthand. "That is a vile slur, sir. I assure you I had no part in their unfortunate demise. You anarchists really ought to keep better track of your villains if you hope to someday be taken more seriously." He replaced the balled-up rag over the bullet wound and motioned over his shoulder. "Allow me to introduce Detective James Bonfield of the Metropolitan Police. James, you should be honored to meet Mr. and Mrs. Fielden. Mr. Fielden is, to my knowledge, the one and only Englishman affiliated with the local anarchist cause. Will you not be terribly lonely after the revolution, Samuel, with no other John Bulls to celebrate with?"

Fielden let out a disdainful chuckle. "Ah, so you are Irish and I am English, so we must hate each other and curse each other and fight to our last day? That is what the bastards in the central police station would have us do, and the bastards with crowns and the bastards with bank titles. Do not be a pawn for them, Irishman. You and I are of the same stock and the cause of the workers should be our clarion call."

Finnegan sighed. "Mr. Fielden, if you were in better condition, I might, conceivably, give you a good drubbing simply for being an Englishman, but as things are, I believe I will simply haul you off. We have a coach waiting down the street. I will take one side and Detective Bonfield will take the other." Finnegan held up a likely looking roll of old bedsheet. "First, we must bandage this leg properly. It will not do to have you bleed to death in transit after all the trouble of coming here to collect you."

Fielden shook his head, grimacing. "You do a disservice to your people today, Irishman. We share a common cause."

Finnegan sighed again and tore loose a section of bedsheet. "I do not recall the workers coming to save me the last time I lay as you do now, Samuel. Now that I think of it, one of your benevolent workers attempted to blow me to smithereens not a few days past. I do not believe these workers you speak of feel as kindly toward me as they do toward you." He gingerly raised the man's leg and began wrapping it. "Or, it may simply be that you are mistaken regarding the entire matter. I suppose time will tell, shortly."

FINNEGAN STROLLED into the alley where Shea stood smoking his beloved pipe and staring at the offices of the Socialistic Publishing Company which produced several newspapers including the *Arbieter Zeitung*, the *Fackel*, the *Vorbote*, and the English language *Alarm*. Printers and their underlings had been coming and going since the dim dawn hours, but the man Shea was in search of had not shown himself quite yet. The print offices occupied the upper story of the rather sprawling brick building. A saloon and a Chinese laundry comprised the street level.

Shea glanced at Finnegan as he and Bonfield approached. "Ah, gentlemen, did you find Mr. Fielden at his morning prayers?"

Finnegan took a cigar from his pocket. "He was not difficult to capture. Some bloke placed a bullet in his leg the other evening."

Shea smiled. "Nice to know some of them end up in the correct location when fired." He motioned to the print office. "There are a goodly number of men working in that place. I would not have thought they would employ so many."

Finnegan lit his cigar. "They produce a number of periodicals. I rather enjoy the *Alarm*. From time to time, they have some lovely cartoons of Queen Vic and her concubine Albert I find quite amusing."

Bonfield looked a bit confused. "You read these anarchist rags, Mr. Gilhooley?"

"Oh, they keep a stack of them at the main office. A man gets pitiless bored sitting around waiting to inform the Pinkerton brothers of what has been discovered. You will be amazed what you find yourself reading after a few more years in this occupation, young Bonfield. I once read the entire Book of Mormon while forced to linger in Missouri."

Bonfield laughed. "How did you come to possess a copy of that?"

Finnegan shrugged. "All the Mormons had moved on and fellow gifted it to me, suspecting that no one else would ever have an interest in it." Finnegan returned his cigar to his pocket. "If I am not mistaken, gentlemen, that is Mr. Spies arriving to begin his day." He motioned across the street. "It is well that his employees beat him to the office. Now we may sweep them all up and possibly discover a few coconspirators to make Detective Bonfield's report truly shine." Bonfield grinned and took a step forward, but Finnegan placed a hand on his shoulder. "Let the man get to his desk and settle in some."

"Ah, yes. Of course." Bonfield stepped back.

"Shea, how many men do you have about here?" Finnegan smiled at the policeman.

"Five or six, unless some have wandered to find lewd women." Shea knocked out his pipe on the alley wall.

"Well, tell at least one to watch the rear of the building and one the front of this place. The rest of us will enter through that saloon, just as Spies did. It appears as though the chap who runs the place is at work already."

Shea nodded. "It does, at that. What do you want with a barkeep?"

Finnegan shrugged. "It is not so much that I want him for anything. I merely intend to bring him along upstairs with us when we go to arrest Spies. I do not know the disposition of the barkeep, but if he is in agreement with Spies on most opinions, I would prefer not to have him behind me or below me. These rascals are too fond of dynamite for that."

"Ah, a good point, yes." Shea slipped his pipe into his pocket. "Very well, then. Shall we?"

"As my sainted mother would say—it does not pay to put things off." Finnegan led the way out of the alley. Bonfield stayed by his side as Shea moved off to the right to inform one of his patrolmen where he wanted the men. Finnegan and Bonfield paused at the saloon door and waited for Shea to rejoin them. "Did some of your men elect to not dally with the girls, Shea?"

"Enough." He nodded. "One will be here, one in the rear. The other two will ascend the back stairs and meet us at the print office."

Finnegan sighed. He disliked working with an overabundance of assistance, but sometime there was little choice in the matter. "Do these men know enough to not fire on us coming from the other direction, Shea?"

The lieutenant smiled at his fellow Irishman. "It is the Chicago Police, Finnegan. The sweet Lord himself cannot say what they will do next with any degree of certainty." He patted the Pinkerton on the shoulder. "If you have begun to worry about such things, perhaps you had better get back to your cattle ranch and leave this dirty business to those not so well favored by fortune."

Finnegan shook his head and drew his revolver. "As usual, I will take that advice into consideration, just after I am done acting foolishly." He opened the door and the group walked into the saloon. A short man who looked not unlike one of the beer kegs next to him wore a surprised look as the detectives crossed the room. Finnegan nodded to the barkeep. "You know the way up to the print office, sir?"

The saloon keeper set down the rag he had been cleaning a glass with. "Yah."

"Then lead the way, sir."

The saloonkeeper glanced from the revolver up to Finnegan. "Yah, I show you."

With the saloonkeeper in the lead, they walked up a cramped staircase to the second story of the building. A strange slapping sort of noise could be heard as the barkeep swung open the door and walked into the print office. The presses were already running with half-a-dozen men standing in front of the wooden frames pulling on steel levers to chuck out the printed pages that composed the various periodicals produced in the building. The press operators looked up from their work in turn and Finnegan herded them toward the front of the loft-like print office. At the far end of the sprawling room the desks of the various contributors to the newspapers and the editor, August Spies, were set in a few rows. Spies wore a surprisingly calm look as the group of detectives and employees crowded into the spaces between the desks.

Finnegan motioned to Spies. "That is your man, Shea. Bonfield, place your manacles on him." Bonfield moved toward Spies, weaving between the desks. "Mr. Spies, keep your hands where they can be seen, sir."

Spies narrowed his gaze toward Finnegan. He was a small fellow, meticulously dressed in the guise of a more well-to-do businessman. His papers returned little in terms of profit, but you would never tell it by the man's clothes. Even his mustache was carefully waxed and curled. "Oh, you worry I may cast a bomb at you..." He glared. "Pinkerton, if I am not mistaken." He kept his hands in view and slowly stood behind the desk. "By your lilt, frock coat, and gun, I would venture a guess and say you are Gilhooley."

Finnegan gave a printer a small shove and moved the employees to one side of the room where they instinctively lined up against the wall. "I am, Mr. Spies."

"You have come to accuse me of throwing a bomb, then?" Spies held out his hands for Bonfield.

Finnegan shook his head and holstered his gun. "It is not my place to ask you about such matters. I would be interested to know if you draw the cartoons of Queen Vic."

Spies nodded toward a man with a desk in one corner. "Mr. Dobson there draws our caricatures."

Finnegan tipped his hat to the man. "Well done, sir."

"A bomb goes off and you men rush to the conclusion that a social revolutionary must be to blame." Spies chuckled while Bonfield set the manacles on his wrists and clamped them shut. "You all assume I am a mad bomber." He nodded toward Finnegan. "Did it occur to you that the man who really threw the bomb may have been with you all morning. These Pinkerton bastards have no scruples. I know for a fact this one here has been shooting men down for Allan Pinkerton since the war."

Finnegan laughed. "You should count yourself lucky that Mr. Pinkerton is no longer with us, Mr. Spies. If he were, I doubt you would be in chains this morning. He had a strong dislike for you and yesterday's unpleasantness would have undoubtedly convinced him to cease showing you deference."

"Ha, there, see, the man admits to being nothing more

than an assassin." Spies held his chin up, seemingly proud to have perhaps tricked Finnegan into the admission.

"I do not know if it would be proper to say I am nothing more than an assassin, Mr. Spies." He shrugged. "As you can see, I have the ability to arrest men when it suits me. As a matter of fact, I have not shot a man all day. I often do chores that do not involve killing men. I will thank you to give credit where credit is due."

"Ah, so proud to be a blunt tool for these damned capitalist swine, Gilhooley. How many men have you killed for your keepers?"

Finnegan smiled. "Oh perhaps a few more than you, Mr. Spies, but then you are only beginning and, as you mentioned, I have been about my work for some time."

"I have killed no one." Spies spit out the words, making his moustache flap.

"No one?" Finnegan took a seat on one of the desks. "Do you not have your very own militia, Mr. Spies? Are they not making ready for your great, grand, glorious revolution? You are so very fond of discussing the matter in your paper. You have not killed one man leading that terrible gang of dragoons?"

"Not one man. We will use no force until the revolution begins." Spies sneered.

"Ah, how lovely for you." Finnegan looked over the office. "So then, Mr. Spies, when we search these rooms, we will find nothing that could hurt a fly, eh?"

"You go to hell, Gilhooley. There is nothing here a man cannot legally possess in a free country. This is a free country, at least it was until you damned Pinkertons began shooting men who only wish for fair pay and an eight-hour day."

"Do you spend eight hours a day here, August?" Finnegan scratched one side of his chin. "It seems to me you left much earlier than all that whenever I was tasked with keeping an eye on you." He motioned to the writers and printers. "We will find no weapons on any of these men? Not a man among you carries a pistol or a knife?"

"These men do as they please; I am not their master, Pinkerton." Spies glanced down to his desk twice, then back to Finnegan.

"Ah, August, do you really keep some of your anarchist toys so close at hand? Finnegan crossed the room to the desk and opened the top drawer. He withdrew a small metallic object and held it out for Bonfield's inspection. "Do you need blasting caps to put out your paper, August?"

"I may keep what I please at hand in my own office, Gilhooley."

"You may indeed, August. Although, your jailer may be in the habit of telling you what you may possess in your cell. Shall we get these men to the police station, Shea?"

Most of the policemen in Chicago would have given their right arms to interrogate the Haymarket bombing suspects. Finnegan Gilhooley had little interest in them at all. As far as Finnegan was concerned, the anarchists and the police were bound to clash, blood was bound to cover the streets, and there was little for a man such as himself to do about it. He would have preferred to distance himself from the whole affair, but was rather unable to thanks to his long career with the Pinkerton firm. For years, Allan Pinkerton had dispatched Finnegan to observe and track the various anarchists and communists that seemed to infest the city of Chicago. While Finnegan did not particularly enjoy the duty, it had given him firsthand knowledge of most of the men the police were currently in pursuit of. Finnegan knew most of them by sight. He would have rather spent his time chasing a bank robber or, preferably, train robber, but that was not an option, and the Pinkerton brothers would have never forgiven poor Finnegan for telling the police to see to their own business when the city was up in arms over a bombing.

Finnegan had found himself somewhat tethered to the police station once the batch of men from the print office were delivered into their cells. It seemed as if nary a minute would pass that some detective was not bothering Finnegan with questions related to the suspects or activities Finnegan might have observed at some point. Finally, mercifully, a beat officer had come into the station and asked Finnegan if he could possibly tear himself away to help a detective down by the St. Paul freight houses. Assistance was needed to identify some men loitering on a bridge. Any excuse would do at that point, so he snatched up his coat and followed the officer.

Finnegan found one Detective Madden huddled by a streetlamp near a stoop. He was gazing down the street at a few men in ragged clothes who seemed deep in either conversation or quiet argument. Finnegan stepped next to the detective and tried his best to appear as though they were only acquaintances meeting on the street. "Madden?" The detective nodded. "I am Gilhooley. You watch those men by the bridge?"

"I have been, yes. They appear to be conspiring in some manner."

"All men conspire given the opportunity, sir. The question is what ends they conspire to achieve. I would say those men are discussing nothing more than a trip to a brothel if I did not know one of them."

"Which man do you recognize?"

"The hulking fellow a head taller than the others. He is hard to miss. Rienhold Krueger, by name."

"He is one of the agitators from the McCormick works, is he not?" Madden seemed quite pleased with himself.

"I am sure he must have been there for that row. The man loves a good fight. Be wary of him; he is quite the thumper when given opportunity for sport."

Madden ceased slouching and stood to his full five-feet-six-inches. "I have done some thumping as well, Gilhooley."

"I am sure you have." Finnegan reached back and felt to make sure the clasp on his holster was not set over the Remington's hammer. "I take it you mean to arrest some or all of them?"

"As best we can, yes. Is the boy who brought you still around here?"

"I sent him down to the lower bridge. He has been told to cross and move to the other end of the bridge those men occupy. I assumed they were your quarry when I first arrived. The young fellow seemed capable of a brisk pace, and I told him not to dawdle. Madden, the anarchists, the communists, and all the union men of every stripe are all fit to be tied this day. We must be careful as to how we handle these fellows. Events can get out of hand quickly on days such as this." Finnegan looked up and down the street, but saw no other people.

Madden pulled a small Colt from his hip pocket. "If these men will not cooperate, I have something for them."

"Detective, both my employer and your captains wish for these men to be collected and captured without undue gunfire. Let us speak with these fellows and ask them to come with us. Most of these fools are guilty of nothing more than standing with their fellow workmen or joining a union. It is only a very few of them we seek for far more terrible deeds.

Watch Krueger carefully, and try not to irritate him. You may find he will come with us quite easily if we are to pass a gin house on the way to the station."

"Gilhooley, perhaps it is not my place to say, but you seem to take these terrorist bastards a bit lightly."

"Terrorists?" Finnegan let slip a small chuckle. "That is what the bloody English called my father when he killed the tax collector. I do not believe I have heard the word since."

"You are a strange one, Gilhooley. If you say we should approach these men with a deft touch I will take your word for it, but one wrong move and I will make them pay for it."

Finnegan shrugged. "We must all pay for wrong moves in this life, Detective."

The two left the stoop and walked toward the bridge. Inside of a minute they were approaching the clutch of men who lingered in close conversation. As they walked up, Madden cleared his throat and held up his badge. "Gentlemen, we wish to have a word with you."

The oversized Krueger turned from his associates and towered over the much smaller Madden. To Finnegan, it looked as if the giant might eat the tiny detective. The thumper spoke down to the policeman with a voice made raspy on many a slaughterhouse floor. "What gives you the right to harass us, peeler. There is no law against standing in the street."

Madden did his best to puff up. "You damn well know there is a law against it, bohunk. You all constitute an illegal public assembly, and you are all loitering."

"Loitering? You upstart little prig, I ought to..." Krueger's thought was cut short by Finnegan's chuckling. The men, Madden included, turned to look at him.

"Ah, sorry, gentlemen, I was thinking of an old joke about an elephant and a scotch terrier. I cannot say what brought it to mind." Finnegan smiled. "Gentlemen, I cannot speak for the detective, but I am not particularly interested in arresting anyone for loitering. I do a fair bit of loitering myself from time to time and would hate to think it had become a punishable offense." Finnegan surveyed the men, trying to appear amiable. "We do not wish to arrest anyone, we merely seek conversation. Would you men be willing to accompany this detective to the police station so that we might have a smoke and a discussion -- or a cup of coffee, if you prefer?"

Krueger loomed up next to Finnegan. "The day I go anywhere or say anything to a goddamned Pinkerton will be the day I swing. I don't know what whore whelps you Pinkerton scum, but she must be the devil's own."

"Ah, Mr. Krueger, why do men such as you always insist on being difficult?" Finnegan drew his Remington and thumped it into the giant's groin. He followed that by kicking the ogre in one knee. When Krueger fell to his knees, Finnegan brought the Remington across the man's face and sent him to the cobblestones. "There, now." Finnegan stared down at the ape. "A man is never so small as when he sinks to rudeness." He smiled at the remaining men. "Madden, if you would be so kind as to manacle Mr. Krueger and watch over him while I obtain an ox cart to haul his large carcass to the station. Unless you gentlemen would care to aid in carrying him." Finnegan settled his gaze on one man, in particular, who was sweating badly in spite of the cool evening air. "You there, are you coming down with the pox?"

"Damn you, Pinkerton swine!" The man drew a pistol just as Madden stepped forward to manacle Krueger. When he fired, Madden fell next to the giant and Finnegan fired into the man's chest.

"Bloody hell." Finnegan stepped to move forward, but Krueger grabbed Madden and flung the wounded fellow into

Finnegan's legs. The Pinkerton fell, snarled akimbo with the policeman. Finnegan lurched up to see the man he shot lying dead, the fellow's friends fleeing toward the city, and Krueger running hell bent for leather across the bridge. "Damned lousy..." Finnegan looked down at Madden. "Are you hurt badly?"

"I will live, get that damned hulk."

"Damn the luck." Finnegan got to his feet and began to give chase. Krueger was not difficult to follow and was not overly fleet of foot. The fugitive decided to give up on fleeing down the street only a block or two after the bridge, noticing that Finnegan was steadily gaining on him. The giant made a hard right turn and burst through the doors of Henry Schroeder's Saloon, a common collection point for various union organizers and agitators. Finnegan followed the giant straight in.

Krueger limped to the bar. "Henry! Give me over your gun."

The bartender, a slim man wearing a lily-white apron was shocked by the request for obvious reasons. "What's that now, Krueger?"

"Damn you, Henry." Krueger leapt across the bar as best he could in his injured state and rolled to the other side, hitting the floor with a colossal thud. He stood, grasping a sawed-off shotgun in one paw. Across the bar, Finnegan stood with his Remington leveled.

"Do not raise that gun, Krueger."

"Go to hell, Pinkerton."

Krueger twitched the hand that held the shotgun and Finnegan fired. He put three bullets into the ogre's chest and one into the mirror behind the bar as the giant fell. Smoke hung in the barroom air and the other residents of the saloon held deathly quiet. Finnegan opened the loading gate on his

Remington and began ejecting the spend casings. They dropped to the wooden floor with dull clinks. "As you men saw, he gave me no choice. I made every effort to..." A massive hand clamped onto the bar and soon enough Krueger's equally massive body came into view. "Ah, bloody hell." The shotgun appeared again as the nearly broken man tried to level it on Finnegan. The ogre fired wide and nicked a customer. "Damn it to hell." Finnegan dropped his Remington and pulled the Colt Frontier Model he kept in a shoulder holster. Being somewhat flustered, he fired a round into Krueger's shoulder, one into the giant's hip, one wide into what was left of the bar and two into the bar top. The ape let out a wet grunt and fell down behind the bar once again.

"Mister?" The bartender motioned with one shaking hand. "He's still drawin' air."

"For the love of St. Michael." Finnegan placed the Frontier Model back in its holster and withdrew the Cloverleaf Colt he kept in the small of his back. He stalked behind the bar and shot Krueger twice in the head. Finnegan looked over the other occupants of the saloon once more. "Yes, well, as I was saying, you all saw that the man gave me no choice. In either instance." He returned the Cloverleaf to its hiding place and withdrew the Frontier Model so he could begin reloading it.

The bartender took a tentative step toward Finnegan and the enormous corpse. "Sir, are you some sort of constable or such?"

It was not always intelligent to mention his employer, but, since he had reloaded the Colt, Finnegan felt reasonably safe in the admission. "I am a detective in private employ empowered by the chief of police in this city for special investigations. I had every right to pursue this man and every right to defend myself against his threatened acts." Finnegan rounded the bar and picked his Remington from the floor. He began reloading that gun, as well.

"I cannot say as I care about any of that rot." The bartender grew a bit churlish. "What concerns me is who will be payin' for my damn mirror."

Finnegan looked over what remained of the mirror. "Aye, yes, that is a pity." He began slipping fresh rounds into the Remington. "Feel free to dig through the man's pockets. If anyone is deserving of his remaining funds, I would adjudge you to be that man." He closed the loading gate on the Remington and holstered it. "If the funds found in his possession do not cover the damages, please feel free to contact the Pinkerton Detective Agency to receive the additional funds. Tell them Finnegan Gilhooley sent you around."

Chapter 6

CHICAGO, ILLINOIS

May 6, 1886

Finnegan sighed and tossed an old musket into the corner of the police station livery stable. It was one of four that had been found during their raid of Zepf's Hall, another well-known meeting place for the anarchists and their related ilk. Finnegan had been hoping for a true arsenal, but had hardly found enough for a proper deer outing, and that would have only been proper thirty or forty years earlier. He leaned against a post and brought out a cigar as Bonfield set to unharnessing the horses from the wagon they had been using the better part of the day.

"These anarchists are proving to be somewhat of a sorry lot, Mr. Bonfield. I am not certain you require my assistance in helping them to clean out their unused storerooms or sweep up their unused firing ranges."

"Mr. Madden is glad you were attending last night, Mr. Gilhooley. When I spoke to him, he made it quite clear that if it had not been for your being there he surely would have perished at the hands of those lowly thugs."

Finnegan lit his cigar. "I would take the man's compliment more to heart if I did not have cause to believe my presence was partially the cause of the unpleasantness. These men we pursue have a deep hatred for Pinkerton agents. With any luck, I will cease to accompany you soon, young Bonfield. I feel you may have easier going without me in tow."

Bonfield shook his head. "My brother has had dealings with both of the Krueger brothers, and he was not a bit shocked to hear one of them had finally met his demise. As John tells it, the man living as long as he did was a minor miracle."

"At the end there, it seemed as though he might live forever." Finnegan blew out his match and cast it well clear of the hay. "Still, I look forward to another assignment." Finnegan turned to see Chicago's Chief of Police strutting toward the stable. The fellow always reminded Finnegan of August Spies. Both men were so overly fastidious about their appearance that one wondered how they operated in the outside world at all. "Stand tall, Bonfield. Your superior approaches."

The young detective stiffened and stood straight. He did his best to remove the hay from his jacket and pants. "Hello, Chief Ebersold; am I needed for something, sir?"

Ebersold checked his boots to make certain the stable had not sullied them and then looked to Finnegan while a smile spread across his face. "No such need, Detective. I merely wish to chat with Mr. Gilhooley for a moment. If that is to Mr. Gilhooley's liking."

Finnegan had seen the police chief many times, but never been formally introduced. He put his hand out to the man most of Chicago hated for one reason or another. "A pleasure to meet you, sir."

"Ah, the same to you, Mr. Gilhooley. And, might I say,

you did a lovely job dispatching Mr. Krueger last evening. The city is a better place for your actions, and I was personally quite pleased to see the man's name appear in the morning report. Krueger was a notorious scoundrel." Ebersold grinned. "If you could possibly find a reasonable cause to shoot his brother this evening, it would be much appreciated."

"We shall simply have to see how the day progresses, sir."

"Mr. Gilhooley, I have been told you own a cattle ranch, given to you by the grateful cattlemen of the Montana Territory. Is there any truth to the statement?"

Finnegan let out a small laugh. "Oh, as with the majority of tales, that one is about half truthful, depending on how you look upon it." He knocked the ash from his cigar. "Some years ago, I was temporarily employed by the Montana Stock Growers Association. I assisted in the capture of a few horse thieves and for wages I receive a small percentage of the increase in the cattle herds belonging to the cattlemen I assisted."

"Ah." Ebersold nodded knowingly. "That must come to no small profit some years, Mr. Gilhooley."

Finnegan shook his head. "It should, come the day I sell my shares and draw upon the funds. Given the inevitable increase in the herds every year, as only nature herself can guarantee, I have so far not felt the need to convert my interest in the operations back to cash money." He smiled at the police chief. "Given my experience with banks and stocks, trusting cattle to answer to their impulses has always seemed the better bet."

"I am sure time will prove you correct, sir." Ebersold withdrew a small snuff can and took a pinch. "Mr. Gilhooley, might you be interested in speaking with some of these various miscreants we have managed to collect thus far?"

Ebersold motioned over his shoulder. "Bonfield and the other detectives are doing a fine job, but there are several more hideouts and pits that require raiding and searching. We're running terribly behind, Mr. Gilhooley, at least from the perspective of State Prosecutor Grinnell."

Finnegan adjusted his hat. "Chief Ebersold, I am sorry to hear you are running behind in your chores, but my speaking with the men you have already brought in might not move you along as you are hoping. The spite these men hold for Pinkertons will undoubtedly color the issue."

"At this time, that may be precisely what is required, Mr. Gilhooley. Perhaps their anger for you will cause them to slip. To you, in a passion, they may make admissions no other detective could illicit. I would not claim it is certain to work, but it is at least worth a try, sir. Would you be willing to attempt it?"

Finnegan took a moment to review his options. If he turned the police chief's offer down, the Pinkerton brothers would undoubtedly keep him engaged raiding more gin joints and dirty holes until every conceivable anarchist hide in Chicago had been discovered and tediously searched. "Uh, very well, sir. I would appreciate keeping young Mr. Bonfield with me for his translation abilities. I am afraid I have no ear for the language of these Huns."

"Ah, certainly, yes. Keep Detective Bonfield for as long as you like." Ebersold seemed quite pleased to have recruited additional assistance. "Now, then, the prime objective in interrogating these fellows is to discover the whereabouts of Albert Parsons, since he is the only member of this vicious little sewing circle we have yet to collect. Personally, I view him as the most likely suspect for actually pitching the bomb. What would your thought be on that matter?"

Finnegan dropped his cigar and stepped on it. "I am not a

bit surprised that Mr. Parsons' has yet to be located. I am certain he has a fine network of places to find succor laid out and is making ready use of them. As for him being the bomber you seek, well..." Finnegan shrugged. "I would not say he is of too high a character for such a thing. He has surely never balked from suggesting others fire bullets or fling bombs. All I can say is that he has certainly had ample opportunity to toss a bomb at the police in the past and has always refused the offering. He may have changed his mind Tuesday last, but I doubt it."

"You feel we seek another man?" Ebersold appeared a bit put out.

"I imagine we do, but as you say, the only way we will discover Parsons or any other man is by continuing. Who is it you would like Mr. Bonfield and I to speak with first?"

FINNEGAN SAT across the table from August Spies. The small fellow still appeared quite well put together, given his current circumstances. Compared to most men residing in a Chicago jail, he seemed remarkably calm and somewhat optimistic at first blush. Finnegan held out a cigar across the table. "Care for one, August?"

The rabblerouser extraordinaire reached out and took the cigar. "Why are you here, Gilhooley? I have heard many tales regarding you, but none of them made mention of your... investigative abilities. You are, at best, a simple tool for bashing other objects. Why are you attempting to trick me into a confession when there are so many policemen crawling about this place? I would think almost any one of them would be better suited to this task."

"Perhaps, but Chief Ebersold felt I would be a good

companion for you to chat with for a while. He felt you might be more forthright with me than you would be with his officers."

Spies sneered and reached out for the match offered by Bonfield. "To me, a Pinkerton is the same low animal as a policeman. You are all slopped from the same trough and are all beholden to the same cruel masters. What difference does it make what badge of disgrace you wear?"

"To most it matters little, I suppose." Finnegan sipped the cup of coffee he had brought with him. "But, I would think you would prefer me to these policemen on account of what became of your brother." Finnegan sipped again. "William was his name, was it not?"

Spies puffed, looking bitter. "His name was William."

"The young fellow was shot down by these policemen, as I recall, but not for the cause of the eight-hour day, eh, August?"

Spies licked his lips and indulged in more cigar puffing. "Poor William fell in with bad company. He had little choice in the matter. In this pitiless Babylon a man can either be a criminal or a pawn of the capitalists. There is not much difference, at any rate." Spies knocked ash to the plank board floor. "These peelers shot him down for reaching in his coat. That is what they told my mother when they brought his body home. Would you have bothered to offer an explanation, Gilhooley? From what I have seen of you Pinkertons, you rarely seem to waste time on such pleasantries."

"I might not have bothered. Although, since I do not work directly for the city, there is rarely cause for me to ferry bodies about." Finnegan contemplated his coffee for a moment. "It is good that we can be honest with each other, August. We are not fond of each other, and it is unlikely we will become friends very soon. I do not suppose you would be interested in telling me the whereabouts of Albert Parsons?"

Spies blew smoke out his nostrils. "Why would I wish to tell you the whereabouts of any man?"

"Oh, I cannot say for certain, but I always got the impression you and Parsons were at cross purposes. Did he not give you trouble about forming your rather ill-equipped militias? Really, August, those muskets were army issue when I was in the service of this nation, but that was many long years ago. I hardly think you would find them fit for toppling the current government."

"Workingmen fight harder than Pinkerton scum. You need not worry for the safety of the men in the coming revolution, traitor." Spies leaned forward a bit. "You truly believe I would inform on Parsons out of spite for some minor slight from years ago?"

Finnegan smiled and finished his coffee. "Before this bit of unpleasantness is at its end, you may wish you had someone to inform on. You yourself said all of you will surely swing when we marched you out of your print shop. Do you now believe some insurrectionists are on the way to save you, August?"

The agitator's lips quivered slightly. "What becomes of me matters little. If Albert lives to see the revolution, then the workers will be all the better to have a leader close at hand. If you seek Parsons, go to hell and look for him, Pinkerton. Take these police and your other bastard brothers with you."

Finnegan sighed. "Lovely chatting with you as always, August."

Finnegan stared across the table at the second man Ebersold had asked the Pinkerton to interview. Adolph Fischer had a hard German face and piercing blue eyes that showed only a fraction of the anger that lurked inside the man. His days in Chicago were not his first fighting what he viewed to be the cruel machinery of the modern world. Finnegan had never met the man before, but he had read of his exploits thoroughly.

Finnegan proffered the man a cigar, just as he had with Spies. Fischer sneered. "I need nothing from you, Pinkerton."

"Ah, very well then." Finnegan lit the cigar for himself and puffed. "I am sorry if I am taking up your time, Mr. Fischer. I have been asked to inquire of you if you saw the man who threw the bomb at the Haymarket. I do not suppose you might be interested in confessing to that particular crime? It would save all parties concerned a great deal of effort and fooling about."

"I confess to nothing." He looked slowly from Finnegan to Bonfield and then back again. "I did not throw the bomb, but if I had I would be proud to say I was the man who did."

Finnegan knocked some ash down to the floor. "You are quite the peripatetic fellow, Mr. Fischer."

Fischer squinted. "What the hell did you call me?"

Finnegan chuckled and turned to Bonfield. "The man is insulted."

Bonfield shrugged. "I might be, as well. What did you say about him?"

"I said he was peripatetic."

"Peri-pathetic?" Fischer was more confused than angry.

"It means that you lark about, move from place to place. It is...pay no mind." Finnegan took a puff from his cigar. "You lived in St. Louis for some time."

"Ya, so what? You don't like St. Louis, Pinkerton?"

"I like it just fine. I have read that you were there during the railroad strike. You were one of the Ring of Five who set up the commune and tried to take over the city. That must be a very impressive credential to your anarchist brethren, eh, Mr. Fischer?"

"I am not an anarchist; I am a communist, Pinkerton."

Finnegan shrugged. "I have heard that you communists do not believe in the good Lord, Mr. Fischer, so perhaps you are not bothered by the notion of being sent to meet your maker."

"I do not fear to die for my cause, Pinkerton. I am not like you. I do what I do for more than money."

"Ah, yes, indeed you do, sir." Finnegan tapped down a bit more ash. "But you are not just a communist, Mr. Fischer. You are also a husband and a father. Why not think of your children for a moment? If they find you guilty of murder you are sure to swing, sir. Why not be a good lad and admit that you were only a witness at the Haymarket? Tell these police who threw the bomb and go about your business setting type for the next silly paper some agitator starts up with his capitalist profits." Finnegan smiled. "Did you know August Spies started his paper with the money he made selling umbrellas, Mr. Fischer? Do you really want to die for nothing more than to offer some company to a damned umbrella salesman?"

Fischer leaned as far forward as the chains he wore would allow. "I die for something you could damn well never understand, Pinkerton."

"That much is certainly true, Mr. Fischer."

THE DETECTIVES of the Chicago Police Department were not afforded anything as fancy as desks. They were allowed a room on the third story of the station where a used dining room table had been deposited by some charitable person, along with a collection of mismatched chairs. This was where they kept the "evidence" collected in any given case and where they ruminated on what to do next to catch various perpetrators.

Finnegan looked over the haphazard piles of household goods, books and various other traps that had been acquired so far during the Haymarket case. The organizational skills of the detectives were not impressive. "Do you not have a file room, Bonfield?" Finnegan scanned the piles, trying to decide if there could conceivably be anything of use.

"A file room?" Bonfield took a seat in one of the chairs. "What for?"

"So that you may determine which of your suspects each pile of refuse formerly belonged to, at least." Finnegan reached down and pulled a book from a collection of clothes. The title was in German, so he tossed it to Bonfield. "Any idea what that reads, Detective?"

Bonfield smiled and flipped through the book a bit. "We have found several copies of this. I believe we took this one off of Fischer. It is called *The Science of Revolutionary Warfare*." Bonfield held up the book and tapped the subtitle with one finger. "A Handbook for Instructions on the Use and Manufacture of Nitro-Glycerin, Dynamite, Gun-Cotton, Mercury Fulminate, Bombs, Incendiary Devices, Poisons, Etc.."

"I am certain every typesetter owns such a book." Finnegan shook his head.

"The majority of the men working at the *Alarm* owned a copy. The work of Johann Most is quite popular with the local newspaper men."

Finnegan nodded and took the book back. "We have a

translated copy of this at the main office. Having read through the brunt of it, I would say these fellows have taken the advice to heart. Chasing them, I have encountered several bombs, plenty of fulminate and more than a dash of gun-cotton." Finnegan looked up from the book as a sweaty policeman barged into the room. "Ah, now there's a lad earning his pay."

The rather chubby fellow caught his breath and looked to Bonfield. "Sir, I been sent to tell you we've captured a fella named George Engel. Lieutenant Quinn sent me, said you wanted to know when he was brought in. We found a goodly stash of bombs at his place, sir, and a few of them Remington rifles like the army uses. Czar bombs and some made from pipes, sir."

"Very good, Carter. Thank you." Bonfield stood. "Go catch a break. You appear to need it."

"Thank you, sir." The policeman turned to leave.

"A moment there, dear Carter." Finnegan walked over to the man and proffered a cigar, which was readily accepted. Finnegan struck a match and lit it for the fellow. "Pray tell, did you search this man's dwelling?"

"I did, sir."

"And you found more than a few of these lead bombs that must be soldered together?"

"Yes, sir, and dynamite and blasting caps."

"Did you find anything about the place that could be used to manufacture the bombs? A vise or irons for leading?"

"Oh, no, sir, nothing of the sort."

"Thank you, Carter. You may be about your business."

The policeman held up the cigar. "Thank you, sir."

When Carter was gone, Bonfield turned to Finnegan. "Manufacturing?"

Finnegan resumed flipping through the book. "It is only

that it bothers me a bit that we have found so very many bombs. We have found bombs and blasting caps at the newspaper offices, more in each man's home. I believe an informant has led your men to a stash of them in a sewer grate, correct?"

"It is."

"And yet, so far, we have not found a single bombmaker. Those ugly little czar bombs are not purchased at department stores. One of these men should possess a furnace for melting lead, and a mold, at a minimum. The men we have in custody thus far seem more interested in flaunting their bombs than exploding them, or saving them for whatever sort of anarchist rapture they expect to arrive. They are the sort of fellows who brew up trouble. The sort of man who builds bombs is who we need to discover. If we can locate our bombmaker, I believe we will be well on the way to..." Finnegan had reached the back cover of the book. He held it open for Bonfield to see. An address was scribbled on the inside. "Any idea who might reside at 422 Sedgwick Street?"

"The address is not familiar to me. Perhaps it is a bookstore?"

"I have never seen a copy of this book next to Moby Dick in a bookstore, Bonfield. I think we would be well served to investigate this."

Bonfield scratched his head. "I was hoping to interrogate Engel."

Finnegan waved one hand dismissively. "Oh, posh, Engel is not going anywhere. He was found in a house full of dynamite. I doubt he will convince the judge he had it merely to remove a stump from his property. Interrogate the man later when he has been properly mellowed by a cell. This address on Sedgwick Street is scribbled in a terribly ominous manner and promises to be far more interesting than yet another dull-witted typesetter hoping to blow up city hall."

"In fact, Engel operates a toy shop."

"Fine then, a dull-witted toy maker. Either way, a man can only stare at fools across that table for so long before he must find new entertainment."

Bonfield looked pensive. "Finnegan, would you mind my asking you a question of a personal nature?"

"If you like, certainly."

"If you do not mind my saying so, you seem to view this investigation as somewhat of a merry chase, a bit of fun. You were nearly blown to bits at the Haymarket, you shot a man only yesterday, now you wish to go fishing for bombmakers at this scribbled address. Do you not find any of this the least bit distressing?"

Finnegan nodded and pulled a cigar from his coat. "Detective, you are too young to recall the war, so you simply have a perspective that is skewed from mine. You are horrified by what that ridiculous czar bomb accomplished a few days past. You have never seen the like of it. On the other hand, I know that a bomb such as that only did the work of a single shell launched at Gettysburg. Now, with all this excitement swirling about, it seems as though the world is nearing its end and may never be the same, but I assure you, the sun will continue to rise and, soon enough, the newspapers will return to petty political squabbles. In ten years' time, not a man among us will recall the events of the Haymarket bombing or care to argue over Mr. Engel's role in it." Finnegan smiled at the young man. "You would do well to keep things in perspective, Bonfield. View this for what it is, a jolly good chance to chase some fellows and have a bit of fun that gets you out of this damned station for a day. Beyond that, such things serve little purpose."

Bonfield chuckled. "My work has never been explained to me in quite that way, sir."

"No, and it is not likely to be by any of your elders or betters. You are lucky to have come across a fellow such as myself who feels no need to glorify matters. Now, let us go see about this address before we are too old to enjoy the outing."

STANDING across the street from the rather unassuming home at 422 Sedgewick, Finnegan was a bit disappointed to see that the place did not much resemble a bad man's lair. A woman could be seen through one of the windows going about her chores and there was a nicely laid out garden in the backyard.

Finnegan sighed. "This does not look to be the dwelling of a proper villain. Then again, many an evil bastard keeps the paint up on his house." Finnegan took the Pinkerton badge from his pocket and pinned it to his vest.

Bonfield shook his head. "What precisely do we tell the lady of the house as to the purpose of our visit? Can you think of some likely excuse for our call?"

Finnegan straightened his frock coat and stepped to cross the street. "I have rarely found need for subterfuge in this occupation, young Bonfield. The majority of people are more apt to be honest if you are honest with them. I will address the lady."

The police detective shrugged and followed. "I suppose, since you have been at this work longer than I have, I will be well served to defer to you, sir."

"You will see, James. Honesty is the best policy." Finnegan

strolled to the front door of the house and gave it a stiff knock. It was only a few moments before a stout woman wearing a flour-covered apron opened the door. Finnegan removed his hat and gave the woman a small bow. "Madam, my associate and I are quite sorry to bother you while you are about your work, but we are detectives and require your assistance."

"Oh, ya, detectives?" The woman had a thick German accent and seemed fairly amazed by Finnegan's proclamation.

Finnegan pulled back the lapel of his frock coat so the lady could see his badge. "Madam, would you mind if we asked you a few questions?"

"Oh, ya, sure. We good people in this house. I got no cause not to talk to police." She cleaned her hands on her apron.

"Madam, might there be someone living at this residence who owns a small lead furnace for casting items, round items?"

"Yah, we rent room to a man named Lingg. I do not care for him, but he pay rent on time every month. He melts lead to make bombs to kill the Kaiser."

"I see." Finnegan nodded as if the declaration was a very common thing to hear. "And does the man ever fuss with dynamite?"

"Yah, he like dynamite. He say he use that to kill da Kaiser, too."

"Is Mr. Lingg home at the moment, ma'am?"

"No, he not been here for a day or two, I tink."

"I see." Finnegan rubbed his chin. "Are the gentlemen's things still in his room, ma'am?"

"Yah, he not get them back if he not pay this month rent, either."

"Aye, very good to be sure, madam. Would you mind if my associate and I looked over Mr. Lingg's room?"

"That fine." She stepped aside. "You come on in. We good people in this house. Got no trouble with police."

Finnegan bowed again and crossed the threshold, Bonfield followed. The younger detective paused as he was passing the lady of the house. "Madam, you say you have no quarrel with the law, ma'am?"

"Yah, no trouble."

"But you let a man live here who wished to blow up Kaiser Wilhelm?"

"Yah. Da Kaiser no live in Chicago. He is none of you concern. You Chicago police."

Bonfield tipped his hat to the woman. "Very good, ma'am. Quite correct."

The lady showed the men to a staircase which led up to the second story of the house. The detectives passed through a slim door and found the large attic formerly occupied by one Louis Lingg. A bed and a table constituted the only furniture. The table was cluttered with the exact equipment Finnegan had been searching for. He sighed and motioned to the discovery. "A lovely clay mold, a small burner, plenty of ingots." He stooped to look under the table. "I would wager the canister down there contains powder." He looked over the remainder of the rather barren room. "We should step lightly in this place, James. He likely has his dynamite concealed under a floorboard or in a wall."

Bonfield looked about furtively. "I must confess a great dislike for dynamite, Finnegan."

"Not all men would agree with you, James. I would imagine Mr. Lingg fairly loves the stuff." Finnegan slowly moved to the opposite wall of the room and gently stepped on a floorboard that sat slightly above the others. "Bloody hell."

He rubbed one side of his face. "I would be interested to know what might be below this board, but I am tentative to pull the damn thing up."

Bonfield took off his hat and wiped sweat from his brow. "I cannot say, Finnegan. You suppose he may have rigged it somehow or other?"

Finnegan chuckled. "Yes, James, that is precisely my worry."

Bonfield pointed to the floorboard. "It is not just being blown to bits that we need worry over. I have heard that only touching the stuff with to bare skin can stop a man's heart."

"Truly?"

Bonfield shrugged. "I cannot say, but that is what I have been told."

Finnegan moved back from the floorboard slowly. "Now that I think on it, there are most likely men in your station or somewhere in the employ of the city who would know more of these matters than we do. Perhaps it would be best to defer to their judgment."

"Yes, I expect it might." Bonfield took a step toward the door. "It may be best to remove ourselves and let a fellow with more experience handle this particular portion of the investigation."

"An excellent notion." Finnegan moved toward the door, as well. "Of course, you understand it is not merely the threat of death that gives me pause, but rather the instant nature of the death. If I were to explode, I would never even have the opportunity to contemplate my stupidity. A man ought to at least have a moment or two so that he might make peace with his own reasoning before passing on."

"I could not agree more, Finnegan. I am certain there must be some sort of powder man about who would be better suited to mucking about with this." Bonfield began descending the stairs. "In terms of policy, I am sure locating the place as we have done is really more the business of detectives than prying up boards, anyway."

"We are in agreement, James."

As the detectives emerged from the stairwell, the lady of the house approached with a boy of about fifteen in tow. She thrust the boy forward toward the men. "Yah, dis is Gustav. He show you where Lingg keep the dynamite."

Finnegan stared at the youngster and pointed upward. "Up there?"

The boy shook his head. "No, sir, under the house. If you like, you may crawl under with me, and I will show you."

Finnegan shook his head. "No, son, it is not my place to go crawling about under houses. That is not the business of a detective." He looked to Bonfield for confirmation.

"Quite right, Mr. Gilhooley, quite right."

Chapter 7

CHICAGO, ILLINOIS

May 7, 1886

Finnegan struck a match and lit his cigar. The flame served a dual purpose, as igniting it signaled Abijah Smith. The young infiltrator moved past an abandoned cattle pen and approached the shed Finnegan lingered by, smoking. When he made it to the shed, the wind changed and Abijah stopped short to cover his nose.

"Good God, Finnegan. What is this place?"

Finnegan smiled and took a step deeper into the shadow where the shed blocked the moonlight. It was an hour past midnight and there was little chance of being noticed, but a man could not be too careful when employed by the Pinkerton Agency. "The tannery keeps the hides here until they are brought into the factory. On the other side they discard the hides which are too far rotted. Those lie there until they can be turned into soap."

Abijah gagged a bit. "That is fascinating." He coughed. "Why are we meeting in this fetid hell?"

"Would you come here on a stroll?" Finnegan offered a cigar. "We will not be interrupted, and you will not be seen."

He grinned. "Take this, it will help with the stink." Finnegan puffed away while Abijah got his cigar going. "How are things with the socialists? Do you have the minor details of the revolution seen to yet?"

Abijah shook his head. His old mentor had never really taken the anarchists of Chicago seriously, and probably never would. "They are a bit disappointed that the rest of the city has not risen to burn the police stations yet. They begin to worry that the Haymarket was only a flash in the pan." Abijah puffed rather vigorously so the smoke would hopefully surround him. "Please say you did not call me down to this brimstone swamp simply to jest about the scruffy fools who plot uprisings from their sleeping rooms."

"I do enjoy such fun, although this evening I have a different purpose in mind. During your time amongst the rebels have you come to know a fellow by the name of Louis Lingg?"

"Lingg?" Abijah gave his mentor a quizzical stare. "Yes, I have met Lingg. He has been in the company of Spies and Fischer a fair amount these last few weeks. He is a bit of an odd man out in their group. He is young and I believe he has only been in the country a few months."

Finnegan nodded. "How young?"

"He cannot be much over twenty. He does not speak much English. It always seemed odd that men like Spies or Parsons would keep him about. What do you want with such a pup?"

Finnegan glanced about to make sure the stench was keeping eavesdroppers away. "Lingg is a pup with useful skills. He has been making bombs and handing them out to your unwashed insurrectionists at an impressive rate. Looking over his room earlier, I got the impression he did not have another hobby to keep him occupied."

"Lingg? Truly?" Abijah shook his head. "These men do nothing but complain of how the working man has no time for leisure in this world, and yet they have so much time for building bombs. I begin to suspect there are some untruths in their proselytizing."

"It is good you have kept your sense of humor, Abijah. Many men lose their ability to laugh in this business."

"As you have often pointed out, Finnegan, there is often little better to do than laugh."

"Yes, well, a man must get by somehow. Do you have a notion as to where I may find Mr. Lingg, now that he has left his room on Sedgewick Street?"

"I may have to think on that a moment." Abijah scowled at the stink once more. "Was the man truly building enough bombs to distribute about?"

"We found much lead, much powder, and pounds of dynamite at his rented room today. He had more stashed under the house. Enough to blow half the city apart and a Remington rifle under the floorboards. Young Mr. Lingg is prodigious beyond his years."

Abijah took the cigar from his mouth. "Well, if he was so very important to their revolution, it may be that one of the elders of the order would be willing to give him aid and succor, now that he has been forced into hiding."

Finnegan nodded. "Or they have set him up in a new place to make them more bombs. Either way, I thought you might have a likely spot in mind."

"I might, at that." Abijah smiled. "Parsons has a cousin, a widow woman who lives in a cottage on Ambrose Street. It is a strange little dwelling with pale blue paint and a garden with trellises out front. Parsons showed it to me once and made a point of saying that a man could find shelter from the woman in a time of need."

"Very kind of the man to look out for you, Abijah."

"Mr. Parsons loves me like the son he never had, Finnegan."

Finnegan shrugged. "And yet, you cannot say where the man might have gotten off to."

"Well, men often run off from their sons. I have checked the cottage on Ambrose, of course, and a few other haunts I thought likely, but it appears as though Parsons has left the city. Your man Lingg may yet be lingering somewhere, though. Peeking through the rear window on Ambrose the other day I saw the bed had been slept in. Parsons' traps, which I damn well know he would not travel without, were not to be seen, so I moved on to other business."

"We shall have to see about Mr. Lingg." Finnegan puffed. "Too bad about Parsons disappearing into thin air. I had rather been looking forward to him being dragged in. Mr. Pinkerton always said that man would hang. It is a pity he will not be here to see it."

"Yes, Mr. Pinkerton did rather despise Parsons. I had difficulty stifling a grin from time to time thinking of the old man ranting, when I was in the company of Mr. Parsons. It is strange how things shake out, is it not, Finnegan? One day I was a wet-eared boy hearing none other than Allan Pinkerton curse a man's name. Now I am grown and have spent many a dull night listening to Parsons curse the memory of Mr. Pinkerton. How strange life is."

Finnegan sighed. "And bound to become stranger still before it is over." He let his cigar butt drop to the muddy ground.

"Oh, by the by, congratulations. I have been told you shot Big Krueger in Schroeder's Saloon. Fine work, Finnegan. I see you have not lost your touch."

"I very nearly lost more than my touch. The behemoth

would not stay down. He raised up like Lazarus until I was nearly out of ammunition. It is becoming so that a man never knows what may happen next in this damned city."

"Perhaps it is time for you to finally marry your schoolteacher and settle into your cattle business, old friend."

"Why is it everyone shows so much interest in my meager share in a few cattle outfits lately? From the number of inquiries, you would think I had invented the cow or held sole knowledge of the animal's workings."

"Perhaps it is simply hard for men to understand why a fellow with another option would continue on as a Pinkerton agent. The stories I have heard of your time in Montana may be the cause of some of your troubles, as well."

"Stories? Ah, what rubbish do the fools claim now?"

Abijah chuckled. "One, in particular, was told to me by none other than Albert Parsons himself, so he might educate me as to the evil nature of the average Pinkerton agent." Abijah wore a playful smile. "As you may already know, once upon a time, Allan Pinkerton dispatched his finest assassin to the wilderness of Montana, so that the fellow might shoot down all the small cattle and sheep ranchers there to make room for the capitalists. The assassin shot and hung more than a hundred men while roaming the territory and was rewarded with a sprawling ranch of his own, and a seat on the Stock Grower's Council. That scourge of small farmers and sheepherders alike is currently worth many a million and the envy of all other Pinkertons who live only in the hopes of emulating the bastard."

Finnegan laughed, but stifled it, lest someone might hear. "Ah, Abijah, Mr. Parsons does weave a fine tale, does he not?"

"He always did, sir. I must admit, I do rather miss hearing his fanciful tales, now that he has departed."

"I would not doubt one of us will see him again someday, Abijah." Finnegan gave the young infiltrator a pat on the arm. "Thank you for the information regarding Lingg."

"That is the purpose of fine young spies such as myself, Finnegan. Are you finding enjoyment in collecting these anarchists? I would think you would after having followed them about and fussed over them for so long."

"Oh, I do my level best to find some enjoyment in my work, regardless of the task." He shrugged again. "I suppose I am glad to see the more smug fellows behind bars. Although, a part of me will miss them a bit when they are gone. I do not know if I will have the energy to keep track of a whole new set of communists when these are inevitably replaced. Perhaps I will search out that schoolteacher you mentioned."

"I have been told a comely schoolteacher is far preferable to a bearded revolutionary."

FINNEGAN FOUND himself standing next to Bonfield outside yet another unassuming house. Abijah had described the place more than well enough for Finnegan to locate it and it appeared as though people moved about inside. All things considered, the prospects of capturing Mr. Lingg were looking up, even if neither of the men were looking forward to the event. The idea of hidden dynamite still lingered in each man's mind.

Finnegan surveyed the cottage. "You do not wish to send one of your underlings over, Bonfield? A man would think you wish to be chief someday, showing so much gallantry."

Bonfield swallowed with an audible click in his throat. "I attempted to pressgang a few of the patrolmen, but there is another row brewing in Packer Town or the McCormick

Works or some damn place. There was not a man to be had." Bonfield scratched his head. "Well, what do you recommend this time? Shall I ask the lady if the mad bomber of the house is home?"

Finnegan shook his head. "No, you may wish to abandon the truth in this instance." Finnegan stared at the house a little more. "Knock on the door and tell the lady you wish to speak with Mr. Lingg."

"What? Are you daft?"

Finnegan smiled. "Give her some Hun name and tell her you wish to speak with Lingg. If she has never heard of a man named Lingg, she will tell you so. If Lingg is hiding within, she will go to fetch him."

"Why would she do that?"

"If you are not a confederate of Lingg's or sent by confederates of Lingg, how on earth would you know where to ask after him?"

Bonfield looked fairly shocked. "By Jove, Finnegan, now and then you truly do come up with a corker." He laughed. "That may do, my friend. What name should I give her?"

"Oh, well, any Hun name will do nicely. Tell her you are Mr. Kruse, that is a fine name for a Hun."

"I knew a Kruse once who claimed to be of French descent."

Finnegan waved one hand. "There is many a communist frog hopping the earth. If it is French, it will do."

"And what will you be doing while I announce myself at the front door."

"Oh, I will scamper around to the back of the house. If your ruse does not work, Mr. Lingg will flee. If it does deceive them, it will only deceive for a moment or two. Be careful mucking about with that bomber if it comes to wrestling him down."

Bonfield wiped sweat from his forehead. "Perhaps it would be better to simply keep watch and shoot the scoundrel when he comes out."

"Oh, come now, James. Your chief and your prosecutor would not like to hear you say such things. Besides, I am sure you will receive a large and quite shiny medal or billowy ribbon of some sort if you capture this fellow Lingg. Would you not like a billowy ribbon?"

"Ah, damn the luck." Bonfield took a deep breath. "Mr. Kruse will do?"

"He will do fine." Finnegan smiled. "Just yell out if you need anything, I will be around back."

Finnegan walked off to enter the alley near the cottage and Bonfield crossed the street on stiff legs. Once in the alley, Finnegan trotted to the rear of the cottage, stepped over the small picket fence that separated the cottage grass from the alley, and made his way up next to the rear door of the place. He pressed one ear to the door and could already hear the sounds of Bonfield in conversation with the widow. The lady sounded amiable enough. Finnegan stole a quick peek through the door's window and saw the lady ushering Bonfield into the house. Taking that as a sure enough sign the woman had at least heard of Lingg, Finnegan drew his Remington and made ready to put his shoulder to the door if it was locked.

There was a knocking sound very close to where Finnegan was hiding. He heard the woman say something muffled and then heard a voice with a very thick accent yell out "Who es Kruse?" With that, there was the sound of some glass breaking and the noise of a scuffle erupted.

"Oh, bloody hell." Finnegan tried the doorknob, found it would not turn, and put his shoulder to the door. It popped open with little force. As he entered, he found, there on the kitchen boards in front of him, Bonfield and Lingg wrestling on the floor. Bonfield appeared quite terrified. Lingg only looked enraged. "Ah, well, if you have not exploded yet, I doubt you will soon, Mr. Lingg." Finnegan brought the Remington revolver down on the back of Lingg's head. The fellow went limp, and Finnegan pulled him off Bonfield.

"The stringy bugger is stronger than he looks, Finnegan." Bonfield lay on the floor, panting for a moment before moving over and putting a set of manacles on Lingg's wrists.

Finnegan sighed and holstered his pistol. "It has been many years since I have arrested so many men in so short a time. I must say, I had nearly forgotten the method."

Bonfield stood and pulled Lingg to his feet. The man's groggy head lolled around as Bonfield held him up. "I have heard you hung a hundred men in Montana. You must have arrested those fellows previous to their demise, eh?"

"Why do men continually accuse me of killing a hundred scoundrels in one way or another? It is the acme of foolishness to accuse a man of such a thing. Ninety-nine or a hundred and one would be far more believable. How would a fellow ever manage to stop at a perfectly round mark such as a hundred?"

Bonfield paused to consider his fellow detective for a moment. "So, you do not deny the base charge, only the quantity?"

"Be about your business with your prisoner, you damned pup." Finnegan leaned against the wall and looked to the widow who owned the place. She stood observing, looking as though she did not know whether to approve or not. "Tussling with dynamiters is a sport for the young. Would you not agree, madam?"

Chapter 8

CHICAGO, ILLINOIS

May 10, 1886

FINNEGAN YAWNED INTO ONE FIST AND RUBBED HIS EYES. For some reason, appearing in the office of his current employer caused a fit of boredom lately. He had always felt a sense of impending excitement when Allan Pinkerton had called for him. When the great man's son William made the same request, it only made Finnegan feel weary. Perhaps it was the inevitable result of replacing a bold adventurer with a rather stodgy businessman. Finnegan reminded himself that the whole world got a bit more stodgy every day and, as such, the home office should be no different.

William Pinkerton checked his watch, sneered, and looked up to Finnegan. "Do you have any idea where Smith might be?"

Finnegan stifled another yawn. "I could not say, William. I have not seen him since the other night when he put me on to Lingg's hideout."

Pinkerton groaned. "It will be a damned nuisance if the boy has been found out or some other calamity. It has taken near on forever to insinuate the fellow into the socialists."

Finnegan chuckled. "He has not been found out. He is merely running late."

"How can you be certain of a thing like that, Gilhooley?"

"If he had been found out, we would have received word regarding a number of anarchists either being shot or exploded, William. I have taught that boy to sell his blood dearly, I assure you."

Pinkerton cupped his forehead with one hand. "Finnegan, I do not wish to offend, I truly do not, but I have always pondered how my father found men such as yourself to bring into his employ."

Finnegan smiled. "As you know, he found me when I was a boy. From there, I can only assume he formed me into the type of man he preferred to have on hand." Finnegan glanced about the office. "Where is dear Robert today?"

Pinkerton sighed. "He was meant to be here by now, as well. He is trapped south of here by the damned railroad strike and a hundred other calamities."

"When troubles come, they are not single spies but in battalions, William."

"What is that?"

"Shakespeare. *Hamlet*, as I recall."

Pinkerton grunted. "I have been told you pursue a schoolteacher somewhere in Montana Territory. Is she responsible for that knowledge?"

"In truth, it was your father who first suggested the bard to me, William."

"Ah, yes, he was a great one for such rot." Pinkerton coughed into his hand and checked his watch again. "Where in blazes is that damned boy?"

"It takes time to place a message in a man's hand in the field, William. The message must be carried to the drop. The agent must visit the drop. If the agent has other commitments, he cannot simply take flight under all circumstances. If you have sent for him, he will arrive, eventually. What is so damn pressing that it requires our attention on a Sunday, anyway?"

"Oh, am I keeping you from Mass, Finnegan?"

"You are keeping me from frittering away my day as I damn well please, William. I can only assume you have good reason." Finnegan rubbed his face. "We have made excellent progress rounding up the anarchists the police wished collected. With Lingg in custody, I see little need to rush."

"Men like you never do."

"I have seen too many men in a rush die to consider it a wise practice."

"Yes, well, I suppose that sort of thinking often poses as an excuse to..." Pinkerton turned to the door that was swinging open. "Ah, Smith, I had begun to think I would have to strike you from the company roster. Where have you been?"

Abijah stepped next to Finnegan and stood at what approached attention. "My apologies, sir. As instructed, I have been making use of my spare time to search locations that might possibly conceal bombmaking operations. I did not receive your message until just earlier."

"Ah, well, just see that it does not happen again." Pinkerton leaned forward in his desk chair. "Now, then..." His nostrils raised and a deep frown formed on his face. "What is that?"

Finnegan turned to his young associate. "Abijah, I hope you do not mind me saying so, but you smell a bit like a murdered prostitute who was drowned in some French concoction."

"Yes, well." Abijah shuffled his feet and looked down at

the floor. "I was searching a factory that perfumes butter just before coming here."

"Perfumes butter?" Pinkerton looked aghast. "What on earth is that, and why does it smell so damned awful?"

Abijah cleared his throat. "Sir, when butter becomes rancid, the dairy sellers scent it rather than throw it out. That is why the smell is..."

"Flowery death is how I might describe it." Finnegan rubbed his eyes again. "That is why I suggested the prostitute had expired. There is a definite sense that whatever has been covered in perfume has begun to decay." Finnegan winced. "I do believe this to be worse than the tannery shed, eh, Abijah?"

"I would, Finnegan."

"Oh, bugger, enough of this foolishness." Pinkerton waved one hand in front of his face. "Smith, do you know a scoundrel by the name of Schnaubelt?"

"Rudolph Schnaubelt, sir?"

"Yes, damn it."

"Uh, yes, sir. Rather, I have met him more than a few times. He is the brother-in-law of Michael Schwab, one of the men in custody already for the Haymarket."

"You could recognize him by sight?" Pinkerton continued to wave his hand.

"Yes, sir."

Pinkerton moved his gaze over to Finnegan. "Do you know this scoundrel?" Finnegan shook his head. "Very well, then. Take Smith here with you and search the bugger out."

Finnegan rubbed his eyes and took a step away from Abijah. "Find him, William?"

"Yes, is that not what the great Finnegan Gilhooley is good for? Tracking men down? Find him and shoot him or drag him to the police station house. One way or another, the city wants him brought to heel."

Finnegan sighed. "The collection of another anarchist ragamuffin is the cause of you bothering me on the sabbath, William? What makes Schnaubelt any different from the rest of the lousy mob?"

"The shiftless detectives of our city's police have settled on Schnaubelt as the man who tossed the bomb at the Haymarket."

Finnegan shook his head. "Is that simply because he has not yet been apprehended? What is wrong with saying Lingg did the deed?"

"Oh, he was many miles from the Haymarket when the bomb exploded, Finnegan. All the socialists in my circle agree on that point," Abijah interjected, looking as if he was having difficulty remaining so close to his own clothing.

"Well, it is a fine thing to know men of such high character have given the rascal an alibi." Finnegan winced again. "Did you roll in the damned butter, Abijah?"

"It is a butter factory, Finnegan. It is difficult to find purchase and I slipped several times."

"I do not care about butter factories." Pinkerton ran a hand through his hair. "The police have found a witness they credit as sober, and the man has identified Schnaubelt as the man who threw the bomb. Finnegan, you have an excellent record of capturing the men you chase, or producing parts of them that can be identified. Smith, you know what the man looks like. Go fetch him, both of you."

"William." Finnegan slipped his hands into his pockets. "This business of infiltrating unions and associations is hardly new to you; surely you understand that young Abijah here cannot be seen to be larking about Chicago next to a

Pinkerton agent. At best, he will be found out. At worst, we will both be hung from a lamppost."

Pinkerton appeared exasperated. "What of all the talk of selling blood dearly?"

"Just because it is our policy does not mean we would not like to avoid it, William."

Pinkerton took to waving both hands. "If Schnaubelt was in Chicago, the damned police would have found him by now. You two are to discover where he has fled and go fetch him. I dare say Mr. Smith is not so well known as to be recognized by a ship's steward in Alaska or wherever the bastard has gone." He paused and gagged slightly. "For the love of God, whatever you two must do to find the fellow, get to it."

"Oh, William, I really think the three of us should remain here to scheme a bit."

"Damn you, Finnegan. Take this rank pile out of here and do not reappear until you have Schnaubelt and have scrubbed this cur red."

Finnegan turned to Abijah. "Truthfully, I would prefer it if you scrubbed first and then we set about finding this last rascal. See to your bath and I will make inquiries with a few people as to where Schnaubelt may have gotten off to. Do the same of your anarchists, Abijah. Do not forget to make them aware that your poor aunt is nearing her demise and you will, in all likelihood, have need to rush to her bedside."

Abijah grimaced at his own stench. "Yes, well, it might be better to tell them I intend to flee the police, given the circumstances, would you not say?"

Finnegan took to waving his hand. "You are the master infiltrator. I defer to you."

"Do as you please." Pinkerton gagged, once more. "Just get the hell out of here. We will have to burn the building if you do not leave quickly." He stood and began fighting to open the window.

THE QUITE DAPPER gentleman came through the door to the dressing room and set his silk top hat on the bureau. He turned to the theater manager. It was necessary to speak up a bit due to the sound of applause that could still be heard from the audience. "Zee to it that I am not disturbed for at least an hour, Maurice. And tell zat scoundrel Jeremiah zat he is paying for dinner zis evening." The man grinned. "Or he vill suffer a wrath zat can only be produced by a man of my talents."

The manager turned a bit red. "Oh, yes, sir. Very good, sir. Um, might I say that it was a very impassioned speech you gave tonight. I am honored to have had such words spoken in my humble theatre."

The man waved one hand dismissively. "It is nothing, Maurice. It is I who am honored to be a guest of zuch a dedicated supporter of ze cause."

"Sir? Do you truly believe that dynamite will act as the savior of the Irish people?"

"Dynamite and true patriots, Maurice." The man patted the manager on the shoulder. "Now, if you please, you know how Mr. O'Donovan Rossa loves to torture me with ze gentlemen of ze press. I must have some time to rest before vee go out for the evening and ze torment begins anew."

"Yes, sir, of course." The manager gave a low bow and backed out of the room, swinging the door shut as he went.

The man chuckled to himself and checked his hair in the dressing room mirror. "Ah, thank the good Lord for placing money in fools' pockets."

"The good Lord watches out for fools, drunks, and all sons of Erin." Finnegan stepped from behind a curtain at the back of the dressing room.

The man spun around and turned a whiter shade of pale. He held one hand up to his face and took a deep breath. "By God, Finnegan, you nearly frightened the life out of me." He looked Finnegan over. "Bloody hell, is there good cause for me to fear?"

Finnegan chuckled. "Do you think I have come to put you down, Sam Rooney? I assure you, times are not so tough that I have taken to killing old friends for money." He took another step forward and extended his hand, which the other man ardently shook. "How have you been, Sam?"

"Never better, as you can bloody well see." Rooney lifted one lapel of his silk-lined frock coat. "Nothing but the best for a true showman."

"Ah, is this what passes for theatre these days?" Finnegan plucked a promotional pamphlet from the dressing room table. "Mr. O'Donovan Rossa and the owners of the Polaris Theatre are proud to present a lecture by the academically esteemed and internationally renowned Professor Samuel Mezzeroff regarding the use of the resources of civilization and how they might be used to further the Fenian cause of independence." Finnegan grinned. "Taking yourself rather seriously these days, Sam."

"Well..." Rooney shrugged. "The proper moniker is half the show, Finnegan." He patted the gunman on one shoulder. "By God, it is good to see you. It is a bloody bore being chained to these revolutionaries. The bastards never crack a smile."

"Not the crowd for the Sam I know. Did you truly believe I had come to shoot you?"

"It is always hard to say who may have become thoroughly convinced by an act. It may be that oh-so-serious William Pinkerton has come to consider me a liability."

Finnegan shook his head. "You should know better than that. I would damn well shoot William before I shot you. Although, this theatre tour might be laying it on a bit thick. Surely, before you are done rambling about the nation, telling every Hibernian on the continent to throw a bomb at Queen Vic, you will find some trouble."

"Bosh." Rooney produced a flask. "It is only smoke and hard talk. If these Irishmen had a mind to sit Vic on some dynamite, they would not be in America. You always were a sour one, Finnegan. What is wrong with making a few dollars from such rot? I would offer to make you a guest lecturer if I had not heard you were too well off for such things these days."

"Too well off?"

"I have it on good account that you killed two hundred men in Montana and received no less than a thousand dollars a head in payment." Rooney sipped the flask and returned it to his pocket. "Although, now that I think on it, if you were near to a millionaire, I doubt you would have secreted yourself into my room here."

"Both the size and reimbursement of the Montana massacre have been greatly exaggerated." Finnegan took out a cigar and offered it to Rooney. "I am fairly certain I have shot more men in Missouri than Montana; why is it so many rumors fly about my short visit there?"

"Exotic locations always put tongues to wagging. What brings you by, Finnegan? Say you have come to have dinner and spend a proper night reminiscing."

"That would be fine, if you feel we can be seen together."

Rooney laughed. "You are Finnegan Xavier Gilhooley,

gun wielding pride of the Irish people. Who better for the notorious Professor Mezzeroff to dine with?"

Finnegan took out a cigar of his own. "If you say so, Sam. I was hoping to speak with your friend O'Donovan Rossa, as well."

"I would not have it any other way; you simply must meet Jeremiah. A finer fellow or one more devoted to the cause you are not likely to find."

Finnegan lit a match for both cigars. "I assume that cause is the same as it always was, Sam?"

"There is no purer cause I can imagine than attempting to get rich, Finnegan. As always, I pray the war will end soon."

Jeremiah O'Donovan Rossa was not nearly as pleased to be taking a meeting with Finnegan as Rooney had predicted. The Irish revolutionary and general rabblerouser actually looked quite piqued to have the famous Pinkerton agent in the same room. The theatre was empty, even the manager had left for the night, but O'Donovan Rossa still worried they might be discovered.

"No, Sam, no. I will not parlay with this...man." Rossa shook his head and held up his hands while standing on the theatre stage. "I do not care where the man was born, we cannot be seen to be...conspiring with his type."

"Conspiring?" Finnegan smiled. "Sir, whether you like it or not, you have been conspiring with me for some time. I might go so far as to say that my previous affiliation with Sam here is the only reason you are still breathing the good Lord's air."

O'Donovan Rossa puffed up, combed back his hair, and

stood to his full six feet. He could be an imposing man when he felt the need. "You, sir, claim to have deferred from killing me, and then ask a favor in return. You are a blackguard, Gilhooley."

Finnegan sighed. "I have not been asked to shoot you down, O'Donovan. Though, someone among my ilk may be saddled with the task if you continue in your ways. What I refer to is my own personal decision to rather editorialize a bit when it comes to the reports the agency issues regarding the antics of you and the good professor here."

Rooney cleared his throat. "Oh, the Pinkerton brothers have you reporting on us?"

"Yes, Sam, for some time now."

Rooney tried a wavering smile. "And who might you be reporting to Finnegan?"

"Well, since you and your friends in the Clan na Gael have chosen to so closely align yourselves with these American anarchists, we report on you regularly to the Prussian Secret Police who, quite quickly, I might add, pass the reports onto the bloody British." Finnegan gave O'Donovan Rossa a hard stare. "I am told you spent some time as a guest of the Crown at Chatham."

Rossa looked truly shocked. "Yes, more than I care to recall."

"Well, if not for me insisting in our reports that both you and Professor Mezzeroff here are nothing more than a couple of dunderheads, pandering in the hopes of turning a profit, I believe the damned English would have fit you for a wooden coat by now."

Rossa continued to look astonished. "What interest do the Pinkertons have in the Clan na Gael?"

"None, so long as you only wish to blow up Englishmen on English soil. Pockmark the whole place with craters as far as I am concerned. It is only bombings on this side of the ocean that concern us." Finnegan turned to Rooney. "Such as the one in the Haymarket." He turned back to Rossa. "Your friends who follow the Black International, the Huns, are all that concern me."

Rossa scowled. "Those men, Huns or not, they only seek freedom, the same as we do, Gilhooley. The yoke of a foreman is no different from the yolk of the damned British."

Finnegan laughed. "I have yet to hear of a foreman hanging a truculent factory worker, at least not here in the city of Chicago. Rossa, the simple fact of the matter is that these Huns you coddle for your own purposes have gone too far. There was many an Irishman among the policemen at the Haymarket. Some have already died, some linger awaiting the reaper. Your war lies on the other side of the ocean; dabbling in war here will only lead to you being run up a scaffold." Finnegan pointed to his old friend Rooney. "The both of you, and there will be nothing I can do to prevent it."

O'Donovan Rossa pursed his lips. He was a man who needed to be careful in his associations, and it seemed he may not have been careful enough in the past. "What is it you require, Gilhooley?"

"I seek the whereabouts of a man named Rudolph Schnaubelt. He is not to be found in Chicago, and the Huns lack the capital to finance the absenting of a man such as him." Finnegan smiled at Rossa. "To my way of thinking, that leaves only the one option for him. His friends in the Clan na Gael were possibly sympathetic enough to purchase him a train ticket."

Rooney held up his hands. "Do not look to me Finnegan. I know no Huns personally, and would not care to."

O'Donovan Rossa rubbed one cheek, considering the

request. "If I do not share information with you, you threaten us?"

"Threaten you personally?" Finnegan shook his head. "No, as Sam well knows, I do my best to avoid shooting my friends or fellow Irishmen. What I will do, if you fail to be friendly to me, is cease being friendly to you. I will allow some other clod in the office to post the reports to the Prussians. If you are no longer painted as proper buffoons, well..." Finnegan hooked his thumbs in his belt. "I am told the Warden at Chatham still holds a grudge against you for flinging a chamber pot at him, Jeremiah. It would be unwise for you to give the British any excuse. They have more than a few men lurking here. They have men lurking everywhere."

"You are a hard man, Gilhooley."

"This is a hard country, Jeremiah. You had best learn it now rather than later. I learned the moment I stepped off the boat, and it has served me well to remember it. What do you know of Schnaubelt?"

O'Donovan Rossa took a deep breath. "Your man, at least I would assume he is the man you search for, came to us a day after the Haymarket, perhaps two days, I do not recall. He begged our protection, and we offered an escape."

Rooney lowered his head. "Jeremiah, why in hell are you giving aid or succor to the damned Huns? They are all crazed and bound to undo any man who flirts with them. What good can come of joining ranks with madmen?"

"We have a common cause." O'Donovan Rossa looked partly stern, partly shamed.

"I do not give a damn for your shared cause, sir. I only care to know where Schnaubelt has gotten off to." Finnegan patiently awaited his answer.

O'Donovan Rossa swallowed and then had out with it.

"West. He claimed to be willing to further the cause in any way, so long as he could depart Chicago." He spoke the words toward the floor. "He claimed you were rounding up the anarchists to hang. What reason did I have to think he was lying?"

"I would not necessarily say he was." Finnegan raised his eyebrows. "West is a direction, not a place, Jeremiah. Where has he gone?"

O'Donovan Rossa sighed. "Gilhooley, you of all men must understand. I cannot...if I tell you of Schnaubelt, I must have assurances that the man traveling with him will be left to complete his commission."

"Commission? Oh, Jeremiah. Perhaps I have not arrived in time to save you from perdition." Finnegan shook his head. "What lunacy do you plot?"

"Plot?" O'Donovan Rossa sneered. "We plot the end of our oppression, the same as ever."

Rooney pulled his silk hat from his head, looking somber. "What have you done, Jeremiah? Who is to die?"

Rossa cleared his throat and looked up from the boards. "By name, Matthew Pendleton. By birth, the eldest son of the Duke of Cumberland. Favorite cousin to the Prince of Wales, eighth in line to the throne."

Both Finnegan and Rooney stood staring, somewhat flabbergasted. Finnegan withdrew a cigar and frowned. "You honestly intend to assassinate a member of the British Royal Family on American soil?" He chuckled and found a match. "It is quite the set of masterminds you have fallen in with here, Sam."

"Ah, bugger it all." Rooney threw his hat off into the theatre seats and clapped his hands over his head. "Finnegan, surely I do not need to tell you that I had no part in this madness."

Finnegan laughed a bit more. "Oh, I know you only look to fill your pockets and little else."

"As any sane man should." Rooney stuck a finger in O'Donovan Rossa's chest. "Jeremiah, you may have well doomed us all, fool. What do you think they will do when the prince's cousin gets blown to bits here on a damned visit? Do you think these Yankees will tell Vic to go hang? It will be us who will hang, Jeremiah. You, I, any friend who has the poor luck to have received a letter from you these last five years. They will hunt us like dogs to the ends of the earth, Jeremiah. Who did you send, damn you?"

"Sam, what other means are at our disposal? Are we to spend the next century with our hand out to the English, begging for our freedom as a vagrant in the street begs for a crust of bread?"

"Oh, do not speak of our disposal or any other shared property, Jeremiah. We are officially of separate denominations, sir. I came into partnership with you in the hopes of making money and assumed you were intelligent enough to share the same goal. This...this insanity...I wish to die old and rich, Jeremiah. Dying with turned out pockets at the end of an English rope is not my preference. Who did you send?"

O'Donovan Rossa took a moment to comprehend what his former associate was saying. "You...you would truly upend our first real opportunity to bring about the revolution?"

Rooney rubbed his eyes and turned to his old friend. "Finnegan, if this man does not give you the name of the fellow he has dispatched, presently, shoot him. I am more than willing to introduce you to those others who might provide information. Eventually, one of them will come to their senses before they are put down."

O'Donovan Rossa stood up at attention with his chin high. "You bluff."

Finnegan shrugged. "Well, if you say there are others who can inform." He drew his Remington, brought the gun up, and cocked back the hammer. "I suppose this one is superfluous."

The attempted revolutionary licked his lips and glanced at the pistol. "Kearney." He licked his lips again. "I dispatched Kearney."

"Lovely." Rooney shook his head once more. "You have doomed us, damn you. Where are they headed?"

"I...you cannot possibly catch up to them."

"Do not vex me, sir." Finnegan moved the muzzle a bit closer to one of the revolutionary's eyeballs.

"They move to intercept Pendleton at a place known as the Infernal Regions. It is in the territories." He moved his head back from the gun.

"The Yellowstone country?" Finnegan lowered the revolver and brought the hammer to half-cock. "This is a fairy tale, Jeremiah. Lie to me and you may wish I had fired this gun."

"I am not lying. I have heard the place called the Yellowstone, as you say. Pendleton practices the science of geology. There are some sort of volcanoes there he wishes to inspect. Kearney and Schnaubelt are to catch him there and finish him."

Finnegan rotated the cylinder of the Remington around so the hammer fell on the empty chamber and returned the gun to his holster. "Why in the name of St. Peter are you trying to kill such a man in the middle of a howling wilderness? Would it have been so terrible to try blowing him up on the damn docks?"

O'Donovan Rossa sighed. "He travels to the volcanos by

way of Canada. We were unaware he was even on the continent until recently. This place you call the Yellowstone is the only spot we can be certain to intercept him. If he has left, Kearney will follow. If he has not yet arrived, Kearney will wait. We will never have another chance such as this. Kearney is a dedicated man, and, as you say, Schnaubelt has little choice but to assist as best he can. His own people lack the funds to steal him away."

Finnegan lit his cigar. "And what of them after the job is done?"

"Done?" Rossa scowled.

"Where do they go after they have detonated the princeling? Surely, they do not intend to return here to Chicago for the parade in their honor."

O'Donovan Rossa sighed, seemingly sad to part with the last bit of his secret. "They are to go south to Mexico. From there, we have people who can smuggle them to Europe or elsewhere of their choosing. I do not know where Schnaubelt might wish to go. Kearney will undoubtedly wish to return to Ireland and continue to fight, if he survives." The plotter rubbed his face. "There. That is all I know."

"We must make all due haste, Finnegan." Rooney pulled off his fancy silk coat. He would not need it for traveling. "Do you have anyone who knows Schnaubelt by sight?"

"Certainly. You remember young Abijah Smith, I am sure?"

"I do. It will be good to see the boy again." Rooney smiled. "Well, it would appear I am to find myself in the service of the Pinkertons once again."

"By God, the world is turned on its head." O'Donovan Rossa gaped at his associate. "You were a Pinkerton agent, Samuel?"

"Did you think I was born yapping rot to union men in theatres, Jeremiah?" Rooney smirked.

"To think that you could betray the cause like this, Samuel. I can understand this damned...mercenary not giving a jot for the fate of Ireland, but you? Your rhetoric inspired even me to greater ends."

"Yes, and I notice that greater end was acting like a jackass and possibly getting half the Irishmen in this country hung for their trouble. You damned revolutionaries need to stop putting so much stock in rhetoric. You, of all men, should know it is spun from whole cloth." Rooney shook his head mournfully. "Ah, it is a damned pity, Jeremiah. Promising these scruffy vagabonds utopia was the finest occupation I ever had. A respectable flow of funds without risking my neck. I will never fathom your motives for fouling this up." Rooney stepped forward and set one hand on O'Donovan Rossa's shoulder. "Was it really so much to ask, Jeremiah? We were not laboring, we produced nothing, our only sweat came when we drank too much whiskey, and yet we were paid. Was it really so terrible?" He flung his hands in the air. "Well, bugger all. There is always some fool who must come along and ruin paradise." Rooney stalked off the stage in the direction of his dressing room.

Finnegan sighed. "Well then, I suppose we must be off, sir. I can only hope that you will be intelligent enough to not attempt any interference with my work." Finnegan shook his cigar at the Irish patriot. "Do not attempt to alert Kearney, do not send men in pursuit of us. This is not the time to attempt salving your conscience, Jeremiah. The men of the Clan na Gael will not suffer a squealer. Speak of this and they will likely teach you more regarding dynamite than you would care to know."

Chapter 9

ST. PAUL, MINNESOTA

May 12, 1886

FINNEGAN RUBBED HIS EYES AND PEEKED OUT THE TRAIN car curtain. He pulled it back, finding the outdoor light too bright for his taste. He was already tired of riding the train, but he knew there were many more weary miles to go before their journey would be even near ended. He consoled himself with the knowledge that it could be worse. If they had been forced to make for the Yellowstone Country by horse, it would take upwards of a month to reach the geysers, assuming all went as planned. Thanks to the marvels of rail travel, they would be there in a handful of days, assuming all went as planned. Of course, knowing he had it easier than he might have did not make him feel any better about being stuck in the train. He reached over and shook Rooney awake where he slept curled up on his side of the berth.

The former Pinkerton agent slowly opened his eyes to stare blearily at the current Pinkerton agent before him. "Oh, sweet mother Mary, I had hoped it was merely a night terror, but there you sit." Rooney lurched up in the berth bed and yawned. "Finnegan, after losing my role as Professor Mezzeroff, I do not know if I will ever feel lighthearted again." He let out a deep sigh and pulled his flask from his vest. "Did you know that we toured from one end of the continent to the other, Finnegan? Everywhere you go in this country there are Irishmen, and every one of them was willing to pay a nickel so that he might learn how to free the home isle. The cheers, the money, the women in San Francisco. Oh, I will miss it all, my friend."

Finnegan gave his face a hard rubbing and stuck a cigar between his teeth. "Sam, you are a damned marvel. Although, when I first learned of your new identity, I clearly recall thinking that I should not be surprised to find you in such a position. You always were one to land on your feet."

"Oh, it was so very fine, Finnegan. California, Denver, New York, New Orleans. The times I had in that town would make the devil himself blush with shame. The French truly know how to live."

"And you truly know how to spin a yarn. What I never fully understood is how you managed to convince anyone you were supposedly the one true disciple of Alfred Nobel. As I recall, you never had much interest in any type of explosive, and no interest whatsoever in using them for something so silly as a revolution."

"The revolution was only stage dressing, but, of course, you know that." He took a long drink from the flask. "As for my deep and abiding knowledge of dynamite and its uses, well..." He pointed to Finnegan's cigar. "Might you have another?"

"Certainly." Finnegan handed it over.

"Yes, well, have you ever purchased a case of dynamite, Finnegan?"

"No, I cannot say as I have ever had cause to." He lit his friend's cigar.

"Well, if you ever have cause to purchase that rather vile compound, I would recommend none other than the Etna Powder Company for your patronage. Each case contains a small pamphlet explaining the general method for the use of both caps and dynamite. It is quite useful."

"A pamphlet?"

"Yes."

"You made use of a single pamphlet to convince the world you were an expert chemist, blaster, and madman?" Finnegan laughed and flopped back in the berth seat. "Well done, Sam. Bloody well done. Though, I must point out, you once again very nearly put your neck in a noose. I would have thought you would watch out for such things after so many of the Mollies swung during your tenure."

"There seemed to be little harm in suggesting blowing up Englishmen in a country so very far from England, Finnegan. I certainly had no cause to worry that one of the drunken sots out in the audience would actually take it upon himself to visit Queen Vic and shove dynamite up her nose. I presumed that if the ruddy bastards had any inclination to free Ireland, they would not have run off from her." He shrugged and stretched. "It would seem I was wrong."

Finnegan smiled and puffed his cigar. "You and I have been in the wrong many times before. Hopefully, we shall live long enough to be wrong a few more times before it is said and done."

"It is good that the occasional mistake arises so that I do not begin to feel infallible." There was a knock at the berth door. "Are we expecting company, Finnegan?"

"Indeed, we are." Finnegan reached out and slid the door open. "Good morning, Abijah."

"Abijah!" Rooney leapt up and gave the young infiltrator a warm hug. "Ah, saints preserve us, it has been too long." He looked Smith over. "You have grown to twice the size you were when last I saw you, boy."

Abijah laughed. "I do not know if I would go that far, Sam. Though, you always were one for going too far. How have you been? I hope you did not spend all our profits from Pennsylvania on a single horse race."

"As I recall, it took more than a few races to fritter it away. Finnegan tells me you have become a master infiltrator during your time with the agency."

"Oh, I would not say I have mastered much of anything, as yet. And what have you been doing to earn your living, Sam? Did you marry a farmer's daughter and take up bartending as you claimed you might?"

"No such thing, young Abijah. Most recently I have been selling revolution under the guise of a fake professor. You may have heard of me, Dr. Mezzeroff?"

"Truly?" Abijah let out a belly laugh. "I will be damned. I hoped to attend your lecture on propaganda by deeds this coming week."

"Ah, that would have been a fine thing, Abijah. It was one of my finer bits of oratory." He sighed. "Due to some recent misfortunes, I am afraid I will not be delivering that particular lecture as scheduled. I fear I may never deliver it again."

Abijah could not stop grinning. "Now that is a pity. Truly a shame to throw away such a well-developed character over nothing more than poor luck."

"He casts the professor aside to save his neck, Abijah." Finnegan stood. "And his luck was set to run out eventually." He stretched. "So long as we are in the station, we may as well look to obtaining some breakfast. This cigar and Rooney's flask are all that has passed for sustenance so far."

After filling their bellies, the three returned to the train and it pulled from the station, belching smoke and rumbling as only a steam engine could. Finnegan and Rooney spent their time reading the papers or conversing back and forth, but Abijah spent most of his time staring out the berth window, watching the countryside roll by. After several hours, Finnegan rolled up his newspaper and gave the young man a soft smack in the back of the head.

"What requires your attention on the other side of that window, Mr. Smith?"

Abijah turned to the other men in the berth, smiling. "Outside that window is the west, Finnegan. I have never seen it before, and we move farther into the west every moment."

Finnegan nodded. "Ah, yes, I forget that you have not yet traveled that widely. Sorry to interrupt, carry on if you like. Although, I might caution you, there will be little else to do but stare out the window for several days, yet. Best not to overdo things too soon."

Abijah motioned out the window. "Is this near the place where you first met your schoolteacher?"

Finnegan thought back. "I believe that is behind us already, Abijah, and she was not a schoolteacher then."

"Ah, I see." Abijah began digging around in the small bag he had brought with him. "Somewhere in here I possess a map. Will we be passing through the area the young lady currently resides in?"

"We will not." Finnegan unrolled his newspaper, looking bored. "I am afraid the Yellowstone lies in a direction that will require us to detour away from the part of the Montana Territory I formerly visited."

Rooney lowered the paper he had been reading. "Finnegan, are you two discussing that doe-eyed temptress who assisted you after you were shot by the James contingent?"

"Well, yes." Finnegan shrugged. "What of it?"

"What was her name?"

"Molly."

Rooney stared with a shocked visage. "You still...? The same woman you were mooning over so long ago when we first met Abijah in St. Clair?"

Finnegan appeared a bit exasperated. "Yes, Sam, the same lady. What of it?"

"You are still...you still pursue her?"

Finnegan shook his head. "I do not know how precisely to describe the arrangement. We remain friendly and correspond frequently, if that is what you are asking."

"Friendly?" Rooney sat up in his seat.

"Yes."

"You correspond with her?"

"Yes, Sam. Has pretending to be a Prussian doctor caused you to lose facility with your native tongue? Should I speak more slowly?"

Rooney continued to stare. "I am sorry, Finnegan. I simply do not understand."

Finnegan looked to Abijah, but the young man seemed to have nothing to add. He turned back to Rooney. "What is it you are not comprehending, Sam?"

"You...you write this woman letters?"

"Yes."

"And she writes to you?"

"Yes."

He brightened for a moment. "Her father is quite rich, and you expect a dowery in short order?"

Finnegan sighed. "Her father is of well, but moderate, means. Though, it does not much matter. I do not foresee matrimony on the horizon." He looked down at his paper, hoping to ignore further inquiries.

"And this is a decent woman of respectable character we are discussing?"

Finnegan looked up from his paper. "Yes, Sam. Of the sort you have seldom had acquaintance with."

Rooney leaned forward, curious beyond caution. "Finnegan, in truth, if the woman is decent, and her father offers little, why on earth do you continue to be friendly with her?"

Finnegan sighed. "Sam, perhaps there are things you are simply fated to never understand."

Chapter 10

COULSON, MONTANA TERRITORY

May 14, 1886

The train lurched and Finnegan was tossed out of his nap. He groaned and looked about the berth. Across from him, Rooney snored, oblivious to the sudden stop. Abijah held a book in his hand and smiled. Finnegan groaned again. "The rail service across the Dakotas has improved greatly since I last made this trip. The last time, I was stranded and we were forced to find venison for our supper several days running." He rubbed his eyes. "Did I already tell you that tale?"

"You did, Finnegan." He shut the book. "But it is a fine tale, nonetheless."

"You are a good boy to tell a rambling old man such things." Finnegan peeked out the window at the darkness. "I hunger, Abijah." He looked Rooney over. "What say we let the professor sleep? We can locate a basket of food in whatever settlement this is and bring some back for him. It is remarkable how many places have grown up around these railroad stops since I was last on this route. The food in that last place rivaled anything a man might find in Chicago."

"Civilization follows the railroad, Finnegan." Abijah put his book in his carpet bag and stood. The two men left the berth and snoring Rooney. As they made their way out onto the platform, Finnegan checked his watch. "We are making damned fine time." He put his watch back. "If there were delays in the past week, we truly might be able to overtake our quarry."

"I do not know if we are that lucky, Finnegan, but I will surely keep an eye out for Schnaubelt at the café." He pointed across the platform to a small building just down the town's main street. "That is the likely spot, would you not say?"

"I would say." They began strolling toward the lights that burned in the windows. The town seemed quiet. If it had formerly boomed, the lull had arrived.

Abijah cleared his throat and put his hands in his coat pockets to guard against the chill. "Do you know I was meant to observe and, if possible, meet Professor Mezzeroff during his sojourn in Chicago?"

"That would have been a bit awkward for both of you, I should think." Finnegan laughed. "Rooney, what will he conjure next?"

"It will likely not be honest labor, that I can assure you." Abijah turned toward Finnegan for a moment as they walked. "The men paying for Rooney's touring are all part and parcel with the Clan na Gael, though I suppose you know that."

"I was aware of that, yes."

"Are you any part of the Clan na Gael, Finnegan?"

The Irishman stopped and glanced over at his young friend. "What would make you ask such a thing, Abijah?" He shook his head and continued walking.

"You told me many years ago that your family fled Ireland to avoid hanging for the death of a tax collector."

Finnegan shook one finger at the infiltrator. "The murder of a tax collector, Abijah. By now you should know the importance of the distinction."

"Very well, then, the murder of a tax collector. At any rate, you can understand how I might suspect you could hold a grudge against the British."

"Abijah, as you well know, I am loath to join any group that does not pay for my labor." He laughed again. "And if I was given to joining such congregations, I should hope I would choose one with better chances for success. The brave men of the Clan na Gael do little other than drink beer and spin fanciful fictions. If they had any intentions of doing more than that they would go back to Ireland instead of sitting here, thousands of miles distant."

"Are we not currently pursuing a man who intends to do much more than drink beer and brag, Finnegan?"

He shrugged. "These fools Kearney and Schnaubelt are aberrations. I would wager that they are simply the two jackasses in Chicago who happen to be most fond of dynamite. Fate has conspired to bring them together and drop them in our path." He shrugged again. "Although, that is an assumption, as well. We may very well reach the end of our journey and find both fools sitting in a saloon drinking whiskey. Many men start out to begin revolutions and end up drunk. They would not be the first." Finnegan glanced at his friend again. "What would you do if I told you I had been initiated into the Clan na Gael?"

"Nothing."

"Nothing? Some damned fine Pinkerton agent you turned out to be. Is it not your place to go about informing on desperate characters such as myself?"

"You do not drink beer. How dangerous a member of the Clan could you possibly be?" Abijah hopped up onto a boardwalk and Finnegan joined him. "How long have you known Rooney was, in fact, the mysterious Professor Mezzeroff?"

"Oh, the better part of a year, at least." Finnegan pulled his frock coat shut. "I saw the daft bastard give a demonstration of the power of dynamite at a union picnic in New York."

"A picnic?"

"Yes. Fried chicken, lemonade, a half-wit blowing a big rock to smithereens, what else would you expect to find at a picnic, Abijah?" He laughed again. "The world is a strange place, and men like Rooney continue to find ways to make it stranger."

"How long would you have allowed him to continue in his fiction?"

Finnegan laughed. "Until perdition set in, or the good Lord called him home. What do I care if Rooney struts about defaming Queen Vic and threatening revolution? In truth, I was a bit shocked to see that he made it all the way to Chicago in his tour. I rather thought he would blow himself to bits long before achieving a full circle." Finnegan held the café door open for Abijah. "After you, sir."

"Many thanks." They stepped into the café and wandered to the rear of the place where a haggard cook stood over a smoking stovetop. Abijah approached the man. "What do you have this evening, sir?"

The man turned and pulled a cigar from his lips. "Beef steak, killed this morning. I still have a haunch left." He looked back into the smoky kitchen. "I have taters and beans leftover, as well."

Finnegan smiled at the decidedly filthy chef. "We will

take two plates full and a third steak with some bread wrapped in what you can part with. If you can produce it all before the train departs."

The cook tossed his cigar to the floor and tossed the steaks onto the stovetop. "Be ready in a moment."

The cook proved as good as his word and the two men were shoving their food into themselves shortly. They sat at a table in the otherwise empty café. Abijah faced the door and Finnegan had his back to it. They had eaten about half their food when the door opened and the small bell above rang. The floorboards of the place creaked as a large man put his weight onto them. Abijah gave the new arrival a quizzical look. "Ah, now there is a frontier type, Finnegan."

"Finnegan?" The new arrival spoke up in a booming voice.

Gilhooley straightened up in his chair and the color drained from his face. "Abijah, what town is this?"

"I saw a sign that I believe read Coulson."

"Ah, damn it to hell." Finnegan leapt from his chair so quickly it was cast aside and clattered over. He turned and drew his pistol to cover the man who had entered the café. "Do not move, Johnson." Finnegan thumbed back the hammer on the Remington. "Come nearer and I will kill you with glee, damn you."

Abijah slowly lifted a napkin to his lips and cleaned his face. "You have visited this town before, Finnegan?"

"I have."

"And you know this large, furry gentleman?"

"I do."

The new arrival gave Finnegan and his revolver a disappointed look. "I did not mean to rile you, Finnegan. I only meant to say hello. Is Mr. Kilkenny with you?" He took a step forward.

"No, he is not, and you would be wise to stay the hell away from me, Johnson. I still regret leaving this place without shooting you."

"I only wish to shut Willard's door." The large man swung the door shut. "If you do not wish to speak with me, that is your concern, but I will be having my dinner about now and you will have to shoot me to keep me from it." He scowled. "What do you have to hold against me, anyway?"

"You nearly split my skull open with a buffalo gun and tossed me in a filthy cell. To say nothing of the fact that you are a confessed cannibal, which is something any man in his right mind ought to take umbrage with."

Abijah raised his eyebrows. "Cannibal?"

Johnson squinted. "Umbrage?"

Finnegan lowered the Remington a bit. "This man is known as Liver-Eating Johnson, Abijah. He is said to have killed many, many Crow Indians and feasted upon them."

"Ah, now, I explained that to you and Ephraim the last time you was here. You know that ain't nothin' but gossip and rot, Finnegan."

"I know well and good that you struck me from behind in this town's saloon and nearly killed me, you bastard."

Abijah leaned forward a bit at the table. "I am sorry to interrupt, gentlemen, but I am not clear on the point of cannibalism you were discussing." He pointed to Johnson. "Does the man eat people, or not?"

"There's a yarn regarding it that explains how it came to pass, young friend." Johnson took another step forward.

Finnegan raised the gun up again. "Johnson, if you tell that revolting story again, I will shoot you dead."

"You are a surly cuss this night, Finnegan. What has you so riled?" Johnson shrugged. "You ain't the first man I clouted with my rifle, and none of them held a grudge, that I know of."

Abijah laughed. "Yes, Finnegan, do not be rude. The man only clouted you over the head. From the sound of it, he has done far worse in the past." The infiltrator grinned and popped a hunk of beef steak into his mouth.

"Cloutin' folks who shoot other folks is my job. I *am* the town deputy." It appeared as though Johnson frequently explained his position and duties.

The young Pinkerton sipped his coffee. "See, there, now. This cannibal is the town deputy, Finnegan. He obviously meant no harm." Abijah set his cup down. "At any rate, he does not appear to be armed at the moment and shooting down the local deputy may cause a delay in our journey." Finnegan groaned in response. Abijah sighed. "If it is truly important, we will likely pass through here again on the way home; you may shoot him then without fear of being diverted from our purpose."

Finnegan groaned again and holstered his revolver. "Very well."

As though not much of interest had occurred in the last minute, Johnson leaned over and righted Finnegan's chair. "Yeah, I recall you being damned surly the last time you was here. I guess travel just don't agree with some people." He set the chair by the table and took up one of his own. "What brings you this way again?"

Finnegan resignedly lowered himself into his chair. He did not much like the idea of discussing matters with Johnson, but could not afford to miss even the slimmest of prospects to catch his quarry. "We come this way searching for two men; I do not suppose I could be lucky enough to hear that you have recently clouted two fellows and still hold them in your tiny jail. As I recall, there is a proper bribery procedure here that must be observed at all costs."

Johnson shook his head. "The jail stands empty. Is most days, now. Town's more or less settling down. Most nights I got little to do other than stare up at the stars and wonder at how much more interesting this country used to be when it was free of civilization."

Abijah slipped the last hunk of steak in his mouth. "I must say, you are surprisingly poignant for a cannibal."

Johnson rubbed his chin. "You fellas use a lot of damned odd words. What kind of men you lookin' for? Just cause they ain't in the jail don't mean they didn't pass through."

"An Irishman; short, thick, with a full beard, and a Hun who is lanky, underfed and probably cleanshaven by now, if he knows what is good for him."

"Hun?" Johnson inquired.

"A Prussian." Finnegan offered, but Johnson shook his head. "A German." Another head shake. "A damned Russian? Have you met no one but myself and Indians?"

Johnson smoothed his beard, deep in thought. "I once knew a man who claimed to be a Dutchman. Are Huns of the same stripe?"

Finnegan gave the deputy a cold stare. "When is the last time you saw the Dutchman?"

"Uh, must be nigh on ten years ago."

"Then I suppose it does not much matter." Finnegan rubbed his eyes.

"You know, if you're out after these fellas, and expect to find them in the territories, I would be of a mind to throw in with you. It's terrible boring around here. What did these boys you chase do to earn chasin'?"

Finnegan wiped his mouth with his napkin and stood,

collecting Rooney's meal from the tabletop. "We suspect them of setting off a bomb in the city of Chicago."

"Ah." Johnson nodded. "They are some of the anarchists that set to bombing Haymarket Square, eh?"

Finnegan paused in his preparation. "You are aware of the incident that occurred in the Haymarket?"

"Been nothing but that in the papers since it happened. We get the papers quite regular these days, and there ain't nothing better to do than read them, damn it. Like I said, it's dreadfully boring round here, lately."

Abijah stood from the table and gave the accused cannibal a warm smile. "We appreciate the offer, Mr. Johnson, but, unfortunately, this investigation is Pinkerton agency business, and, as such, must be handled by agents of the company. I am sure you can understand, given your profession."

"No, but it's nice of you to put it so nice, anyhow." Johnson leaned back in his chair, looking sullen.

Finnegan narrowed his eyes and stared hard at the mountain man. "Mr. Johnson, how long would it take you to make ready to accompany us?"

Johnson perked up. "Uh, I'd just have to grab my traps out the jail and get on back here."

Finnegan smiled. "Then see to it, sir. Your train ticket will be compliments of the Pinkerton agency. I assume you have visited the Yellowstone country previously?"

"Was practically the first man in it." Johnson lunged up out of his chair and took Finnegan's hand. "Damn glad for the diversion, friend." The ogre lumbered out the café door and could be seen fairly running toward the small cabin that served as the local jail.

Finnegan stood in the café, looking quite pleased with himself. Abijah looked quite shocked. "Finnegan, do you truly intend to bring that...well, I do not quite know what to call him...you intend for him to accompany us?"

"Yes, of course."

"What on earth for?"

Finnegan motioned toward the jail. "That Barnum's attraction might appear useless, but I know to a certainty that he has spent his entire life wandering this country. We will need a guide in the Yellowstone country, unless you intend to simply wander the wilderness yelling out and hoping that Kearney or Schnaubelt will be kind enough to answer."

Abijah laughed. "Yes, well, I suppose that is true, but why that fellow? I am sure that between here and the Yellowstone region there are many men who could serve as guides. You very nearly shot him down two minutes past, and now you intend to employ him?"

Finnegan shrugged. "Abijah, I will be frank with you: these last few days, tromping about Chicago looking for hidden dynamite, it has come to my attention that there could be great utility in having a fellow around who does not understand the intricacies of dynamite. Perhaps it would be best to have a man such as Johnson on hand to enter rooms, camps, or such places first."

Abijah raised an eyebrow. "You intend to make use of that man the same way the miners make use of canaries?"

Finnegan shook his head. "This is slightly different; the canary does not explode, but Johnson well may." Finnegan took out a cigar. "You have met the fellow, can you imagine a more useful role for him to fill in this world?"

"Nothing leaps to mind."

"Very well. Ah, here he comes. Let us keep talk of dynamite to a minimum, shall we? No need to unduly agitate the poor fellow."

Abijah sighed. "Finnegan, it is not always a simple matter to be your friend."

ROONEY AWOKE in the berth as the train pulled out of the station. He sat up and looked across the small space at Johnson, who occupied the seat Finnegan and Abijah had held when he had dozed off. Johnson smiled and held out the steak sandwich wrapped in cheesecloth that had been procured in Coulson. Rooney rubbed one eye and nodded to the new arrival. "Hello, sir."

The furry mountain man smiled through his scruff. "Good nap?"

"Well enough."

Johnson thrust the sandwich forward. "Gilhooley says this is your'n."

Rooney slowly took the sandwich and gave it a brief inspection. "I see. Where is it Mr. Gilhooley has gotten off to?"

"He's making arrangements with the conductor to get me another berth, him and that young Abijah fella. Going to be a might crowded in here, now that there's four of us."

"Yes, four." Rooney extended his hand. "Sam Rooney, proud to make your acquaintance."

"John Johnson." The mountain man slowly shook the proffered hand. "You ain't heard of me?"

"No. My apologies, Mr. Johnson. I am new to the territories and not overly familiar with the residents here. Are you well known in these parts?"

"Too damn well known." He sat back in the berth seat, looking quite satisfied. "Be damn fine to be amongst them who don't know me for a spell."

Rooney nodded and began to unwrap his sandwich. "Oh, I can bloody well sympathize with your plight, Mr. Johnson. Confidentially, I have been enjoying the trip thus far for the same reasons." He grinned.

"Yes, sir." Johnson leaned forward. "I been waitin' for you to wake up so I could ask. Finnegan, he says you're a professor, like a schoolteacher, and you've got a mind to blow up the queen of England. That true?" The train rattled and Johnson took a moment to better secure his filthy travel bag and immaculate Sharps rifle.

Rooney took a bite of the sandwich. "As with most statements, there are elements of truth to it and some falsehoods scattered in. What is it you do to make your living, Mr. Johnson?"

"Up until this evenin' I been the city deputy at Coulson, but the settled life ain't been agreein' with me of late, so I throwed in with Finnegan when he asked. I'm to guide you boys through the Yellowstone."

"I see." Rooney wiped his mouth with one coat sleeve. "You are an experienced guide?"

"I am."

"And a deputy?"

"I am." He rubbed his chin. "I imagine I will be again when this little lark is over. I can't imagine I'll be gone long enough from Coulson for the sheriff to take notice. Even if he does, I doubt he'd find another man willing to tolerate him. Nice enough fella most of the time, but when he gets in his cups and takes to cheatin' at cards, he's a difficult man to suffer."

"Yes, well..." Rooney took another bite. "Some men should not indulge." He munched on the steak and bread while assessing his new friend. "Mr. Johnson, you will have to excuse me for being so bold as to ask, but if you are an experienced scout and the citizens of...what town was it you hail from?"

"Coulson, presently."

"Yes, the citizens of Coulson have seen fit to let you serve as deputy -- if that is the case, what gives you the notion that you have a bad reputation, sir?"

Johnson nodded solemnly. "I reckon most of it is on account of them that call me cannibal doing so damn much gossipin'. Seems like once people get to flappin' their lips about something, it just never ends and follows a fella around like that the rest of his days."

"Yes, it is a terrible thing to find oneself slandered." Rooney leaned forward a little. "Sir, did you say you stand accused of cannibalism?"

"Them in Coulson say it whether I'm standing or not."

"I see." Rooney folded the sandwich back in the cheesecloth.

"Ain't true, of course. Not like they tell it, anyhow. You see, the trouble really started many years ago. I was down on the Missouri, or was it the Judith? Hell, I don't recall, and it don't much matter. I was cuttin' firewood for the steamers. Damn things burn ten cord a day, and..."

Rooney held up one hand to stop the man mid-revelry. "Sir, I am certain this is a fine tale you intend to relate, and I look forward to hearing the details of it, but before you continue, I really must insist on you answering a question."

"Oh, certainly, Mr. Rooney."

"Where did you obtain the constituents of my dinner?"

Chapter 11

LIVINGSTON, MONTANA TERRITORY

May 15, 1886

As the train labored its way across the lower portion of the Montana Territory, Johnson steadily regaled the other members of the party with tales of his life on the frontier. While Finnegan had never much enjoyed Johnson's story describing how he had received his moniker, the Pinkerton grudgingly began to take an interest in some of the man's other yarns. To say the least, Johnson had been around and had seen his fair share of the world. The man had left his boyhood home in New Jersey to join the Navy and fight in the war with Mexico. After that, he had meandered his way through the majority of the west, more or less settling in Montana, for seemingly no other reason than that was where he had been when the trapping industry experienced its final days along with the true mountain men.

One of the topics Johnson took particular time to expound on was the beauty and uniqueness of the Yellowstone country. From the way he spoke, it was apparent that seeing the country again was the primary motivation for accompanying the Pinkertons in their quest.

"I'd wager it's been at least nigh on to ten, maybe fifteen years since I passed through the geyser country down that way. I came through with a mind to shoot a few buff, but there was a few others of the same mind and not many buff left to speak of. Wouldn't give more than a few dollars and a handshake for a hide by then, anyhow."

Finnegan nodded. He harbored a slight jealousy for any man who had shot a buffalo. His first trip to the Montana Territory had afforded him his first chance to try hunting, and he steadily plotted to try it again someday. "What year was that, Mr. Johnson?"

Johnson rubbed his beard thoughtfully as the train rocked from side to side. "Was after the war, the war between the states, mind you, not the Mexican war. Call it '70, '71. It was before they started all the talk of turning the place into a park for the lawyers and dentists in New York to come gawk at, I'll tell you that for certain."

Rooney nodded. "Yes, I have heard that. A few fellows have gotten together and convinced those drunken sots in Washington that there can be no possible use in developing the place, so it is to be set aside for...well, for some sort of picnicking or such, I suppose."

Abijah left out a laugh. "My goodness, what silliness will they think of next? Who would possibly wish to travel thousands of miles to picnic in a howling wilderness full of wild beasts? A man would have to be daft to even contemplate such a thing."

Johnson shrugged. "I always swung through the Yellowstone looking to fill my larder or get hides. Damn place was always full of bears. Oddest damn thing, just flush with 'em. Couldn't tell you why. 'Course, since, I think it was '72, they started yappin' all that park foolishness, you can't hunt nor trap it no more."

"No hunting at all." Finnegan shook his head. "Ridiculous."

Johnson waved one hand absently. "Well, it was just talk, is all. A man could go down there and do as he pleased, so long as he stayed out of sight or pressed a few coins into the hand of the...I'm not sure what the fella who ran the place called himself, some sort of Indian Agent or other. At all events, you could bribe the scoundrel and do some huntin', but that cuts into a fella's profits mightily." Johnson sighed. "'Course, that's all over and done now, too, from what I heard. Damn Army's comin' in to run the country." The mountain man shook his head. "Once the Army encamps in a place, the fun's all over, boys. I seen it before, and it'll be the same damn thing in the Yellowstone."

"The Army?" Finnegan puffed his cigar. "What fool conceived of that notion? Why would they put the Army in charge of watching over a park?"

Johnson continued to stroke his beard. "They say it's to keep the hunters out. They call 'em poachers, now, of course. You ever heard that word, Finnegan?"

"I have." He puffed and smiled. "A poacher is a man who would dare to kill a king's deer."

Abijah nudged his old friend with an elbow. "Probably better the king's deer than his tax collector, eh?"

Finnegan snorted. "I say first one, then the other. You were saying, Mr. Johnson?"

Johnson pursed his lips. "I don't know much about kings, but I know they got in a regular dither about folks shooting bears in the Yellowstone." He laughed. "As though there was any other damn thing to do with a bear. They make a damn poor housemate, I can tell you that for certain. So, yeah, I heard they got in a regular snit over it and kicked that crooked Indian Agent out to make room for a regular U.S. Cavalry

Regiment. They aim to build a town to house 'em by some of the hot springs down there and everything. Couldn't tell you what the purpose of having an Army encampment in the middle of a park is, but that's what they're doing."

Finnegan pondered the statements. "I heard many wonderous tales regarding the Yellowstone Country during my last visit here. I must confess an interest in seeing the place firsthand."

Johnson frowned beneath his beard. "I must confess an interest in seein' the place one more time before the damn bankers and railroad men set to ruinin' it. One thing I can tell you boys for sure, once the soldiers arrive, the rest of that horde of yappin', botherin', mulein', sons a bitches that make every parcel of God's green earth unlivable ain't far behind. You just watch. In ten years' time, there won't be a spot in the whole of the Yellowstone where a man can find some peace. I seen it happen in every decent bit of country I been in since I mustered out the Navy."

Finnegan knocked some ash out the train window. "How old are you, Mr. Johnson?"

"I don't rightly know, for certain." He rubbed his greying beard. "What year is this, now?"

Finnegan grinned. "It is the year of our Lord, eighteen-hundred and eighty-six."

"My, the years do slip past. Couldn't tell you what year I started to deputy at Coulson." He scratched the back of his head. "I reckon I must be into my third score by now. Maybe a bit more, even."

"You are holding up rather well, in that case." Finnegan knocked more ash out the window.

"It's livin' in towns that ages a man." He gave the declaration a bit more thought. "It's livin' in towns the way fellas prefer to live in town that ages a man. Too much whiskey, too many chippies, too many scuffles over women and whiskey. A few months of that straight and a man looks well beyond his years and can't hardly make it up a hill at a good gait. Damn sad thing to see what becomes of a man when he gets civilized."

Rooney leaned toward the mountain man. "I am sorry, Mr. Johnson, but we cannot all spend our days killing Indians and eating them. I am sad to say that if it were not for the pursuit of whiskey and women, the majority of men would have nothing to do all day long the world over."

Finnegan raised his cigar to get the floor. "Mr. Rooney, I would submit that some men would explode boulders in public parks for the amusement of labor agitators."

Rooney shook his head. "Alas, dear Finnegan, that was only a means to the end of obtaining more women and whiskey."

Chapter 12

GARDINER, MONTANA TERRITORY

May 16, 1886

The burgeoning town that greeted the Pinkerton men at the end of the Northern Pacific spur line was not precisely what any of them had been expecting. In single file, they departed the train and stepped onto the platform, a structure that still had pitch leaking out of the rough-cut planks. Gardiner appeared quite similar to the other towns they had passed through with the notable exception that a half dozen or so extremely large buildings on what passed for the town's main street were currently under construction. Carpenters and masons scurried about the place in a fervor, all seemingly racing the others.

Johnson surveyed the scene and groaned through his beard. "By God, last time I was near here I don't think there was more than a few miner's tents. Damn shame, boys; I believe I'm too late."

"Yes." Finnegan set his valise and the wooden canvas-covered case he carried down on a platform bench to avoid the pitch. "It would appear civilization has quite beaten you to this place, Mr. Johnson. Not only has the whore arrived first, she has settled in considerably." He motioned to the thick clouds of smoke and red glow emanating in the distance to the south. "Is that the result of the volcanos I have been hearing about?"

A rather spry fellow with a flat brimmed hat, short beard, and glasses covering bright eyes let out a laugh and turned from where he stood on the platform. "Volcanos, did you say?" He grinned at Finnegan.

"Yes, I had been told there were volcanos hereabout."

"There are geysers aplenty, but those are a different animal from a volcano, sir." The man pointed to the south. "What you see there is the smoke from a large fire, or set of fires, burning in the forests all around the area." He extended his hand to Finnegan. "Will Wylie, pleased to make your acquaintance."

Finnegan shook his hand and he nodded to the rest of the group. "How is it so many fires were ignited at one time, Mr. Wylie? Is it the result of widespread storms and lightning?"

"It is the result of man's stupidity. A collection of fools in these parts have intentionally set the forests ablaze. Supposedly, to dissuade the Army from taking over management of the park. If they cannot have the area for poaching, apparently, no one will."

Finnegan shook his head. "I wish I could say this was the most gross example of stupidity I have seen, but it only ranks among many." He tipped his hat. "Finnegan Gilhooley." He pointed to the assembled men with him. "The young man is Mr. Smith, the thin fellow is Mr. Rooney, and this rusticated frontiersman is Mr. Johnson."

The fellow brightened. "Ah, from your accent, sir, I will venture a guess and say that you are another portion of the Pendleton Expedition."

Finnegan, never one to miss seizing an opportunity, nodded emphatically. "We are indeed, sir. Dispatched all the way from Chicago."

"Yes, excellent. Mr. Kearney came from Chicago, as well. That city must fairly overflow with students of geology." Wylie chuckled and glanced around the platform one last time. "Well, the Covington Party must be continuing to run late." He pulled a watch from his vest pocket and shook his head. "Life is full of minor difficulties. A man simply must rise above them. If the Covingtons are not of a mind to perambulate with the Wylie Camping Company today and view the natural curiosities of the park, I see no reason why you gentlemen should not take their place."

"Their place, sir?" Finnegan smiled at the man.

"Yes, I can offer you and your party transportation to Camp Sheridan, where the Army has encamped. From there, it should only be a matter of determining where the Pendleton Party has gotten off to and tracking them down. I keep some stock at the livery for fellows just like you who are in need of traveling where the coaches cannot go." Wylie tipped his hat to the group. "We aim to please."

"You seem to offer just what a man might require." Finnegan glanced over to the rest of his party and back to Wylie. "It would appear fortune has smiled on us."

Wylie grinned. "Of course, fortune is greatly improved when you have the funds to make your own luck."

"We are sufficiently funded, I should think." Finnegan gave the matter a moment's thought. "Sir, has the Covington Party paid for their transportation in advance?"

Wylie rubbed his chin. "Yes, I believe they did."

Finnegan nodded. "In that case, I would like to amend my previous statement. We are, in fact, the Covington Party and would appreciate it if you would make good on your contractual obligation."

Wylie laughed. "Ah, if only life were so easy." He motioned to the town's main street. "Come this way, fellows. Just after all these very fine hotels currently under construction we will find my livery and feedlot. It is a pity that you will have to pay, but you will, hopefully, find the means of transport comfortable enough that you will not regret the expense."

Wylie and the party of Pinkertons made their way down the street to the livery and reviewed the collection of rather well-equipped coaches there. It was agreed by everyone that traveling into the park with the Wylie Company was assuredly the way to go. Finnegan set his valise in one of the coaches and then set his wooden, canvas-covered case on a nearby workbench. He opened the case to reveal the three components of his English express rifle. The Pinkerton snapped the barrels onto the action before setting the forearm in place and tightening it down. He smiled at the assembled weapon.

"By God, Finnegan, that is a fine rifle." Johnson ogled the dark maple of the stock.

The others gathered around to gaze on the great gun. "Yes, she is truly the belle of the ball wherever she goes." Finnegan broke the gun open and inserted two of the 500 Express cartridges into the twin bores. "Ah, she is my darling."

Abijah surveyed the rifle. "Finnegan, is that a Purdey?"

"It is." Finnegan closed the rifle's action and checked to make certain the safety was engaged. "How is it you know of English gunmakers, Abijah?"

"Oh, I have gazed and wished at them many a time in the

downtown shops." Abijah rubbed his chin. "If you do not take offense to my asking, how is it you came to possess a gun of that...expense?"

"It was a gift for services rendered. Ephraim Kilkenny equipped me with it so that I could guard the members of our expedition from bears the last time I was in this territory. He gifted the rifle to me when the expedition came to a close. It is a highly effective means of defense against large animals."

"Shot many bear with it?" Johnson was comparing the express rounds to one of his Sharps cartridges.

Finnegan cleared his throat and thought back on his time with the Purdey. "Well, no bear, as yet, but I have used it to great effect on several large beasts and have no complaints as to its performance."

Wylie approached and looked over the gun. "Um, Mr. Gilhooley, that is a truly fine rifle, but, I must inform you, it is illegal to shoot any game within the park boundaries. The entire purpose of the Army coming here is to put a stop to the poaching within the park. They will not allow any shooting, and neither will I, sir."

Finnegan smiled at the guide. "Mr. Wylie, I assure you, I have no intention of using this rifle unless it is absolutely necessary to our safety. I have been told that the Yellowstone country is overflowing with bears, is that not true?"

"It is."

"Then, I give you my word as a gentleman that this rifle will only be used under duress." Finnegan set the rifle case in the coach, but kept the Purdey in his hand.

Wylie nodded. "Very well, your word is good enough for me, sir." The guide walked off to the other side of the feedlot to see about the stock.

Abijah patted Finnegan on the back. "Very well done, my

friend. That was a masterful bit of subterfuge about the bears." He moved a bit closer to his mentor. "I understand the claim regarding our safety, but you could have told him that in regard to any rifle. Why did you bring that massive thing?"

Finnegan gave the young man a most quizzical look. "I...I brought it for the bears, just as I told Wylie. For the love of St. Peter, do you not understand that the bears inhabiting this bloody place can practically swallow a man whole?"

"I suppose I had not paused to consider it, Finnegan."

"Well, if you do not believe me, consult Mr. Johnson. I would consider him an authority on the matter." Finnegan turned to the mountain man. "Mr. Johnson, are not the bears of this place well-known to be maneaters?"

Johnson shrugged. "They'll damn well gnaw on a man if he gives them half a chance. Best to keep a wary eye for them. Now and again, one'll come out of a brush bottom and be on you 'fore you even hear 'em. Wouldn't think an animal that big could be so fast, or so quiet, but the damn things can be. The sows are the worst. Get between a sow and her cub and the bitch'll kill you every time."

"Very well, then." Finnegan raised up the Purdey a little. "Carrying a rifle such as this is very reasonable indeed, I assure you, Abijah."

Abijah glanced around to make sure Wylie was out of earshot. "It is a fine bear gun, Finnegan, but it would be preferable to have a repeater or two to deal with Kearney and Schnaubelt, correct?"

Finnegan sighed. "Sam has no less than two disassembled Greener shotguns concealed within his luggage and, of course, we have our pistols. Shooting down either Kearney or Schnaubelt should not be particularly difficult, Abijah. To my knowledge, neither fellow is much of a gunman. The difficulty lies in finding them. Running across this Wylie chap is quite the boon. If all goes well, he can lead us to Pendleton and Kearney." Finnegan shrugged. "Hopefully, the Englishman has not been exploded yet." He shook his head. "I never would have thought to utter those words. It is nearly inconceivable that an Englishman being blown to bits would not be in the public interest, but, alas, here we are."

Wylie had invited Finnegan to ride in the lead coach with him. He assumed this was partially because the guide wished to bring points of interest to the attention of the fellow who had proffered the money, and partially so Wylie could keep an eye on Finnegan. The lead coach contained Wylie, Finnegan, and the party's gear. The coach to the rear contained Abijah, Rooney, Johnson, and Wylie's hired man. As they made their way along what Wylie referred to as a road, Finnegan had to admit the country was quite beautiful, although, as yet, there did not seem to be an appreciable difference between the much lauded "National Park" and the lands Finnegan had been staring at out the train window for many days.

Wylie motioned to some spires on a ridgetop. "Those are limestone remnants from the last ice age, at least that is what I have been told by others of your line, Mr. Gilhooley."

"My line?"

"Geology, sir. Since you wish to find the Pendleton Party, I assumed you, too, are of a mind to investigate the secret doings of rocks."

Thanks to previous experience, Finnegan had a reasonable response at hand. "I serve in more of an administrative capacity and leave science to those men more knowledgeable than myself."

"Ah, then we have something in common. I am the administrator for the school district in this portion of the territory."

Finnegan grinned. "This territory has an intriguing selection of school administrators. I once had cause to spend time in the company of Granville Stuart. He, too, serves as a school administrator, while he is not tending to his cattle."

Wylie turned to Finnegan with a truly intrigued look. "Granville Stuart? I have always had an interest in that fellow, or men of his type, at any rate. Tell me, did he strike you as quite ordinary, or did he attempt to hang you?"

Finnegan laughed. "Like most men, he is extraordinary in some regards and quite ordinary in most ways. His duties to the local school district did not seem to take up much of his time. I believe it only contained the one small school."

Wylie nodded and produced a cookie from beneath the wagon seat. "Care for one?"

"No, thank you."

"My district contains several schools, and they all seem to be in a constant state of turmoil. Though, I shouldn't complain. As you have probably discovered, if all goes well, the administrator's job is the first to become imperiled."

"A very astute observation, sir." Finnegan took a quick look around for bears and adjusted the Purdey next to him, planning for any eventuality. "You say you escorted Mr. Kearney and Mr. Schnaubelt into the park?"

"Yup." Wylie munched his cookie. "Took them in...now that you mention it, I do not recall how many days back it was. Cannot have been more than a week. I do recall telling them they were at least two weeks behind Pendleton and his bunch." Wylie finished the cookie and wiped crumbs from his lips with one gloved hand. "You gentlemen are awfully spread out in your wandering."

"Yes, well, circumstances made it impossible for us to leave Chicago as a body."

"I do not envy you the task of locating all or any of the men you will be searching for. By now, Pendleton could have wandered all the way to the coast and Kearney and, Sherbet..."

"Schnaubelt."

"Yes, Schnaubelt. They could have wandered nearly as far." Wylie coughed into one hand and looked glumly around the valley they traveled through. "I suppose your man Pendleton could not care less, having come here to stand next to a brimstone pit all day, but this smoke is going to do murder to my summer's business. Once word of it gets back east, the dandies will burn up the telegraph wire cancelling their engagements here." He coughed again. "I cannot say as I blame them."

"It is unfortunate." Finnegan pulled a cigar from his pocket and sparked a match for it. He leaned over and cupped his hands to get the smoke ignited. Puffing and shaking out the match, he noticed Wylie was giving him a strange look. "It is hardly the same sort of smoke, Mr. Wylie. I dare say if that was a tobacco field burning in the distance you would see a marked increase in your business."

Wylie laughed. "Probably so; folks do enjoy tobacco." He shook his head. "I am ardently hoping for rain. It would be a pity to have all these old, lovely trees burn, over nothing more than a squabble between a few men over something so petty."

"It is a shame that most men cannot look far beyond what is in front of them at any given moment." Finnegan surveyed the area once more, somewhat searching for signs of bears, but also taking in the scenery. "It is a fine thing that some fellows are possessed of the foresight to set a place like this aside." He pointed behind them with one thumb. "Although,

Mr. Johnson seems to be of the opinion that this place has already become far too civilized. He would prefer to do without the town of Gardiner, the Army, and likely, you, as well." Finnegan chuckled.

"Um, yes." Wylie rubbed his bearded chin. "I have been meaning to inquire regarding that gentleman. Where, precisely, did you come into his acquaintance?"

Finnegan smiled around his cigar. "He joined our party at Coulson."

"I see." Wylie gave the reins a small snap. "Many years ago, I heard a tale of a man named Johnson who was a well-known Indian fighter with...irregular habits." Wylie glanced over at Finnegan. "I would say it is likely not the same gentleman who rides behind us presently. The man I heard of would surely have passed on by now."

Finnegan sighed and knocked the ash from his cigar. "I am afraid the gentleman from the stories you have heard is likely the same man in the coach behind us. He is known as Liver-Eating Johnson, although he prefers to be called John, by his friends."

"Truly?"

"Indeed. The man has been regaling me with tales of these western territories for several days now. If he is not the man from your stories, he is certainly the inspiration for them. He is also past sixty years of age. Quite spry, is he not?"

"I should say so." Wylie chuckled a bit. "Although, that would be in keeping with the legend regarding men such as him."

Finnegan smiled. "There are other men such as him?"

"I refer to the act of...well, dining on your fellow man. The legend is that it keeps you young, ageless, after a fashion. The Indians have a tale or two regarding men who... overindulge in such a diet and are transformed into evil spirits or monsters. The precise name of the beast escapes me just now."

Finnegan shrugged. "His being spry may not be solely the result of Indian magic. An Army cook once spent the better part of a day relating the healthsome benefits of liver to me."

"Perhaps it is nothing more than that." Wylie snapped the reins again.

Finnegan puffed away on his cigar. "Pendleton and his people stayed at this Camp Sheridan for a time?"

"For a few days, yes."

"So, then, they likely gave some indication of where they were headed from there to someone?"

"I should think so, yes." Wylie shrugged. "If not, when we arrive you will find your men Kearney and Schnaubelt sitting on a couple of upturned buckets looking sour. One way or the other, you should be able to locate some of your people."

Finnegan smiled and knocked more ash. "Just so long as we locate a couple of them, that is the important matter." He glanced about for bears once again. "What sort of place is Camp Sheridan?"

"At present, a couple of lowly plank board buildings and a collection of tents. If the Army has their way, someday, it will be a proper town. The Army has its needs and prefers to have them tended to. They fancy a town to go with their forts."

"You would prefer otherwise, Mr. Wylie?"

"The purpose of setting this place aside was to keep towns from being built inside the boundaries of it. Even the damned fools from the Interior Department were at least bright enough to understand that concept." Wylie scowled. "On occasion, it seems to be that we are always trading one devil for another in the Yellowstone country. We managed to force out all the loggers and trappers by making the place a park, but then we were left with the drunken scoundrels the Department of the Interior would send us. Now we are rid of them but saddled with the Army and all that comes with soldiers tromping about."

Finnegan shook one finger at the man. "Mr. Wylie, if there is one thing I have learned to a certainty during my years in this country, it is that if you involve yourself in any way with the government of this country, you will be brought first to frustration and eventually to tears." He grinned and gave his cigar a puff. "Although, I would imagine you consider that proposition a fair trade for your park."

"You have me there, Mr. Gilhooley. I am never so happy as when I am in this country. If I can make a few dollars profit at the same time, more the better." He pulled another cookie from under the coach seat. I am sure you can appreciate the sentiment. Your work has brought you here, as well."

Finnegan scanned for bears and smiled. "Yes, it is always hard to say where a man's work may take him."

"You folks are quite the collection." Wylie laughed. "An English lord, who drags that odd Italian fellow around with him, and all that claptrap."

Finnegan nodded. "Lords never travel light."

"The next two were a funny pair, as well. Kearney and Schnaubelt barely had a bag between them. The only thing they worried over was the crate they had with their instruments."

"Instruments?"

"Scientific instruments of some manner, I would suppose. What is Mr. Kearney and Mr. Schnaubelt's area of expertise? You would have thought that crate was full of eggs the way they babied it."

"Yes, well, some equipment is sensitive to rough handling." Finnegan jolted up in the coach seat and raised the Purdey a bit before identifying the creature that sprang from the creek bottom below. "I'll be damned, is that an elk?"

Wylie nodded. "It is, indeed, sir. Many thousands of them in the confines of the park."

"Are we likely to see buffalo?"

"Oh, you'll see some." Wylie laughed. "They've a devil of a time keeping the Indians and the poachers away from them, so the department of the interior men have them all corralled up by the Mammoth Hot Springs, near the Army camp."

"All the buffalo?"

"All that remain. The ones at Mammoth are fewer every year, as well. I harbor a suspicion that the Interior men were selling them when they get the opportunity. I can only hope the Army will put a stop to those irregularities." He shrugged. "Or they may increase. It is always hard to say what might occur in this place." Wylie looked over at Finnegan for a long moment. "Do all administrative men in your line wear two pistols?"

"Chicago is a rambunctious town, sir."

Wylie nodded. "I read in the papers that a hundred policemen were blown to bits there just the other day. I suppose if I frequented such a place, I might begin to carry a pistol, too."

"I am more than a bit surprised to find that you do not carry a rifle in this place. Johnson tells me this country overflows with bears. Do you not have the least concern?"

"Oh, I have concerns, and I have taken precautions. I have simply seen to different preparations."

"What preparations?"

"I live and work in this country every day. I can run up

one of these hills quite quickly. I can climb any of these trees in a split second."

"More quickly than a bear?"

"Mr. Gilhooley, I do not need to run up the hill more quickly than the bear, I only need to ascend it more quickly than you."

Chapter 13

CAMP SHERIDAN, WYOMING TERRITORY

May 17, 1886

WYLIE HAD ALLOWED FINNEGAN AND THE OTHERS TO spend the night at the camp he had put together just outside the area where the Army was bivouacked. The guide seemed to be interested in avoiding the soldiers, or keeping the soldiers away from his clients, at any rate. Having spent more than his fair share of time in Army camps, Finnegan could not blame the fellow. When the morning dawned, Finnegan walked down the road to the Army camp to locate the commanding officer, who would, theoretically, know where the Pendleton Expedition had gotten off to. With any luck, following the lord would lead to the Irishman and the anarchist Finnegan sought.

It was a half mile from Wylie's campsite to Camp Sheridan, but Finnegan made the stroll happily. He carried the Purdey in one hand and took in the country as he went, glad to be off by himself for a short time. As the Army camp came into view, he could see that it was not an overly large operation. The Army of the Potomac had spread out over many miles when it came to rest. Camp Sheridan looked to be home to only one troop of cavalry numbering fifty or sixty men at most.

It had been Finnegan's experience that an Army troop of any sort would quickly fall into laxness and patent laziness when they found themselves in any sort of posting far from a fort or their home barracks. The soldiers of Yellowstone seemed to be of a different sort, though. Either that, or their commander kept after them quite regularly. Even in the early morning hour the enlisted men were up and moving in groups under the careful watch of sergeants. The whole troop appeared busy as bees. Finnegan walked up to the closest sergeant and offered the man a smile as his men chopped and notched logs.

"How does the morning find you, Sergeant?"

The NCO pulled down on his forager's cap. "Very well, sir. How may I help you?"

"I seek the man who commands here."

"That would be Captain Moses Harris, sir." The sergeant pointed past a long line of white canvas tents toward a two-story structure formed from rough cut lumber, but not yet painted. "His office is on the ground floor. He is normally just finishing up officers' call about now, sir. Please look through the window and check to make certain they are finished before entering, if you would be so kind."

"Certainly, Sergeant." Finnegan tipped his hat. "It has never been my habit to interrupt officers. Doing so can only lead to receiving orders, and then...well, I am sure you know the kind of predicaments a man can find himself in then."

"To be sure, sir." The NCO motioned to Finnegan's right hand. "That is a fine rifle."

Finnegan smiled again. "Thank you, Sergeant." Finnegan continued on his way and made it to the front door of the one and only building just as three lieutenants came walking out.

They all nodded to Finnegan in their turn and made directly from the captain's office toward the mess tent with nothing further. They seemed rather inured to odd characters visiting their commanding officer. Finnegan gave the door a quick knock.

"Come."

Finnegan swung the door open and entered. Inside the office, he saw a trim fellow with a surprisingly clean uniform and what appeared to be freshly starched shirt cuffs extending from the sleeves. Captain Harris sported a bushy mustache and close-cropped hair. He took a quick glance at Finnegan, took a second glance, and then raised his eyebrows. "Is there something I can be of assistance with, sir?"

Finnegan leaned his rifle by the door and took a step forward, closing it behind him. "That would be my ardent hope, Captain. I am seeking a group of men who passed through here some time ago and I have been told you keep track of such matters, as well as any man can, of course."

"I attempt it, or have been the last few weeks. Whom do you seek?"

"The Pendleton Party, or more specifically, two men who were following up the Pendleton Party."

The captain rubbed his chin. "Many parties pass through here, sir. You will have to offer a few details to jog my memory."

"Pendleton is an English lord, come here to investigate the volcanos."

"Ah, yes. That will do." Harris smiled. "Mercifully, we have very few members of the royal family pass through, at least during my brief tenure here." He tapped a pencil on the top of his desk. "Pendleton and his group were making for the Firehole River and the Geyser Basins." Harris grinned. "I always thought of such oddities as volcanos, as well." He leaned forward and lowered his voice. "However, speaking such blasphemy here can practically lead to a lynching. You have never seen so many men so inexplicably obsessed with a few spurting mudholes of hot water. The way they act, you would think the door to heaven lay inside one of those pits."

"I would think the door to hell would be the more likely portal." Finnegan withdrew a couple of cigars from his vest pocket. "Care for a smoke, Captain?"

"Oh, don't mind if I do." He motioned to the chairs before his desk. "Please, sit, sir. Did you mention your name?"

"Finnegan Gilhooley." He lowered himself into the chair and passed the captain a cigar.

"Gilhooley?" The captain took the cigar, looking pensive. "That is a very uncommon name." He rubbed his chin yet again. "Oh, yes, are you not the Pinkerton agent who spent so very long pursuing the James brothers? I apologize if I am being discourteous in bringing the matter up. I recall it was quite well covered in the *Police Gazette*." He shrugged and lit his cigar. "There was a time when I had such free and easy access to newspapers." He sighed. "Now, I can barely recall the name of the President."

Finnegan shrugged and lit his own cigar. "If you have lost track, I am sure there will be a new one soon enough for you to read about. They come and go quite regularly."

Harris laughed. "They do, indeed. So, are you in fact the famous Pinkerton agent whose adventures so thrilled me in years past?"

Finnegan nodded slowly, tentative to discuss the matter, but finding himself with little choice. "I am, sir, though, the *Gazette* frequently...enhanced certain aspects of my work to sell additional papers. I assure you, pursuing the James brothers was rarely thrilling."

Harris scrutinized the gunman. "So, then, you tracked the James brothers many a weary mile and now you find yourself in search of an English lord?" Harris let out an earnest laugh. "I must say, Mr. Gilhooley, the company you wish to keep has taken quite a turn."

Finnegan smiled. Being posted to the wilderness had not affected the captain's humor. "I would have to agree with you, sir." He knocked ash to the captain's floor. "Sadly, I have not come here to collect the Englishman. I am in search of the two men who previously came in search of Pendleton."

"The Irishman and the Hun?"

"Indeed."

Harris puzzled for a moment. "Those two seemed harmless enough. Rather out of sorts in this open country, but not dangerous."

Finnegan shrugged. "The Hun set off a bomb killing half a dozen policemen in Chicago, the other man intends to dynamite Pendleton."

Harris raised an eyebrow. "It would appear I misread them."

"Yes, that will happen from time to time." Finnegan removed his hat and set it on his knee. "I thought it would be best to come here and inform you as to the situation. If you alert your men to the circumstances, it may be a great deal easier to keep Kearney and Schnaubelt from any further mischief."

Harris smoothed his mustache. "Mr. Gilhooley, my men are soldiers, not sheriffs." He knocked ash of his own to the floor. "We have been given the commission of rounding up the vagrants engaged in poaching in this area, and I am sad to say we are ill-suited to the endeavor. There is much ground to cover, and we are few."

"Yes. I could not help but notice you are only a single company."

"Not even that when you deduct the men on the sick list." Harris shook his head. "I take it you were formerly in uniform?" Finnegan nodded. "Then you understand the propensity of the average soldier to get himself in trouble from boredom or poor judgement." Finnegan nodded again. "So far, Company M has lost men to the usual number of accidents with the stock and the wagons, but we also must contend with the construction difficulties."

Finnegan motioned over one shoulder, back toward the camp. "I meant to inquire about that. How ever have you kept those men working so assiduously? The soldiers seemed to spend most of their time drunk or asleep at the territorial forts I have visited previously."

Harris grinned. "And therein lies the secret to troop morale here. There is no fort, as yet. No barracks. Nothing but thin canvas tents." He puffed his cigar. "These men all come from Fort Custer. They have all spent at least one winter in this country and know full well they will be spending another here. They have been informed that if they are to spend the winter indoors, it will be due to their diligence in building the fort and barracks that will house them."

Finnegan returned the captain's smile. "Fear of freezing to death will motivate a man."

"Quite." Harris puffed again. "What were we discussing... oh, yes, my troop and the sick list. Unfortunately, this country offers many difficulties I had not predicted. Men are injured working on the barracks. Men are injured on these damnable trails." He shook his head, looking sullen. "And it is the devil's own trouble keeping them from fooling with the damn volcanos. The enlisted men are drawn to them like a moth to a flame. The pools appear quite inviting, but...the burns are horrid things to inspect. Do not approach any of those damn hot springs while you are in this vicinity, Mr. Gilhooley."

"I will use the utmost caution, Captain. It is regretful that you are short of men, but I fail to see what that has to do with my commission here."

Harris shook his head. "Oh, do not misunderstand me, sir: if it were within my power, I would give you every assistance in locating and capturing these men, but I simply lack the resources. I send out patrol after patrol seeking to apprehend poachers and they always return emptyhanded. These men have yet to fully learn the country and, as I said, they are soldiers, not sheriff's deputies. They know nothing of capturing criminals."

Finnegan chuckled. "No need to complicate the issue, sir. If your men locate them, no one will trouble them about shooting the rascals down. If I encounter them, that is certainly my intention. I see no reason for your soldiers to hold themselves to a higher standard."

Harris sighed, looking deeply exasperated. "Oh, Mr. Gilhooley, if only life were so simple. Hearing you speak so makes me long for happier times chasing Indians. In those days, I only worried over losing my hair. Now, I worry I may lose my sanity. I can no more order my men to shoot the miscreants you seek than I can order them to shoot the poachers. The soldiers stationed here may not initiate an engagement. How can we? We have no enemy to engage. We are to keep this park and the various animals that inhabit it secure. If you know what on earth that means I wish you would tell me, because I am at something of a loss when it comes to deciphering it."

Finnegan rubbed his eyes. "So, you can offer me no

assistance? I am to attempt searching this vast wilderness with nothing but the three men with me?"

Harris sighed again. "Do any of the men in your party know the area at all?"

"We have brought a man named Johnson with us who was formerly one of these mountain fur trapper types. He hunted here many years ago."

Harris arched his eyebrow again. "Johnson?"

"Yes. John Johnson."

"The deputy from Coulson?"

"Yes."

"I have heard a few...disturbing rumors regarding that man."

Finnegan nodded. "They are all true, I assure you."

"Well..." Harris raised his hands in resignation. "If he is half the frontiersman I have heard he is, you should be well set when it comes to navigation. The man can surely find the Firehole River if he managed to find three hundred Crow to kill. I assume your other companions have their uses."

"They are both Pinkerton Agents, yes."

"Then you are better off than you would be dragging a few of my soldiers along behind you. Most of my men, excepting the non-commissioned officers, are not good for overly much. The lieutenants are fresh from West Point. The privates and corporals are farm boys shipped here after the Indians had been corralled. I do not trust most of them with the axes or hammers required to build our encampment. Aside from the sergeants, I do not trust a one of them with a loaded arm."

Finnegan nodded sullenly. "I see. Yes, well, we all have our cross to bear, I suppose. Perhaps you are correct. I may be better off with my own fellows and the mountain man."

Harris puffed his cigar to the halfway point and motioned

behind Finnegan. "Is that one of those English guns they refer to as a double rifle?"

"It is."

Harris pursed his lips. "Now that shows a great deal of forethought on your part, sir. I refuse to travel anywhere in this wretched place without a rifle. The place is absolutely filthy with bears, and I would congratulate you if you removed a few from the area during your travels."

Finnegan smiled. "You might. I doubt our esteemed guide Mr. Wylie would hold the same opinion."

"Ah, Wylie. He brought you here?"

"In one of his rather fine coaches, yes."

Harris grimaced. "The people who inhabit this place are strange, to say the least. Are you aware that fellow is in command of every school in the territory, or near to?"

"Yes, he mentioned that."

"His wife is some sort of schoolteacher, as well. Educated people, far more so than you or I, Mr. Gilhooley, and they lark about this wilderness as though it were some sort of...I do not know what to call it, some sort of amusement folly. They watch these giant bears play. They give visitors tours of the smoldering gates to Hades and revel when boiling water is blown at them. It is madness, Mr. Gilhooley. I daresay, hearing that an Irishman and a Hun have come here to blow up an English lord is the first sensible item I have been privy to in nearly forever."

"It is strange to me that anyone would wish to visit a place so full of volcanos and bears."

"Much less pay someone like Wylie to show them around the place." Harris shrugged. "The world is a madhouse, my friend."

BACK AT THE WYLIE CAMP, Finnegan broke open the action on the Purdey and set it across his knee before sitting down by the small fire Wylie had going for cooking. He sighed and looked over to Rooney. "Well, the Army will not be assisting us in our search."

Rooney moved down the log bench he was seated on so that he could answer in a low tone. "Did the commandant give any indication of where Pendleton might be?"

"Some lovely place known as the Firehole River. The lord has scampered there to investigate his beloved volcanoes. Kearney and Schnaubelt presented themselves at the captain's office just as I did and made the same inquiry."

Rooney squeezed the bridge of his nose and scowled. "Damn it to perdition. Why does there always have to be a man like Kearney in every crowd?"

Finnegan cast a skeptical glance at his old friend. "Sam, are you not the rabblerouser who gathered the crowd?"

"What? Oh, you of all men would not put the blame for this on my shoulders?"

Finnegan shrugged. "You were rather specific regarding the possible uses for dynamite in the changing of governments."

Rooney waved one hand. "That is merely theatre, Finnegan. You would not blame me if a fellow stabbed someone after watching me perform Julius Caesar, would you?"

Finnegan rubbed his face. "No, I suppose I would not. Though, one who did not know you as well as I do might argue that a man who suggests the immolation of English royalty, again and again, in most of the larger cities of this nation, twice a day for a year, should not be surprised when one lonely fellow takes him up on the suggestion."

Rooney stared into the fire, looking quite serious.

"Finnegan, if this fellow Kearney kills Pendleton...chances are I will be in a cell just down from those anarchists from the Haymarket, awaiting the rope."

Finnegan waved a hand in response. "You worry over nothing, Sam. I would wager you have simply grown too settled and..." He grinned at the former Pinkerton. "Perhaps a bit soft living the theatre life. If Professor Mezzeroff finds himself accused of complicity in some vile act, he will simply disappear in a puff of smoke as so many of your varied aliases have before him." Finnegan chuckled. "William Pinkerton might even be persuaded to bring you back into the fold, now that you are so well versed in the current condition of the Irish revolutionary movement. Convince him the sons of Erin are somehow plotting with the Knights of Labor and you will be set for life."

Rooney laughed. "Ah, now there is a thought. Yes, you are quite right. I am being dreary to no purpose. If Lord Pendleton finds himself in various pieces it is none of my affair." He sighed. "Oh, but it would be a pity to leave Mezzeroff behind. It was a grand sort of charade, Finnegan."

"Somehow, I doubt Kearney exploding the Englishman would be your only difficulty in resuming your career as a showman. Mr. O'Donovan Rossa may be loath to partner with you after learning your history."

Rooney waggled one finger at Finnegan. "Ah, but there is something you have never been able to fully appreciate. All is subterfuge with these types, Finnegan. They weave a tapestry of lies and one day they cannot quite recall what the purpose of it all was. I could easily convince O'Donovan Rossa to provide the financing for another tour."

Finnegan shook his head in amazement. "I do not know if Mr. O'Donovan Rossa will be overly interested in backing you financially, now that he is aware that you were formally a Pinkerton man, and never a professor."

"He always knew I was not a professor, or a Hun." Rooney poked the fire a bit. "As for my affiliation with Mr. Pinkerton, that is a small matter. If my former business associate reveals my history to the Clan na Gael, I will tell the others that O'Donovan Rossa is, in fact, an agent provocateur of the Pinkertons." Rooney smiled. "If I am to remain quiet, my friends must do the same."

Finnegan cleared his throat. "So, then, your future plans are, essentially, to do nothing more than kill Kearney to put a stop to this foolishness, and then resume pretending to be a Teutonic professor hell bent of the destruction of the British and the other assorted monarchs?"

Rooney nodded. "Yes, that will do nicely."

"Sam, O'Donovan Rossa has been the Clan na Gael's firebrand and rabblerouser for more years than I care to recall. Why in the name of St. Peter would they ever believe the man is a Pinkerton operative?"

Rooney showed a toothy grin. "They might believe it quite readily, if Allan Pinkerton's own good hammer were to tell them it was so. I dare say all it would take would be for you to swing by O'Donovan Rossa's hotel room at an inopportune time."

"You are a devious man, Sam. It has always been your most impressive trait." He attempted to look more serious as he continued. "Sam, is this Kearney fellow knowledgeable enough regarding dynamite to assassinate that damned Englishman?"

Rooney bit on his lip, contemplating the question. "Well, he knows what I taught him. Although, dynamite is not the most complicated of instruments. If he does not, I suppose simply shooting the bastard is a workable option. Dead is dead, Finnegan. It is who kills a man like Pendleton that matters, not how the limey bugger dies that is important. In truth, if we can shoot down Kearney and Schnaubelt still manages to murder the Englishman, I could not care less. A Hun killing an English lord should have little effect on my well-being." Rooney brightened a bit. "Now there is a thought. Shall we swear, here and now that, regardless of what becomes of Kearney, we shall tell all interested parties that Schnaubelt is the murderer? It would seem to be the most convenient method to relieve us of our troubles, Finnegan."

"I suggest shooting and you suggest lying. Our respective specialties have not changed noticeably over the years, Sam."

"We are creatures of habit who gravitate toward what has been proven effective."

"Yes." Finnegan tossed a small branch into the fire. "It would appear we must locate both Pendleton and Kearney of our own accord. When we do locate Kearney, you can recognize him by sight?"

"Certainly."

"Will you shoot the blackguard?"

Rooney moved around uncomfortably on this log bench. "Would it not be better for you to see to that particular bit of business, as always?"

"Oh, make no mistake, my friend, I have no intention of procrastinating on that score. I would merely find comfort in your assurance that if you do find yourself in Kearney's company you will do more than cry out my name and hope I deliver you from your current predicament."

Rooney appeared quite confused. "My predicament? Is this not a predicament for us both? You are commissioned to find Kearney, and Finnegan Gilhooley always gets his man."

Finnegan shook his head. "You, of all men, know that is a

ridiculous fabrication. I chased after the James brothers seemingly forever, and I did not capture or kill either of them. I have chased more than a few men who have given me the slip." He raised his eyebrows. "Letting Kearney slip will in no way ruin my legacy, Sam, but it may see you fitted with a hemp collar."

"Damn O'Donovan and damn Kearney." Rooney pounded one fist on the side of the bench. "When I began this, it appeared as though it would be a perfectly safe and profitable venture. Why must fools always allow themselves to be swept up in hysteria?"

Finnegan had to chuckle. "I would agree it was profitable, Sam, but I would hardly call it safe. You were roaming the earth teaching ruffians the use of dynamite. How can such a thing not end badly?"

"My key error was in choosing my associates." Rooney looked perfectly serious. "The next time I ought to partner with you. Finnegan Gilhooley has done many things, but losing his head is not one of them. I could at least trust you not to arm and fund fools such as these we pursue."

Finnegan rubbed his eyes. "It is always difficult to say what a man might do if he finds himself in possession of disposable funds." He sighed. "But speaking of pursuit, I believe we should look to procuring a few mounts from Mr. Wylie and getting to our business. We shall soon discover if Mr. Johnson recalls the path toward someplace called the Firehole River."

Rooney scratched his slowly forming beard. "They do enjoy descriptive titles here in the territories. Why would anyone wish to visit a place called the Firehole River?"

"I cannot say as I would, on my own account, but that was Pendleton's stated destination. That is the likely spot to begin our search."

"How long is the journey?"

"Captain Harris tells me that if we depart this morning, we should reach the river in two full days of travel. Although, it seems doubtful Mr. Wylie will be able to locate enough stock for us today. I heard him complain that his horses and mules are very rarely where he left them."

Rooney grimaced and glanced about. "We will be spending the night in the open, in this wilderness?"

"You spent the night in the open every night for several years during the war. What are a few more nights roughing it?"

"Pennsylvania was not quite so populated with bears."

Finnegan patted the Purdey over his knee. "There are palliatives for that condition, as well. Though, I must admit, I share your trepidation."

Chapter 14

GRIZZLY LAKE, WYOMING TERRITORY

May 18, 1886

THE LIGHT WAS BEGINNING TO FAIL WHEN THEY STOPPED to make camp. Johnson expounded on how the lake had received its name and then set to seeing about the stock. He had apparently given Wylie his personal guarantee that nothing untoward would occur with the horses. Rooney began building a fire and pulling various items from their one and only mule's pack. Finnegan stood guard, nervously glancing about with the Purdey clutched in his hands. Abijah vigorously rubbed his backside after a long day of riding he was quite unused to.

"It is a terrible inconvenience that these scoundrels have chosen to do murder so far from a rail line. Riding no longer seems to agree with me." He continued to rub his lower back.

"I only wish they had chosen a location with fewer murderous beasts." Finnegan moved his gaze from the surrounding woods to his old associate Rooney. "And what is it you are engaged in?"

"I am working at making our supper, Finnegan. Unless

you plan to live off the land like a red Indian. We have some canned things here and a side of salt pork."

"You intend to cook something?"

"Yes. Is it so inconceivable that I would know how to fry salt pork?" Rooney glanced between Finnegan and Abijah. "This cannot be the most astonishing action you have ever discovered me to be involved in."

"Sam, I have known you since we were little more than boys, and I have never seen you place the smallest victual in a fry pan." Finnegan returned to surveying the country.

"I learned a great many things during my absence from the agency, Finnegan." Rooney flipped the lid off one pack box. "Why don't you two make yourselves useful and locate some additional firewood. We will have need of it before it is dark."

Abijah ceased rubbing. "Certainly, Sam." He looked over the general vicinity. "This must be a common choice for camping. The wood seems to have been mostly picked over." He shrugged. "Finnegan, we should investigate that stand of brush there by the lake. The branches from those fir trees down there should make fine fodder."

Finnegan swallowed and grimaced. "Yes, very well." He took a few steps toward the copse of trees.

"Finnegan?"

"Yes, Abijah?"

"Will you not find it difficult to carry wood along with your rifle?"

Finnegan stared at the young fellow quizzically. "I will not be carrying wood. You will carry wood and I will watch over you with the rifle to make sure you are safe."

"Safe?"

"From being eaten by the bears."

Abijah slowly turned his head from side to side. "I see no bears, Finnegan."

"That is how they fall upon you. They keep hidden until you are within striking distance and then...you are no more than a few large gulps."

Rooney sighed and shook his head. "Indulge him, Abijah. I cannot say why he has chosen these bears to fixate on, but he does. Let him guard you while you collect sticks."

Finnegan cast a truly irritated look toward Rooney. "Sam, I would remind you that we are camped at a place named Grizzly Lake, named after the grizzly bear that formerly ate all who passed this way. Johnson has just finished admonishing us as to the danger."

Rooney rubbed his tired eyes. "That is not what Johnson said. If the bear ate all who passed this way, how is it anyone would reach civilization to relate the tale?"

"Sam, I do not take much comfort in knowing that the bear could not find room in his gullet for the twenty-first man after ingesting the first score."

"That is not what Johnson said, either."

Finnegan shook his head. "We have a need for firewood. Abijah and I will collect it." He waggled one finger at Rooney. "When I return, we shall finish this discussion."

Finnegan and Abijah made their way down toward the lake shore and entered the stand of willow by way of a game trail, weaving their way along toward a stand of fir trees. Abijah traipsed along the slim path as though he did not have a care in the world, but Finnegan was considerably more cautious. Abijah turned around and noticed Finnegan lagged behind by the better part of fifty feet. He turned fully in the path and raised his hands a bit. "Finnegan, truly?"

"Abijah, you have not been in this country previously. You cannot fully appreciate the peril we face."

"Finnegan, you yourself have told me that you failed to encounter a single bear the last time you traveled to this territory. If it we so very full of these murderous beasts, do you not think you would have seen at least..." Abijah paused, noticing the look of rather abject terror that had passed over Finnegan's face. It was a visage he had never before viewed. "Finnegan?"

"Abijah. Jump from the path."

The young man slowly turned to look behind him. All that was visible through the brush was a gigantic swath of brown fur. The beast's breathing could be easily discerned. "Bloody hell." Abijah dove into the brush on one side of the path and did not see Finnegan fire the Purdey, he only heard the report from first one barrel of the gun and then the other. Not being one to foist work entirely onto another fellow, Abijah pulled the Colt from his hip and the Smith & Wesson from the small of his back. He fired a round from each in the general direction of the beast, then sat up and took proper aim for four more shots. He paused, indecisive as to whether he should run the risk of expending all his ammunition. "Finnegan?"

"Yes, Abijah?"

"Is it dead?"

"Dead as charity, my friend."

Abijah released a long breath and set his guns down on the ground next to him. "I dare say that must be the largest bear in the territory. Did you see the size of the creature, Finnegan?"

"I did."

"And its fangs, enormous." Abijah hung his head. "It must have only been a trick of the light, but I swear I saw blood dripping from them as it crouched in ambush for us."

He looked up to his old friend who appeared somewhat pensive. "Are you all right, Finnegan?"

"The beast has no fangs, Abijah."

"What?"

"It is a buffalo, Abijah. I have no idea why it felt the need to lurk in this brushy bottom, but it is a buffalo, nonetheless."

Abijah turned and sat up fully to better inspect the corpse. "I...well now, that is a rare accident, I suppose."

"Oddly enough, much the same thing happened to me on another occasion, but it is hardly of consequence now." He broke open the Purdey and pulled the empty cases from the gun.

Abijah got to his feet and began reloading his revolvers. "I must admit, I am at a bit of a loss as to what we should do next, Finnegan."

Two fresh rounds went in the Purdey and Finnegan snapped the action shut. "I see no reason to not make use of the beast. Come, I will show you how to remove the better cuts of meat from an animal such as this. I became rather well practiced with it during my last journey to these wild environs. Did I ever tell you how impressed I was with Ephraim Kilkenny's abilities to remove the hide from animals? That drunken Irish lay-about could remove the skin from an animal with no more effort than it takes you to change your shirt."

Johnson bit off a small hunk of buffalo tenderloin and placed the remainder back on his plate. It had come as something of a shock to the entire party, but Rooney had done a fine job of cooking the meat. Johnson, especially, had enjoyed it.

"Been many years since I tasted the sweet meats of a buff. I do miss it." He popped the rest of the tenderloin into his mouth. "Damned odd. Wylie told me all the buff were rounded up and kept in pens of late back there at the Army camp." He chuckled. "Looks like they missed one."

Rooney nodded. "It is well they did. This is fine meat."

Johnson grabbed another hunk from the frypan. "It is, but that Wylie fellow will be damned soured if he hears of this. Not supposed to be shootin' nothin' in here, let alone these precious few buff. I been hearing there ain't but a few hundred of them left between here and...well, whatever the hell is above the British up there."

"The North Pole?" Abijah smiled and plucked a potato from the fry pan.

"I suspect." Johnson grinned. "Can't say as I ever had much interest in goin' up to inspect Canada. Like I told you boys, I come up about this far and the damned winters just about couldn't be suffered. Don't know what the hell they do farther north."

Finnegan set his empty plate on the ground and sipped his coffee. "They get by in various ways. It may be hard to credit, but the human race inhabits areas very far to the northern extremes. Very nearly all the way to the pole Abijah mentioned. Have any of you had chance to read of the exploits of the Englishmen who were so ardently searching for the Northwest Passage some years ago? Two of them, Franklin and Parry spring to mind." The group shook their heads. As always, they appeared a bit surprised to hear what Finnegan did with his idle hours. "Yes, well, these two fellows: the one, Franklin, he pursued the Passage by searching on foot. He walked all the way from Hudson Bay to the northern extreme of the British lands to the north. Parry sailed a ship through the ice flows above Hudson Bay. At any rate, they both encountered people as they traveled north and did not cease to encounter them during their journeys. The human body is capable of enduring great strain, especially if the frame has been inured to it."

"I reckon so." Johnson tossed a log on the fire. "We may have a few difficulties to endure, as well."

Finnegan drained his coffee cup. "Such as?"

"Well, like I told you earlier, this is griz country. I don't know if we ought to keep camp near a dead buffalo. Griz'll be on that like flies on a...well, a dead buffalo."

Finnegan sighed and threw what remained of his coffee into the fire. "Mr. Johnson, I grow damned weary of this."

"Of what, Finnegan?"

"This damned yarning regarding the danger of bears. Everywhere I travel in this cursed territory I hear nothing but warnings of these ephemeral bears, but they never materialize. So far, these warnings and threats have cost the life of a moose, a very fine bull, and that misbegotten buffalo. A member of a very nearly vanished race, I might add. I am finished, do you hear me? I am done, sir. No longer will I live in a state of constant anxiety looking out for an imaginary foe that is so often replaced by innocent victims. No more." He spoke the last words looking quite stern.

Johnson licked his furry lips, looking confused. "A bull?"

"Do not burden your mind with the details, Mr. Johnson. Only take note of the end result. We are not moving camp, we are not sleeping with one eye open, and I am no longer living in a state of excitement for no damn reason." Finnegan tossed down his plate. "I am going to sleep. Bother me no further."

Abijah looked up at his mentor. "A moose?"

Finnegan scowled. "Bother me no further."

Chapter 15

GRIZZLY LAKE, WYOMING TERRITORY

May 19, 1886

Finnegan had slept like a rock, so he was more than a bit perturbed to feel one of his compatriots shaking him awake. Instead of rousing, he pulled his coat tighter around him and flailed one hand about. Despite his protestations, the shaking continued.

"Leave me be a moment." Finnegan squeezed his eyes shut and attempted to roll over, but found he was not able to leave his back. Very slowly he let his eyes roll open. He stared up into the early morning light. Above him, standing with its front paws planted on his chest, a not overly large grizzly bear stared down into Finnegan's face. The gunman emitted a small grunt which the bear seemed to take interest in. "Sweet Mary mother of God." Finnegan hissed out the words and slowly pulled his Remington revolver from his bedroll beside him. Showing great restraint, he brought the muzzle of the pistol up until it nearly touched under the bear's chin. A small amount of pressure was just being applied to the hammer spur of the weapon when Abijah appeared and aimed the Purdey rifle at the back of the bear's head. Finnegan sucked in a small breath. "Abijah, please, hold fire."

"But, Finnegan, I must...it is right on top of you." Abijah clearly felt compelled.

"Abijah, that gun has shot through every damned thing I have ever fired upon. If you fire you are sure to kill me, as well." He pulled back the hammer on the Remington far enough to hear the first click. "I will see to this." Oddly, the bear appeared to find the two men and their hijinks rather amusing. Finnegan brought the hammer back to the second click just as Johnson called out from the other side of the camp.

"Finnegan, it might not be my place to say so, but you ought not shoot that bear under the chin like that."

Finnegan drew in a short breath and closed his eyes for a moment. "Why is that, Mr. Johnson?"

"It's just that them griz take a might bit to die, even head shot, and it very well may get to tearin' on you before it passes."

Finnegan swallowed. "All right, Mr. Johnson, if it would not be too much trouble, could you please tell me what in the bloody hell you would recommend?"

Johnson sat up out of his bedroll on one elbow and took in the full scene. "Mayhap you ought to just clout the damn thing with your pistol." He nodded at his own suggestion. "Yeah, give 'em a rap on the skull with that fine pistol of yours and see what it does. It ain't a very big bear. It'll most likely run off."

Finnegan bit back the urge to release several vulgarities toward the mountain man. "Most likely?" A globule of bear drool fell down onto his face.

"It ain't like I know what in the hell the intentions of any given bear might be. Give it a try, if it don't work let the kid shoot and kill you clean."

Finnegan sighed. "And so, it has come to this." He brought the Remington back and drove it forward onto the side of the bear's head. The beast let loose an agitated grunt and hopped off of the gunman. Finnegan scrambled to his feet and stood with his pistol leveled on the bear.

Abijah held the Purdey on the animal, as well. "Do I fire, Finnegan?"

Over the years, Finnegan had shot a number of men with considerably less provocation than had been offered up by the bear. In spite of that, he lowered the hammer on the Remington and kicked a rock in the direction of the bear. "Well, damn it, be gone!" The bear snorted and loped off into the trees, presumably to resume dining on the buffalo. Finnegan let out a long breath and holstered his pistol. "Bloody hell. That is a hard thing to awaken to."

Johnson slowly left his bedroll, carrying his Sharps with him. "I got to say, in all my days I have never quite had a similar experience." He rubbed his face. "Playful thing, weren't it?"

Finnegan cleared his throat. "Mr. Johnson, I am quite grateful for the advice, but I am not in the mood for conversation this particular morning. Please forgive my rudeness."

Johnson nodded slowly. "That is the sort of notion I can surely understand, Finnegan. Years back, I knowed a man who had a gangrenous foot and while he was fevered some damn rats came along and chewed the most of it off. That fella didn't say a word to hardly a soul for months after that, and when he did, they wasn't pleasant words, neither."

The whole group's attention was brought toward Rooney's bed roll. The former Pinkerton had let out a yawn and was in the process of removing himself from the folds of his wool blankets. He yawned once more and surveyed his friends. "My goodness, you men look awfully serious for such an early hour. What has you all so agitated? Did no one ever tell you that such seriousness is best kept for a later hour?" He loosed himself from the roll and stood, stretching.

Finnegan shook his head. "It must be marvelous to go through life as you do, Sam. I am fairly envious."

It did not take long for the men to resume traveling after the incident with the bear. Abijah returned the Purdey to Finnegan and the gunman rode in wary silence for the remainder of the morning. Being pulled in one direction and then another regarding the bears, Finnegan was left with nothing but ambivalence. At all events, the issue was laid to rest quickly enough. Contemplation of the bears soon gave way to interest from the entire group in the bubbling mud pots, jets, and other steaming vents that populated the Monument Geyser Basin. After crossing the Gibbon River, Johnson brought his horse up next to Finnegan. The aged mountain man appeared to be somewhat relishing his return to the Yellowstone country.

"Ought to be comin' across your man Pendleton at some point now, Finnegan."

Finnegan rubbed his eyes and set a cigar between his teeth. Every time the wind changed, the smoke from the fires in the distance was either relieved or increased. Between the smoke and the emanations from the mud pots, it truly felt as if they were riding through Hell sometimes. "Are the animals drawn here for the minerals in these pools, do you think, Mr. Johnson?"

The mountain man shrugged. "I always figured it was

just a hot place to spend the winter, and the most of them weren't inclined to roam away when spring come. It sure is nice to get into a piece of this country the damn Army or them damn campers hasn't settled into." He shook his head. "Time that Wylie is done preserving this place, or whatever the hell he called it, it'll be nothing but ruined." He spit down into the sagebrush. "Don't know why the hell people got to always be trying to fix this country. Be a lot better if they'd stay in their damned eastern towns and leave it the hell alone."

"I cannot help but agree with you, Mr. Johnson." Finnegan lit his cigar and tossed the match down into a steaming pool. "I often feel as though events might unfold altogether better if I were to cease interfering in them, as well."

"Been meaning to ask you about that."

Finnegan eyed the mountain man. "About what, Mr. Johnson?"

"This fella Pendleton must be damned important for you to go so damned far to find him and keep him from getting killed. Folks get killed every day. What makes this one man worth the trouble?"

"Nothing in his personal character makes him worth any effort, or so I would imagine, Mr. Johnson. Like most things in Mr. Pendleton's life, the plot to kill him is an accident of birth, and our efforts to save him could be classified the same way. Somewhere, far back in antiquity, one of Pendleton's relatives declared himself king of some rude little huts and muddy quarters in what I can only assume was a lousy and musty portion of Britain. Since then, they have been nothing but trouble."

Johnson grunted. "If that's all it is, why not let the fella get killed and be done with it? I imagine you get paid either way, eh?"

"I will be paid, yes. The trouble with men such as Pendleton being murdered is not that it would have much effect on myself. No, the trouble lies in the general view the human race takes of men such as Pendleton. If he is killed by an Irishman, the British will visit some form of vengeance for the killing on the Irish race, in one way or another. Likely, the Irishmen punished will have had nothing to do with the actual murder of Pendleton, but they will be punished just the same. Other Irishmen will visit vengeance upon unrelated Britons in response and on and on it shall go." He puffed out smoke. "All men engage in such foolishness. You have heard of the James brothers?" Johnson nodded. "They claimed to have begun their predations to punish the Union. I attempted to punish them for the predations. They robbed and murdered more to punish the Pinkertons. On and on. It is how men spend their lives, I suppose." Finnegan reviewed the grizzled frontiersman next to him. "What, pray tell, was your motivation for killing all those Indians, Mr. Johnson?"

"Motivation?"

"Why did you kill them?"

"Oh, uh..." He smoothed his beard and gave the question the consideration it deserved. "A good many of them I got to fightin' with due to personal squabbles. Pelts unpaid for or transgressions of rudeness. I had a woman and the Crow killed her."

Finnegan nodded. "That is a pity, Mr. Johnson."

He shrugged. "Can't blame my whole feud with the Crow on it. She was Blackfoot and Crow kill Blackfoot when they get a chance. I killed Crow when I got a chance. Damned odd thing about it, though. All them years they tried to lift my hair and I'd take a shot at 'em whenever one'd get in range. Went on like that a score a years, and then one day I just left off of it and they chose to do the same, I reckon."

"Left off of it?"

"I quit. Saw a Crow buck one day and instead of shootin' at 'em I let 'em ride on by. Did that for a month or two and one of them comes over and wants to trade some pelts. That buck traded with me all summer. Never mind I probably killed his very own daddy. Folks can leave off of feuds, Finnegan. Maybe you Irishmen ought to try the same thing?"

Finnegan knocked the ash from his cigar. "Unfortunately, Mr. Johnson, the Irish have not placed me in command of the entire race." He sighed. "I would be hesitant to take the position if it were offered. I have little choice but to attempt to save this worthless Pendleton and most likely kill another Irishman to do it. It is strange what a man must do from time to time. Perhaps you were the luckier man. Your feud was a personal matter. In a case such as this, I am not the master of my own destiny."

Johnson snorted. "You're damn well old enough to know better than that. No man says where he goes or what happens next. Luck, or God, or what have you, makes the choice there."

Finnegan nodded, thoughtfully. "Yes, I suppose that is true. Some days a man finds himself the seeming lord of all creation, other days he awakes with a bear on his chest. It is hard to say which will occur next."

THE SMOKE in the distance from a few campfires was difficult to discern from the forest fire smoke, but it was possible when the wind was right. As they approached closer yet, Finnegan and Rooney observed the camp with a telescope and determined that the large conglomeration of lily-white canvas tents and fancy expedition gear bespoke of the kind of wealth not generally possessed by wilderness transients. Finnegan pulled the glass from his eye and turned toward Abijah and Rooney.

"We know our quarry by sight, gentlemen." They both nodded. "We also know that the one man is responsible for a cowardly and low act, perpetrated for no reason. His companion plots an equally vile act. We are well within our rights." He turned to Johnson. "You may feel free to remain out of the fray, Mr. Johnson. You were commissioned to guide us, and you have done that. Anything more cannot be asked of you."

Johnson shrugged. "If you fellas find yourself in trouble, I'll throw in." He rubbed his furry chin. "Ain't there only two of 'em?"

Finnegan nodded. "Yes, I would assume we can handle two lone souls." He sighed and checked his pistols before picking up the Purdey. "Very well, then." He motioned to the horses. "We will approach the camp on foot. If you would be so kind as to see to the horses, Mr. Johnson?"

"I'll take care of 'em."

"Thank you." Finnegan rechecked his equipment. "Yes, fine. We have traveled far, gentlemen. Let us put an end to this."

Rooney rather nervously checked over his shotgun and offered Finnegan a somber smile. "I suppose it is time to find the corner I have painted myself into."

The three men walked down the creek bottom toward the large camp. Johnson was in the rear leading the animals. Finnegan did his best to appear amiable as they neared the collection of gaudy tents and sleek stock that were obviously well cared for and groomed daily. When they were little more than fifty yards from the camp a man emerged from one of the tents, spotted the approaching group and waved to them. Finnegan waved back and walked to the fellow, smiling. "Good morning, sir." Finnegan waved again. "Might we enter your camp? We are in search of a few friends who might have passed this way."

The man, who was dressed more for a dinner party than a wilderness excursion, sported a silk vest and spotless trousers. The dandy raised his eyebrows and extended a hand to Finnegan. "Oh, yes, of course." He shook Finnegan's hand vigorously and spoke with a thick British accent. "I am very pleased you are here. I did not know if the poor man's cohorts would ever arrive. He rants you see, from the pain, I imagine. We have done what we can for him. It is fine that you have arrived."

Finnegan let go of the man's hand. "Um, well, yes. Thank you."

The man motioned to the interior of the camp. "Yes. This way, please. I am glad some of his countrymen are here. When I heard you speak, I was quite relieved, chaps. A man ought to be with those of his acquaintance in a condition such as the poor man finds himself in. It is a sad thing to find oneself amongst strangers when so mortally injured."

Finnegan began following the man toward one of the larger tents. He glanced back and gave Abijah and Rooney a confused look. "Yes, of course. We did not know what had become of him. We will do all we can to succor the poor fellow." He stuck close to the well-spoken guide. "What occurred, sir?"

The man paused at the tent flap and leaned close to Finnegan. "I am sad to say, I believe it was an accident brought about by either ignorance or hubris. The chap was mucking about with some dynamite, and it detonated. Most assuredly, well before the fellow intended it should. I cannot say why he was fussing about with it." The man grimaced and adjusted his vest. "Some men take an unhealthy interest in such things."

Finnegan nodded. "Yes, well. Thank you for caring for him. He is inside?"

"Yes."

"Thank you again." Finnegan motioned for Abijah and Rooney to come forward. "If it would not be too much to ask, we would appreciate a private moment with our friend."

"Certainly." The man nodded. "If you require anything, I can be found in the cook tent."

"Thank you, again." Finnegan ducked through the flap along with Abijah and Rooney. Light filtered through the canvas of the tent, barely illuminating the interior. On the far side, a cot held a man fairly swaddled in bandages. The crippled soul slowly turned his equally bandaged face toward Finnegan. It was hard to say, but there seemed to be fear in the man's eyes.

Rooney walked forward to the cot. "Kearney, what have you done?"

The swaddled form hissed up at his compatriot. "Mezzeroff? What the hell are you doing here?" He tried to raise himself from the cot, but could not. "Have you come to finish the bastard?"

Rooney shook his head. "Even now, you are a fool, Kearney." He squatted by the cot. "You fumbled the dynamite meant for Pendleton?" Kearney gave a small nod. "Damn it to hell. Where is Schnaubelt?"

Kearney groaned. "He is gone. He ran after...he does not give a damn about the cause. He lacked the courage." His eyes narrowed beneath the bandages. "Your language, you no longer sound Prussian."

"Insufferable jackass. Where has Schnaubelt gone?"

"Mezzeroff, you must finish this. You must finish the English dog."

"Saints preserve us." Rooney hung his head.

"You must finish the Royalist swine, Mezzeroff. Please. I cannot." He attempted to raise his extensively bandaged arms, but could only make them tremble, for the most part. "My hands are gone, Mezzeroff. I made a misstep. I do not know how it occurred. I studied by your side so diligently."

Finnegan did his best to stifle a chuckle. Rooney gave him a hard glare. "My apologies. I am certain the accident was unavoidable."

Abijah sighed. "Gentlemen, this is not our purpose here." He motioned to the dying man. "We must locate Schnaubelt."

Rooney groaned. "Kearney, I damn well know you must have had a plan for removing yourself from this place. You surely confided it to Schnaubelt. Escape can have been his only reason for accompanying you. Tell me where he has gone."

Kearney's face contorted in pain. "Mezzeroff, please, tell me you will finish the English dog. I cannot." He moaned. "My hands, Mezzeroff, my hands."

"For the love of all that is holy." Finnegan took a few steps forward and knelt by the man's cot. "Kearney, you damn peat chopper's son, listen to me." Finnegan pulled the maimed fellow's head over so he could look him in the eye. "I intend to kill that English bastard for you straight away. I would be happy to blow him to kingdom come or shoot him in his empty head. Truly, whatever you prefer, but you must first tell me where your Hun friend Schnaubelt has fled to. You had a plan for escape. Someone was to assist you, Kearney. Who was to help you flee?"

"The Frenchman." Kearney hissed through the bandages. "He is to pay the Mexicans."

"A Frenchman? What damn Frenchman? What is his name?" Finnegan offered a warm smile to the soon-to-be departed. "The Frenchman's name, Kearney?"

"Simon Sebag." Kearney grimaced again. "He is a Jew, but a believer in the cause."

"Grand, Kearney, just grand." Finnegan continued to smile. "Where were you to meet him? How were you to find each other?"

"To escape!" Kearney tried to sit up, but could not.

"Yes, to escape, Kearney. We must be off, after I finish the English dog. How do I find Sebag?"

"Armstead." Kearney gritted his teeth. "Rossa made me remember. I should not have told Schnaubelt. If I had held my tongue, his hand would be forced..."

"What in hell is Armstead?" Finnegan was not in the mood to suffer the man's last regrets.

Kearney glared at the Pinkerton. "It is a town, a town on the railroad. The Frenchman will meet me there. He will take me south to Mexico." Kearney's eyes brightened. "From there, from there to London. I will feed that old bat a stick of the little giant. It makes all men equal, my friend." He slowly let out breath and sank into the cot.

Finnegan stood. "Courage makes men equal." He smoothed his frock coat. "Does the name Armstead mean anything to either of you?"

Abijah shook his head. "Surely Johnson or one of the men in this camp would know it."

Finnegan licked his lips. "These anarchists are a spry bunch." He looked to Rooney. "Well, here is the man you sought, Sam. I would say he is no longer much of a danger to his lordship. Do you have a preference as to what becomes of him?"

Rooney stood and stared down at the mangled revolutionary. "It is a sad end for any man, even one such as this fool." He rubbed his eyes. "It may be best to put him down. If we leave him here to rant in this manner, he will eventually mistake one of his nurses for one of us and...well, I can see no profit in allowing the whole ugly matter to become common knowledge."

"Put him down?" Abijah looked from Rooney to Finnegan and then back again. "Meaning what, precisely?"

"Well..." Rooney shrugged and motioned toward the dying man. "As they say, we should, uh, loose his mortal coil... leave him over to God."

"Kill him?" Abijah looked to Kearney as he said it.

Rooney sighed. "It would obviously only require a small push in that direction. The idiot has done most of the labor himself already."

Abijah rubbed his face. "I do not consider the labor to be the definitive issue in the matter, Sam. I have never killed a man and I dare say I have never considered killing one as pathetically maimed as this. If you wish for this man to die, you must see to it yourself."

Rooney chuckled. "No such thing, Abijah. I am certain Finnegan would be happy to handle the matter."

"What?" Finnegan took a step back. "Why do you assume I will be so willing to smother this simpleton on his death bed?"

Rooney appeared somewhat astounded. "I am sorry, Finnegan, but honestly, what difference can it make to your soul? With all you have done, I am not certain God would even take notice of this small act."

Finnegan stared at his old friend for a long moment. “Sam, I would point out that, by and large, you have no bloody idea as to what I have done or not done in this life. I would also suggest that it is hardly your place to speculate on the nature of the Almighty.” Finnegan nodded to the cot. “If you want that man dead, see to it yourself as the boy suggested.”

Rooney cleared his throat. “I am...I am not certain I can do such a thing, either.”

Finnegan turned toward the tent flap. “Then you shall simply have to trust in your luck. Perhaps the secrets of Professor Mezzeroff will die with him. Perhaps they will not.”

FINNEGAN WALKED to the edge of the camp where Johnson waited with the horses. Abijah and Rooney had gone off to speak with the Brit at the cook tent and question him regarding Kearney and his stated destination. Finnegan petted the horse he had been riding. He had learned over the years that it served a man well to show kindness to borrowed stock.

Johnson heaved himself up off the log he had been seated on. “You find the fella you was after?”

“We did indeed.”

“I didn’t hear a shot.”

“He was in no condition to cause further trouble.”

“He explode the English fella already?”

Finnegan shook his head. “The wretched fellow made an attempt and was undone by his own dynamite. He lies in wait of the Reaper in one of the tents. Little remains of him. Certainly not enough for further misconduct.”

"He exploded his self?" Johnson grimaced and crooked his head. "Hell of a thing to have happen to ya."

"Yes, I would imagine it was quite disconcerting." Finnegan sighed. "Are you familiar with the location of a town called Armstead?"

"It's south and west of here. Rail line runs through it headed south. What of it?"

Finnegan sighed again. "We found the Irishman, but not the Hun. The Hun has scampered again. Presumably to Armstead to meet some damned Frenchman. We must give further chase to finish this particular hunt."

Johnson shook his head. "You do find your way into some damned odd troubles, Finnegan." He chuckled. "You intend to give chase?"

"It is what I do."

Johnson snorted. "Well, best of luck to you. It would be a pity if you did not find the man after such a long chase."

Finnegan turned to the mountain man. "You do not intend to accompany us further?"

"The railroad, last I heard, runs all the way from Butte down to Denver. I reckon you can't hardly miss it if you ride west. I was of a mind to have a bit of an outing, but I can't say as I'd like to spend the whole spring chasing some funny Dutchman around God's creation. This has been a decent diversion, but I ought to get back to Coulson while my regular pay is still waitin' for me."

Finnegan nodded. "I suppose all men must look to their own commitments. I am obliged to you for your assistance, Mr. Johnson." He grinned. "Most especially with the bear. For all my worry and preparation, I was sorely ill-equipped when the moment arrived. Thank you."

"Aw, that wasn't much. If I hadn't been there, you would

have come up with somethin'. Hell, it was just a bear. One's much like the next in my experience."

Finnegan grinned wider. "Despite your initial habit of clouting me over the head, I have to say that I will miss your company, sir. You have always offered up such rarified conversation."

"I reckon I have enjoyed your yarning, as well, Finnegan. You're the only live Pinkerton I ever had a chance to chat with. Likely the only one I'll ever yarn with. You think you'll ever pass through the territories again?"

Finnegan smiled, somewhat embarrassed to discuss the subject. "I should definitely hope so. I have an interest in several cattle ventures in the area. I am owed a portion of the increase of the herds for the work I did here during my last visit."

"When I whomped you with my buffalo gun?"

"Yes, during that excursion." Finnegan rubbed his head, recalling the incident. "I entered into a contract with the Stock Growers Association and am owed a significant sum by this time. I intend to return to these territories someday and enter into the cattle business in a proper manner."

Johnson nodded approvingly. "That seems a fine thing to do, Finnegan." He smoothed his beard. "Uh, Finnegan, if you don't mind me askin' if you got a pile of cattle and such riches just waitin' for you to take possession, what the hell are you doin' chasing some fool dynamiter around the earth? You think this is some kind of amusement?"

Finnegan contemplated the question. "It is, from time to time, amusing." He thought on it a bit more. "Although, it is not nearly so boisterous as it once was. Mr. Pinkerton, the elder Mr. Pinkerton, provided me with rather more... purposeful work." He shrugged. "I take little pleasure in chasing deceitful mail clerks or spying on union presidents. Have you ever met a union president, Mr. Johnson?"

"No, I cannot say as I have."

"They strikingly resemble the men they represent, around the time union elections near. After they are elected their manner changes considerably. I have never seen one that is not a lowly creature. Their poor character can only be rivaled by that of an even more vile creature, the corporation president. Have you ever met the president of a corporation?"

"I do not believe such men pass through Coulson all that often."

"And a lucky man you are in that respect. The presidents of corporations know no decency, Mr. Johnson. They are composed solely of guile and nothing more. Their warring with union presidents may someday lead to this entire nation being set to flames and, when it is, neither set of presidents will either admit responsibility, or much care if they are not personally ignited."

"That does all sound like dastardly behavior, Finnegan." He scratched his head. "I got to say, hearin' you tell of all that makes me curious, yet again, as to why the hell you'd want to keep doin' what you're doin'?"

"The root of the problem may very well lie in the fact that I have never done otherwise. Like most men, I am hesitant to change until my hand is forced." He considered the matter further. "Though, soon enough, it may not be my choice. The younger Mr. Pinkerton does not extend the same courtesies to me that his father once did."

Johnson wore an extensively confused look. "So, you don't care for what you're doin' but you just keep on doin' it?"

"Well, yes, I suppose that would be how to put it." Finnegan moved on to petting another horse. "I would wager you did not always enjoy your life in the wilds, but you continued on with it, just the same."

Johnson nodded. "I did keep at it a long time, but I didn't have a hell of a lot of choice in the matter. It ain't like a man can just throw down his traps one day and go be a damn shopkeep. When your pockets is empty a man goes on as he is, whether he cares for it or not." He chuckled. "If you took note, I wasn't trapping beaver no more when you found me, neither."

"No, you were not." Finnegan rubbed the horse between the eyes, and it nuzzled him in return. "In proper honesty, I should also mention that there is a woman."

"A woman?"

"For a long time now, I have pursued a particular woman. We near...we have approached forming a union on occasion and then...she tends to shy away from the proposition. I have long felt that I should not leave my present occupation behind until she is prepared to join me in new endeavors."

Johnson had appeared confused previously, after hearing Finnegan's admission he switched to astonishment. "A woman?"

"Yes, Mr. Johnson, a woman. The female of the species. I am certain you are familiar with the term."

"I know the word." He scratched his beard. "I kept many a squaw. I just...If you can't get the one to share your bed, seems you ought just to go and find another more amenable to the request?"

"Another?" Finnegan turned away from the horse. "Mr. Johnson, I am not the sort of man who simply abandons a task when it proves difficult. I have come a great distance, and do not intend to retreat now."

Johnson sighed. "Do you intend to show the same devotedness to chasing that dynamiter?"

Finnegan nodded. "Naturally."

Johnson shook his head. "Finnegan, if you don't mind me sayin' so, I believe you often make matters more difficult than they need be. Possibly you seek more sport than the world commonly provides?"

"That could be said." Finnegan extended his hand to the mountain man. "I wish you luck, Mr. Johnson."

"I wish you the same, Finnegan."

ROONEY TOSSED another small log onto the fire and sat staring as the flames began to lick from it. He had prepared dinner for the party once again and had seemed to grow more melancholy as the sun sank lower. Now that it was fully dark, the shadows made him look as though he had slipped into sadness. He pulled out the bottle of Tennessee bourbon Pendleton's valet had been kind enough to gift to the party. "Finnegan, I know you do not partake, but perhaps, in just this one instance?" He held up the bottle.

"No thank you, Sam."

Rooney looked to Abijah. "For your health, young fellow?"

"I still abstain, Sam. Feel free to indulge. An oddity in our characters should not steer you away from what you prefer."

Rooney pulled the cork from the bottle and let some of the fine brown liquid flow down his throat. "Ah, those limey bastards do know their whiskey." He sighed deeply. "A pity Mr. Johnson elected to return home." He drank again and wiped his mouth with one coat sleeve. "He was a pleasant companion in this unsettled country."

"Each man has a right to look to his own best interest."

Abijah slid down and reclined against a conveniently located boulder. "This expedition of ours does not offer the man much in the way of steady wages."

Finnegan nodded. "In all the time I conversed with him, the man never mentioned having a house or lodgings. I believe the small cabin that serves as a jail there in Coulson is the man's only shelter. Winter will arrive inevitably, whether we follow Schnaubelt to the end of the earth or not. Johnson cannot afford to shirk his duties."

"Perhaps it is for the best." Rooney took a small sip from his bottle. "The poor man did seem quite displeased to discover how this country has changed since he last visited. The way he spoke, the establishment of the park did not suit him. I can sympathize with him in that regard. It is difficult to face changing times. For myself, I have decided to fight against the changing tide. I simply refuse to be relieved of my means of support without making some sort of fuss. Especially now that I have labored so diligently to repair the damage that was done."

Finnegan groaned. "Sam, truly? How can you even contemplate returning to Chicago? Of all the mad schemes you have attempted over the years, your masquerade as Professor Mezzeroff was undoubtedly the most foolhardy. It is nothing short of miraculous that you were never shot down by some waiting assassin while you masqueraded, and now that your own associates likely wish you dead you intend to return to their midst? Are you overcome with a sense that you have lived too long and wish to act to correct it?"

Rooney waved one hand dismissively. "Those men are the worst kind of paper tigers. They would not raise a hand against me, beyond the hand of oratory, perhaps."

Finnegan shook his head. "Is that not precisely what you

thought regarding men like Kearney, previous to his taking up the sword?"

"That is a different matter entirely. Kearney was an aberration. A man nursed on far too much rhetoric and idiocy."

Finnegan reached out and took up the coffee pot that still simmered by the fire. "Sam, I have known you many a weary year. You know I always attempt to give you good counsel. Do not return to Chicago. At least not in the guise of your damned professor. If you continue with us, I am certain you could resume your old position with the company. William is not the equal of his father, but his employ is preferable to being murdered by your fellow schemers and charlatans."

Rooney's countenance brightened. "Ah, but why not attempt both?"

Finnegan filled his coffee cup and returned the pot to the fire ring. "Sam, I do not know what precisely you are suggesting, but it is sure to be a terrible notion."

Rooney grinned in the firelight. "Yes, of course. I cannot conceive of why it has taken me so very long to realize the possibility existed. It seems so obvious once the idea has taken root."

Abijah stared in wonderment. "Sam, is life really so toilsome you wish to throw it away?"

Rooney laughed. "I wish to avoid toil, and this new addition to my old scheme will serve quite well. What I propose is this, Finnegan: I will resume my role as Professor Mezzeroff, after properly browbeating O'Donovan Rossa, of course."

Finnegan sipped his coffee. "Ah, that should be a simple matter now that he knows you were formerly a Pinkerton."

"Pish posh, not everyone holds such things against a man, especially when they learn it may be in their own best interests. The second portion of the plan hinges on you, my friend." Rooney waggled one finger at Finnegan. "You will go to your keepers, William and Robert, and inform them that one of their former employees has valiantly insinuated himself into the very inner folds of the dreaded Clan Na Gael and is currently capable of furnishing them with information regarding all manner of plots and murderous endeavors. Between the sums accrued as Mezzeroff and the sums purloined from the Pinkertons, we shall be rich as Midas in no time, Finnegan."

The gunman nodded, looking quite skeptical. "I can only assume you intend to proffer wholly false information to the Pinkerton brothers?"

Rooney chuckled. "It is certainly an easier commodity to come by. It also has the added benefit of being created promptly when a fellow is without funds."

Finnegan nodded. He was more than familiar with his old friend's methods. "And, of course, O'Donovan Rossa would require a share of the earnings?"

"Naturally."

"And, of course, it would be careless not to include young Abijah here. He has been privy to our scheming. It is pay him or kill him by this juncture." Finnegan smiled at his younger counterpart.

Abijah grinned back. "You gentlemen should not be so quick to include me in your plans. I find certain aspects of this caper morally reprehensible. It is one thing to defraud the Pinkerton firm. As far as I know, near constant defrauding is budgeted for by the bookkeepers. It is another to defraud the Clan Na Gael. From what I have seen they are a group of quite innocent men and only capable of hurting themselves."

Rooney shook his head and sipped more bourbon. "You two should not jest. There is much money to be made in this game, mark my words. I have seen plenty already and intend to see more still to come."

Finnegan tossed his old friend a cigar. "Smoke that, Sam, and consider adopting the country life as a farmer."

"Finnegan, I appreciate you looking to my well-being, I truly do." He paused to light the donated cigar. "But I will be damned if I will abandon a practice so lucrative as being Professor Mezzeroff, simply because a few short-sighted individuals have chosen to make life difficult. I cannot, I will not, allow such a thing to pass."

Finnegan lit a cigar of his own and sighed. "Sam, you damn well know the duration of some trifle such as your playing Professor Mezzeroff has nothing to do with your personal preference. Even if you could resume your charade, can you truly tell me it is wise to travel about inciting these fools to violence? Kearney was only a danger to himself; the next man may be far worse." Finnegan tapped some ash into the fire ring. "The Clan Na Gael, now there is a bunch I have never fully understood. Not them, not the White Shirts, none of them. They wish to drive the English from Ireland. They rant, they rave, they throw bombs. None of it has ever led to much. The occasional tax collector meets a sad end. If they are lucky, they cast dynamite at a second cousin twice removed from the Queen's nephew. I have more royal blood in me than the last fellow they detonated." Finnegan took a moment to puff his cigar. "The other oddity I have never had explained to me regarding these revolutionaries is just what exactly they wish to replace the damned British with. Do they honestly believe that damned rabble we Irishmen call a race could field something as coherent as a government? If they ever did manage to kick the British into the ocean, who the hell would take charge? They would likely be lazier or worse than the damned Brits."

Rooney stared at the gunman. "Finnegan, for the love of all that is holy -- I am discussing the time-honored and highly respectable business of scheming to gain money. You are ranting about governments and the Irish people. No wonder that Minnesota lass continues to spurn your proposals. You are incapable of facing reality. Who gives a damn about the Irish?"

Abijah laughed. "Sweet mercy. I have never seen two men talk longer and say less. Is this what you two did every evening during the war?"

Finnegan grinned and shook his head. "No, we split our time evenly between scrounging food and plotting desertion. I rather miss those old days. I believe we were both closer to our right minds when the rebels were trying to kill us on a daily basis."

Chapter 16

WEST YELLOWSTONE, WYOMING TERRITORY

May 20, 1886

Finnegan slowly let his eyes roll open to see a man sitting on the log Rooney had occupied the previous evening. The fellow had long black hair that ran all the way down to his shoulders. He wore the blue coat of a Union soldier, along with the black knee-high boots of a cavalryman. A necklace of what looked to Finnegan to be little more than bits of trash hung around his neck, and he cradled a Henry rifle in his hands. Behind the visitor Finnegan could see several other men, some staring down at Abijah and Rooney. Some were investigating the picketed horses.

Finnegan rubbed his eyes and slowly sat up in his bedroll. He kept the Remington concealed beneath, for the moment. "Good morning, sir." Finnegan nodded to the coffee pot. "If you light the fire, I can offer you breakfast."

The fellow eyed Finnegan. "You men sleep well. You must all be good Christians."

"We certainly try." He did a quick count and determined six men had come into the camp without his noticing. "And are you and your friends Christians?"

"We have been taught the ways. Some stray more than others."

"That is unfortunate." Finnegan gave a glance to his two traveling companions. If their chests did not move slightly, they could have easily been mistaken for dead men. Finnegan smiled to the visitor. "Do you live in the area, or are you merely passing through?"

"We are passing through." He seemed to give it some thought. "We are always passing through."

"I see." Finnegan rubbed his face with his left hand. "Well, if you do not care for breakfast and we do not happen to be camped on your land, I cannot help but wonder why you are here, sir?"

"My land?"

"Yes, your land."

"It is all my land, white man."

"Ah, perhaps therein lies the problem." Finnegan smiled at the fellow. "I was discussing much the same conundrum with my associates last evening before turning in. You see, I was born to a people who have lost their lands to another people. They continue to worry and moan regarding it, never once pausing to consider that they might be far better off to simply let the matter be and get on with their lives, as it were. Have you ever considered that solution, sir?"

"Considered what?" The fellow wore a truly inscrutable look.

"Simply admitting that your lands are no longer your lands. Admitting that they have been lost. Would it not be superior to traveling about with this handful of playmates pretending to be savages? You ride stolen stock from ranches. You wear clothes purloined from the Army. You are speaking to me in English, or what passes for it in this territory. Why not admit that you are far more the product of this current world than the world your grandfather knew? You may find great solace in it."

"You are rather surly for a man outnumbered and still in his bed." The fellow rubbed his chin. "Who are you?"

"Finnegan Xavier Gilhooley, at your service."

The fellow nodded. "There are many who hate you Irish more than us."

"And there are many Irishmen who richly deserve it. Did you mention your name, sir?"

"Simian White Feather."

Finnegan arched an eyebrow. "Simian?"

"You hardly have reason to throw stones, Mr. Gilhooley."

"That much is true." Finnegan grinned. "What brings you by today, Simian?"

"We require a few of your animals. Ours are becoming weak. I am sure such a kind man as you would not begrudge us a few horses."

"Unfortunately, I would." Finnegan shrugged. "The animals are not mine to give. They belong to the Wylie Camping Company and the proprietor of the company expects their prompt return. As soon as I can locate a suitable fellow to lead them back to the park, of course. I hope to hire one in Armstead. Would you mind telling me how far we are from that particular town?"

"I would say about thirty miles."

"Thank you. It is hard to judge such things in country one is unfamiliar with."

"Think nothing of it." White Feather rubbed his chin again. "No horses?"

"No horses. I am afraid you will have to wait and steal them from the man I hire on the return trip."

"In my experience a man caught napping rarely has the gall to set terms."

Finnegan nodded. "Quite true, and if you had possessed the forethought to murder me while I slept, we would not be debating the point now. But you did not murder me, and you did choose to wake me. This is where we find ourselves, Simian. I have no less than two pistols concealed under this blanket. I have been assessed to be an excellent shot over the years. Of course, the report of my first round will undoubtedly wake my associates, who are also fine marksmen. We will be three against six, but that should hardly matter to you, since I fully intend to fire on you first." Finnegan held up his left hand. "Keep the rifle where it is."

White Feather's lips spread into a wide smile. "You have some damn gall; I will give you that." He kept his rifle across his knees. "What will you give me?"

"Ah, a fine question." Finnegan pointed to one of the pack boxes. "Open that." White Feather leaned over and gently raised the lid. He reached inside and pulled Rooney's bourbon bottle out. "That is yours."

"Tennessee." White Feather nodded approvingly. "Better than my usual rotgut."

Finnegan motioned to the box again. "Dig a bit. There should be a box of cigars."

The visitor dutifully dug and located the box. "This?"

"That is the item. You may have six. One for each of your men."

"Six?" White Feather continued to smile. "Not the whole box, but only six?"

"That is as generous as I am prepared to be, sir. You may take the offer or leave it."

"Mr. Gilhooley, are you really in a position to be stingy?"

"You are well within range, Mr. White Feather. Are you in a position to complain?"

"I suppose not." White Feather motioned to his compatriots. They stood staring for a long moment, seemingly confused as to the direction and obviously perturbed by the suggestion to leave the horses. After an elongated staring contest, White Feather shook his fist at the most adamant man and that appeared to end the argument. The other men in the party mounted the horses they had arrived on and sat waiting for White Feather. "Your friends sleep very soundly."

"Their souls are not burdened by guilt."

"If they spend all day napping, they would have a hard time finding sin to commit, at any rate."

Finnegan nodded. "Perhaps we would all be better off if we slept the day away."

"Sleep too long around here and a bear will come along and eat you." White Feather placed six cigars in his jacket pocket and slowly stood, holding his Henry in one hand and the bourbon bottle in the other. "Thank you for the fancy whiskey."

"It is not mine. I do not partake."

"Then I understand your willingness to part with it." He stared down at Finnegan. "You truly do not care that other men possess your land?"

Finnegan shrugged. "I am a rare case. It was never my land. This I sit on is not my land."

White Feather raised the bourbon bottle a bit, smiled, and nodded. "It is hard to rob a man who has nothing. Good day, Mr. Gilhooley."

Finnegan sat and watched the Indian party ride off in the direction of the park. He lit one of his cigars and, after about an hour, both Abijah and Rooney began to rouse themselves. Rooney was the first to abandon his bedroll. The former professor slowly got to his feet and shuffled over to the pack box. He rummaged around inside and then turned to Finnegan, looking quite vexed. "Finnegan, where the hell has my bourbon gotten off to? I know you did not drink it. You are not nearly so entertaining."

"I gave it to a rogue Indian in payment for passage through his grandfather's lands. You would prefer I had allowed him to slit your throat while you slept?"

"Compared to an entire day without libation? Yes, I would very nearly prefer it."

FINNEGAN STARED into the bleary eyes of the railroad agent. The man's hat was cocked to one side, and it was clear that the fellow had not passed the saloon by on his way to the railroad office. He seemed more than a bit confused by Finnegan's questions. "It is very simple, sir. I am asking if you have sold tickets to a Frenchman and a Hun in the last few days. This place is not Philadelphia; surely you would recall such an odd pair."

"I...I do recall one odd fellow." The agent removed his hat and tousled his hair. "Strange sort."

"What about him was strange?"

"He come to town..." The agent hiccupped. "Holed up in the hotel and only come out once a day, that I know of. He come here when he did."

"To what end?"

"Fella had me sending telegraphs."

"Telegraphs? Sent where? I will need to see them."

The agent rubbed his festering eyes. "I can't show you other folks telegrams. I took a damn oath."

"Damn your oath." Finnegan pulled his badge from his pocket. "I am a Pinkerton and agent of this railroad."

"That don't make you an agent of the telegraph company."

"For the love of St. Peter." Finnegan squeezed the bridge of his nose. "Do you have a marshal or deputy or constable in this town?"

"You think he'll make me show you them telegraphs?"

"No." Finnegan motioned to the cluttered office behind the agent. "I am merely attempting to determine if, after I shoot you, I will have time to sift through all that before someone arrives to interrupt my work." He gave the agent a quite unconcerned look.

"Uh, well, seein' as we ain't got a marshal -- last one died of flu about six months back -- and the sheriff only comes by about once every two months..." He licked his lips. "I guess there can't be no harm in lettin' an agent of the railroad take a little peek."

"I appreciate your forthrightness, thank you." Finnegan watched as the agent dug through a small wooden filing cabinet. He soon produced half a dozen yellow sheets and presented them to Finnegan.

"Never did get a reply. He'd just come down here and send one of them off every day for the better part of a week. Last day he was here, he come down and bought two tickets and sent that last message you got there in your hand."

Finnegan flipped through the pages. They all read HOLD and lacked a signature. The final message read RECALLED TO LIFE. Finnegan sighed. "Oh, how very droll." He glanced at the header of the pages. "El Paso, Texas?"

"Every last one of 'em."

"The name of the recipient is not listed."

The agent shook his head. "Didn't bother, never do with Mr. Smith."

"Mr. Smith?"

"That was what the Frenchman asked for. He wanted

them sent to the El Paso office, care of Mr. Smith. Most times it's a Mr. Smith sendin' something care of Mrs. Smith, if you get my meanin', but it ain't my place to ask. Until you come along and threatened to shoot me, wasn't my place to say nothin', either."

"Yes, well, it is always difficult to say what new adventures will present themselves from day to day. I take it the Frenchman and his associate were traveling south when they boarded the train?"

"They was."

Finnegan held up the telegraph sheets. "I will keep these."

"Don't much care what you do with them, so long as you don't shoot me over 'em."

Finnegan nodded to the agent. "Thank you for your time." He left the tipsy agent to his work and walked down the platform to where Rooney and Abijah awaited him. Holding up the fistful of telegrams, he did his best to sound hopeful. "They have been in contact with someone in El Paso."

Abijah let his eyebrows raise. "El Paso, Texas?"

"It is very nearly Mexico." Finnegan shrugged. "For the moment, it still resides in Texas."

"And we give chase?"

"We do, young man." Finnegan smiled at Abijah's excitement. "This news pleases you?"

"I have never traveled to the southern states. In truth, I have seen little of the world beyond the coal patch you found me in and the filth strewn streets of Chicago. I have seen more of the continent in these last weeks than my entire preceding life. My worldly experience grows daily."

Finnegan shook his head. "Yes, it is a miraculous life we lead. A pity you slept through our being accosted by savages."

Abijah grinned. "I will be sure to take the time to view the next group. The southern border still possesses quite a lot of them from what I have read."

"Ah, youth." Rooney slapped Abijah on the back. "Oh, to be young again, eh, Finnegan?"

"I could ill afford to be young again. I was far too stupid." Finnegan assessed his old friend. "Speaking of stupidity run rampant, I sense you are about to broach the topic, Sam."

Rooney nodded, sullenly. "I would prefer not to, but I must, Finnegan."

"Must? In the decades I have known you, I have rarely seen you bend to what must be done. You know as well as I, you go to do what you intend to do out of greed, nothing more." He held up one hand to stifle Rooney's objection. "I am aware most of what men such as us engage in is rooted in greed. There is little purpose in denying it. We are not saints, but gunmen and scavengers and charlatans. It is inevitable that you should dabble in endeavors such as pretending to be a mad professor, but you must show some damn sense, my friend."

"Is it not sensible to attempt the resumption of my most profitable endeavor to date?"

"Sam, if you return to Chicago and attempt to resume your activities, you will be doing little else but waiting for your associates to gather their courage to do murder."

Rooney waved one hand. "You overestimate Professor Mezzeroff's handlers. They were really nothing more than playactor revolutionaries. I would hardly credit any of them to be capable of murder."

Finnegan grunted and pointed east. "An attempted murderer from among them lies dying somewhere out there as we speak."

"Kearney? Piffle. As you say, he was only capable of

attempted murder, and he was the worst of the lot, I assure you."

Finnegan rubbed his eyes and shook his head. "Sam, there is no need for this. Accompany us. It is a far preferable option."

Rooney chuckled. "Is it truly? You travel south to a place overflowing with miscreant bandits, former confederates, bushwhackers, and the last truly savage Indian tribes. I would wager I am in considerably less danger strolling the cobblestones of Chicago. Honestly, Finnegan, is it not hard to say which of us will die first? The lions I go to bait are considerably more tame than those you intend to face."

"Sam, if fortune smiles on us, I shall step off the train at some station south of here, spot Schnaubelt, and shoot him down. There should be no bandits, no Indians, no hazard of any sort."

Rooney nodded, grinning. "And I intend to be welcomed back into the fold among my counterfeit revolutionaries with an equal lack of excitement. What we plan and what occurs is rarely the same thing in this life, Finnegan." Rooney extended his hand. "I wish you luck, wish me the same."

Finnegan took his hand. "I always do." He patted the charlatan on the shoulder. "You will likely reach Chicago before we reach our goal. The northern railroad will take you straight there, or nearly so. Send a wire if you require assistance. We will not be hard to locate on the southern route."

Rooney gave a pat to Finnegan's shoulder in return. "Do not hesitate to wire if you require my assistance."

Finnegan sneered. "I believe I should be able to locate help if I cannot get a cork removed from a truculent bottle."

"It can be more complicated than you might imagine, especially for a man with no practice." Rooney turned to

Abijah. "My young friend, I am so very pleased to see the man you have become. Please keep a close eye on Finnegan for me. You know how he tends to become mired in predicaments when left to keep his own counsel."

"I will do my level best to keep him within sight and within reason."

"That is all any man can ask of another." Rooney took his hand. "Safe journey. Oh, I would hope you will find the time to attend one of my upcoming lectures once all this foolishness comes to an end."

"It would be my absolute pleasure, Professor. Assuming, of course, that Finnegan is incorrect regarding your imminent demise."

"Finnegan is normally quite incorrect. I see no reason this time should be any different."

Finnegan pointed to the approaching train. "Should you not about be on your way, then?"

"I surely will. Ah, it was a fine thing to be on the trail of some rascal with the two of you again. I must say, from time to time I do miss the old days, even if I constantly lacked for funds and was forced to live by my wits from day to day."

"I fail to see as circumstances have changed much." Finnegan laughed. "Ah, Sam, I pray you find safe harbor in Chicago and that we will see each other yet again. It is always entertaining to be in your company. Safe journey."

Finnegan and Abijah watched in silence as Rooney purchased a northbound ticket and boarded the train. After taking on water, the giant iron behemoth began to labor out of the station once again with Rooney ensconced in one of the travel cars. Abijah sighed. "I will miss Sam. That fellow is one of a kind."

"That fellow is several men who are all one of a kind. It is endlessly entertaining, but a bit complicated." Finnegan turned up the collar on his coat. "Let us see to our transportation. It may also profit us to wire the branch offices that are located farther down the southern route we must travel in search of Schnaubelt. They can dispatch men to the train stations along the way and possibly intersect our quarry." He sighed. "Mr. Rooney may not wish to rejoin the ranks, but even so, we still have many fellow agents out there. We may as well get some use out of the poor fools."

Chapter 17

POCATELLO, IDAHO TERRITORY

May 21, 1886

The train rocked back and forth violently, and Finnegan was slung against the side of the Pullman car. He grunted, put out a hand to keep himself upright, and then swung his eyes over the cabin. It took a moment for him to realize where he was and recall that he had been napping. On the seat opposite, Abijah sat staring at his old mentor with a book in his lap.

"These western tracks are not near so smooth as the mainlines in the east." He placed a small bit of ribbon in the book and closed it. "I tried sleeping but kept being jarred. You keep your balance well while unconscious."

Finnegan smiled and steadied himself as the train slalomed again. "It is a skill refined over many years." He chuckled. "A few pennies can be folded into a man's purse if he foregoes the purchase of a sleeping berth."

"While placing the cost of a sleeping berth on his account with the agency?"

"Ah, you have learned much in your time under the Pinkertons." Finnegan rubbed his face and looked out the window at the early morning dawn. "Another day is upon us, Abijah. How far south are we, by your reckoning?"

"I believe the conductor said something related to Utah being forthcoming soon." Abijah smiled, seeming quite pleased. "Another territory I have never seen before."

"It is new ground for me, as well." He sighed and removed a cigar from his pocket. Coffee would be preferable, but tobacco would do. "A pity we will not have more time to look the place over. I am told the desert of the Mormons is quite beautiful. Sadly, unless fortune smiles on us, we will likely only see what passes out that window."

Abijah shrugged. "We could simply take a detour from our route, view the country in our own good time."

Finnegan lit his cigar and gave the young man a confused look. "Our own good time? You may recall we have business farther down this railroad, Abijah."

"We have our assigned commission farther down the line, Finnegan. The business belongs to other men."

Finnegan rubbed his eyes again. "Perhaps my wits are not yet fully with me, Abijah. To what do you refer?"

Abijah sighed and stared out the window. "While you slept, I had time to weigh Sam's words upon parting with us. You were correct to counsel him against returning to Chicago, but he was not mistaken in all matters."

Finnegan shook his head and grinned. "Our friend Sam is so frequently mistaken it is difficult to notice when he is correct. On what matter was he in the right?"

"He was undoubtedly correct when he stated that acting as a shoddy charlatan might make him a rich man, whereas acting as a Pinkerton detective will never profit us much more than it currently does." Abijah pointed a finger at his mentor. "I would surely venture to say that since the elder

Mr. Pinkerton has passed to his reward, you stand little chance of promotion."

Finnegan nodded. "Even when he lived it was a scant possibility."

"Yes, I would readily agree." Abijah set his book to one side on the seat. "Given my current assignments, I would also venture to guess that the best I can hope for is to someday be gifted the management of a branch office. At best, we may someday aspire to admittance through the front door of the houses the lawyers, bankers, and railroad barons we serve reside in. All while the Pinkerton brothers grow rich on the backs and blood of men such as us."

Finnegan groaned. "Abijah, perhaps you have been spending too much time amongst the anarchists. You are beginning to mimic them in speech."

"I would readily agree I have spent too much time among them. Far too much to suit me."

Finnegan blew out a plume of smoke. "Going on without sleep often makes a man melancholy, Abijah. You should try to rest."

"I am not downtrodden, and I am not fatigued."

"You have not mentioned these complaints before. Why bring them up now?"

"I did not think it right to discuss such matters in Sam's company. He is no longer in the employ of the Pinkertons. You and I remain in their keeping."

Finnegan rubbed one temple. "Do not misunderstand me, Abijah; I can appreciate the rigors of an assignment that does not please. I have suffered through more than my fair share of them in my time. Long months in hostile environs truly wears on a man. While I would freely admit that, I would not go so far as to suggest you and I have ever or will ever find ourselves in some sort of servitude to the Pinkerton agency."

"You would not frame it as such?"

"Abijah, when Allan Pinkerton found me, I was little more than a ragged child forced into a man's partial uniform. When I found you, you dwelt in a belfry. Now then, if you are aware of a more lucrative form of labor for men such as we are, I would dearly appreciate you telling me of it. I, for one, have not stayed with the Pinkerton agency all these years solely out of a sense of obligation to the elder Mr. Pinkerton. I have no interest in rejoining the army or becoming a street sweeper. Do you suggest another occupation?"

Abijah cleared his throat. "For the most part, I was considering a change more along the lines of a modification, while you slept. We are finally in the west, Finnegan. This is the place we both have long thought to seek our fortunes. Why not make inquiries or even attempts while we find ourselves here? The Pinkerton brothers would be none the wiser."

Finnegan smiled. "I do not know if I have ever paused to consider whether the Pinkerton brothers were wise or not." Abijah did not appear to appreciate the jest. "Abijah, my preference is to finish a task, once begun."

"My friend, what difference can it make? It will not matter a jot to the Pinkertons if this man Schnaubelt is gunned down by you in the next station or alludes us and lives for many years in a monastery in Mexico. It is likely a safe assumption that the fool has done all the evil he possesses courage to attempt. He certainly elected to pass unnoticed by Pendleton and his expedition."

Finnegan shrugged. "It is hardly my place to predict who may or may not do violence to their fellow man in the future, Abijah. I simply know the man has done violence in the past and must be brought to answer for it, if it is within my abilities." He scratched his chin and puffed his cigar. "Abijah, some time ago, you made mention that you had come to believe the work of infiltration was a far better path to promotion within the firm than...well, than the kind of work I labor at."

Abijah nodded rather slowly. "Infiltrating various organizations has led to promotion for more than a few men. When I first began, I had every reason to believe it would lead to greater opportunities. As time passes, and I continue to plug along, I cannot help but wonder whether I am being passed over in favor of other men who have given less service and showed less loyalty."

Finnegan puffed a few times and let a small groan escape. "Ah, Abijah, perhaps I did you a disservice when I brought you into the fold at the agency." He held up a hand to stop the young man's response. "I cannot help but think you might have been better off if I had suggested you engage in my specialty. I will grant you, there are a great many unfortunate aspects to my work, but there is also the occasional satisfaction in a job well done and, of course, the cold comfort of finality. It is hard to put a price on such a thing. Infiltration is a grubby little bit of business. I would not go so far as to say that it is not fit work for a decent man -- all men must do what they must to fill their coffers -- but given an alternative, I have always chosen the alternative. I can easily understand how you have come to be disenchanted with it."

Abijah pondered the remarks. "And yet you would counsel me to continue the pursuit of Schnaubelt even as more profitable ventures pass us by?"

Finnegan shook his head and tapped ash into the tray built into the wall. "Abijah, I would counsel no such thing. As you know, I myself have never been opposed to pursuing other ventures in conjunction with my usual labors. You have even been a party to my digressions in the past."

Abijah chuckled, thinking back. "Yes, I certainly have."

"Yes. As I told you long ago, all men must look to their own best interest, the interests of their family, those they consider to be family. I consider you to be within that fold, Abijah." He tapped more ash into the tray. "I am not suggesting that if fortune should present us with a gold mine or a great windfall in the course of our journey that we should not take full advantage of it. Only a fool passes such things by out of stubbornness or some other contrived idiocy. What I would surely council is that it is also a fool who bites the hand that feeds him, before first locating another source of food. Unless you suggest robbing the train we currently ride on, I see no other source of funds presenting itself currently."

Abijah sat forward in his seat a bit. "Finnegan, did you not find yourself in possession of shares in several cattle operations in a way just such as this? You left Chicago on an errand for Mr. Pinkerton and then deviated from your path to pursue the other venture. Has it not proven quite profitable for you?"

Finnegan stubbed out the cigar in the tray. "The amount of profit I will enjoy remains to be seen, Abijah. Even the willingness of the various members of the Stockgrowers Association to make good on their obligations." He grunted and smiled. "For all I know, I may have to return to the northern territories and throttle my money from several highly esteemed gentlemen." He sighed. "Financial wellbeing is promised to no man in this world, Abijah. Banks fail, investments go sour, charlatans prove effective. There is little men such as ourselves can do to prevent any of it. We must simply soldier on and always keep careful watch for opportunities."

He grinned. "You may recall that William Pinkerton had more or less relieved me of my duties just previous to the unfortunate incident in the Haymarket. I did not return to my duties because I gain so much enjoyment from them. The Pinkertons merely provide the best possible opportunity presently."

Abijah sighed. "Perhaps I allowed my passions to get the better of me momentarily."

"It will surely happen from time to time."

"It could simply be that you are correct in regard to my having been with the anarchists too long. Their chatter does wear on a man's mind after enough hours. They begin to make a fellow feel as if he truly is being abused by his masters, even if his work is tattling to those masters." Abijah laughed. "Quite naturally, the incongruity confuses matters. By the time a month has passed a fellow barely knows where he stands anymore."

"In that case, our present chore should be somewhat of a comfort to you. There are few labors with more purity than running down a man and shooting him. Beyond all else, we can be certain of what we wish to achieve."

Abijah nodded and took up his book once more. "It should surely prove more pure than spending my days whispering secrets gleaned from corrupted tongues into corrupted ears. A minor assassination such as this may do me good."

Finnegan stood on the platform in Ogden, stretching out his back as best he could. Abijah had gone off to see the local telegraph clerk and inquire as to whether or not news had been sent across the wire yet. As Finnegan worked the kinks out of his lower extremities, he could not help but contemplate the fact that it was far easier to move east or west along the nation's railroads than it was to travel north or south. The national obsession had been joining the Atlantic to the Pacific. Little thought had apparently been given to traveling from the British possessions in the north to Mexico in the south. If Finnegan and Abijah were to continue on their path they would be forced to move from branch line to branch line, moving both east and south at the same time.

Finnegan stopped stretching and was letting his eyes roll over the area of town around the station. His belly wished for food and his bleary mind wished for black coffee. He was turning to see if Abijah had exited the telegraph office yet when he saw a man standing and watching him. Finnegan's hand strayed ever so slightly toward his Remington before tallying up the fellow's appearance and determining that he was surely not Schnaubelt. The man raised a hand to Finnegan and crossed the platform. He wore a bowler hat and kept glancing about somewhat nervously.

"Would you be Finnegan Gilhooley?" He smiled, which brightened his rather chubby cherubic face.

Finnegan let his eyes stray over the platform, checking to see if the man had confederates. He did not appear to. "I am. Who are you, sir?"

"Oscar Demery. The company has me here checking ledgers on mail clerks. The telegraph clerk could not think of anyone else to give your wire to. You are chasing some sort of Hun?"

Finnegan nodded. "I am."

"I am sorry to report he must have passed through already. You are the only two men I have seen loitering about the platform since I received the message. Do you know precisely how far ahead your man might be?"

"Too far for you to have seen him these last few hours.

Our hope is that he has been delayed and his description will raise the alarm with some member of our flock. I assume no Huns have become delayed in this town and taken up residence just lately?"

"No. I cannot say as such."

"Well, a man cannot be lucky all the time." Finnegan looked back to the telegraph office again, but saw no change. "How is it you know who I am?"

"I have been receiving wires for the last week saying that Finnegan Gilhooley has come west to give chase to a man or men wanted in Chicago. Until the last wire, I did not know if you would make landfall here or not." Demery smiled and nodded. "Of course, I rushed to the train platform. I have always harbored a desire to shake your hand. I am sorry I could not have been of more assistance."

Finnegan took a moment to think on what was occurring. "Well, at least the men up and down this line have been roused. It will make matters hot for Schnaubelt if he does find himself delayed." He rubbed his face. "Or it may motivate him to seek a different form of transportation."

Demery motioned about. "If the man enjoys riding, he is welcome to obtain a horse here, same as anyone else. If he enjoys a good jaunt, he may purchase boots. Although, the train is the far preferable option, as you know. You have some inkling of where the man is headed?"

"Mexico."

Demery frowned. "Ah, well, it is a pity you cannot whittle that down a bit. A whole country is a rather large proposition."

"El Paso is suspected." Finnegan saw Abijah emerge from the telegraph office and begin to cross the platform. From the look on his face there clearly was no news of use to them. "My associate has finished his business and the train will soon be ready to depart once more." Finnegan put out his hand. "Thank you, Mr. Demery. Any assistance is appreciated."

Demery gave the gunman's hand another firm shake and nodded. "Quite obviously the least I could do, sir. If you travel so far, Mr. McParlan himself intends to greet you on the platform in Denver and offer whatever assistance he may."

"Lovely." Finnegan did his best to hide his grimace. "Well, thank you again, Mr. Demery."

Demery left the platform just as Abijah was arriving. The young man pointed to the departing one. "Who might that fellow be?"

"The esteemed Pinkerton representative for this hamlet. Nice enough sort; I cannot say how he might have been stuck here." Finnegan raised an eyebrow. "He took the time to inform me that all the varied and sundry Pinkertons on the road south have their hackles up. Though it may not do us much good."

Abijah shrugged. "They do enjoy pitching in. Even when it is not entirely useful."

"He also informed me that when we pass through Denver no less a gentleman than James McParlan will be there waiting for us."

"Sweet mercy, I had not thought of that scoundrel in some time."

"Nor I," Finnegan sneered. "I suppose there is not much reason to think of him."

Abijah shook his head. "I cannot help but wonder if he ever thinks of old Jack Keogh's widow. Do men like McParlan ever pause to think of the damage they have done, Finnegan?"

The gunman leveled a cold stare on his young apprentice. "Is McParlan a different sort than we are, Abijah?"

"I believe you have suggested that very thing frequently, Finnegan. Is there not a great gulf between your work and the work of infiltrators?"

"There is a great gulf between what an infantry soldier does and what a cavalryman does, but there is little difference regarding the result. The dead men left on the field likely do not take note of the methods employed in their demise. McParlan hung a few men in your hometown. I have shot many more. Who is the greater devil, Abijah?"

"Finnegan, you shoot men down in your own defense, or to end their predations. McParlan hung those men in St. Clair to line his pockets and gain a desk to sit behind. There is no other explanation."

Finnegan rubbed his chin. "And the men you have been spying on in Chicago, are they any different from the Molly Maguires old McParlan condemned?"

"The men I have been keeping watch over are confederates and conspirators of Schnaubelt. They murdered policemen and women and who knows who else. If those anarchists hang, they will have earned it. We both know the Mollies likely never did more than imbibe too much and indulge in rough talk."

Finnegan took on a bit of a morose visage and watched the train they were about to board take on water. "In truth, I would wager that before William Pinkerton is through, the Molly Maguires will be a mere drop in the ocean compared to the men who will eventually perish. How many have already died in this last strike? How many died in the Haymarket or will eventually die of their wounds? It is sad to say, Abijah, but the hangings that took place in St. Clair when you were a boy may be little recalled or little noted compared to what is bound to follow in the years to come. The day may come when neither of us much cares whether McParlan gained his desk through evil or not. We may only be glad to conceal we were ever Pinkerton men and find ourselves thankful to have survived."

Abijah laughed. "Finnegan, the things you sometimes suggest. Truly, what could possibly occur that would make the men of the esteemed Pinkerton agency hang their heads in shame?" He grinned. "I would imagine if it were possible for the company to be adjudged immoral, it would have surely happened by now."

"Abijah, there were thousands of men at the McCormick Works. There will be many thousands at the next strike line. Someday soon, hundreds of us, armed with Winchesters, will face thousands of workingmen. Both sides will lose."

"What a desperate picture you paint, Finnegan. I will admit, I am not looking forward with glee at the prospect of shaking hands with McParlan, but the thought of it does not have me predicting the end times."

"Only the end times for our kind, Abijah. Make no mistake: as far as most of the world is concerned, all men under Pinkerton employ are to be judged the same. They will lump us in with him, sure enough, when our day finally comes."

Abijah did not seem to give much weight to Finnegan's doom and gloom prediction. "I would not worry too much, old friend. You have never been the kind of man to stand about and allow himself to be judged. I am sure you will find a way to slip the noose."

Finnegan patted the younger man on one shoulder. "That is what Jack Keogh thought. That is what men like Parsons are thinking as we speak. When my day comes, I will likely tell myself the same. All men wish to slip the noose."

"Would you wager McParlan will slip it?"

"He is the type of man who generally does. I wonder if he has changed much since I last saw him. He had a tendency to be a bit of dandy in his younger days."

"He tended to dress like a coal miner when I saw him."

"Yes, well, it was in his best interest, I am sure." Finnegan thought back on his association with McParlan so many years earlier. "The fellow was near obsessed with counterfeit money. I always got the sense he wished to prefect the manufacture of it for his own personal reasons. When that proved too difficult, he was forced to turn to his own particular brand of detective work to make ends meet."

"Was McParlan the first of Pinkerton's infiltrators?"

"Not by a long stretch. Mr. Pinkerton rather prided himself on having at least one fellow dug into every organization of interest at any given time. McParlan was merely the first to make a true name for himself. The press covered the Molly trials quite thoroughly. For a time, McParlan was a famous man. Surely the most famous Pinkerton."

"With the exception of Fearless Finnegan Gilhooley."

Finnegan shook his head. "Ah, and even that glory fades. It is my poor luck that another man came along and finished Jesse James off. Although, I privately consider it a bit of fortune. Let Robert Ford worry over every bump in the night until his dying day." Finnegan smiled, considering Denver. I would assume Mr. McParlan feels much the same way regarding the remnants of the Molly Maguires."

Chapter 18

ROCK SPRINGS, WYOMING TERRITORY

May 22, 1886

FINNEGAN SAT NEXT TO ABIJAH ON A LARGE BOULDER BY the side of the railway. To their left, back in the direction of Ogden and ground already covered, a collection of inert railcars sat in abeyance. To their right, the locomotive loomed with its cowcatcher buried in the far end of a dry creek bed. The rear of the contraption sat at a steep angle, still on the tracks. The far end of the bridge across the gully had collapsed and caused quite a hard stop to occur. The occupants of all the cars had been thrown about and a few minor injuries had resulted. The train crew had suffered worse. On impact, the engineer was thrown from the cab. Some of the passengers found him in the creek bed with a broken neck. The coaler was slammed against the boiler and badly burned. A few men who fancied themselves carpenters were building a travois for the man so that he could be transported the remaining miles to Rock Springs. A shimmer of the town could be seen in the distance, but that meant little in the endless prairie.

Abijah sighed and puffed the cigar Finnegan had

provided him with. "This Schnaubelt is making a damned nuisance of himself, forcing us to chase him in this manner. If we keep after this much longer the cursed railroad will kill us both."

"The more time one spends on trains, the more frequently the railroad will attempt your murder. Such is the lot of the traveler."

Abijah sighed again. "Oh, perhaps it does not matter much. If we do not die crushed in a wreck we will only return to Chicago and, likely, be killed by anarchists or former rebels. The first will inevitably discover me and the second will surely never forgive you. Who can say? The quick death of a train crash may be far preferable to the slow death resulting from shoddy marksmanship."

"Abijah, it has been said that I am a rather morose fellow most of the time, so you should give my statement great weight when I observe you seem particularly glum these last few days. Under most circumstances, I would not remark on it -- a man's disposition is his own business -- but it is beginning to make you a bit wearisome as a traveling companion. I would appreciate it greatly if you would either come out with what has you in such low humor or get the hell away from me until your mood improves."

Abijah shrugged and knocked ash from his cigar. "I received a letter from Mrs. Wallace the other day. You recall Mrs. Wallace?"

"Certainly," Finnegan nodded. "Lovely woman. Perhaps not as given to minding her own affairs as I would prefer in a landlady, but nice enough." He smiled. "I still receive correspondence from Annabel Lee, on occasion. Formerly, I received missives from Mrs. Wallace, before she taught Annabel to write, of course."

"Yes, well, I took a bundle of letters and stored them in

my valise just as we were leaving Chicago. I did not have cause to think of them until we resumed traveling by train these last few days. The letter from Mrs. Wallace informed me that Father Mulvaney has passed to his reward."

Finnegan rubbed his chin where he had thumped it falling during the wreck. "The priest from the church in St. Clair?"

"The very same."

Finnegan thought back on the fellow. "Well, Abijah, it is unfortunate that the man has passed, but he was already rather aged the nine or ten years past when I met him."

"Oh, it is not that he was taken too young. If he did not receive his three score and ten, he must have come close. It is not his passing that has been rather gnawing at my nerves these last few days. What has caused me some bother is thinking back to the last time I spoke with him before leaving St. Clair. It is odd that I should think on it, so many years hence, but I ponder it rather continually."

"What is it you discussed upon your parting?"

"I offered the father remuneration. He had been more than kind to me. I know for a fact he fed me many times out of the meager supply of pennies cast into the collection plate in a town as poor as St. Clair. He likely went hungry himself more than once to keep me in victuals. It was only natural that I should feel I owed the man. I knew I would be receiving wages from my employment with the Pinkerton agency and I asked the father how he would prefer to be repaid." Abijah assumed a strange inscrutable look. "Father Mulvaney told me that all I need do to repay him was to follow God's will and be a good man. That was all. He asked nothing else of me."

Finnegan scratched his head. "Such a memory as that agitates you?"

"Somewhat, yes."

"Why?"

"Finnegan, ever since learning of the Father's passing, I cannot help but think I have failed to live up to his wishes. I never saw the man after that last conversation, so from my perspective it was a last wish. A man's last wishes should be honored, should they not?"

Finnegan shrugged. "I suppose that is best. Assuming the dying man does not ask too much." He rubbed his injured chin again. "I still do not quite understand in what manner you feel you have failed to make good on the priest's request. All men follow God's will, whether they like it or not. Do you honestly not consider yourself a good man?" Finnegan grinned. "You are hardly a saint, but, believe it or not, I have met a few men who were greater sinners than you, Abijah Smith."

Abijah rubbed his eyes. "I suppose it does not matter whether I consider myself a good man, but rather whether Father Mulvaney would concur. He spoke over many of the Mollies when they were laid to rest. The Mollies were members of his congregation. He baptized them and their children. How would he view my current occupation, Finnegan?"

"Father Mulvaney was not the first priest to have some of his congregation face the rope. I would think a priest could appreciate the vagaries of human nature better than most. While I knew the man, he did not repudiate my position with the Pinkertons." Finnegan gave the question some further consideration. "Abijah, in my youth, in the war, I took notice of a trait in men that I found most interesting. I took note of the fact that it is not so much what other men think of our actions that concerns us, but what *we* think of our own actions. Our opinion of ourselves is what tends to keep a fellow up at night. Is it that you worry over what Father Mulvaney's opinion of you would be, or do you ponder what your own opinion should be?"

Abijah nodded very slowly. "You may be on to something there, Finnegan."

"Yes, well, since I have accidentally managed one piece of advice, let me offer another. I have always found it is better to keep about one's business rather than loitering about endlessly mulling such things." Finnegan pointed to the group wrapping up work on their travois. "Let us lend a hand tugging on that contraption. With some aid, that man may reach the town before he expires." Finnegan smiled at his young friend. "If we assist in dragging him, there will be one fellow who considers us to be good men, regardless of past deeds."

"Ah, Finnegan, always finding the silver lining."

Chapter 19

DENVER, COLORADO

May 24, 1886

The sun beat down unmercifully hot on the station platform. Finnegan had a hitch in his step as he disembarked from the train. He had managed to slip and bash a knee helping to haul the coaler into town, and it had been aching a bit ever since. The train wreck, combined with the uncommon exercise of lugging an injured man, had put the Pinkerton in a bit of a mood. He groaned as he set his bags down and looked to Abijah. The much younger man was in fine form and suffered no aftereffects from the manual labor. Noticing it irked Finnegan, though he could not say why.

"Abijah, this journey begins to weary me, as well."

"It would be preferable to not change trains so often."

"Yes, and these damned..." Finnegan looked across the platform where a man with a grey head of hair and grey mustache stood with one hand raised. It took a long moment, but Finnegan finally placed the face with the name. The fellow had put on some weight and lost his mop of black hair since last Finnegan had laid eyes on him. "Our fellow detective has come to meet us, Abijah." Finnegan motioned to the far side of the platform. "James McParlan is here."

Abijah stared at the man. "Yes, well, speaking of the damned."

McParlan came across the platform. He carried a walking stick he did not appear to need, but which matched his suit and bowler hat quite well. The former coal mining Pinkerton was still fond of fashion. He squared up in front of Finnegan and extended his hand. "Mr. Gilhooley, I hope the years have treated you well."

Finnegan gave the hand a quick shake. "To still be living is well enough treatment." He motioned to his right. "This is Abijah Smith, another of us."

McParlan nodded and extended his hand again. Abijah hesitated, but finally shook. "Pleased to make your acquaintance, Mr. McParlan."

Finnegan made an attempt at stretching out his knee. "Mr. McParlan, it is quite decent of you to meet us, but it is hardly necessary. We must switch to the other rail line and be on our way as quickly as possible."

"Yes, well..." McParlan stared down, contemplating his walking stick. "I had intended to merely say hello after so many years, although, matters have now progressed."

"Progressed?"

"We have reason to believe your man Schnaubelt is here in Denver, Finnegan."

"Here, in Denver?" Finnegan glanced to Abijah and back to McParlan. "Based on what information?"

McParlan let a small smile play across his face. "We keep a close eye on all labor agitators in the general vicinity. They are constantly attempting to bring the miners into unions, along with any other scruffy worker they can lay their hands on. Our people are well embedded inside the local organizations, as the local outfits are affiliated with the anarchists. The one often grants aid and succor to the other. We receive word when anything of note occurs." McParlan seemed rather proud of the machine he had built. "We have received word this very day that a Hun has taken up residence at one of the tenderloin flop houses that fancies itself a depository for communists and those of like leanings."

Finnegan was not impressed. "Mr. McParlan, I would assume there are more than a few Teutons lingering about the local flop houses, especially if you happen to have a population of anarchists in this town. Why do you assume the fellow here is Schnaubelt?"

"One of our agents is formerly of Chicago. He has identified him."

Abijah could not hide his shock. "Identified him?"

"Yes. Is that not what our people are trained to do?"

"I suppose that is meant to be one of our skills, but Schnaubelt has not been in the country all that long and only in Chicago for a short time. How well did your man here know him?"

McParlan shrugged. "Presumably well enough to spot the man." He slowly looked between the two new arrivals. "You are not pleased to be informed your pursuit will likely end here?"

Finnegan removed his hat and scratched his scalp. He would have been far more pleased to hear a bath might be in the offing. "Mr. McParlan, it is not that we do not consider your information to be welcome news, it is only that we have traveled far and have received similar news several times already."

"Yes, I would assume your voyage has been rather grueling." McParlan took a moment to adjust the various parts of his outfit from his vest to his bowtie. "There is no reason for haste. I have several men monitoring Schnaubelt. We can take custody of him whenever you prefer."

Finnegan located a cigar in his vest and got the smoke lit, hoping the stimulant would perk him up. "If you have men watching him, and you are certain he is the man we seek, why have you not collected him already?"

McParlan cleared his throat. "We have been waiting for you to arrive."

Abijah could not hide his confusion. "Why on earth have you been waiting on our arrival?"

McParlan took a long moment to choose his words carefully. "We have awaited your arrival simply because Mr. Gilhooley has accumulated an impressive record dealing with men such as Schnaubelt. Of course, we also assumed you would prefer to finish your task once begun."

Finnegan stared through his cigar smoke with disdain. "Do not bother to obfuscate, Mr. McParlan. Your men are a pack of sneak thieves, back shooters, and barroom sweeps. They are afraid of Schnaubelt because he is known to possess dynamite." Finnegan turned to Abijah. "Mr. McParlan gave consideration to the problem and came to the conclusion that it would be best if we exploded instead of him, or his underlings."

McParlan cleared his throat once again. "Well, Schnaubelt is your commission, not mine."

Finnegan smiled and nodded. "Yes, and all men must see to their duty. It is good to see you have not changed much over the years, Mr. McParlan. I agree that it is important to be consistent in such matters."

Finnegan sat on the wooden bench just outside the half-wood and half-canvas structure he had purchased a biscuit and a cup of coffee from. The proprietor was obviously more inured to serving the needs of mining camps. The fact that Denver had degenerated into a city around him seemed quite a disappointment to the fellow. He had scowled the whole time he poured the coffee and then requested that Finnegan take it outside and return the cup when finished.

Across the street from the less-than-amiable eatery stood the hotel McParlan had mentioned. Finnegan sipped his coffee and surveyed the structure. "Do you believe that these places are cheap because they cater to communists or that only penniless communists would stay in such a hovel, so they become the favored haunt?"

Abijah grinned. "Ah, the chicken and the egg. Who can say?" Abijah looked around to make certain neither McParlan nor any of his associates were within earshot. As far as he could see, they all still waited inside the eatery attempting to procure victuals. "Our old friend from the coal fields has not assembled a very impressive group here."

Finnegan sighed. "As I said, they are likely sneak thieves, drunkards, and the last batch ejected from the state prison. There was a time when Mr. Pinkerton worked to keep the majority of such men out of our profession. His sons tend to rely on them. They are not detectives, nor infiltrators, or even assassins; they are thugs and nothing more. I have been saddled with them all throughout this most recent railroad strike and have not missed their company during our journey."

"I fail to see what use these apes might serve."

"They are the proper choice for shooting down unarmed men on a picket line."

"That may be. What purpose could they possible serve for us today?"

Finnegan chuckled. "If Schnaubelt runs into a shed they will be the ones sent over to extricate him." He looked behind him to see McParlan approach. The aged infiltrator had switched out his bowler hat for a slouch and had the collar of his coat up, partially concealing his face. He sat on the bench next to Finnegan. "Your man lingers inside?"

McParlan nodded. "He has been told to periodically check outside. When he sees us waiting, he will come and report." He gave Finnegan an irritated glance. "Do you never attempt to conceal your identity when in public?"

"What's that now?"

"You and I are the two best known agents of the Pinkerton firm. I would think you would attempt to keep a low profile, just as I do."

"I am afraid I do not follow."

"You have no anxiety regarding being recognized or fallen upon by one of your former nemeses?"

Finnegan smiled. "You truly believe some fellow from the coal fields will approach here and put a bullet in you?"

"The Mollies were only beaten down by my efforts, Finnegan. They were not eradicated. The Confederate cause certainly did not die with Jesse James. We have cause to worry, sir." He glanced about, checking for the Molly Maguire that could be currently stalking him. "Do you not even bother to make use of a false name?"

"Well, no, not in most cases, at any rate. For the most part, I have found making mention of my name aids me in my work. More than a few scoundrels have been quite helpful to me in the simple hope that I will be on my way when my work is complete." Finnegan rubbed his chin. "I would not think you would have much cause for worry. Do you not spend most days in your office?"

"Of course, that is my preference."

"Well, then, aside from the occasional murderous impulse from your secretary, you should be quite safe." He motioned across the street. "Is that your man?"

"It is." A fellow in a dirty suit with black fingernails emerged from the hotel and crossed the street to the eatery. He strolled past McParlan and Finnegan without giving them a second look and disappeared into the tent-like restaurant. McParlan slowly climbed to his feet from the bench. "I will get his report."

Finnegan remained silent until McParlan had followed his agent into the eatery. He turned to Abijah. "Well, that answers my question regarding his memories of the coal patch."

Abijah nodded. "It is rather fascinating to hear he still considers himself both famous and hunted. He is a goodly distance from Pennsylvania for that sort of silliness."

"Some twenty men swung in the coal patch based solely on that man's word. I would wager he will never be far enough from Pennsylvania for his liking." They sat for some minutes until McParlan returned. The grey-haired Pinkerton resumed his seat next to Finnegan. "And what did your man have to say?"

"Schnaubelt is in the hotel. Room 405. My agent believes he may have turned in just now. He has been listening from the adjoining room for some time."

"Lovely." Finnegan sighed again and slowly stood. "Room 405?"

"Correct."

Finnegan tried not to smile. "So, then, you will lead the way?"

McParlan shifted on the bench. "I have located the man, the next step is within your purview, not mine."

"Your consistency astounds once again." Finnegan ran his hands over his various pistols. "Come, Abijah. Let us go see what sort of fellow this mad bomber is. As you know, I am finicky about my company."

McParlan licked his lips. "I will keep my men posted just outside the hotel to make certain Schnaubelt does not escape." He scanned over the streets once more. "I will remain here to make certain nothing goes amiss."

"Thank you, Mr. McParlan." Finnegan and Abijah crossed the street and entered the dingy hotel foyer. Before them, a staircase ascended to the upper floors and the two Pinkertons began trudging up the four flights. Finnegan glanced over at his young associate. "I would assume you have not placed many men in custody so far?"

"It is not frequently part of my duties."

"If he sleeps, we will attempt to bind him while he is still out of his wits. If he is roused, we take every advantage to keep him from gaining a weapon. We will refrain from killing him unless absolutely forced. Many in Chicago wish to interrogate this man and place him before the bar. It is not our place to cheat them unless forced."

"I understand, Finnegan." They reached the fourth floor. They slowly moved down the filthy corridor until they stood before the door marked 405. Instead of a knob or lock, the door only had a hole with a length of rope slung through it. The rope had been tied on the inside to guard the resident as he slept. Abijah knelt by the door and produced a small pocketknife. Slowly, but surely, making as little noise as possible, he sawed through the length of hemp rope. When the knot on the end fell to the floor Abijah stood and quietly drew his pistol.

Finnegan drew his Remington and, ever so gently, gave the door a small push with his free hand. It swung open a small distance and did not emit a creak. Another small shove moved it enough so the two men could enter. Inside, they found the especially spartan chamber a man on the move normally settles for. There was nothing for furniture other than a tick matress and a chair that was missing some rungs. It only took a moment for both men to let their eyes roll over the small space. It was noticeably empty. Abijah was just opening his mouth to speak when Finnegan held up his hand and pointed to the curtain on the opposite side of the room that appeared to conceal a closet. Finnegan was just moving one foot forward to approach when a voice came from behind the curtain.

"Do not come any closer."

Finnegan paused, mid-step, and lowered his boot back to the planks of the floor. "Hello, there." He let his thumb move up to the hammer of the Remington.

"If you fire on me, you will not live long enough to regret it."

Finnegan offered what he hoped was a comforting smile to the curtain. "And why would I wish to fire on you?"

"You are Pinkerton swine and wish to murder any man who would better himself and his fellow workers. You have erred in coming here. I will not be put down like some dog in the street. If this is my last day, I will be leaving with you two in my company."

"And how is that, precisely?"

A hand appeared and drew back the curtain. The man standing in the closet was of average build, wore the ratty clothes of a mason or some such worker, and had a clear glass bottle clutched in one hand. Under different circumstances, Finnegan would have assumed the bottle contained nothing more vicious than a road show medicine. The fellow smiled with what teeth he had and held the bottle up slightly. "You gentlemen are familiar with nitro-glycerin?"

"Ah, bloody hell." Finnegan slowly looked over at Abijah. "This represents a problem."

Abijah offered a complimentary smile to the man and then craned his head slightly toward Finnegan. "There is a further complication."

"Perhaps now is not an opportune time to discuss it."

Abijah grimaced and attempted another smile. "I only make mention of it as we may not be alive to discuss it later. That man is not Rudolph Schnaubelt."

Finnegan glanced from Abijah to the man in the closet and then back again. "He is not?"

"No. He is too short, has an entirely different accent, and looks nothing like the man I met in Chicago."

"Perhaps he has shaved?"

"And shrunk?"

Finnegan gave the closet dweller a hard look. "You are not Rudolph Schnaubelt?"

The fellow seemed more than a bit confused. "No. I am... it is none of your damn business who I am, but I am not Rudolph Sch...noblat, or whatever it is you said. I have no idea who that is."

Finnegan nodded. "I see." Quite slowly he brought his Remington back and slid it into the holster. "Well, then, I suppose we will be on our way."

Abijah's head swiveled over to stare at the gunman. "What's that?"

Finnegan cleared his throat. "Dispose of your pistol, Abijah. I believe the preferable course of action for all parties concerned would be for us to make ourselves scarce from this gentleman's room so that mister...whoever you might be, can resume his business uninterrupted."

"Finnegan, he has a bottle of nitroglycerin."

"And a fine little bottle it is. Holster your pistol."

"Finnegan, what are you suggesting?"

"I am suggesting that this fine fellow is, as you mentioned, not Rudolph Schnaubelt. Since he is not Rudolph Schnaubelt I do not much give a damn what he has in his hand, what he does in his closet, or if he wishes to be sent to Congress. Put your pistol in your belt so that we may be on our way." Finnegan looked to the man in the closet. "I would assume that course of action would be amenable to you, as well."

The man blinked a few times. "You do not wish to kill me?"

Finnegan shook his head. "No."

"You do not even know who I am?"

"No, nor do I wish to."

"What do you want?"

"My only interest, currently, is to be off." Finnegan glared at Abijah.

The young man returned a rather plaintive look. "Finnegan, we cannot leave this madman standing in a closet holding a bottle of nitroglycerin."

"Why not? This chamber is his room. Why should he not be allowed to do as he pleases?"

"He is endangering every person in the hotel."

"Which is precisely why I wish to leave the damned hotel."

"But..."

"Abijah, it is rude to accost a man in his rented room based upon mistaken identity. If you do not holster your pistol and back out of the room, well, you will be remaining here alone. I do not intend to continue this discourteous behavior." Finnegan took a step back. With no other option Abijah holstered his Colt and moved backwards, as well. Finnegan took hold of the door and gave the man one last smile before departing. "My apologies for disturbing you, sir." He drew the door shut and straightened his frock coat. "Ah, well, shall we get back to the train station, then?"

They descended the four floors to the street and exited the hotel to find McParlan still seated on the bench across the street and his various men still lingering by the hotel's doors. Finnegan removed his hat, scratched his head, and replaced the hat once more.

"Finnegan, I...I am not certain we acted correctly just now."

"We are still in one piece and drawing breath, I would say we acted quite flawlessly. Go to the station and make arrangements for our departure. I will have a few words with Mr. McParlan before joining you."

"Finnegan, should we..."

"Go to the station."

Abijah shrugged. "Very well." He turned and strolled off down the street in the direction of the railroad.

Finnegan crossed over to the bench where McParlan still resided. He sat down next to his associate and pulled a cigar from his pocket. McParlan leaned forward a bit and watched as Finnegan lit a match. "I did not hear the shot."

Finnegan puffed out smoke and shook out the match. "There was no shooting."

McParlan sat back and crossed his arms, obviously perplexed. "If you did not kill the man and he is not in your custody, what the hell has become of him?"

"I would assume the gentleman still lingers in his rented room pondering what to do next. He is undoubtedly aware that Pinkertons have him under watch, or should be, by now."

"Gilhooley, what is this business you are playing at? I found your man for you. All you need do was to fire your gun once and declare victory. Are you out of your damned head?"

"The man in that hotel is not Rudolph Schnaubelt. The lousy damned spittoon man you have hired as an agent lied to you. Likely to curry favor." Finnegan smiled and puffed out blue smoke. "I cannot help but wonder who gave the man such a notion. Honestly, lying to feather one's nest. Who could ever sink so low?"

"Not Schnaubelt?"

"My young friend Mr. Smith knows the fellow quite well, and assures me the grubby miner concealed in that commune is not the man I seek."

"I...I do not know what has transpired, but...who the hell is the man in the hotel?"

"He did not offer his name, nor was I interested in pressing the subject since he has rather barricaded himself in a closet with a vial of nitroglycerin. I would agree that his refusal to give his name was somewhat rude, but, as I did not wish to ride the building down to the street to make him amend his behavior, I chose to depart."

"Nitroglycerin?"

"The key component in dynamite, as I understand it, dear James."

"You left him there in the closet with his explosive? What the hell are you thinking?"

Finnegan shrugged. "Finding Schnaubelt is my commission. I would say sorting out that madman in the hotel falls firmly within your commission." He stood from the bench and straightened his guns. "Good day, Mr. McParlan. It was lovely seeing you again. It seems to me that the better part of a decade is a proper amount of time to pass between our visits. Perhaps I will see you again before the century turns." He knocked the ash from his cigar and strolled off toward the train station in search of Abijah and the tickets for the next leg of their journey.

FINNEGAN WATCHED the sun sinking through the train car window. Abijah was perched on the opposite side of the berth giving him a rather stern look. The gunman licked his lips and considered his words carefully. "Something vexes you, Abijah?"

"Finnegan, you honestly believe we should have left that lunatic to do God knows what in that hotel?"

Finnegan sighed. "First, my young friend, I suppose we can both agree that we did not hear a massive explosion while we awaited this train. In all likelihood, that fellow scampered out the rear door of the place as soon as McParlan departed. If he did not, the safety and well-being of a hotel full of sardonic communists is hardly my concern, or yours. We did not invite those people to board there and they surely did not consult us when they chose their neighbors." Finnegan scowled at his associate. "More to the point, what action would you have preferred? I am only a mortal man, Abijah, with the same slim options as any other. If I had shot the fellow, he would have dropped the vial and we would be conversing while we awaited St. Peter. Discretion was our only choice. Do you conceive of another?"

"Well...no."

"Then please cease glaring at me so. I am aggravated enough having been in the company of that damned McParlan. I loathe the sight of that twit and had rather hoped to go the rest of my life without seeing him again. I did not care for his company before he hung the Mollies and I do not care for it now."

"He is a rotten sort."

"And all that damned prattling on about being recognized and fearing an assassin might hide behind every corner. What has that fool gotten into his head? As if anyone recalls men such as us for more than the time it takes to kindle a fire from those damned newspaper fables. The very fact that the man has nursed such idiocy for so long fairly turns my stomach. It is a great pity Mr. Pinkerton is not still with us. If he were, I would use what influence I had to get that cur thrown out in the street where he belongs. Honestly, to think anyone would recall a scoundrel the likes of James McParlan. Hell's bells, there is hardly a man alive who recalls my name and I dare say I have accomplished a bit more than that low rascal. I have half a mind to telegraph Robert Pinkerton and at least attempt..." Finnegan paused in his ranting when the curtain to the berth was torn open. Two men stood in the train car isle with pistols leveled. Finnegan scowled. "Bloody hell."

The two men were doing their best to keep their armament concealed from anyone else who might happen down the corridor. They both appeared to be some version of miners by trade. The dirt on their clothes and mud running in streaks up their pant legs was an excellent indicator. The accents in their speech betrayed them as southern men.

"That's him right there, Cletus. I told you, on my momma's grave I'd know the whore's son anywhere. I seen him kill my own good uncle wearing that same damn frock coat."

Finnegan sighed. "Bloody hell."

"I'd be careful cursing, Mr. Gilhooley. You'll be meetin'

your maker real soon and you can't afford the stain on your soul, you son of a bitch."

Finnegan rubbed his eyes with his right hand and sat forward a little in the berth. "It is as though the fates conspire to make me look foolish. And who the hell might you gentlemen be?"

The taller and slightly cleaner of the two spoke up, proud to be queried. "I am William Robert Younger, and this here is my cousin Cletus Payton. You done much harm to our family, Finnegan Gilhooley, and we aim to pay you back."

"Ah, you are a member of that most remarkable Younger clan. Abijah, you should take note of this fellow; the men in his family live just long enough to make asses of themselves and are then shot down. Presumably, directly after breeding, so that the line may continue to plague the earth."

"You lousy bastard." Cletus shoved his revolver forward, but William Robert stopped him short.

"Now, don't let him rile you, Cletus. We got a good plan here and there ain't no reason to go upsetting the works." He smiled as well as his missing teeth would allow. "We gonna ride down the line here nice and quiet and when we get to the next stop, we gonna disbark this here train and find us a decent spot for you two to rest eternal."

Abijah sighed. "Disembark."

"What's that?" William Robert raised his eyebrows.

"The word is disembark. You disembark from a train, you do not disbark."

"Well, ain't you the uppity sumbitch."

"It is not uppity to know proper English. Although, I suppose that is too much to ask of you damn rebels."

Finnegan chuckled. "Oh, now you are being discourteous, Abijah. This man cannot help his upbringing."

"I suppose not." Abijah smiled at the two would-be assassins. "Perhaps we should all share a cigar and forget the whole disagreement." He reached into the inside of his coat.

Just as Abijah was reaching, Finnegan fired the Cloverleaf Colt from behind his back. It was a rather awkward position to be shooting from, but at a range of only two feet he was near-certain of a hit. The .44 caliber bullet slammed into William Robert's pelvis and tossed the poor fellow back against the train car wall. Just then, Abijah withdrew the Smith & Wesson from his jacket pocket and shot Cletus twice in the chest. Finnegan stood, brought the Cloverleaf around to his front, and shot William Robert in the head. He brought the stubby gun over to cover Cletus, but the assassin appeared to be breathing his last. Finnegan stared down at him. "Is there a stain on your soul, sir?" Cletus's breath ceased and Finnegan looked over to Abijah. "Well done. Splendidly executed."

Abijah got to his feet and braced himself against the rocking of the train. He stared down at the still men. "Um, they are quite dead?"

Finnegan nodded and began reloading his Cloverleaf. "I should say so. Fine marksmanship on your part."

"I...what did he say his name was?"

"I believe he said he was William Younger, of the Younger clan. You may recall they were closely affiliated with the James family. I would suspect the fellow felt compelled to avenge what he perceived to be my predation of both those families."

Abijah continued to stare down. "No, the other fellow. The one I..."

"Hmm." Finnegan replaced the small pistol in the back of his belt where it rode. "Cletus, yes, I am quite sure he said Cletus Payton or something very similar. I am not familiar with the Payton family, as such, but it is probably safe to assume they are somehow related to the Youngers, I suppose." Finnegan glanced up and down the corridor to see if anyone was approaching. "Why do you ask?"

"Well, he is, or rather he was, or I should say he is...I have never killed a man, Finnegan."

The gunman stared at his young associate with something close to awe. "Never?"

"No."

"I suppose it had not occurred to me that...well, I imagine it does not come up much in your line at the agency."

"No, it does not." Abijah looked up from the bodies. "Cletus Payton. It strikes me that a man ought to remember the name of, at a minimum, the first man he shoots." Abijah shivered and set his gun on the berth seat. "It is a strange sensation that grips me, Finnegan." He swallowed and rubbed his face. "Do you recall the first man you shot?"

Finnegan pondered the question for a long moment. "Um, well, I recall the first instance when I had cause to fire on men. I could not say if any of them were hit by the ball. I could not claim to know if they were killed. As I recall, the first man I ever knew by name was a Colonel Richard Duran. Mr. Pinkerton dispatched myself and an older agent to sort the fellow out. He had been selling troop information to the rebels."

Abijah looked a bit shocked. "A Union Colonel?"

"He betrayed his own men to the enemy. I felt no compunction about the matter. You should feel no compunction regarding this...useless cur who lies here dead. You may have delivered him to his fate, but he chose it himself."

"I...I do not feel particularly conflicted regarding the necessity of the act. It is only the oddness of the sensation that bothers, not guilt or regret."

"Yes, well." Finnegan glanced around the train car once

more. "I suppose the first killing is always somewhat off-putting." He motioned to the rest of the car. "Are there no other passengers in these berths?"

Abijah leaned forward far enough to look into the corridor. "I suppose not. I would think they would have made some inquiry by now if there were."

Finnegan sighed. "Perhaps it would be best to simply cast them out and give the pretense that nothing has occurred when the conductor comes through. It would allow us to avoid the endless nagging such men always feel the need to indulge in after a shooting."

"Cast them out?"

"Yes, toss them off the train."

"Finnegan, we cannot go about dropping dead men off into the countryside along the railroad tracks. My God, we have to show a little respect for the dead."

Finnegan shrugged. "Since this is your first killing, I will abide by your wishes. After you have shot a few more men and grown weary of the endless questioning and meaningless drivel that inevitably follows, you will become a much preferable traveling companion."

Chapter 20

EL PASO, TEXAS

May 26, 1886

The land around the train depot could not have been more different than from where their journey had begun. They had gone from the swamps of dreary Chicago to the endless sand and emptiness of the Texas border country. Finnegan's mind fairly boggled at the speed with which the trip had transpired. He felt as if he had been picked up by a whirlwind. Abijah's disposition did not help settle his agitation. The young man had been oddly quiet since the shooting on the train.

The aftereffects of the shooting had been more than enough to cause aggravation. When the train had pulled into Pueblo, it seemed every railroad employee for miles around had felt the need to pass through the befouled Pullman car and investigate the corpses. All the while, the engineer had insisted on waiting for the country sheriff to be found and had refused to move the train further until given permission by that esteemed potentate. If Finnegan had possessed greater knowledge of steam engines he would have simply shoved the fellow off to the side and gotten things moving along, the sheriff be damned. Unfortunately, he knew little of the workings of steam and could not conceive of how he might shovel coal and operate the train engine at the same time.

Standing on the El Paso platform, the country had obviously changed, but the feeling that he was on an endless journey had not. All the platforms looked the same, and all the café meals had begun to blur together. Finnegan longed for the trip to end. He fervently hoped the border would at least mark some sort of change. Anything would be preferable to further train travel. Since the railroad did not extend south into Mexico, that, at least, seemed likely.

Looking over the platform, it was not difficult to sight the Pinkerton man who had been dispatched to meet them. Finnegan was not precisely in the mood to speak with yet another member of his ilk, but there was little choice. He waved to the fellow and the man approached. The operative was somewhat fleshy and would have made a better newspaperman than a detective, at least based on first appearances. His clothes were well kept, and his bowler hat was spotless.

"Finnegan Gilhooley?"

"Yes, unless you happen to be of a lineage that includes the British crown or certain strains of southern rebel. If that is the case, I would be obliged if you would consider me a salesman of ladies' hairbrushes and allow me to be on my way without incident."

The man was a bit taken aback, but did not pause for long. "I am an agent of the company, Clyde Gordon." He glanced over to where Abijah was removing the last of the luggage from the train. "That would be Mr. Smith? I was told he was young."

"Only compared to some."

"Yes, well, I also received a telegram that you would not

be coming. It stated that the man you seek, Schnaubelt, had been located in Denver and your chase was at an end."

Finnegan sighed. "That proved to be incorrect." He squinted in the sun. "If you were told we were not coming, why are you present?"

The detective shrugged his wide shoulders. "I knew the information was not correct."

"How did you come to that knowledge?"

He rubbed his slightly flabby face. "I knew because I have it on good account that Schnaubelt passed through this place not more than two days past."

Finnegan eyed the fellow suspiciously. "You have good reason to believe this?"

"The finest. I received the news from a man who rather depends on me for funds to supply his laudanum habit. A man in such a state cannot be trusted for much, but is terribly dependable when it comes to trading for his ration. Your man Schnaubelt was on this very platform, met by men who greeted him by name. Hours later, he returned and boarded a train going west. Likely to Deming."

Finnegan was more than a little surprised by the man's thoroughness. "You were unable to put the man in custody?"

"I receive information, but not always in a timely fashion." He took a moment to pick something from his teeth with one fingernail. "While the man is not yet placed in your clutches, you may be glad to learn that I have knowledge of where Schnaubelt spent his idle hours while in town, and the fellow he spent them with likely possesses information regarding his eventual destination."

"His eventual destination is Prussia."

Gordon grinned. "This local fellow should have knowledge of a few of Schnaubelt's stops previous to Prussia. Unless you fancy following him all the way to...wherever the hell Prussia is. My guess would be it is farther off than Deming."

"It is, in fact." Finnegan extended his hand to the other detective. "It is good to make your acquaintance, Mr. Gordon. I dare say you will prove more useful than the other Pinkertons I have met on this trip."

Gordon laughed. "Yes, I am told you were to cooperate with McParlan up in Denver. Is that scamp still scared to cross the street for fear a coal miner will run him down with a beer wagon?"

"He is. Oddly so, given the passage of time."

"Some men have difficulty with the admission they have been forgotten."

Finnegan grinned back. "Some men dearly long for it."

THE BARBERSHOP WAS A LARGE AFFAIR. There were no less than three stories of wood stacked up to form it and there was a brightly painted barber pole affixed to the front entrance. Finnegan walked in with Abijah by his side. Gordon had, rather wisely, opted to be absent for the interrogation. Finnegan and Abijah would soon be on their way, but Gordon would remain stationed in El Paso for some time. There was good reason for him to remain in the background.

There were three chairs and three barbers on the main floor of the shop. All three were idle when the detectives arrived. A rail thin gentleman with slicked black hair offered a small bow. "Haircuts or shaves, my friends?"

"Shaves." Finnegan returned the small bow and placed his hat on a nearby peg.

"Ah, very well." The barber spoke with what could not be taken as anything other than a French accent.

"Are you the owner of this establishment, sir?"

"Pierre Canin, at your service."

"Very good." Finnegan took a seat in the nearest chair. "If there is no dispute, I always prefer to receive a shave from the proprietor. I have found the responsibility of ownership often makes a man more cautious in his actions."

Canin found a sheet and cast it over Finnegan before gathering one end around the gunman's neck. "You may be correct in your observation, sir. Although, I must say that I have often known the weight of responsibility to make a man's hand shake. I am not certain you will always be better off seeking the services of proprietors."

"Does the weight of ownership weigh heavily on you this morning, Mr. Canin?" Finnegan watched as Abijah silently lowered himself into another one of the chairs and one of the spare barbers draped a sheet over him.

"I do not sense the burden so keenly, just now, sir."

"Then I suppose it is moot point." Finnegan craned his neck back as Canin lathered him. "I take it you are not a native Texan, Mr. Canin."

"I was born in Lyons. My family moved to the capital when I was but a boy." He smiled to Finnegan and then to Abijah before returning to his work. "There were many bouts of unpleasantness in France. After the last upheaval, I boarded a ship. When it landed, I began moving to the west and now I am here." With only a few quick movements the barber removed all the lather and beard from one side of Finnegan's neck. "If you do not mind my saying so, you do not sound much like a native of these parts, either. How is it you came to this far-flung land?"

"Oh, much in the same way you found your way here. I recall a boat. General westward movement, with fits of eastern retreat." With a few quick strokes, Finnegan found his throat, cheeks and upper lip cleared of lather. The barber offered up a hand towel, which Finnegan used to clean his face. He returned the towel and Canin held up a hand mirror. "Ah, expertly done."

"Cologne?"

Finnegan inspected his face closely, but did not see a single nick. "I do not believe it is required, sir. Very expertly done."

"Such matters are my lifelong vocation. I would hope I have reached a level of skill that is satisfactory to the majority of my clientele."

"Of that, I am certain." Canin withdrew the sheet and Finnegan climbed from the chair. He produced a silver dollar from his vest pocket.

"The charge is twenty-five cents."

"A well-deserved gratuity." He flipped the coin to Canin, then turned and flipped a coin to the still-idle barber.

The idle man caught the coin and smiled. "I have yet to perform a service to earn a tip, sir."

"Some men prosper through guile, some through skill, yet others through luck. There is no reason to question the path." Finnegan flipped another coin to the barber just finishing with Abijah's shave. "My only caveat for the gratuity is that you both retire to the saloon to celebrate your newfound riches. I wish to have a word in private with your employer."

The two barbers looked to Canin for confirmation. "It is alright, boys. Enjoy a break, but do not overindulge. You will return just past lunch."

The two spare barbers nodded and shuffled out the door, still clutching their coins. Finnegan watched them go and straightened his coat, looking in the mirror. "Fine fellows."

"They perform their duties admirably and with little complaining as to wages. It is hard to ask more of a barber."

Canin leaned against one of the shop's counters and took a broom in his hand. "What, pray tell, would you care to discuss, gentlemen?"

"I seek an acquaintance who passed through this town recently. I am told you assisted him in his travel arrangements and wish to know where he is currently headed."

"Ah, and the name of this acquaintance?"

"Schnaubelt. Rudolf to his better friends."

Canin's eyes narrowed. "So then, if I were to ask your opinion of the Black International, you would say...?"

Finnegan sighed and looked to Abijah. "Do you have anything to add, Mr. Smith?"

"The man obviously queries for a password of some sort. I am not familiar with the Black International." He shrugged. "I cannot know the intricacies of every beer garden bred secret society."

"Perhaps it is better this way. I do so loath subterfuge." Finnegan knocked the broom from Canin's hand, grabbed him by the lapels, and swung him into the closest barber chair. "Sir, my name is Finnegan Gilhooley. I am an agent of the Pinkertons. I seek the creature Schnaubelt and you will assist me."

"To hell with you, Gilhooley." Canin writhed in the chair, but Finnegan held him fast. "I should have slit your damn throat while you lay in this chair."

"We all have regrets in this life, which is why I make use of every opportunity -- or try to, at a minimum." Finnegan plucked a straight razor from the countertop and flipped it open with one well-practiced thumb. "Lay still, Mr. Canin. It would be a pity for the barber to die in his own chair, would you not say?"

"You cannot do this. I will get the sheriff on you."

Finnegan smiled. "Sir, I am no more opposed to shooting

down the sheriff of this lousy, dusty, misbegotten hole in the earth than I am of opening your windpipe. Now..." Finnegan patted the barber's chest and took up the lather brush with his left hand. "As I said, lay still, lest you be cut." He slopped the lather onto Canin's face before pushing the chair back as far as it would go. When the lather was roughly even, he put the brush back in its receptacle and leaned forward over the barber. With one steady hand he began drawing the blade down Canin's cheek. "I might mention that you are not the first man whose throat has been under a blade with me. Early in the war, when I was quite young and uninitiated in the ways of the world, we charged a rail fence with bayonets fixed. I made it across the fence, many of my comrades did not. When I found myself on the other side, a fellow in grey -- much older than me, mind you -- ran at me. I brought up my musket and the fellow planted his throat on the iron just above his Adam's apple. As we fell together, he planted his bayonet down into my shirt and coat so that we were rather stuck together there in the lee of the fence." Finnegan finished with one cheek and moved on to the other. "Such unfortunate incidents change a man's thinking. Such deeds make a man different, more capable in some respects, more incapable in others. Is there an incident that made you the man you are today, Mr. Canin?"

The barber stared up from the chair at his assailant. "Yes. Of course."

"Stemming from a war?"

"Of a sort. I was a barber then, as I am now. We were attempting to flee the capital. The royalists had the republicans at their throats once again." Hate shimmered in his eyes. "I had gone ahead to secure our belongings and make certain we would not be left to the cold. When I returned..." His lips quivered and Finnegan paused in shaving for a moment until he regained control. "You are good with a razor, Mr. Gilhooley."

"I see to my own face every day, when another is not available. Please continue."

"There is little to tell. When I returned, the royalist guards had made sport of my wife and daughter and killed them when they had their fill. Since that day, I damn all aristocracies and aid all those who would damn them with me." He pitched his head back, exposing his throat. "Do what you will, Pinkerton."

Finnegan used the razor to clear the lather from the barber's neck, and nothing more. He wiped the razor clean on a nearby towel and tossed it down onto the counter. "Mr. Canin, a man such as yourself deserves to find his due and proper bit of vengeance someday. I would also freely say that your loyalty is misplaced in a loathsome bastard such as Schnaubelt. That cur only cares to throw bombs and revel in the carnage produced. He does not hunt aristocrats, but settles for whatever poor wretch is close at hand. In Chicago, he killed not just policemen, but women and children. Thanks to that particular son of a bitch, many an honest working man did not make it home to his wife or child that night. That is the sort of man you aided, sir."

Canin sat up and righted the barber chair. He slowly ran one hand over his face. "You give a decent shave, Mr. Gilhooley." He rubbed his neck. "Did Schnaubelt truly kill children?"

"When a man throws a bomb into a crowd, all manner of people are killed, from the bomb, from the chaos that is sure to ensue. At the Haymarket, Schnaubelt even killed or maimed several of the anarchists whose purposes he claimed to have served. Some men kill for necessity, others for a cause, some, merely because it pleases them. Schnaubelt is of the latter sort."

Canin stood from the chair and ran a towel over his face. "In that case, he is no better than the bastards who killed my family." He shook his head. "It is so very hard to find people worth saving in this world. Have you ever noticed that strange fact, Mr. Gilhooley?"

"Frequently, much to my continued disappointment."

"Yes, well." Canin leaned against the counter, almost exactly where he had begun the conversation. "Schnaubelt travels west to Deming. Once there, he will meet with a revolting fellow known as Ben Huxley. He is what they call a mescal man. He brews Mexican whiskey and sells it to the Indians, the half breeds, the dregs of society all along the border. He often supplements his income by smuggling wanted men into Mexico. He often brags of having affiliations with sea captains and others who would be of use getting fellows to Europe or beyond. He has never asked for a grooming in this establishment. If he did, he would be denied. He would surely befoul my chair beyond reclamation." Canin shrugged. "Feel free to kill him, too, if you like. It would be something of a service to all mankind."

"We do not intend to kill Schnaubelt." Abijah had been rather sullenly watching the proceedings, but felt the need to interject. "We intend to transport him back to Chicago to face a jury."

"Ah, I see." Canin pointed to Finnegan. "You must not know the reputation of your fellow traveler very well, young man." Canin put some aftershave on his hands and smacked his face. "I have read of more than a few of your exploits, Mr. Gilhooley. You are much hated by more than a few men I have met. You pursued the James and Younger families through this very town, I believe."

"I did."

"Yes, and in all my reading and in all the tall tales I have heard of you, never once have I heard or seen a word regarding your delivering a man to the bar of justice." Canin cocked his head to one side. "Much has been said and written regarding your shooting and killing of the men you pursue, but I know nothing of the other practice. If this young fellow truly thinks you will be manacling either Schnaubelt or Huxley, he must be a very cheerful and hopeful young fellow, indeed." Canin turned to Abijah. "Though he does not seem to be. What troubles you son? Was the shave not to your liking?"

Abijah ran his hand over his face. "The shave was satisfactory. I am simply suspicious of a man who switches allegiances so quickly. How is it you have decided to turn on your friends and associates so easily?"

Canin allowed himself a chuckle. "Ah, yes. I can see how it may be difficult for a man of your lean years to understand. Even saddening, perhaps. My son, as you go through life you will find yourself moving from one cause to another. One belief to another. One idol to another. As you are beaten down, disillusioned, or the idols are proven false, you will move on and on. Eventually, you grow to rather expect to be proven a fool and you take it in stride. Mr. Gilhooley has shown me the error of my ways. As a well-worn fool, it does not take more than a moment for me to come to my senses. Or did you truly believe he intended to slit my throat?"

"I gave up the practice of attempting to predict Mr. Gilhooley's intentions long ago." Abijah sighed. "There is a good distance between Deming and the border proper. How are we to locate Huxley or Schnaubelt if they are no longer in the city?"

Canin held up his hands. "I cannot aid you in every

detail, young man. I am only an agent provocateur and a barber. In matters regarding the searching of deserts, you will have to seek assistance elsewhere." He reached into his pocket and produced a quarter. He flipped the coin to Finnegan who caught it. "For the shave."

Finnegan put the coin in his vest. "Many thanks."

Gordon sat down at the table Finnegan and Abijah occupied in the backroom of a small café. Their train was not scheduled to leave for more than two hours and both men wished for some sustenance before embarking. They also wished to pick Gordon's brain regarding the continuation of their chase.

Gordon surveyed the café and grimaced a bit. "It is customary for visiting representatives of the firm to buy the resident agent dinner."

Finnegan nodded. "That seems perfectly reasonable, though you do not seem pleased with our choice of establishment."

"Oh, well." Gordon sighed. "It is not that the establishment does not offer decent fair. It is only that when I receive a free meal, I prefer a place that sells beer."

Finnegan set a silver dollar on the table. "Take that in good conscience and spend it as you please after we have left."

Gordon took up the dollar. "To what do I owe the largesse?"

"I offer it in the hope that you will be able to assist us further." Finnegan forked a portion of pork loin into his mouth.

Gordon rubbed his jowl. "I would be more than happy to

accompany you on your trek. Although, I cannot say as I would know more than either of you when it comes to the proper strategy to wander about in the desert. Moses would be a better choice."

Finnegan ingested a potato and nodded again. "You are a capable man, Mr. Gordon. I would not be opposed to you accompanying us, if you wish. You are, however, correct in assuming that your particular skills might not be of much use in the desert. My inclination would be for you to offer help in another manner. Do you know of someone in this vicinity with a thorough knowledge of the border country below Deming? Someone who could serve us in the capacity of a guide?"

Gordon thought on it for a moment and then nodded vigorously. "As it happens, I am aware of a fellow who might fit your bill quite well. He is a young man, quite vigorous, and has just recently left the employ of the army. He served as a scout and interpreter, but has become embittered. He is mining just now and, if his mining operation is like the majority of them, he will be in need of funds."

Abijah smiled. "Mining is not lucrative?"

Gordon shrugged. "It can be, if a man can figure a method to eat until the motherlode is reached."

Abijah sipped his coffee. "Why did the fellow become disgruntled with the army?"

"As he told it to me, the poor man was continually bedeviled by both generals and newspapermen until he was at wits end. The generals harassed him for results which could not be delivered, and the newspapermen accused him of collusion with Geronimo."

"Geronimo?" Abijah appeared more than a little shocked. "The last of the Indian chiefs still raising Cain?"

"The very same." Gordon turned and motioned to the

waiter. "It is said that Tom Horn is the only man the old scamp will palaver with. Not that it has done anyone much good. Geronimo will someday be remembered as a mediocre war chief and a great liar, if you ask me. One day he agrees to live on the reservation appointed to him, the next he runs madcap. I can readily understand how Horn grew weary of it."

"That would make for vexing labor." Finnegan tried more pork. "How do we find him?"

"If he has not starved, I would wager he can be found digging his hole in the Aravaipa Canyon. The area is not difficult to locate. Going south from Deming and asking the way should suffice for directions." Gordon gave up attempting to get the waiter's attention. "So, I take it the barber offered something of use?"

Abijah felt the need to field the question. "He informed us, after only the slightest cajoling, that Schnaubelt is currently in the company of a whiskey peddler by the name of Huxley. Do you know of the man?"

Gordon groaned. "He is not much of a man, to be sure. A more filthy specimen you are not likely to encounter. Although, he has amassed a rather impressive record shooting men down. Last I heard, he was credited with more than thirty victims. At least, that is the chatter in various saloons. Even if it is simply idle talk, you would be well served to approach him with caution."

Finnegan shook his head. "I have no commission to arrest whiskey peddlers who happen in my way. I have no intention of approaching Huxley at all."

Gordon chuckled. "No, I suppose you would not. You can take comfort in knowing that Horn will give you no trouble on that score."

Abijah raised an eyebrow. "He is given to shooting men?"

"It would be better to say that he does not shy away from it when pushed. I have never had cause to witness it, but I am told he is an uncommonly fine rifle shot and somewhat obsessive about his equipment, both horses and guns." Gordon smiled at Finnegan. "You two should hit it off famously."

"Perhaps so." Finnegan finished his pork. "Do you believe you will starve before that waiter gives you your due and proper?"

"I may be forced to take up mining to make ends meet before he notices me. I pray he comes to his senses soon. It would be a pity to miss my opportunity for a free meal due purely to his incompetence. I should hate to waste a portion of my dollar gratuity on food."

Finnegan tossed another dollar onto the table. "Take that, as well. I would hate to be a party to such a tragedy. Thank you for the assistance, Mr. Gordon."

Chapter 21

ARAVAIPA CANYON, ARIZONA TERRITORY

May 31, 1886

THEY WERE SLOWLY BECOMING ACCUSTOMED TO THE color green once again. The trip from El Paso had been comprised of nothing but dull desert with bland cliffs thrown in now and then for variety. Deming had not been of much note. Just another barren outpost in a barren land, as far as the two Pinkertons could tell in the dim morning light. They had made use of the town only to procure horses and glean a bit of information from the local blacksmith who did a steady trade in horse flesh. One day earlier, the grizzled iron monger had fitted out a man with a thoroughly memorable stench, and a queer Hun, with horses and a pack mule. Their stated intention was to swing both north and west to collect several squaws and whiskey stashes, then descend in a southern direction rapidly. Finnegan had paid the man an extra five dollars for that precious tidbit, and directions to Aravaipa Canyon. The blacksmith had assured the Pinkertons that the canyon would be hard to miss and the men they had inquired about were likely to make it part of their route, as well.

Finnegan knew William and Robert Pinkerton would consider the five-dollar gratuity money well spent.

Once the Pinkertons had left the desert for the cool and very nearly lush canyon, they began to feel considerably better about their journey. They began encountering mining claims almost as soon as the landscape had changed. All the miners consulted recalled the fragrant whiskey peddler and the Hun. As they traveled the canyon further and further, they began to suspect the hounds might be gaining on the prey, in spite of their difficult trail.

The last batch of miners queried had identified the next claim down the creek as belonging to Tom Horn and his cohorts. As Finnegan and Abijah made their way toward the outfit, they took great care due to the rounded river rocks that formed the trail and posed a continual stumbling hazard for the horses.

"Do you ever pause to wonder how a man finds his way to such a place, Finnegan?"

Finnegan glanced back at his partner only for a moment before answering. "Such a place?"

"Yes, this seems to be a canyon rather placed at the end of the world. Was this Horn fellow born in this area, or did he wander here from elsewhere? If he wandered here, did he set out with this destination in mind, or is his residing here pure happenstance?"

Finnegan pulled his mount off to the side and entered the creek to avoid a boulder. "I would not think you would ponder it much. More than a few times we have both remarked on the possibility of discovering a gold mine. Mr. Horn has simply gone beyond mere conjecture and made a formal attempt." Finnegan brought his horse back up onto the creek bank. "From what we have seen, he is hardly the only one."

"Yes, this canyon seems a popular choice."

"They appear to need a ready water supply to work their equipment in many instances. They may find themselves here more out of convenience than anything else."

"That would go a long way in explaining why they do not appear overly prosperous. So far, none of the miners we have encountered appear to be wealthy or near to becoming so. By my count, half have inquired as to whether or not we can provide employment or hope of work."

"I would say your count is correct." In almost every claim one or more of the men had asked whether the Pinkerton pair required assistance in their traveling, freighting, guiding, or an assortment of other odd services. The gold was obviously not forthcoming or not forthcoming in large amounts. Like opium addicts, the miners clawed for an opportunity to continue in their obsession. They all had the look of devoted disciples, true believers. If they could only find a way to continue a bit longer, dig a little deeper, fortune awaited them. Part of Finnegan sneered at their foolishness. Part of him recognized it from his own foolhardy schemes.

He brought his horse to a halt in a wide portion of the trail and Abijah came up next to him, tugging their pack mule. "Ah, this would be the Horn estate, then?"

Finnegan surveyed the small collection of buildings hewn from the surrounding woods. There was a low, dug-out cabin that was apparently the main living quarters, a small corral, an equally small lean-to, and a privy. While the structures were not overly impressive, the setting amongst the cliffs, trees, and creek could not have been more prosaic or beautiful. "Well, it is not much, but I dare say it is more than either of us possess in the way of a home. Do you still dwell in rented rooms in Chicago, Abijah?"

"I reside in only one room, Finnegan. I have never seen reason in the waste of funds on extravagance."

"Nor I." Finnegan gave his horse a small kick and they continued on to the collection of buildings. Above the constructions, piercing the wall of the canyon, a mine shaft could be seen with the requisite pile of tailings pushed out from it. Men could be seen moving in the opening of the shaft from time to time, transporting buckets of earth out, one by one. Finnegan brought his horse to a stop and watched the work for a moment before offering a wave to one of the laborers. The man raised a hand in response, yelled something to the others, and soon enough three men could be seen descending toward the cabins below. "These men all certainly seem to value a visitor."

"As I recall, the miners back home placed a high value on a bit of distraction. Life in a shaft becomes monotonous in short order."

"Yes, well, even at its worst, I have always preferred the work of a Pinkerton to that of a miner." He smiled at Abijah. "I have often said I wished to possess a gold mine. You may notice I have never expressed any interest in the physical act of mining." Finnegan pulled a cigar from his pocket. "I always imagined my position in the mining industry to be more closely akin to the work practiced by those railroad barons you and I are always lamenting. A man who gains money from railroads, but has not the foggiest idea as to how the train operates."

Abijah grinned. "I would wholeheartedly agree. If a man could profit from a mine without ever gaining a knowledge of shovels, that would be a fine thing."

"I should say so."

A young man, looking to be of similar age to Abijah, approached the Pinkertons with one hand extended. "Tom

Horn." He offered a quite genuine smile and appeared to be in very fit condition. The only oddity was a slight premature balding that shown on the forefront of his exposed head. "If you boys have come here to purchase this fine mine of ours, I can tell you right now that I am of a mind to sell and would be happy to be named foreman so as to boss the rest of these rascals to their death, presently." He turned to grin at his fellow miners. That done, he made a lengthy assessment of the Pinkertons. "If you boys won't take offense, I'll say outright that you don't look much like mine speculators."

Finnegan puffed out a plume of smoke. "All men are speculators, Mr. Horn. They merely seek gold in other forms from the one you seek."

Horn appeared to be amused by the Irishman. "That so? And what kind of gold you currently seeking?"

"A stench-ridden whiskey peddler and a Hun would do nicely."

Horn nodded. "You'd be describing Mr. Ben Huxley and..." Horn rubbed his chin with one dirty hand. "I do believe I was told the other fella's name, but I'm rather at a loss to pronounce it."

Abijah sat forward a bit in the saddle. "You know Ben Huxley?"

"Every man in this border country that's ever pulled a cork knows Ben. He's mean as a damn snake, but every now and then he brews a batch that won't make a fella go blind all at once, so we tolerate him."

"We are pursuing Mr. Huxley and his Teutonic companion. We were told in El Paso that you might have an interest in assisting us." Finnegan pulled the cigar from his lips.

Horn squinted and grimaced. "Well, now, friend, don't misunderstand me: I'm sure as summer that you likely got a real good reason to be chasing after Ben and that other fella.

Ben's real good about giving folks reason to chase him. Thing is, I just left off doing that sort of work for the army and I'm looking to settle down a bit. That's to say nothing of the fact that I got no quarrel with Ben or that other fella. If I'm to be keeping steady house around here, I'd prefer not to rile folks when I don't have to."

Finnegan licked his lips. "I will give you fifty dollars."

Horn nodded without pause. "When you frame it that-a-way, it makes for a better picture. Would you prefer to shoot Ben Huxley, or do you want me to do it?"

Finnegan grinned at the fellow. "Whatever way proves to be of greatest convenience is more than acceptable to me, Mr. Horn."

"Always nice to work for a fellow who's not too stringent. What did you say your name was friend?"

"Finnegan Gilhooley, pleased to make your acquaintance."

"Gilhooley." Horn rubbed his face once again. "Ah, yeah, I read about you in the *Gazette* once or twice. I reckon you likely don't care much who shoots who as long as the shooting gets done."

"A very succinct way to put it, sir."

Horn shoved a Centennial Model Winchester into the scabbard on the side of his horse and turned to the other miner behind him. "See to it that them others don't slack off, Timothy. I'll be returning promptly with enough money to keep up the works for some time. Though, I expect you'll hit a big vein while I'm away and take all the credit for yourselves."

Timothy, an older man with a bum shoulder grinned and

clapped Horn on the back. "Gold or silver, by your reckoning?"

"I got no more idea what lurks in that hill than you do. By now, I'd settle for lead, least ways we might save a little money on ammunition." Horn swung up into the saddle. "Take care, Timothy. I'll be seeing you soon." He turned to the Pinkertons. "That is, unless you'd prefer to give up chasing outlaws and take up digging for a profession. We're always willing to take on partners. Getting harder and harder to find folks dumb enough, lately."

Finnegan smiled and shook his head. "We will give your offer proper consideration when our present work is done." He nodded to Timothy and gave his horse a kick.

The trio had descended a few miles of the canyon before they came to a spot wide enough for the three horses to fit abreast of one another. Abijah was the first to ask a question of their new recruit. "Mr. Horn, if you would not consider it discourteous to ask, I am interested to know what you consider the prospects of your mine to be?"

"That is something I spend a great deal of time contemplating my own self, Mr. Smith." Horn removed his hat to rub his balding head a bit. "I guess the best way to put it would be to say that my present mining endeavor has more or less the same potential to produce riches that my previous mining ventures held. You gentlemen ever heard of a little city called Tombstone, not so far from here?"

Finnegan nodded and passed Horn a cigar. "I have heard of it. The place is rather famous for silver strikes and gunfights."

"The cemetery grows by leaps and bounds, I am told." Horn took the cigar and nodded thanks. "I wouldn't know much about that, though. I ain't been through Tombstone in some time. I only mention the place because Mr. Smith's question brought it to mind. See, me and the boys founded Tombstone, many years back, of course."

Finnegan struck a match on his saddle horn and cupped his hands around the flame. "It is my understanding that Tombstone has become a substantial settlement, Mr. Horn. I would think the founding of a town such as that would be a point of pride for a man."

Horn laughed. "Oh, they give me quite the reception whenever I happen through. Likely continue to so long as there's somebody about to recall my name. What brought it to mind was that we ended up in Tombstone, well the pile of rocks that'd become Tombstone, right after I up and quit my government scout position and went forth to make my fortune." He got a match of his own going. We wandered out into the desert like them lost tribes in the bible and thought Tombstone looked like a likely place to dig." He grinned, puffing smoke. "Not that a one of us knew a thing about silver or gold, aside from maybe seeing a ring or bauble made from it once upon a time. We camped out there until we was about ready to eat our boots, then pulled up stakes. As I recall, it was about two months later a fella brought in the first big silver strike." He shook his head. "I was back with the army by then. Won't lie to you, felt a bit riled when I heard the news."

Abijah took a moment to try and appreciate the tale. "Yes, I imagine it did. And now you have resigned your position to attempt prospecting once again?"

"I have. Hard to say how many times I might go back and forth yet. Hard to say how long it might take for a man's luck to crop up. Hard to say if it ever will."

Abijah shrugged. "I suppose a man has little else to do in this world other than to make attempts and try again. If there is an alternative, I am not aware of it."

"Nor am I, Mr. Smith."

Finnegan sat up in the stirrups to see farther down the trail. "Mr. Horn, if you would not consider a second question discourteous, I would be interested to know if you have already formed a theory as to where in the hell we are headed? You have some inkling of where Mr. Huxley is bound, I take it?"

Horn nodded. "Oh, I reckon I know exactly where he's off to. If he's trying to pack that Hun off to Mexico, he'll likely swing past his mescal still and pick up some trading fodder for the road. From what I understand, he uses that snake oil of his to sort of pay his way south with the Apache and the...I guess you could call 'em Comancheros. Half-breeds. There was a time when the Mexicans didn't much care who came or went, but they're plum particular lately."

"Yes. I am told they no longer tolerate men attempting escape from American justice. The few officials I had cause to speak with some time ago held that castoffs from Texas and other parts did nothing but cause trouble and invite further immigration of ruffians." Finnegan thought back on his pursuit of Dave Rudabaugh. "They have become quite stringent in their policies."

"Well, it ain't just them that are fleeing jurisprudence." Horn puffed his cigar and looked to be thoroughly enjoying it. "Every gully south of the line has got Mexican troops in it these days. I guess they don't care to have Geronimo and his raiding parties stop by for supper whenever they please. Can't say as I'd feel any different about it if I was them. Old Geronimo's played his string out just about as far as a man can. He's got two armies fussed and bothered with him and every white man in the territory looking to hang his head on a hook." Horn laughed. "Ornery old bugger never did know when to quit."

"So, Mr. Huxley must walk softly to smuggle his charges into Mexico these days?" Finnegan tossed ash from his cigar.

"Oh, that's a polite way to put it." Horn motioned south. "He'd better watch his backside, doing what he's doing. The Mexican army, the Apache, the half-breeds, and any other scoundrel in this desert will be trying to lift his hair and take his mescal, way things are right now. Who's the Hun?"

It occurred to Abijah right then that they had not bothered to fully explain their commission to Horn, and he had not bothered to ask. "His name is Schnaubelt. He is a bomber. Wanted for murder in Chicago."

"Bomber?" Horn stared quizzically.

"Yes, he threw a bomb into a crowd during a union rally."

"What precisely would a bomb be?" Horn looked back and forth between Finnegan and Abijah.

Finnegan fielded the question. "An explosive, Mr. Horn. Not unlike the dynamite used in mining. I am sure you are familiar with that."

"Yeah, that I've seen plenty. Wish I could get my hands on some of it every time we get into the hard rock. A fella really tossed a stick of that stuff into a crowd?" Finnegan nodded. "Is the fella wrong in the head?"

"I believe that would be the polite way to put it." Finnegan steered his horse around a boulder. "Do you believe we will catch Huxley before they make the border? From what you have said, it would be preferable to take them on the American side."

"If we step up quick once we're out of this canyon, we got a real good chance of doing that very thing. Assuming Huxley is headed for the still I suspect he's headed for."

Abijah's horse gave a small start, but he calmed the beast. "Huxley keeps more than one encampment?"

"A smart fella don't keep all his eggs in one basket in this country. Of course, the more a fella spreads things out, the greater risk that somebody will run across the stash and make off with it." Horn began laughing around his cigar. "I knowed this fella down around Tucson way, he was terrible worried all the time that somebody was going to make off with his spare picks and shovels and other accoutrements when he wasn't looking. For peace of mind, he'd sneak out in the night and bury the stuff out in the scrub brush. Thing was, when he'd wander out to get some of what he'd buried, poor bugger never could find any of it. He'd hid it so good even he couldn't say where it was at."

Abijah gave a chuckle. "That would pose a great difficulty. Did he ever arrive at a solution?"

"Nope. Spent the rest of his days looking for gold and them shovels." Horn pointed south again. "If you boys wish to make up the time we're running behind old Huxley, I would recommend we ride all night and that ought to put us in the vicinity of his still not long into morning. As I recall, when I saw them two, they wasn't in any particular hurry. They didn't seem to know anybody was chasing them."

Finnegan nodded. "If Schnaubelt had cause to believe he was being pursued, I would have to think he would have disabused himself of the notion by this time. He has been in transit a good distance and has not been harried."

"All the way from Chicago, you say?" Horn spoke the words with a bit of awe. "That is a goodly distance."

Abijah laughed. "By way of the Montana Territory and Denver it is even further."

"I should say you boys have had a trip. You know I ain't never been to any of them places."

Finnegan shrugged. "You are not missing much. Then again, it is always difficult to say what type of country will please a fellow. Where are you from originally, Mr. Horn?"

"Scotland County, Missouri."

"Ah, I have passed through Scotland County in the commission of my duties."

Horn turned in the saddle. "Yes, indeed you have. You shot down a lousy cur by the name of Dan Cooper right in my hometown of Memphis. That was just before I left to go west."

"I recall Mr. Cooper. He was affiliated with the James contingent."

"Sure enough was." Horn turned to Abijah. "You heard tell of what occurred between this fella and Dan Cooper?"

Abijah glanced at his mentor. "I do not know if he has ever mentioned Mr. Cooper, specifically."

"Well, it truly was something. The cowards came for him while he was attempting to take his dinner at the one and only café in town. Cooper and no less than six men burst into the place and beget to firing on Fearless Finnegan Gilhooley with rifles. Well, let me tell you, that was the last mistake they was ever involved in. That there fearless Pinkerton raised up from his dinner table with pistols blazing and shot down the whole bunch of 'em without even spilling his coffee. At least, that's how it was described in the *Memphis Daily Dispatch*, which was carefully read to me by a nice old fella used to linger around the general store. Took note of your name when I heard it ever since, sir."

Finnegan offered a somber smile and shook his head. "It is a thrilling tale, Mr. Horn, but lacking much resemblance to my memory of events."

Horn rolled his free cigar from one side of his mouth to the other. "If you wouldn't mind too much, Mr. Gilhooley, I'd be obliged to hear the tale from you. I've pondered on the event quite frequently over the years. It was the first shooting scrape I was ever made privy to."

Finnegan rubbed the back of his neck and thought back. "Well, as I recall, Mr. Cooper was wanted for relieving a mail hack of its contents somewhere outside of St. Louis. I had been chasing him about for some time and was rather nurturing a hope that he would be foolhardy enough to lead me to the more well-known members of the James contingent. Although, on the day you referred to, I believe I had somewhat forgotten about the fellow or lost track of him. I certainly did not have him on my mind when I exited the café."

"You was outside?" Horn sounded slightly disappointed to hear his childhood myth had not occurred according to script.

"Oh, yes. I had finished my meal. Mr. Cooper and a single associate had taken up a position in the livery stable loft across from the café. I walked out onto the boardwalk and one of them fired at me, I could not say which, of course. Regardless, the ball missed me and passed through the planks of the wall into the gentleman who owned the café. He was killed, stone dead, preparing the next fellow's noontime repast." Finnegan shook his head. "I could not tell you how many innocent people fell to bullets fired by the James brothers or their cowardly associates in haste or panic. In some of their robberies, they appeared capable of only hitting those poor people they were not aiming at."

Horn was beginning to enjoy the tale. "So, what'd you do after they began firing at you?"

Finnegan continued. "I ran to my horse and retrieved my Spencer rifle. They were a good bit off, and I knew that firing pistol shots at them would be a fool's errand. I got my Spencer and drew a careful bead on Cooper's accomplice." Finnegan rubbed his chin. "If I ever knew the man's name, I have long since forgotten it. At any rate, I fired on the man and the bullet went wide. It struck the beam next to him without drawing blood." Finnegan shook his head. "The near miss flustered the fellow a great deal. He stumbled, lost his footing and fell from the hay loft. Broke his bloody neck when he hit the ground."

"Broke his neck!" Horn brought his horse to a stop, dumbfounded. "The hell you say?"

"On my sainted mother's soul, my bullet never touched the man."

"Well, now, that is truly a tale. What happened with Cooper?" Horn seemed near gleeful.

"Cooper elected to take flight. He had placed his horse in the livery and came riding out, mounted, but hanging off to one side to avoid my fire."

"Silly sod." Horn shook his head. "You shot the horse?"

"Of course. What else?" Finnegan smiled, seeing he had met a bit of a kindred soul. "I placed several bullets in the animal and it fell to the mud. It begat to kicking Mr. Cooper in its death throes, and there was barely a need for the ball I placed in his head when I reached the place he had fallen." Finnegan shrugged. "So, there you have it, the thrilling tale of Finnegan Gilhooley and the Cooper Gang that never was."

Horn shook his head grinning, and got his horse moving once again. "Well, that sure ain't the way I heard it, but I'm damn proud to be able to say I heard it straight from your lips. Fell out the hay loft and broke his neck, if that don't beat all."

"I have found there is often a great gulf between what actually occurred and what is transcribed in newspapers, Mr. Horn."

"Ain't that the truth?" Horn tossed his cigar butt down into the creek. "Them newspapers are most of why I had to leave my post as a scout this last time. Did nothing but print lies. Claimed I was in the pay of Geronimo." Horn scowled.

"Never did mention what he might be paying me with. I'd wager the advance you give me for this pursuit is more money than that old chicken thief ever had in his life. Nothing but lies, but them at the forts kept whispering them over and over again until I just couldn't stand it no more. Got out for my own good before the general started believing the lies, too."

Finnegan had more than a little experience with the sort of menace Horn described. "Yes, those who print periodicals can work terrible mischief and likely never pause to consider the damage they do."

"Ah, well..." Horn adjusted his hat. "I was bored with eating dust and watching Geronimo go over the next hill anyhow."

"And you have your mine," Abijah interjected. "I would imagine it is a fine thing to have a mine, in such a manner as you do. Every new day offers a new chance for fortune."

Horn grinned. "And eating dirt instead of dust."

Finnegan grinned back. "Just so long as a man eats, that is the important matter."

Chapter 22

MICA MOUNTAIN, ARIZONA TERRITORY

June 1, 1886

Horn handed Finnegan's binoculars back to him. They had their horses concealed in a small declivity and Horn had momentarily ascended the gully wall to take a peek at the mescal still above them on the hill. "That is a mighty fine item, Mr. Gilhooley. Does the Pinkerton company purchase such things for you?"

"Oh, the company might be convinced to foot the bill for such items, if an agent could conjure a reasonable cause. In this case, they were a gift from an Irish whiskey baron I once escorted through the wilds of Montana."

"A whiskey baron?" Horn rubbed his face and smiled at the Pinkerton men. "You mean a man whose as rich as a railroad baron, but from selling whiskey?"

"I do indeed. Ephraim Haig Kilkenny."

Horn nodded slowly. "He's the old boy that makes Kilkenny whiskey, then?"

"To my knowledge, he had very little to do with the daily operation of the company, but, yes."

Horn nodded again. "In that case, he deserves to be rich.

That is some damn fine whiskey." He motioned up the hill. "A sight better than whatever we're likely to discover in that shack up there. The tis-win these failed sheepherders brew ain't nothing a man would care to admit to drinking. Although, as pappy used to say, bad whiskey is a sight better than no whiskey at all."

Abijah patted Horn on the back. "Well, if we do discover a stash of whiskey above, you are more than welcome to it, Mr. Horn. Finnegan and I do not partake."

Horn arched one eyebrow. "That a requirement for being a Pinkerton man?"

Abijah laughed. "I should think if it was, Finnegan and I would be the only two men still inhabiting the company payroll."

Finnegan eyed the scout. "Might you have an interest in working for the Pinkerton firm, Mr. Horn?"

"I suppose I might. This don't seem too particularly arduous of a way to make a living, and it's nice not to have some half-wit lieutenant bossing me like he was my pappy. You two are plum affable in comparison. If the pay on something like this came in regular, it would suit me real well." He pulled his Winchester from the scabbard and motioned up toward the mescal still again. "You two got a preference on how this is to be handled? There's smoke rolling from the chimney and a few horses picketed outside. I'd wager there's somebody in there; might be Huxley and your Hun, might only be a couple of squaws left behind fer being too ugly to make fer trading fodder." He shrugged. "You wouldn't think a man would be too fussy regarding female company down in that border country, what with it being hard to come by, but a lot of 'em are."

Finnegan pulled his Purdey from the scabbard. "If you and Mr. Smith would be so kind as to find positions on each side of the structure, I will approach the front of the place and announce myself from behind that large boulder. We will give them an opportunity to surrender themselves. If they are not amenable to the offer, it should be a simple matter to fire into the shack and kill them."

Horn pointed to Finnegan's weapon. "That boulder's at least fifty odd yards back from the shack. That shotgun ain't gonna profit you much from back there."

Finnegan withdrew one of the Nitro Express rounds from his pocket. "This is not a shotgun. It is a British-made rifle with dual barrels."

Horn slowly reached out and took hold of the three-inch long cartridge. He stared down at in in a state akin to wonder. "Well, I'll be." He looked up at Finnegan. "That is an impressive case, sir. At least the equal of the Sharps, I would say."

"It is, certainly."

"Does it give good accuracy at range?" Horn handed the cartridge back.

"It is a bit difficult to use at long range. Mostly due to the central positioning of the sights. The rear aperture of the Sharps is more useful for that sort of shooting than the V-notch arrangement. Even so, I have taken game with this rifle out to two-hundred yards making use of the added leaves, and, I assure you, these rounds will handily penetrate that flimsy shack."

"I would certainly hope so." Horn laughed and worked the action on his Winchester. "You Pinkertons got some interesting equipment." Horn pointed up the gully. "You reckon you'd prefer the right side, Abijah?"

The young Pinkerton checked the action on his aged '73 Winchester and nodded. "That will suit me."

"Very well, then, I ardently hope that damn Hun is in there. I would enjoy the chance to look on him once."

Finnegan watched as his two partners climbed up and out of the gully, making use of what cover there was to reach the opposite sides of the small cabin. When it appeared as though they had climbed high enough to cover the rear of the building as well as the sides, Finnegan began his climb moving from rock to rock until he reached the final boulder in front of the shack. The building before him was only about ten feet by ten feet wide with a small collection of flat rocks serving as a set of steps to reach the one and only door. Finnegan settled in behind the boulder and got a fairly good rest on one side of it. He cleared his throat and stared down the barrels of the Purdey. "You there! You inside the shack! You are surrounded. Come outside without weapons and you will not be harmed." He sat in the perfect silence of the high desert mountains for the better part of a minute. "You there, answer me or you will be fired upon!"

Another long minute of silence passed until it was broken by Horn calling out from above. "Mr. Gilhooley, I know it ain't really for me to say, but you might could be yelling at an empty shack."

Finnegan sighed. He looked at the smoke coming from the shack's ragged chimney. He looked to the picketed horses. "Such things will occasionally happen, Mr. Horn. Could you suggest a method to test your hypothesis?"

There was a long pause. "Say what now, Mr. Gilhooley?"

"Fire a round into the shack, Mr. Horn. Abijah, please do the same." Finnegan readied himself to fire at the shack door and watched as bullets thudded into the structure on both sides. He could hear them thud into the planks and logs that formed the walls. Aside from the dust the projectiles raised, nothing moved around the shack.

Horn yelled out. "You want more fire, Gilhooley?"

Finnegan rubbed his face. "No. Hold where you are."

Quite slowly, Finnegan emerged from behind the boulder and began walking toward the shack. He could see both Abijah and Horn making ready to fire if he encountered any difficulties. When he was in front of the door, he reached out and tore the thing open, bringing the Purdey up to his shoulder one-handed while he did it. With the door open it only took a moment for him to survey the interior of the tiny building. He lowered the Purdey and swung the door shut again. "Mr. Horn, Abijah, I believe you may come down now." Finnegan walked a short distance from the shack and took a seat on the remnant of a tree stump. He put the Purdey across his knees and lit a cigar.

Abijah arrived first and stopped short of looking inside the shack. "What lies within, Finnegan?"

"Many bodies, my friend." Finnegan puffed out smoke. "We will have to look them over to determine if our Hun lies amongst them." He sighed. "Give me a moment. I dislike rummaging through corpses and grow less fond of it as time passes."

Horn ambled up to the shack. "We got troubles, gentlemen?"

Abijah motioned to the shack. "The shack contains bodies, Mr. Horn."

"Bodies?" Horn scratched his chin. "Round about how many?"

Finnegan shrugged. "I did not take the time to make a precise count."

"Well, is one of 'em the fella you're looking for?"

"I am working up to it, Mr. Horn." Finnegan puffed his cigar. "Feel free to make an inventory, if you like."

Horn leaned his rifle against the shack. "I got no problem moving bodies so long as I'm the one who keeps what they got."

Finnegan emitted a small laugh. "This is a hard country, Mr. Horn. If one of the deceased possesses something worth keeping, you are more than welcome to it. Consider it a gratuity on top of your wages."

Horn opened the shack door. "You're a right fair employer, Mr. Gilhooley."

FINNEGAN STARED INTO THE FIRE. Horn had hauled no less than six bodies out of the small cabin, four men and two women. He had laid them out in front of the shack in a manner that suggested he had done much the same, many times before. The methods he employed going through what remained of the departed's belongings was regimented and thorough. When finished, he had simply announced that Huxley and the Hun were not present, and it would be best to move down the trail some distance before making camp.

Settled in for the evening, Finnegan felt it was time to make a few inquiries of the man who had more experience in the border country. He lit a cigar and passed one to Horn and Abijah. "Would you care to venture a guess as to who is responsible for those bodies, Mr. Horn?"

Horn took his cigar and lit it with a burning stick from the fire. "I'd put my last nickel down and say it was Apaches. Most likely Geronimo's band. They had their tailfeathers ruffled a piece back against the mescal brewers." Horn puffed out a plume. "Good smoke."

"Chicago offers an excellent selection." Finnegan tossed another small log on the fire. "What did the mescal men do to offend the Indians?"

"Some of the Apache come into El Paso. The mescal brewers got them all liquored up and killed 'em. I've been hearing rumors that Geronimo's been going around burning them out and killing them off ever since."

Abijah sighed and got his cigar lit. "You did not believe it was pertinent to mention such a thing before we began our journey to this mescal still?"

Horn shrugged. "Geronimo or some other war chief looking to make a name for himself is always raising some sort of hell in this country." He chuckled. "There's a reason the army's been chasing them all over creation for ten years and trying to keep 'em locked up on the reservations. Telling you the Apache's riled up would be like telling you it might rain while we're on the trail."

Finnegan nodded grimly. "What effect will these matters have regarding our search for Schnaubelt?"

Horn scratched his head. "Uh, well, I guess I wouldn't know how to say. I guess it don't much matter if Huxley came by before or after they was killed. Although, I reckon he would have taken the extra stock if he'd come by after. Now that I ponder matters, I suppose Huxley and your Hun come by, got whatever traps they were there for, and moved on." He puffed his cigar. "Them two women weren't much to look at. Could be they left them for the amusement of them other mescal men. It's probably safe to assume old Huxley and your man are none the wiser. Though they might suffer trouble on the trail."

Finnegan knocked ash from his cigar. "Huxley is well known in these parts?"

"I'd wager just about every man, white or red, knows old Huxley."

"So then, if he is seen by Geronimo's men, they will fall upon him and likely kill him?"

Horn shrugged again. "Likely. That make much difference to you?"

"I suppose it does not make much difference in the grand scheme of things. So long as they do not butcher Schnaubelt so much that he cannot be identified properly."

Horn sneered. "I'd say it's rare for the Apache to mess up a corpse quite that far. Assuming we find the bodies quick, which is likely what with us being right on their trail." Horn smiled. "I reckon we ought to do all right."

"I often wonder if men are capable of much more than killing each other." Abijah was staring into the fire and had not yet bothered to light his cigar.

Horn laughed. "I seen 'em drink whiskey, make babies, and blaspheme God, but mostly I'd say they're just productive at murder, Mr. Smith. If you expect much more of them, you're bound to find yourself disappointed." He finished drawing on what remained of his cigar and tossed the butt into the fire. "Well, I suppose I'll get some shuteye. Not much purpose in trying to find Huxley in the dark. A man on the run ought to have enough brains to run a cold camp." He rolled over onto one side and pulled a wool blanket over himself. "Just before first light we can begin again." He closed his eyes and pulled the blanket over his head.

Finnegan tossed his cigar butt into the fire, as well. "Yes, well, another pleasant day in the employ of the Pinkerton agency." He stretched out on the bit of tarpaulin he had laid out and brought his own blanket over himself. "Good night, Abijah."

"Good night, Finnegan." Abijah moved down onto the ground and placed his unlit cigar by his saddlebag. "Mr. Horn, I do not mean to disturb you, but if it is such a bad notion for Mr. Huxley to have a fire, why do we have one?"

Horn squirmed a bit in his blanket and answered without uncovering his head. "We got nothing to worry over. Geronimo's already killed everybody around here he meant to, so there's no reason for him or his braves to be about. Now, Huxley, six hours or more down the trail -- that man ought to worry."

Finnegan sat up and drew his Purdey rifle a bit closer to him. He reviewed the positioning of the gun. "Yes, that is preferable."

"I just got done saying there ain't no Indians about, Mr. Gilhooley."

"It is not the red savages but the bears that agitate me, Mr. Horn." Finnegan patted the rifle. "I will not be embarrassed again."

Chapter 23

SKELETON CANYON, ARIZONA TERRITORY

June 2, 1886

FINNEGAN WIPED THE SWEAT FROM HIS BROW AND moved over to be deeper in the shade of the large boulder they had the horses picketed behind. The poor beasts had been pushed hard in the last six or seven hours. Horn had announced they were closing in on Huxley in the morning and eventually there had been signs along the trail that even an untrained eye could assess. Three hours earlier they had passed a still smoldering cigar butt.

Horn had called a stop to the forced march at the mouth of a large canyon. The horses were unsaddled and given water from a small spring while Horn went on ahead on foot. Finnegan and Abijah had dutifully waited the better part of an hour for him to return and could see his grey hat bobbing toward them amongst the boulders and scrub brush.

Abijah took a long drink from his canteen. "I believe it could be said that Mr. Horn rather enjoys this sort of employment."

Finnegan nodded and accepted the canteen. "He is a man practicing a trade to which he is well suited. There is no reason I can think of that he should not take a bit of enjoyment from his work. At his age, I took occasional pride and, dare I say, enjoyment in my work, as well." He took a drink and returned the canteen.

"And now?"

"Now?" Finnegan gave the younger man a quizzical stare.

"You no longer find satisfaction in your work?"

"Satisfaction and enjoyment are hardly the same animal, Abijah. I suppose I might say that even a fine chase such as the one we are currently engaged in amounts to something like drudgery. Still, there is always a chance Mr. Horn will bring news of something of note, and that keeps my spirits up, after a manner."

"Finnegan, why have you not married that schoolmistress you pursued to Montana?"

Finnegan smiled at his friend. "Many an odd notion flits through your mind today, Abijah. What prompts that question?"

"Perhaps this damned sun has made me mad. Would you mind telling me?"

He shrugged. "There is not a great deal to tell. I followed the woman to Montana and made a proposal to her when I located the lass. She declined the offer under the most amiable terms." He shrugged again. "I correspond with her on occasion and intend to renew my suit when she is, perhaps, more apt to entertain it."

"And then what?" Abijah raised his arms, then let them slap down to his sides. "What follows matrimony?"

Finnegan rubbed his chin and assessed the young man. "Um, well, it is interesting that you should raise the matter, actually. As I recall, that was the crux of Miss Meagher's reasoning for refusal. She is rather satisfied in the role of an unattached schoolmistress and did not find the idea of home-life with children underfoot inviting, at least not at the time I inquired." Finnegan puzzled a bit more. "Abijah, what has prompted this? You seem both agitated and despondent of late. What is vexing you? Is the passing of the priest on your mind again?"

Abijah rubbed his eyes. "I am only somewhat confounded as to our purpose."

"Our purpose?"

"Yes. I cannot help but wonder what purpose any of this madness serves. We are chasing this fool Schnaubelt to the end of the earth, finding nothing but a collection of dead bodies. Some are the product of our actions, others the product of other gunmen. But what purpose does it serve, Finnegan?"

Finnegan removed his hat and wiped his brow once again. "Abijah, I would tell you that Schnaubelt requires capture simply because he is a bad man. I would tell you that the pursuit of bad men is a duty to men such as ourselves capable of pursuit. I would possibly tell you any number of things to explain this elongated and, frankly, quite arduous journey, but at its base, we chase because we are paid to chase and nothing more. I do not wish to butcher cattle for a living, and you did not care to dig coal. Whatever we do today we do because..." He trailed off as Horn came trotting into their small patch of shade. The scout smiled and dropped down to the ground next to Finnegan. "What news, Mr. Horn?"

"Well, it's good news, if looked at correctly." Abijah handed him a canteen, which he promptly pulled the cork from. "Ah, many thanks." He took a long draught. "Old Huxley's down in the canyon there with three ladies of questionable character and a pack mule fairly overloaded with mescal. There's also a darn funny looking gentleman in traveling clothes and a bowler hat. Looks plum out of place, if I do say so myself."

Finnegan grinned. "Ah, so, Schnaubelt is still in his company."

"Surely looks that way." Horn smiled again. "That Hun must not be too dumb. I'd bet you anything if he'd paid Huxley already, he'd be moldering under a rock by now instead of dallying with them lewd ladies."

"The intelligent method, when dealing with men such as Mr. Huxley, would be to place the money on account in a bank. Preferably near the boat Mr. Schnaubelt intends to board." Finnegan let out a satisfied sigh. "Well, then, shall we get to our labors and go collect our much-hunted Hun before the heat of the day becomes intolerable for vigorous activity?"

Horn held up one finger. "Unfortunately, Mr. Gilhooley, there's a bit more to the tale that must be passed on before you go and decide what we ought to be doing with our afternoon. See, old Huxley ain't the only party currently residing in Skeleton Canyon right now. There's a pack of Geronimo's boys moving in on Huxley's camp. They're taking their time and sneaking up around him real quiet like. Looking things over to make sure old Huxley ain't more than he appears to be." Horn shrugged. "Once they realize that there's only two men down there and a handful of whores, well, I wouldn't give a hoot for Huxley's chances after that. Where did you say that Hun fella was from?"

"Prussia." Abijah answered.

"And that's way over yonder by Europe and England and them places?"

"It is, indeed." Finnegan adjusted his hat.

"It's something to ponder, ain't it? To be born way off, just about as far from Skeleton Canyon as a man can probably get, and to end up here either killed or spirited away by

Apaches, or caught by Pinkerton men. Heck of a thing to ponder."

Finnegan raised one eyebrow. "Spirited away?"

Horn rubbed the back of his neck with one leather gloved hand. "What's that, Mr. Gilhooley?"

"You said the Indians may choose to either kill Mr. Schnaubelt or may spirit him away?"

"Uh, huh." Horn nodded. "Yup, often depends on what mood strikes 'em. See, they ain't got a lot of..." Horn rubbed the side of his face. "What's the word for it when you do something the same way again and again?"

"Consistency," Abijah ventured again.

"Yup, that'd be it. Apaches got no consistency. One day they'll kill every last soul in a party, even the women, even though they could sell 'em. Next day, they'll haul the whole passel off to Mexico and trade 'em for horses or burn 'em out in the desert where nobody but nobody will ever know."

Finnegan scowled. "Mr. Horn, I believe I have informed you that I require this man Schnaubelt, or, at a minimum, a large piece of him. Now you would tell me that there is a chance he will be carried off into the wastes and we will not be able to locate him?"

Horn nodded. "That having occurred to me, I made my way back here quick as possible, Mr. Gilhooley. The way I figure it, we can put off them Apache and scoop up your man Schnaubelt."

Abijah raised both eyebrows. "Now you wish to engage the Apache?"

Horn rubbed his brow. "Engage?"

Finnegan smiled. "Fight them, Mr. Horn. You are suggesting we fight them?"

Horn chuckled. "Well, talking sense to them is rarely

effective." He shrugged. "Can't be much more than ten or twelve of 'em."

"You..." Abijah glanced between Finnegan and Horn. "You wish for us to engage ten or twelve Apache braves? Finnegan, I have read quite extensively regarding the Apache; they are said to be the finest fighters in the world and only a fool, a very great fool, would ever enter into the fray against them when outnumbered."

Finnegan pulled a canteen from a nearby saddlebag. "You have read more than a little regarding me over the years, Abijah. How much of it would you say is true?"

"That may be, but..." Abijah turned to Horn. "What would your assessment be?"

"Oh, well," Horn kicked at the sand a bit. "See, the trouble with such things is that, when a man fights, he more or less wants folks to be under the impression that he's fighting somebody worth a scrap." Horn grinned. "I mean, I wouldn't go so far as to say the Apache are bad fighters, they got a lot of scrap in 'em, that's for sure and for certain, but when it comes to calling them great fighters, or the greatest in the world, I guess if I was one of the generals fighting 'em, I'd say that too."

Finnegan stared at the scout for a long moment. "So, you would say we have a good chance of chasing them off, Mr. Horn?"

"Uh, to be perfectly honest, Mr. Gilhooley, that's another matter these Apache ain't too consistent in. Some of 'em are right cowardly. You take a shot at 'em and the whole bunch will let out and you got to chase them for a week and then find new mounts to get them back to the reservation when they surrender. Others turn out to be quite stubborn and fairly insist on getting killed if they can't drive the whole cavalry troop into the river."

"This is the acme of foolishness, Finnegan." Abijah seemed less than optimistic regarding their chances.

Finnegan held his hands up and let them drop. "No, in point of fact, this is precisely the interesting occurrence I referred to earlier, my young friend. We began the day with nothing on the horizon beyond eating more sand and chasing this damned Hun to the southern pole. Now, we have the opportunity to shoot a few Apache war braves, which is an opportunity never before afforded to me, or you. I dare say, I never thought I would find myself in this position as a lad in Ireland."

"And I cannot say as I wished to find myself here as a lad in Pennsylvania." Abijah shook his head.

Finnegan grinned at Horn. "What would you say the chances are that any of those Indians down in the canyon have met a man from Pennsylvania?"

"Uh, about the same as them having met a man from Prussia." Horn smiled back. "You fancy a scrap, Mr. Gilhooley?"

"In most instances I do my level best to avoid such idiocy, but I will not have this farce end in the same manner as my pursuit of Dave Rudabaugh."

Horn's eyes narrowed. "You knew old Dave Rudabaugh?"

Finnegan shook his head. "Much to my aggravation, I never made the man's acquaintance."

"Oh, I was wondering if maybe you was the fella that chopped his head off." Horn glanced between the two Pinkertons. "What with you mentioning how you might only need a big hunk of a fella to get paid."

The three men eased into a crevasse between two large boulders. Horn raised his head above the rocks and then pulled it down in a flash. He scowled and flipped up the tang-mounted peep sight on his Winchester. "I can't help but wonder what makes them Apache choose what to steal and what not to steal when they're stealing." He shook his head. "They'd have an easier time of things if they'd just steal one damn spyglass between 'em. At least they wouldn't have to practically creep into a camp to see who they're aiming to murder."

"I suppose every man is apt to his own inclinations." Finnegan wiped dust from the receiver of the Purdey. "I cannot help but notice that you have chosen to not purchase a timepiece, Mr. Horn."

The scout carefully edged back the action of his Winchester to make certain a round was chambered. "I suppose I never felt the need to have one after noticing that the sun drops around the same time whether I got a watch in my pocket or not."

"You have a very unique way of assessing matters, Mr. Horn." Abijah checked his rifle, as well. "I cannot say as I ever thought of the ownership of a watch quite the way you..." Abijah craned his neck up to look toward the top of the crevasse they had massed in. His eyes took in a set of bare legs, a long ragged poncho of a sort, and the body of a rather grumpy looking fellow clutching an old Springfield.

Seeing his compatriot was ill at ease, Horn glanced up. "Oh, hell. That's a bit embarrassing." He swiveled his head to view the other three men who stood above them. "Our goose may be cooked, boys."

Finnegan grimaced and looked the collection of braves over before turning to Horn. "Not to disparage your services, sir, but I dare say Abijah and I could have found our way into this discomfiture without you." He looked back to the braves, but they only stared down stoically. "Perhaps it is best I have not paid you in full yet."

"If we live to see sunset, I'll be sure to make proper apologies." Horn puffed out a breath of air. "I reckon there were a few more than I wagered."

Abijah continued to stare from brave to brave. "What sort of practice are we currently involved in, Mr. Horn?"

"Well, that's hard to say."

Finnegan smiled at one of the braves. "I believe it is safe to say these men are not here to recruit us into the temperance union."

Horn chuckled. "No, they ain't. At best, they'll be taking all our guns and water and stock and leaving us out here for the buzzards. If they're in a mood, they'll likely skin us before being charitable enough to kill us. I guess I ought to have gone back to Missouri."

Finnegan chuckled in return. "Well, as I am sure Mr. Smith would be likely to attest to, I have never been taken captive and do not much care to change my ways this afternoon. I would assume these gentlemen do not speak the King's English?"

"And probably not Spanish worth a damn." Horn did his best to sound calm.

Abijah closed his eyes and sighed. "Finnegan, this may not go as you hope."

"It will regardless be preferable to skinning." Finnegan took a deep breath and stepped just slightly forward holding the Purdey out to one of the braves above with his left hand. "You there, chap, you must be able to appreciate the fine wood-to-metal fit of this weapon? Would you not care to be the fellow that possesses it? Unless I am very much mistaken, it would be the finest gun in your whole tribe." The brave seemed to welcome the offer. He knelt down to take hold of the rifle. When he was at his lowest point, Finnegan drew his Remington and shot the brave under the chin. Instantly, Finnegan swiveled and fired on another brave just as Horn and Abijah began to fire, as well. Finnegan fired, holding the front sight of the pistol on any visible target. The Indians managed to only fire one round down into the crevasse before being killed. Two braves fell into the crevasse and two simply slumped over the rim of the depression. Finnegan lay on the bottom of the crevasse with one dead man on top of him. He dropped his Remington to the sand and nudged the dead man over enough to wrestle his Colt free. "Bloody hell, did we get them all?"

Horn shoved a dead brave to one side. The scout's face was covered in blood that readily flowed down onto his shirt. "I think, I think maybe so." He jammed the dead brave over onto Abijah and leapt up on a small rock to look outside the crevasse. "I don't see no more right off."

Abijah slowly slid up one wall of the crevasse. "By God, Finnegan, I am not finding much enjoyment in this outing."

Finnegan gave his young associate a rather horrified look. "Abijah, are you injured?"

The junior Pinkerton patted about himself with one hand. "I do not believe so."

"There is a hole in the brim of your hat."

Abijah removed the slouch hat. "I will be damned." He stared at the hole in wonderment.

Horn hopped down and began helping Finnegan free himself from the dearly departed. "Damned or not, I owe you one for that, Mr. Gilhooley. You're mighty quick with that pistol. I guess there's a reason they put you in them nickel books. I don't know if I ever seen nobody shoot that fast and hit something they wanted to hit."

Finnegan got free of the brave and stepped off to one side in the small hole they all occupied. "Thank you, Mr. Horn. Although, as time goes by, I feel it would be better to be intelligent enough to simply avoid situations that require speed with a firearm." Finnegan holstered his Colt, picked up his Remington and knocked sand from his blood-covered clothing. "Mr. Horn, would you not say that we should move from this declivity? Our adversary is bound to have heard the gunfire."

"Hell, I almost forgot. I'd gone and gotten all set to die and now here we are back at work." Horn smiled and began climbing up out of the crevasse.

Finnegan turned to his young associate. "Abijah, we are departing." Smith continued to stare at his hat brim. Finnegan smacked him along one side of the head. "Abijah!"

The young man swallowed and looked up from the hat with a shocked expression. "My apologies. That hole is closer than I would prefer, Finnegan."

"Get your wits about you or the next may find its mark. Let us be off." Finnegan set the Purdey on the rim of the crevasse and climbed out to where Horn was concealed behind yet another boulder. The sound of gunfire could be heard in the canyon below. "I do rather detest the border." He flopped down and began reloading his Remington. "I take it the Apaches and Mr. Huxley are now having a tiff?"

Horn looked over the boulder and then drew back again. "That'd be how I would describe it." He peeked over the boulder again. "There are a few more of them red men around here than I reckoned, sir, and that ain't necessarily the worst of the news, either."

Finnegan groaned and replaced his Remington in the holster. "Pray tell, Mr. Horn."

"I think old Geronimo might be down there shooting at

Huxley and, knowing him, he'll be mighty upset with us when he's done with Huxley." A bullet slammed into the opposite side of the boulder they hid behind. "Or he might get after us while he's getting after Huxley." Horn sighed. "I musta set down to supper with Geronimo five, maybe six, times, still couldn't tell you what he's gonna do next. That old horse thief is just crazy as hell."

Finnegan put his head up over the boulder and then withdrew it as several bullets collided with the rock. "Oh, well, yes, there are a goodly number of red men out there, Mr. Horn."

Abijah came crawling over to the boulder, pulling two of the rifles from the braves with him. "How many do we face, Finnegan?"

Finnegan shrugged. "From what I saw during my brief glance, there is most of what constitutes the Apache nation, minus four, of course."

"Ah, well, that is a bit discouraging." Abijah hunched up behind the boulder.

"Take heart, young Abijah. Mr. Horn informs me that the great Apache war chief Geronimo may be among their number. You may have the honor of meeting a famous personage before you die."

"I have already met the famous Professor Mezzeroff. Is that not enough for one journey?"

"Apparently not." Finnegan glanced about at the surrounding maze of boulders and sand that hung on the canyon wall. "Mr. Horn, I have found it is best to take the initiative in such situations. I would like to reach our man Schnaubelt before the Indians. At the very least, we should move about some to avoid being surrounded once again. Would you agree?"

"I damn well would. I'd hate to have you save my cur life

twice in one day, at any rate." He motioned to one side. "There's a few little washes that run down the side of the wall. If we each take one and do our best to move when we don't see Indians or when the other fella's shooting, well, I'd give us at least even odds of living past sunset."

Abijah looked over the gullies. "What occurs at sunset?"

Horn smiled. "Ah, that's when I crawl outta here on my belly whether you boys are alive or not."

"I am certain Mr. Smith will have dispatched most, if not all of the Apaches by that time, Mr. Horn." Finnegan gave his Purdey a brief inspection. If you find yourselves in dire straits, call out. We may be able to hear each other as we progress." He sighed and looked over the gullies. "Mr. Horn, you are fleet of foot. Would you care to try for the farthest wash? Abijah and I will provide fire to distract the Indians."

Horn shook his head. "I guess this is my own damn fault. A grown man ought to know better than to go into a place called Skeleton Canyon and not have trouble." He got into a crouch and made ready. "See you in a piece, boys."

"Good luck, Tom." Abijah slapped the scout on the back and Horn broke into a run toward the farthest gully. Abijah leapt up and fired one of the borrowed Trapdoor rifles down toward the canyon floor. Finnegan came up as Abijah ducked down and fired off two rounds from the Purdey. As he ducked, Abijah came up and fired off the second Springfield.

Finnegan watched as Horn dove into his chosen gully. "Our friend is ensconced, Abijah."

"Ah, good." Abijah set the second Springfield to the side and took up his Winchester. "I do not believe I hit much of anything, for I have no idea where those rifles may hit."

Finnegan shrugged. "I had the sight on one fellow where it belonged. He was not there after the recoil." He shrugged again and broke open the Purdey to reload it. "You may pick your destination, my young friend." He slipped two long rounds into the double rifle and closed the breech. "Just so long as you do not choose the closest declivity. As the oldest man in the group, I claim that hole as my privilege."

"I do not know if you are quite old enough to be claiming privileges as yet, but you are welcome to it, just the same." Abijah fed two cartridges into his rifle to replace the ones he had used in the crevasse. "Good luck to you, Finnegan."

"And to you. Be careful not to become lost on the way to the canyon floor. Just keep in mind the proper direction of travel is the one to which falling is easiest."

"You have always chosen to jest at the oddest times, Finnegan."

"Such is my habit. I will fire when you begin and, if you would be so kind, I would appreciate some fire when you reach your declivity."

Abijah got into a low crouch. "Happy to oblige." He grinned at Finnegan and took off running. Finnegan jumped up and fired both barrels from the Purdey, then lowered the gun and fired off his Remington twice for good measure. Abijah disappeared into the rocks in one of the gullies.

Back behind the boulder, Finnegan reloaded his pistol and the Purdey. He made certain he had all his equipment and that the thongs were over the hammers of his various revolvers. When every item seemed secure, he got into a crouch just as his associates had. "Abijah, can you hear me?"

"I can."

"I am on the move."

"Go now." A shot rang out.

Finnegan took off and covered the small distance to the gully nearest him in only a few seconds. Even so, the Indians below had caught on to what the men above were doing, and they were ready for another runner to emerge. Bullets thudded into the sand and whip-cracked off rocks all around Finnegan. The fusillade did not cease until he had made it to the depths of gully and had been out of sight for some seconds. He gave his clothing a quick review and noticed two holes in the tail of his frock coat. "By God, it is a bit sporting out here."

Abijah voice came over the rocks. "Are you free and clear, Finnegan?"

"I am in my declivity, and I still draw breath. Though my coat has suffered much."

"It is hardly the first garment you have sacrificed." Abijah let a small laugh slip. "Shall we begin our descent?"

"I can think of nothing else that ought to occupy our time." Over the eons, water had occasionally run down the canyon wall and slithered its way between the boulders and escarpments that made up the landscape. Finnegan slowly and surely made his way down the wash, moving from cover to cover and keeping a sharp eye on the opposite canyon wall and what little he could see of the canyon floor below. He had made a handful of moves downward when he dropped into a new hole and looked across to see an Apache who was partially concealed on the opposite wall. More from reflex than malice he brought the Purdey to bear on the man and squeezed the trigger. When he brought the gun down, he could see that the fifty-caliber round had done its work. The Apache slid forward and then tumbled down from where he had been perched on the wall. Bullets began hitting the rocks above and below Finnegan. He ducked down as low as he could in the wash and waited for the firing to abate. He faintly heard either Abijah or Horn fire off a few rounds in response. One of the final rounds from below found its way into the wash and sprayed dust over the side of Finnegan's face. "Christ preserve us." He wiped the dust away and began surveying his next drop.

"Finnegan, are you still in good humor?"

"I am uninjured." He wiped more dust from his face. "I sent one of them to meet his maker."

"I may have taken one as well. I believe I saw Horn hit at least two. He is doing quite well wherever he is set."

"I am in absolute rapture to know he is having a fine outing." Finnegan sighed. "I intend to descend once more."

"Very well. I too."

"Good hunting."

"You, as well."

Finnegan slid down to the next crook in the wash and brought the Purdey up to cover the other side of the canyon. Finding it clear of Indians, he slowly leaned forward around a rock face to get a view of the canyon floor. He had lost a fair amount of elevation so far and was within rifle range of the bottom when it came into view. To the left, he could see where Huxley had built a kind of stockade with rocks, pack boxes, and the carcass of one mule. Finnegan could see one man leap up and put sporadic fire into the rocks on both walls of the canyon. If he was aiming, he was very quick about it.

"Abijah, can you hear me?"

"I can." The voice was quieter. The two washes had moved farther apart.

"Can you see Huxley's fort?"

"I can."

"Can you see Schnaubelt?"

"I cannot see if the man firing is Schnaubelt or the whiskey peddler. What do you propose, Finnegan?"

"We must gain ground and get to Schnaubelt before the red men."

Horn leapt into the wash next to Finnegan and wiped

sweat from his brow. "I ain't sure that's the best idea, Mr. Gilhooley."

Finnegan stared blankly at the scout for a moment. "How the hell did you get here?"

"Well, you know, over and around and like that. See, the trouble we got is that there are just a whole passel of Apaches right in this particular canyon. Old Geronimo must have brought every damn buck this side of Missouri down here with him." He rubbed his chin. "Could be Mr. Huxley's the fella that shot them bucks in El Paso and this whole time Geronimo's been trying to tack his hide to a wall. You suppose our luck is that bad?"

Finnegan shrugged. "My luck has always held quite well. Your luck is what may be at fault here." He stuck his head up and glanced around before ducking back into the wash. "I would pose a more pertinent question. If we do not attempt to cross the canyon floor and reach Huxley's little enclosure, what in the name of Saint Peter have we dropped into this damned declivity for to begin with? If we were to cease our attempts, I would have greatly preferred you to suggest it this morning so that we could have returned to Deming and found proper lodging."

Horn smiled. "When you put it like that, I reckon we really ain't got much else to do today." He sighed. "What you wanna try?"

Finnegan leaned the Purdey against one side of the gully and pulled off his frock coat. "I will not be needing this for the moment." He folded the garment and placed it on a rock, then adjusted his pistols and checked the spare ammunition for the Purdey that he had in the pockets of his vest. "Well, since I am the most amiable of our group, and the senior representative of the Pinkerton agency available, I will amble over to Mr. Huxley and inquire as to whether or not Mr.

Schnaubelt wishes to turn himself over to the auspices of the law."

Horn raised one eyebrow. "You had better do more than amble."

"I was being jocular, Mr. Horn."

"What you should be is damn quick." He checked over his rifle. "I guess if you want to go running out there to see what being properly surrounded looks like, me and Mr. Smith can put down some fire for you. It would only be Christian."

Finnegan took up the Purdey once more. "Thank you, Mr. Horn." He reviewed his guns and ammunition yet again. "I believe one more good drop down this declivity ought to place me near the valley floor, is that correct?"

"It'll get you right close, yup."

"Very well. I will yell out when I intend to begin running."

Horn nodded. "Good luck. Don't be afeared to get near them boulders down there on your way. Although, with the number of Apaches up in these rocks, I couldn't tell you which side you might want to linger on. You might be a damn lonely man if you get to where Huxley's at. One of them braves will get around to finding a way to shoot down into that sad little fort. I know old Huxley a bit. He's a good dry gulcher, but a poor marksman."

"I have known many a man who cannot hit a barn from the inside who lived to a ripe old age on guile alone. I myself largely prosper from audacity. Good day, Mr. Horn." Finnegan leapt down two crooks further in the wash and found himself nestled in a fairly nice bit of cover in the floor of the canyon. By peeking around the corner of one boulder, he could see down to the fort Huxley had constructed from freight and carcasses. It appeared to be roughly two hundred yards distant. Most of the firing had died off for the moment, and only the occasional bullet would thud into the sand or stones around the enclosure. "Are you ready, Mr. Horn?"

"Yup."

"Ready, Mr. Smith?"

"I am, Finnegan."

"Very well, I am off." Finnegan broke from cover and began running through the sand as best he could. In spite of the lacking traction, he was making good time and most of the fire came from Horn and Abijah as he began to close the distance to Huxley's hideout. As he neared a large boulder, a bullet from above collided with the rock and sent dust into Finnegan's eyes. He stumbled and fell down, crawling to the base of the boulder and wiping at his face. Without further pause, he got back to his feet and began running once more. He was only exposed for another few moments before leaping over the dead mule and landing inside Huxley's enclosure. He took a deep breath and looked over at the remarkably filthy man who held a Sharps rifle to one shoulder and was using the dead mule for a rest. "Might you be Benjamin Huxley, sir?"

The grease clad man gave Finnegan a shocked stare. "Last person to call me Benjamin was my dear departed mother."

"Well, if it holds ill memories for you, I would be happy to address you simply as Mr. Huxley." Finnegan reviewed the contents of the small stockade. Inside the scant few yards there were two bodies. One belonged to a young Apache brave who could not have been more than fifteen. The other was an older man in a dark suit.

"Bloody hell. Schnaubelt is dead."

Huxley took his cheek away from the Sharps and rubbed his chin. "Naw. At least he wasn't last time I gave his throat a feel. Still draws breath and there's a heart pumpin' in there somewheres. That injun hopped in here and gave him a hell of a bop on the head 'fore I shot him. Used the only two shotgun shells I had for the scattergun. Ain't much good with nothing but that scattergun and the other mule with all the shells been purloined by them damn savages. Hey, how the hell you know that fella's name?"

"I have been sent here by the Pinkerton Detective Agency to capture him and return him to Chicago for trial. Is that likely to cause a quarrel between us?" Finnegan posed the question as if he were asking the man his preference in coffee.

Huxley pursed his lips and thought on it for a moment. "Well, most times I'd tell you to kiss my sister's black cat's ass and try to shoot you over a declaration like that, but you've surely caught me at the proper moment to find me amenable to being friendly." A bullet thudded into the dead mule. "Tell you the truth, mister, I ain't real sure what either of us would like makes a tinker's damn bit of difference. I believe this time them damn Apaches have got me. Awful decent of you to stop by for a visit, but I doubt we'll know each other long."

Finnegan shook his head. "It is a gloomy race that inhabits this desert. Everyone out here is always awaiting death so presently." He rolled onto his back and withdrew a cigar. "It must me a frightful way to go through life."

Huxley pointed to the cigar. "Might you have another one of those?"

"Are you amenable to allowing me to depart with Schnaubelt, or his corpse, if that is how matters stand?"

"Mister, if you give me a cigar and suggest a method any of us can depart this damn place, you can have what you want."

Finnegan handed him a cigar. "You are a practical man, Mr. Huxley."

"Didn't live this long being picky, that's for damn sure."

Finnegan glanced about the small space. "Mr. Huxley, did you not previously have women in your company?"

"Despite my cautionary advice, they run off down the canyon and are likely now either official squaws or dog meat." He held up the cigar. "Looks like a damn fine smoke." The cigar disappeared along with Huxley's thumb and forefinger. "Hell and perdition on them damn savages!" He dropped down to the sand and gripped his injured limb. "I wish I'd killed every damn Apache I ever seen."

Finnegan assumed Huxley's former position on the dead mule and aimed the Purdey downrange. It was not difficult to find a target. Several Apache braves were approaching the small, improvised fort, moving from stone to stone. As they stalked closer and closer, they were careful to keep boulders between themselves and the fire Horn and Abijah sent down from above. Finnegan placed the front sight of the Purdey on one brave's chest and fired. A bullet thudded into the dead mule from the opposite direction just as he was coming down from the recoil. "Bloody hell."

"Them savages have got around us." Huxley pawed a Colt Peacemaker out from between two crudely built whiskey crates. He gripped the gun in his good hand and grimaced from the pain. "They got around the back of the damn canyon. We'll be skinned fer sure. We got to get the hell out of here, partner." He rolled onto his other side and got his legs underneath him and Finnegan switched sides in the fort to fire on the new threat to the south.

"Do not attempt flight, Mr. Huxley." Finnegan fired at another brave and was rocked back by the recoil of the big gun. "We have good barricades here and men above who can give us covering fire. Do not attempt..."

"Burn in hell you savage bastards!" Huxley launched himself up onto the collection of crates at the rear of the fort. He very nearly cleared the hurdle before the first bullet struck him in his wide chest. He winced at the first hit but continued to clamor on the crates. He fell to the sand just outside the fort as more bullets hit him in the arms and legs. He made only a few staggering steps before falling to the sand and being hit with a litany of gratuitous rounds.

Finnegan ducked down to reload the Purdey. "Bloody hell." He shoved two rounds into the express rifle and slipped above what remained of the crates. The gunman fired off his two rounds at the two Apache braves he could see and then flopped over to the dead mule, drawing his Remington. He fired off six rounds at the Indians who continued to creep closer. He thought he had scored at least two hits as he moved back to the crates and drew his Colt Lightning from its shoulder holster. He fired the revolver double action at the braves who had moved up to within a scant twenty yards of the fort. When the gun was empty, he turned back to the dead mule to see a brave climbing over the poor beast's corpse. Finnegan jerked the Cloverleaf from the small of his back and shot the man in the chest three times before dodging to the side as he fell inside the fort. The last round he put between the eyes of another brave who charged the stockade. The brave fell face down in the sand, revealing another brave behind him. Finnegan leveled the Cloverleaf on the brave, cocked back the hammer, and squeezed the trigger to produce a dull click. The click of Finnegan swallowing was only slightly louder.

The Indian who stood before Finnegan was older than

his fellows and lean from obvious privation. He had an angry, but controlled, look in his cold eyes. He raised a Winchester rifle and aimed at Finnegan. The brave was far too close to possibly miss. Finnegan held his chin up a bit as the man pulled the trigger and got a click similar to the one Finnegan had produced. Finnegan let out a breath and smiled at the brave. "I suppose we are both a bit embarrassed."

The brave grunted. "Mala Suerte."

"Yes, certainly." Finnegan sighed and watched as the brave began to dig around in a small bag he wore on his side. "Oh, bloody hell." Finnegan dove down into the stockade and retrieved his Purdey. With all due haste, he broke the gun open, tore out the two spent casings and pulled a round from his vest, all the while watching the brave. Finnegan's opponent had made slightly better time and had discovered a cartridge. The man slipped it into the rifle's loading gate, worked the action and brought the rifle up just as Finnegan was raising his gun. Both men fired. The brave fired too soon and hit the dead mule. Finnegan's bullet streaked along the brave's cheek, leaving a red welt instead of a bullet hole. Both men stared unbelievingly at the other for along moment.

Both men were broken out of the mutual stupor when Schnaubelt somewhat miraculously came back to life on the floor of the fort. With his black travel suit appearing rather grey from the alkali dust, he leapt to his feet and began babbling to both men in in what Finnegan could only assume was German. Finnegan and the brave both stared on in ignorance of what the hell the fellow might be saying. Seeing that neither the strange white man or the Indian had any insight into what was happening, Schnaubelt chose discretion as the best option and dove over the crates at the rear of the fort. He began running south at an impressive pace, to say the least.

"Damn you, Hun!" Finnegan sighted on the man and put his finger around the rear trigger of the Purdey, but was answered with yet another dull click. "Bloody hell!" He watched as the Prussian disappeared amongst the boulders to the south. He slowly turned to the brave. "I can hardly credit the audacity of that man. Fleeing after I have pursued him so very far."

"Hombre blanco loco."

"You may say that again, sir." Finnegan nodded and was about to offer the fellow a cigar when both men jumped from incoming rifle fire. Rounds from braves were hitting about the fort and rounds from Horn and Abijah were impacting near the brave. Finnegan ducked down into the fort and the brave ran past the small enclosure. Finnegan fought two fresh rounds into the Purdey before slowly bringing his head up a bit to survey the canyon floor. All remained still for several minutes while Finnegan continued to crane his head around, looking for targets that seemed to no longer exist. Finally, above him in the canyon wall he heard a rock fall and a voice call out.

"Finnegan, are you injured?"

The Pinkerton considered the question. "My pride has taken a beating, Abijah."

"We are coming down to you."

Finnegan sighed, realizing that the declaration indicated the engagement was at an end and Schnaubelt was still not in his possession. "Very well." More rocks cascaded down to the canyon floor as the two men descended. After a few more furtive surveys, Finnegan raised up to his feet and stood in the fort. The presence of the dead braves, along with the ripening dead mule did not make for a lovely atmosphere. "To hell with this hole." He hoped over the dead mule and took a seat on a boulder some distance from the fort. There, he lit a cigar, leaned the Purdey against the rock, and began reloading his pistols. Buzzards had begun to gather overhead.

Horn and Abijah came ambling over and took up seats on the rock Finnegan occupied. Horn wore an inscrutable look on his sweat-drenched face. "Now that is something I won't be forgetting any time soon."

Finnegan puffed his cigar. "I would not imagine there to be anything too noticeable regarding this small tiff with some savages. I would think a man of your profession would experience such incidents frequently, Mr. Horn."

"Oh, the Apaches trying to jump fellas in these canyons ain't of much note. What I'm talking about is you standing toe to toe with Geronimo like that and you both walking away. I swear, you must have a guardian angel, Mr. Gilhooley, and that old horse thief must have a heathen one to match. Did my eyes deceive me or did you shoot that scoundrel in the head with your big gun?"

"I believe he received something of a kiss from the bullet, Mr. Horn. A love memento he is not likely to forget and, as you say, miraculously lucky to have been given. I must say I feel rather fortunate to have survived, myself. The gentleman was at quite close range when he fired."

Horn shook his head. "That ain't all that miraculous. It's a well-known fact that Geronimo shoots worse than old blind grandma."

"Well, at any rate, it did cause me a moment's consternation." Finnegan placed his Remington back in the holster. "Did you have a view of what became of Schnaubelt? Is there still cause for pursuit?"

Abijah shook his head. "Mr. Horn does not believe so, Finnegan. We witnessed Schnaubelt being clouted by one of the braves once again and he was slung over the back of one of their ponies. They have carried him off, Finnegan."

"Damn the luck." Finnegan sneered and pulled his Colt from the holster to begin reloading it. "Mr. Horn, do you believe we might retrieve the fellow's remains?"

"Uh...well..." Horn pulled his hat from his head and tousled what was left of his hair. "Now, I wouldn't go so far as to recommend we follow up close and try to jump or dry gulch them savages. There's still a hell of a lot more of them than there are of us. If we trail on behind them, just following up, so to speak, we might be lucky enough to find what's left of your Hun, wherever they decide to leave him."

Finnegan placed the Colt back in its shoulder holster. "If that is the case, we should probably pursue."

Horn cleared his throat. "Uh, well, now, Mr. Gilhooley, there might be a few other matters to take into consideration before we go and do a thing like that."

Finnegan raised an eyebrow. "Such as?"

"Well, oftentimes, them Apache, they get it into their heads to skin and burn a fella they find particularly vexing. My guess would be that Hun yelling in his funny language is gonna be vexing. They're also not too apt to be fond of him, seeing as he was found in the company of the whiskey peddler they burned half this desert looking for. I would venture a guess and say there ain't gonna be a lot left of Mr. Schnaubelt when we run across him." Horn shrugged. "And then there's the other troubles down south."

Finnegan sighed. "Other troubles, Mr. Horn?"

"Yeah, see, the trouble is, these Apache, they tend to know what's up ahead of them and send fellas back to see what's trailing them, too. I've chased them up and down this border for weeks without them letting an army troop get close or get too far behind to give up. If they notice that the three of us are trailing behind them, they're awful likely to lay up somewhere and knock us out of our saddles before we even know the fight got going. It's a simple bushwack. Any fool could do it."

Finnegan groaned. "Yes, that is true."

"And, of course, I really ought not be running around in Mexico chasing Apaches right now." Horn offered a sheepish smile.

Finnegan adjusted his seat on the rock and gave his cigar a puff. "And why is that, Mr. Horn?"

Horn shrugged again. "As I recall, and my recollection might not be the same as some other fellas, we followed old Geronimo down into Mexico and we sort of bumped into some of them Mexican army regulars. Now, keep in mind, I been kicking around this country a long time and I hadn't ever gotten a glimpse of a military patrol up along the border. Well, them boys took umbrage with us being in Mexico chasing Indians and got to shooting at us before we had a chance to figure out who they was, or why they was shooting."

Finnegan knocked ash from his cigar. "I take it you returned fire?"

"Wasn't much else to do. We let off a few rounds at them and might of touched one or two. We scuttled off after that and got on home, but their captain was one of them that got nicked and took it damn personal, as a fella is apt to do when it's his arm that got removed from the rest of the frame."

Finnegan sighed. "Yes, that will tend to perturb a man."

"It sure did. Before I knew what was what, they was calling it an international incident and had me up for court's martial. Only reason that didn't work out to my disfavor is cuz General Crook told them other fellas I wasn't never in the army and scouts can invade Mexico anytime they like, I reckon." He licked his lips and stared down at the sand on his boots. "Long and short of it is that if I chase Indians down into Mexico again anytime soon, them Mexicans are apt to fit me for a rope without asking permission. Probably do the same for any man caught with me."

"I see." Finnegan tossed his cigar down into the alkali. "You might have mentioned that minor fact before contracting with us, Mr. Horn."

Horn grunted and placed his hat back on his head. "Truth be told, it didn't occur to me right off that we might have to push on into Mexico and...well, by the time it seemed likely, it seemed like a shame to let a little thing like that stand between me and fifty dollars."

Finnegan rubbed his face and stood to stretch. "Yes, well, you are nothing if not honest, Mr. Horn. Abijah, what would you prefer? Should we abandon the chase or go on alone to face the savages and the Mexican Army?"

Abijah simply stared at his mentor for a long moment. "My preference is to not die in this damned desert." He emitted a chuckle. "Would you have another cigar on you, Finnegan?"

"I might, at that." He removed two cigars from his vest pocket and handed one to Abijah and the other to Horn. "This does seem to be a reasonable time to leave off our pursuit. I do not know about you gentlemen, but I am sorely low on ammunition, and we are dangerously low on tobacco."

Horn smiled and began looking through his pockets for a match. "I wouldn't count on finding any useful ammunition in Huxley's stores, but it would be quite irregular for him to travel without a bit of tobacco for trade." Horn found a match and lit his cigar. "You boys may as well check over his traps. I'll give a once over to the Apaches scattered about. Now and then a fella finds a right profitable bobble hung around a neck or a decent rifle."

Finnegan returned to sitting. "Mr. Horn, if you do not mind my saying so, you are somewhat too carefree for my taste when it comes to the harvesting of corpses."

"A fella's got to be around here, Mr. Gilhooley. Dead men are about the only thing this damn place produces."

Chapter 24

DEMING, NEW MEXICO

June 10, 1886

THE SOFT GURGLE OF THE WATER TOWER COULD BE heard as the train crew filled the boiler, making ready for the forthcoming departure. Finnegan wiped a bit of dust from the wooden case he used for transporting his beloved Purdey. He smiled and let out a small laugh. "I do not always take the greatest enjoyment in these journeys, but I come to regret their brevity the instant I become aware I must return to Chicago."

"Don't care for the place, Mr. Gilhooley?" Horn lingered on the platform with his thumbs hooked in his belt.

"Chicago is a fine city for a railroad baron or a millionaire. Sadly, I am neither." Finnegan shook the scout's hand. "Thank you for all your assistance." He reached in his pocket and removed a ten dollar gold piece. "A gratuity from the firm. Please spend it wisely and continue to look out for my associate. I may have need of both of you someday hence."

Horn held the gold piece up to the sun. "I got to say, Mr. Gilhooley, as free as your Pinkerton outfit is about throwing around money, I'd be more than happy to answer the call of duty."

"It is always pleasant to know a man who is honest about his motivations." Finnegan turned to Abijah. "My friend, I did not imagine you would ever leave my side to be a miner, but in this life all things are possible. I truly pray you find one of those motherlodes I only read about in the papers."

Abijah nodded. He had accepted Horn's offer to partner in the gold mine in the Aravaipa Canyon and Finnegan had even gone so far as to make a small loan to the young man to supplement the initial investment. "Well, by the time we discover the great vein you will undoubtedly be a cattle baron and have little care for the minor trifle of income produced by a venture as meager as a gold mine."

Finnegan grinned. "Yes. If that is the case, please show the good manners not to bother me with telegrams announcing your paltry successes." Finnegan took Horn's hand once more and gave it a shake. "It has been a unique experience traveling with you, Mr. Horn. I look forward to our next adventure, although, I will require a bit of rest before we embark again." He patted the scout on the shoulder. "Would you mind terribly giving young Abijah and myself a bit of privacy before I am on my way?"

Horn tipped his hat. "It has been a pleasure, Mr. Gilhooley, and I would welcome another outing." He gave his new business partner a pat on the back. "You need only pass into the saloon to find me when you're ready, Abijah. I believe I will work on investing my newfound wealth while you two make your goodbyes."

Abijah smiled. "Try not to overindulge. I do not know the way back to our mine and do not much fancy the notion of wandering this desert like Moses in search of it."

"It is poor practice to make promises a man cannot keep." He tipped his hat again and meandered off toward one of the local saloons.

Abijah sighed. "I do not know how useful he will prove to be as a business partner, but he is entertaining, and that is all anyone can truly ask of a man." He turned more serious. "Do you believe the Pinkerton brothers will hold that I have not met my obligations, Finnegan?"

The elder detective shook his head. "If they do, it is not by right. Whatever you owed, you owed to their father, and he is long past caring. You should take enjoyment in your new opportunity here, Abijah. So few men ever take such chances. You should be proud to be among them."

"Thank you, again, for the added funds. I appreciate the loan more than you can know."

Finnegan grinned. "Show your gratitude by paying me back, someday."

"Of that you may be assured." The young man shrugged. "It may not be formed from mining profits, but I shall sort it out somehow."

"Do not let it burden you." Finnegan patted his shoulder. "I am quite proud of you, Abijah. Seeing you again will be far more pleasurable than receiving the funds."

Abijah assumed a coy smile. "Finnegan, an odd thought occurred to me while we were traveling back from the canyon."

"What might that be?"

"It seems to me that once or twice you have seemed a bit...displeased by the fact you were supplanted as the man who shot Jesse James."

Finnegan shook his head. "Far from it. I wish Robert Ford all the luck in the world assuming the title."

"Well, be that as it may, you are now, surely, the only man

alive to have shot both Jesse James and Geronimo. Now there is an accomplishment to ponder."

Finnegan chuckled. "Yes, well, I suppose I am. Assuming Robert Ford does not take it upon himself to travel to this desert and shoot that old Indian for no good reason."

"I would say the chances of that are slim, my friend." He stared down at his boots for a long moment. "I wish you would take another train and go to your schoolmistress and your cattle, Finnegan. You have always had a charmed life, but luck runs out for all men eventually. It will be that much more difficult for you in Chicago without me to watch out for you."

Finnegan chuckled again. "You watch out for me? Who is the teacher and who is the pupil here, young man?"

"Who was the fellow underneath the bear?"

"Ah, you make a good point there." Finnegan rubbed his chin and withdrew a cigar. "It may all be a matter of small import. The Pinkerton brothers may permanently relieve me of my duties when I arrive. Pursuing men such as Schnaubelt is all I am useful for in this new age of labor uprisings, and I have failed to capture the prey. You may see me again sooner than you think, young Abijah."

"I do dearly hope that is so. You are a better man than your labors suggest."

Finnegan laughed. "Ah, well, I suppose every man has someone who thinks well of him. I am glad to have you occupy that position, Abijah." He gave a look to the surrounding desert. "This is a far cry from Pennsylvania, my friend. Do you believe you will find a good life here?"

The young man shrugged. "If I do not, I suppose I can recall the way back to Chicago. Though I dearly hope it does not come to that."

The boiler of the train let out a sprawl of steam and

smoke while the conductor began to roam the platform. "Well, I must be on my way. Take care of yourself, Abijah."

"Do the same, Finnegan."

Chapter 25

COOK COUNTY JAIL, CHICAGO, ILLINOIS

November 10, 1887

As with any proper jail, the Cook County jail had cold stone walls cut from the rocks that had been unearthed while the city had been built. It served to hold those who were pending trial, those who waited to be transferred to Joliet Prison, and those the state had sentenced to be executed. The lot where the scaffold resided was hidden from the nearby street by a tall wooden fence. Those on the outside could not see the collection of beams and planks that served to mete out a man's last punishment, but the prisoners could. Most of the jail's cells looked out into the wind-strewn courtyard. Nooses did not swing in the cold fall breeze; rather, the severed ends of what had formerly been nooses, cut so that the dearly departed might fall to the ground, swayed back and forth. In many ways, the frayed ends of the ropes served as a better reminder to those within the jail walls than any prettily tied noose might, proof the state had made good on its threats and intended to in the future, as well.

Finnegan strolled down the upper level of the cells and came to a stop where a jailer serving as his guide directed.

Finnegan nodded to the man, and he departed. Inside the cell, Finnegan could see a fellow he knew well. The prisoner sat on a cot, nose in a book, reading by the light of an oil lamp. Finnegan took a cigar from his pocket, lit it, and tapped on the cell bars with his match case. "Are you of a mind for conversation, Mr. Parsons?"

The prisoner looked up from his book. "Conversation with an old adversary, on the eve of my execution? Yes, I should think that would be fitting." He closed the book and stepped to the bars. "I must say, I was not expecting you, Mr. Gilhooley. I thought your employer might grace me with his presence."

Finnegan offered a sad smile and shook his head. "You were his father's nemesis, Albert. William Pinkerton does not indulge in such behavior."

"A pity." Parsons rubbed his eyes. "I hated that old Scot bastard, but he at least stood his own ground. Old man Pinkerton always said I should be hung, without specifying a reason, of course. I wonder if this would please him or if he would mourn the loss of an opponent."

Finnegan puffed his cigar. "I could not say. At any rate, I thought it proper for someone from the agency, someone from past days, to come and say goodbye, fare thee well."

Parsons laughed. "Fare thee well. That is a fine thing to hear from Finnegan Gilhooley, Allan Pinkerton's finest assassin. And do you mean it, Finnegan? Truly?"

"It was the elder Mr. Pinkerton who believed you were the devil's own disciple, Albert, not I. In truth, I always considered you and your anarchist chums to be a pitiable bunch with your ragged suits and strange newspapers. I would not wish what awaits you on any man, but it cannot be said I brought it on you, either."

Parsons raised an eyebrow. "If not the esteemed Pinkerton Agency, then whom is to blame, sir?"

"Albert, honestly, any fool can see that you have brought this on yourselves. You intellectuals wished to stand too close to the flame. You bedded down with revolutionary, bloodthirsty dogs, and now you have fleas. This is not so very complicated."

"Damned be the State. The State says I must die, so be it. For if I were to live, I would be dutybound to kill the State."

Finnegan smiled again and gave his cigar a small draw. "Ah, then all is as it should be."

"Is it?" Parsons assumed a rather sly look. "And what of you, Finnegan? Your sort cannot be tolerated forever. Someday they will come for you, as well."

Finnegan nodded. "That may be."

"And what then?"

"As all men do, I will fight as best I can and likely die." He gave the cigar another puff. "Just as you will die tomorrow, Albert." He withdrew the cigar from his lips and rubbed his chin. "I cannot help but wonder, sir: would you mind terribly if I asked you a question?"

"You may ask. I cannot guarantee an answer."

"Why did you hand out bombs to men such as Schnaubelt? Would it not have been far safer and more satisfying to you to sit in your newspaper office, prattling out drivel? Would you not have lived a long and happy life if only you could have been more satisfied remaining a purely theoretical revolutionary?"

Parsons chuckled again. "I very well may have, but you well know what fools men are. We so rarely pause to consider the costs or the consequences. We allow our passions to rule us." He glanced up and down the cell block to make certain a guard was not eavesdropping. "I have offered no confession, nor will any of us, but I will tell you something, so that you may contemplate it as time goes by." He smiled. "In years to come, I will be remembered as a martyr, a man who lived and died for a cause. I will be eternally linked to a bomb, a bomb cast into a crowd. The report of that explosive will likely echo through the whole history of this nation. That echo and my name will live on." He grinned. "But bombs never crossed my mind in my newspaper office. All that nonsense is the product of other men and other passions. You should speak with Lingg if you wish to discuss bombs."

Finnegan knocked the ash from his cigar. "You truly believe you will be remembered for this, Albert?"

Parsons stood a bit straighter, a bit prouder. "They will speak of us in the same breath as Marx, or even Washington. We will be the founders of a new order. The spark of a revolution. If you live to see the completion of it, you may look down to see my portrait on the coin in your pocket. How will that strike you, Pinkerton?"

Finnegan shrugged. "As always, I shall simply be glad to have a coin in my pocket and give small consideration as to whose likeness it bears. I suppose such great and grave matters are best left to men such as you, Albert. Perhaps that sort of grand contemplation is what made Mr. Pinkerton consider you to be a proper villain, suited to his talents. It is a shame he cannot stand here in my stead. I apologize; I fear I am a sorry substitute."

Parsons put his hand through the bars. "You are not the man your employer was, Finnegan, but such matters are out of our control. I thank you for the visit, at all events."

"Safe travels, Mr. Parsons." Finnegan shook his hand and turned to go.

"Finnegan?"

"Yes."

"You really ought to say goodbye and safe journey to Mr. Lingg before you are on your way. After all, he is, more than any other man, the fellow who made all this possible."

Finnegan nodded. "Very well. I suppose you are correct." He nodded again and walked down the cell block to the three walls of stone and one of iron occupied by Louis Lingg. Finnegan dropped his cigar to the stone floor and stepped on it. Lingg stood in the cell. It appeared as though he had been listening to the conversation down the block. "Hello, Mr. Lingg. How does the evening find you?"

He offered a cold stare. "You kill Schnaubelt?"

Finnegan rubbed his chin. "Now that you mention it, I am not certain the man is dead. I saw him carried off by savages in the southern desert, but that hardly seals a man's fate." Finnegan grinned. "For all I know, they may have made that damned Hun their king."

Lingg sneered, obviously not in the mood for humor. "You kill workingmen?"

"Workingmen, bank robbers, whiskey peddlers, the occasional railroad baron or policeman. I tend to kill those who force me to the action, or those who have labored long and hard to earn such retribution."

"You will not kill me."

Finnegan eyed the fellow. "No, I will not. You hang in the morning. The hangman will kill you."

"Hangman kill Parsons and Spies. He not kill me." Lingg let his jaw hang open after finishing the statement and rather elegantly placed a small, tin object in his mouth.

Finnegan cocked his head to one side, staring at the object. "Is that..."

Lingg snapped his jaw shut and a small explosion of blood and bone erupted from what had once been his face.

The man fell to the floor of the cell and began flopping around in the grips of his death throes.

Finnegan grimaced and turned away from the cell. "Sweet Mary preserve us." He walked back down the block to Parsons' cell.

The former newspaper editor stood by the bars, trying to peer down toward Lingg. "What was that sound, Finnegan?"

"Mr. Lingg has chosen his own way to martyrdom. I believe he bit down on a blasting cap."

Parsons closed his eyes and drew in a breath. "He always claimed he would choose his own way out of these walls."

Finnegan straightened his coat and looked back down the cell block. "The eventual destination is the same, Albert. I believe you revolutionaries give too much weight to the journey. The destination is the same for all men."

A Look at: As the Crucible Closed (Finnegan Gilhooley 4)

The frontier's fading. He's not ready to let it go.

Finnegan Gilhooley doesn't care for the modern world. The Pinkerton Agency no longer has use for his kind, and the wild places he once knew are vanishing fast. No longer under regular contract, he's taken to bounty hunting in the last rough corners of Indian Territory—until even that begins to disappear.

Just as the law closes in and the wilderness recedes, a telegram arrives from his old friend Molly Meagher. She's in trouble out in the high desert of Nevada, and Finnegan doesn't think twice. With his guns packed and doubts in tow, he rides west one more time—to see if there's still any wildness left worth saving.

The maps may be filled in. But not every trail has ended.

AVAILABLE MARCH 2026

About the Author

R.F. Ryan lives in Montana with his beautiful wife and comparatively ugly gun collection. When he is not writing, he can usually be found out in the woods hunting. He's currently retired from a variety of odd jobs that have interfered with his free time, including (but not limited to): ranch hand, green chain operator, bounty hunter, private investigator, and process server. Robert has written over twenty books in multiple genres, both fiction and non-fiction, and has penned hundreds of outdoors-focused articles for websites and print magazines.

www.ingramcontent.com/pod-product-compliance
Lightning Source LLC
LaVergne TN
LVHW040215110826
845146LV00005B/1294

* 9 7 9 8 8 9 5 6 7 2 6 1 7 *